DRAGON FLAME

RIDERS OF JADE & FIRE BOOK 2

MELANIE ANSLEY

WRITING ROOSTER MEDIA

For Susan

CHAPTER 1

*J*in had never feared the dead. Until now.

He was standing just beyond the clearing, half hidden in the fading dusk behind a scattering of trees near a turret wall, smiling at her with that same look he'd had when he thought he'd sent her to certain death. His hair was pulled back into an official's bun, white hairs dusting the temples. And though his lips didn't move, she heard his last words to her: "You are like your mother, nothing more than a common murderer."

He's not real. Gao's not there.

As if on cue, her old enemy dissolved like ash and scattered on the wind. The long, lurking shadows meant anyone glancing over might have thought it was a trick of light. But no one saw. Everyone's attention was on the game of gold ball two dragons were playing in the clearing below them, in the pooling shadows here beneath the Great Wall.

Gao again? Her own dragon's voice spoke to her.

Yes, she answered. *Perhaps it's my getting less sleep.*

She looked over to where the dozen dragons were spread out and easily found Rayshan, who was rubbing one jade-colored shoulder against a groaning pine trunk. He was the only green in a gathering of blacks, bronzes, silvers, and golds, most of whom were roaring approval at the latest score. A jade dragon only hatched every twenty to twenty-five years.

You will grow used to it, this needing less sleep and being more like a dragon.

Good. Though I'm not sure what's worse, the dreams or the hallucinations while I'm awake.

Dealing with the changes brought on by their blood bond hadn't been easy. The dreams, full of dark figures and snippets of her past, had started soon after their return from their final test to become Dragon Class riders. She had so far explained the hallucinations away as her reaction to a week of deprivation in the desert of Singing Sands. Heavily drugged by Gao and left for dead in the middle of nowhere, Jin and Rayshan had almost died. Their bones would still be out there, bleached by the sun, if not for their blood bond. But after weeks of these dreams and waking visions, she wasn't sure they were entirely due to her ordeal in the Singing Sands.

And now, standing here on this northeastern

stretch of the Great Wall that marked the end of the Tang Empire, she looked over the winding ribbon of stone with its turrets and the vast, expansive plains beyond, toward the northeastern fortress of Karahag. Where a monster awaited them.

Are you thinking of Baikalan or King Ulagan? Rayshan asked.

Both.

Another cheer arose, and she saw that the metal helmet being used as a ball had hit the mark in a nearby tree, scoring a point. The gold dragon Bayan huffed in defeat as his opponent, another muscled gold whose name Jin couldn't remember, trumpeted in glee.

Jin spied a tall, dark-haired rider striding over to her from the soldiers' hut where her wing mates had gathered for the night. All were relishing a last dose of Han hospitality from the fellow soldiers who manned this wall before heading into foreign territory at dawn.

Aadan's scent reached her before he did—the outer layer of smoke, bread, and cornmeal from what obviously was being served for dinner, and underneath that, warm sandalwood mixed with something earthy. It had always made her senses flicker. But now, with the blood bond, his scent had tripled.

"The cook asks if you're not eating." Aadan's dark, curly hair was pulled into a ponytail, how he always wore it when he rode. His dragonrider leathers carried a light coating of dust, and his sage-colored eyes squinted from a long day riding in the sun. But otherwise, he was, in her view, better looking than he had ever been in the palace.

Jin shoved the thought from her mind. Harder to tame, however, was her pulse's reaction to his scent. She was almost glad when Panshalar, a giant of a man and one of their wing mates, strode by, the heavy evidence of his favorite foods—roast mutton and garlic—oozing from him to overpower every other odor. She wrinkled her nose, which Aadan seemed to interpret as directed at him.

"I will stop disturbing you." He gave a stiff nod and left before she could reply. She had made the right decision that night in the palace, but by the eight levels of hell, she missed what might have been. Especially as Aadan had grown much more aloof since then. *It's for the best*, she insisted to herself.

What future could they have, after all? In the space of a year, Jin had stolen a dragon egg, trained as the empire's first female dragonrider, and inadvertently foiled a coup from the Minister of War, Gao Shihong, who had been determined to prevent women from entering Dragon Class. Or from occupying the Dragon Throne. And now, they were going to hunt Baikalan, the fiercest dragon in the realm. Having a relationship with another rider was not a complication she, or Aadan, needed right now.

A drawn-out breaking of wind shattered her thoughts, and the accompanying stench made the previous odor of lamb and roast garlic far preferable.

"Sorry," Panshalar apologized, though his grin was less sheepish than relieved. "My northern gut has gotten too used to southern food." He indicated the game. "What did I miss?"

"Bayan lost a point," Jin said. "And he's not taking it well."

They watched Bayan smash his opponent with his tail before glaring at the helmet that had lodged in the tree. It dislodged itself with a shattering of wood and circled up into the sky before barreling down toward his opponent's head. The other gold dodged just in time, then threw his jaws wide to send a stream of fire Bayan's way.

"No flames!" Panshalar yelled. "That's cheating!"

Jin couldn't tell what was cheating. The resident gold dragons had introduced the game to Panshalar's gold, Bayan, and all the rules seemed to change on their whims.

"His metal skills are improving every time I see him," Panshalar gloated.

Jin's mood dampened, but Panshalar didn't seem to notice. All the dragons in her wing had already manifested their abilities: golds like Bayan had the power to manipulate metal, blacks manipulated air, silvers controlled water, and bronzes could triple their sizes. Only Rayshan remained a mystery.

Rayshan grumbled, and she answered soothingly, *Yes, I know. I need to be patient.*

An irate soldier appeared on the wall, yelling at

both dragons. Apparently, the helmet was his. Both beasts ignored him and kept at their game, sending the helmet flying toward various targets. At one point, the "ball" hurtled past the soldier's head, and he dove for cover.

Laughter rang out from the watching sentries as another of Jin's wing mates joined them. As small as Panshalar was large, Jao had a dark, thin face, a permanent frown, and a general dislike for his fellow humans. He held out a jug of yellow wine to Jin.

She was about to refuse, but then took it and sipped. Jao had presented a hostile front the first day she arrived at Dragon Class, but the Singing Sands had changed that. He barely spoke to her now, but he also didn't insult her, which she had learned was his form of friendship. That and offering her wine.

"Think they're giving us this vintage because it'll be our last?" Panshalar took the jug from her and drank. "The whole garrison likely thinks we're going to our deaths."

With a scowl, Jao turned his gaze north, as if he, too, could spot the far-off fortress.

"Just because Baikalan's escaped doesn't mean he's invincible," Jin said quietly.

"Maybe Rayshan will have the power of mind control and make Baikalan purr like a kitten," Jao said.

Jin tried not to let the reminder of Rayshan's unknown skill get under her skin. She fingered the scar behind her ear, as she always did when trying to figure out a puzzle. Jade dragons like Rayshan didn't manifest special abilities at specific times like other dragons, and even when they did, it varied from dragon to dragon. Baikalan, the last jade the empire had seen, could turn invisible, and the head teacher of Dragon Class, Emar, had told her that others could travel instantly between places. Despite everything after the Singing Sands, Jin still felt mounting pressure to uncover Rayshan's power.

"But what are we going to do?" Panshalar insisted. "None of us have ever fought Mengkhis Lai."

"Not true," came a voice.

They turned to see Ezho walking toward them. Where others had a distinct scent, their wing leader had barely any except the soap he used, for he bathed stringently. Tall and lean as a dart, Ezho wore his hair slicked back into a long braid. He leaned against the side of the wall, taking in the dragons' game, then looked up toward the upper guard tower. There, the silhouettes of a middle-aged, broad-shouldered *huren*, or foreigner, and the mage attending him were just visible in the dusk.

"Emar fought Mengkhis Lai?" Panshalar asked, incredulous.

Ezho scoffed. "Your history is worse than mine. He fought Mengkhis Lai and lost."

Understanding dawned on Jin. "Mengkhis Lai killed his dragon?"

"According to stories my cousin heard, they fought

near the palace on the night of Prince Tai's birth. Rumor is Emar was winning until something changed, and Mengkhis Lai was able to attack." He paused, making sure he had their full attention. "He ripped out the dragon's heart."

They all looked up at Emar's outline, his head bent as the mage's hands passed above his neck. If something like that happened to Rayshan . . . Jin's own heart tightened, for nothing seemed as horrible as the death of one's dragon. A rider who lost his dragon usually died himself within the year. Emar had cheated death this long using opium, magic, and what almost seemed like sheer spite.

"Food's almost gone," Ezho said. "You'd better eat while you can."

"In a moment." Panshalar shifted in a way that warned Jin of what was coming.

She moved toward the kitchens before the giant filled the air once more, and ducked into the dimly lit guard tower.

Inside, braziers burned to give light and warmth, for this far north, the summer nights turned cool once the sun fled. Her eyes adjusted almost immediately, another trick for which she could thank the blood bond.

She noticed Aadan first, sitting on a wooden stool opposite one of the newly appointed mages, a wide-eyed man with a pockmarked face named Yao Bing. He smelled of herbs, oils, and smoke and had unusually broad hands for such a slight man. He reminded Jin of a puppy, eager to please and full of enthusiasm for even the driest of subjects, peppering Jin with questions at every opportunity.

"Ah, the girl rider!" The cook lumbered forward, a bowl in one hand and a ladle in the other. He had the ruddy face many northerners bore, and his eyes disappeared into cheeks the size of *mantou*, those bland northern dough rolls that Jin had eaten so many of on this trip she didn't care to see one again in her lifetime.

The cook worked as a cook, soldier, and horse hand up here, where everyone had multiple jobs. The crew stationed here never tired of lamenting how the empress had let the once mighty wall fall into disrepair, along with its staff. Empress Wu had wrought peace through trade and diplomatic negotiations so that the northern tribes didn't raid and the southern tribes grew subservient. But such progress didn't please everyone. In fact, it made the men at the wall restless.

"Lamb, lady rider?" the cook said, ladling the stew out from a nearby pot without waiting for an answer. He shoved a mantou at her as well, and she took it, sighing.

Jin saw a smile play at Aadan's mouth and knew he'd caught her lack of enthusiasm.

She sat next to him and tried to avoid the young mage's gaze. He must have been skilled, having been chosen for this mission along with the dozen other mages, but Jin found his constant scrutiny tiresome.

She preferred the head mage, Grand Master Gu Ben, a quiet man here to both tend to Emar's white disease and advise them once they reached the Well of Ice. For mage magic had held Baikalan for twenty years. But no more.

Somehow, the most feared dragon in the empire had escaped magical bonds and was now free.

Jin glanced at Aadan, who was deep in conversation with one of the soldiers about the benefits of northern irrigation systems. Aadan had an enviable understanding of every area of study and devoured books on all subjects. In contrast, Jin had just learned to read last year, and only with Aadan's aid.

She swallowed a mouthful of the mantou, her hunger overwhelming her distaste.

"You have a very healthy appetite," Yao Bing said, eyeing her with great interest. She tried to gauge any suspicion in his voice. But the boy simply seemed genuinely fascinated with the only female rider in the wing.

"I eat less than Panshalar."

He chuckled, for they both knew that was like saying she ate less than an elephant. Panshalar, the biggest threat to the cook's rations, had been repeatedly beaten back from the kitchens.

"I've never seen a woman eat so much food," the young mage insisted, watching her with an interest Jin found disconcerting.

"Magic must require much food as well," she

replied. Her blood bond made her hungrier than before, to the point where she'd sometimes thought she could eat a whole deer. She had started hiding rations away any chance she had to avoid being detected. But she couldn't let anyone, even a young mage like Yao Bing, know her secret. "You must have done well to reach your level." She forgot what level he was, but hoped an opportunity to boast would steer the conversation from her appetite.

"Best in class," he said with pride.

"What made you join the mages?"

He shrugged. "What makes many of us join. Unlike the Dragon Class, we come from poor families. Families with nothing to offer but our manhoods and our time."

He rubbed one cheek with a hand that was smooth, unlike his face. She guessed his story, one typical for so many of China's poor: he was no doubt one child of many, born to parents who had barely enough to feed and clothe their children, never mind secure them employment somewhere. His parents could have chosen to sell him, give him to the temple to be raised a monk, or send him to the Ministry of Mages, where boys could join the mysteries at eighteen by being castrated.

Even in the dimming light, he looked barely nineteen, which meant he hadn't been a full mage for long. Perhaps he had never even left the capital. "And what powers do you learn, exactly?" Jin asked.

He shrugged. "There are three levels. Most achieve Raven Class, where you can do all the basics—keep people looking young, change properties, that sort of thing."

This genuinely piqued her interest. "Change properties? Like making things lighter or heavier?" She remembered when she had stolen Rayshan's egg and how the box containing him had been lead lined but surprisingly light.

"Exactly." He scraped his chair forward and began listing on his fingers. "Make things hot or cold. Soft or hard. If you can master those skills, then you'll likely find employ with the richer traders in the empire. They will pay top coin for someone who can make their goods lighter and travel faster, or who can keep their foodstuffs cool on the long journeys up and down the canals."

She nodded at the crane emblem sewn on his purple robe. "I assume you're in the Crane Class, not Raven?"

He beamed. "Yes, only a fraction advance to Crane Class," he said, the pride in his voice unmistakable. "We train in binding. Do you know much about it?" Without waiting for an answer, he continued, "Like dragon binding and unbinding, along with dragon healing. The Crane Class's finest can perform intricate magic, like the spells that trapped Baikalan in the Well of Ice, or Mengkhis, wherever he may be."

She wiped a smudge of food from her chin. "Do you regret joining the mages?"

He shrugged. "The alternative was starvation. So, no."

Jin understood that logic. Before Dragon Class, she had been a thief, and her options were similar. It was starve or steal; ethics never played a role.

He looked about to ask her something, but to her relief, the head mage's voice barked from outside. Yao Bing scrambled to his feet. "Excuse me, it is time I help my master see to Emar."

She watched him go, relieved she wouldn't have to field more questions.

"He's not bad once you get to know him."

She turned to see Aadan putting away his empty bowl and chopsticks.

"I don't want to know him. I just asked him questions so he wouldn't ask me any."

"Good to see you are still yourself." He stood.

"Join me for another round?" she blurted impulsively.

He considered and then firmly shook his head, pulling at a scroll in the pack he'd left by the stool. "I am behind on my reading."

She watched him go, berating her sense of disappointment. Of course he preferred his books. She was getting along with others in the wing, but none were Aadan. Aadan, who had answers for so many things.

Aadan, who listened. Except he didn't want to listen anymore, not to her. He preferred his scrolls now.

Well, he wasn't the only one who had brought scrolls.

An outside thought pushed at her, berating her and Aadan for their stubbornness.

Wanli, she sighed mentally, *please stay out of my head.*

Since she had blood bonded, she could communicate with dragons other than Rayshan. Most rarely listened to her bond, speaking only when needed. By contrast, Aadan's silver Wanli had, to her exasperation and occasional amusement, proven to be a veritable busybody, deliberately honing his ability to listen to her thoughts. She had learned to block him, but sometimes he caught her off guard.

Wanli grumbled in protest but sank back into silence.

She finished another round of food, then went outside. The dragons were quiet and settling now. Apparently, the soldier had wrangled his helmet back. The stars blinked lazily, and the moon was clearly visible over the hills to the west. She reached out for Rayshan and heard the comforting answer of his mental hum, then went to the soldiers' quarters, but felt too restless to lie down and read. Instead, she took her pack and pulled it out onto the wall, ignoring the deepening chill of night.

She discovered a secluded part of the wall, where a bench overlooked the illuminated ramparts adorned with torches and bonfires. These towers snaked into the distance, beyond her vision—which was far, given her blood bond. And though her blood bond allowed her to read reasonably in the dark, she chose a spot under one of the torches and unrolled the scroll.

Prince Tai had given her the key to his private Dragon Class library after she had saved him and the empress during Gao's attempted coup. She had spent what spare time she stole searching through the books for clues as to blood bonding and Mengkhis Lai. When the summons to the Well of Ice had come, she had hastily taken a few of the more promising scrolls with her.

There had been so little time before leaving. She had been just as surprised as everyone else in Dragon Class when Emar insisted on taking her wing with him to Khitan instead of other, more experienced wings. He had also insisted on only one other wing of riders, composed wholly of transport bronzes, in order to not pull any other military Dragon Class members from Parhae, where new riots had broken out, or from the Tibetan empire border. Rumors claimed the empress feared for her life and wanted to keep the majority of dragons defending the palace, but Jin knew the empress enough to dismiss these claims as unlikely. In any case, the empress had followed Emar's wishes and ordered the veteran dragonrider to pick his wing and depart without delay.

Jin tore her thoughts back to the scroll and forced

herself to concentrate. *The Complete History of Blood Bonding* was thin, probably because so little was known about blood bonding. Jin unrolled the scroll, making sure to keep the title of it hidden in case of prying eyes. She didn't need to answer questions about why she was interested in a taboo subject.

She resumed reading where she left off, sharing her thoughts with Rayshan.

The first blood-bound riders emerged in the time of the first emperor, who defied the Dragon Queen's orders and deliberately bonded his best riders to their dragons. Over five of them were thus bonded, and the emperor formed them into a special force to police the others and the empire.

I have not seen that in the Firesong, Rayshan said, interest rising. The Firesong, a collective memory of all dragons, was Rayshan's access to knowledge passed down through generations of his kind.

It says that these five riders terrorized the empire and grew so powerful that the emperor himself had to kill them. He knew they could not be killed naturally, and so pitted them against each other. When only two remained, he gave them a choice: survive by not using their poisoned arrows against each other, or kill the other and guarantee their own immortality.

Rayshan rumbled, *I think I know the outcome.*

She read on, grim. *The two riders loosed their arrows at the same time, thereby eliminating all blood-bonded riders. From then on, the emperor decreed that no one would blood bond, on pain of the chariot punishment, where both rider and dragon would be dismembered by horse-drawn carts and buried in the four directions of the empire, never to reunite and fly again.*

She swallowed. Clearly, much thought had gone into how to punish those who couldn't die, which made eternal life more like a curse than a gift.

I wonder why the empress didn't adopt this punishment for Mengkhis Lai, she said. *Certainly, a dismembered Baikalan would have been harder to resurrect.*

Rayshan sighed. *But also brutal. She is not so heartless, surely.*

Jin wondered. Her friend Meipin, with whom she had shared quarters during her first year of training, had hinted that the empress was much more cold-blooded than she seemed. Jin read on. *Though immune to death except at the hands of another blood-bonded rider or dragon, the pain blood-bonded pairs experience is immense. This is thought to be because they now share all thoughts, blood, and sensations, doubling their pain and passions. Therefore, though it is hard to kill a blood-bonded rider or his dragon, it is, ironically, easier to torture them than a regular victim.*

This will help with the nightmares, she thought wryly.

You don't need much sleep, Rayshan said. *But you still need some.*

I'm not tired, she retorted, pushing on with the scroll.

The next thing she knew, however, a large meaty hand had fallen on her shoulder.

"You look worse than I do after a night's drinking," Panshalar said at her bleary-eyed glare.

She rubbed her face, looking out at the dark outline of the horizon. "It's not dawn yet."

"Emar woke us early," Panshalar said. "Best get moving. Says he has something to show us."

CHAPTER 2

*P*anshalar led her down the wall steps to the officer quarters, where Emar had his private room.

It was tiny, dank, and sparse, but better than the riders' quarters and probably second only to the mages'. A carved bed in the corner had a clean pallet and furs and even a northern *kang*—a brick bed over a space where firewood and coals burned to warm the occupant above. A brazier burned in another corner while a bottle of *baijiu*—a strong wine made of sorghum—and untidy sheaves of paper sat on the desk.

Aadan, Ezho, Panshalar, and Jao had already gathered, and they ranged around the room with barely suppressed curiosity.

Emar closed the heavy door behind them. Jin tried to catch Aadan's eye, but he gave a slight lift of one shoulder. He didn't know why they were here either.

The stocky man limped to the desk. Jin had been repulsed when she had first met Emar, for he looked half statue, half man. But she had grown used to his face's marbled left side and the milk-colored orb with no pupil that served as his left eye. Even at this time of morning, their teacher wore black gloves, with his Dragon Class seal in its usual place around his neck.

He poured himself a generous cup of baijiu. No one commented that it wasn't even dawn. Jin wondered if he had been up all night or was simply enjoying an Emar-style breakfast. She had never figured out whether Emar ever became drunk or whether being inebriated was simply his normal state.

When his words came, they were slurred, but not more than normal due to the white disease that paralyzed half his face. "There's something you all need to know."

"At this time of the morning?" Jao muttered.

Emar placed his cup of wine down gently. "Yes. This wall separates the Tang Empire from Khitan. We're about to enter foreign territory, and I cannot have a team divided."

The riders glanced at each other. Jin frowned. Was this about the team accepting her as a woman? Though she would hesitate to call their relationship a "friendship," she did feel she had won her wing mates' acceptance.

"Some of us have been keeping secrets."

Before Jin could process the words, Emar pulled a

dagger from seemingly nowhere and hurled it at her head.

Jin's instantaneous reaction was still too late. A blinding pain shot through her hand where the dagger stuck from it, blood running. She bit back her scream.

"What in—!" All the riders had jumped up, and Aadan darted toward her, but Emar held him back.

Jin clutched her hand, forcing herself to think past the pain.

He knows!

Hearing her distress, Rayshan called out, but within half a breath, Emar was before her. He whipped out a handkerchief from his inner robe and began staunching the wound.

"My apologies, this might sting," Emar said, then pulled the blade out of her hand with one smooth motion. She gasped at the fresh blaze of pain as he bound the handkerchief around her hand.

"What are you doing, Master Emar?" Aadan's voice sounded as stunned as Jin felt.

Emar looked her in the eyes. "She and Rayshan are blood bonded."

Her mind skittered, but before she could deny it, Ezho spoke up.

"How do you know?"

Emar kept his gaze on Jin, his one good hazel eye so like her own, a mark of their huren, or foreign, ethnicity. "Because I was once blood bonded too."

There was a confused silence. As Jin looked at him, she knew it was true.

Emar held up Jin's hand. "Tomorrow, her hand will be healed, and you'll all realize she's blood bonded. Blood-bonded riders recover faster."

"Is this some kind of Dragon Class test?" Ezho asked tentatively, brows knit as if Emar were posing a trick question.

"Yes, it is," Emar said. "A test of whether you can stand together as a wing and keep each other's secrets, keep each other safe."

"How can you have broken the taboo, Master Emar?" Aadan said, his eyes still on Jin.

Emar's diseased eye glinted in the lamplight. "You don't honestly think Mengkhis Lai was the only rider to have ever blood bonded?"

"You defied orders?" Ezho said, still clearly struggling to comprehend this flouting of rules.

"No, I was following them."

Jin digested this new information. Jao was staring open-mouthed at Emar, and the others seemed similarly lost for words.

Emar offered her a cup of his wine, and she took it with her uninjured hand. The burn helped distract her from the pain, which had turned into a vicious throb. "When Mengkhis Lai began his Age of Chaos, the empress knew he had to be stopped. And only a blood-bonded rider could kill him."

Jin had read this, but why had it never occurred to her that the empire would then respond with another blood-bonded rider? Their history teacher had drilled into them how this was one of the most sacred of taboos, never to be broken. She couldn't imagine anyone, much less the empress, breaking the rule. "Just you? And why you?"

"Not just me," Emar said. "There were five of us. A wing."

"Your wing?" she asked.

Emar nodded. "They all joined me once I volunteered."

Everyone held their breath, waiting. Seeing their expectant looks, Emar poured himself another cup of wine. "They all died. One didn't survive the blood bonding. One became too unstable after the blood bonding and killed himself. The rest of us fought Mengkhis and lost."

"He killed them all?" Panshalar asked.

Emar nodded. "As well as my dragon, Yalongma."

"Then how did you capture and imprison him in the Well of Ice?" Aadan glanced away from Jin.

"While occupied with killing Yalongma, Grand Master Gu Ben was able to bind him."

Jao crossed his arms. "Why didn't you kill him then and there?"

Emar's face clouded. "By then, the whole wing of blood-bonded riders was dead. I lost my powers once Yalongma died."

"And the empress didn't command another wing to blood bond?" Aadan asked.

Emar shook his head. "The empress didn't want to risk more lives, when we had Mengkhis and his dragon subdued."

Such a show of mercy didn't quite fit the woman Jin knew. Did the empress want to save Mengkhis, and if so, why?

"Master Emar, with all due respect . . ." Panshalar cleared his throat. "How does no one know about this?"

"It's been erased from the history books, hasn't it, Master Emar?" Aadan said, voice soft.

Emar regarded the Persian shrewdly. "Blood bonding is forbidden to all of you. But it has been done." Emar turned to Jin. "And I hope you all can understand why Jin did it."

Jin began to protest, but Emar held up his good hand.

"If anyone had reason, it was you. Gao sent you out to the Singing Sands, drugged and left for dead. Anyone would have done the same if their dragon had the courage to attempt it. As I said, not everyone is lucky enough to survive. And I want to give you all some advice, advice you won't find in your history lesson with Master Fu."

He looked at them each in turn.

"Jin cannot be killed except by another blood-bonded rider, but it doesn't mean she doesn't feel pain." He turned back to Jin. "Because of your heightened senses, you will feel everything more keenly: touch, taste, appetite, sight, sound, smell. And pain."

A thought occurred to her. "That means that your white disease . . ."

"Is double the pain that a normal rider would experience? No, all my blood-bonded abilities left with my dragon's death."

A wave of pity gripped her, but he must have sensed it, for he scowled. "Look at me like that again, and I'll slice your other hand. I make do with the poppy and the drink. We'll see which kills me first."

Death, she thought, might be a relief to him. The prospect of living twenty years without Rayshan was unbearable. She had once asked Emar what kept him going, but he had never answered.

"I tell you all this for two reasons." Emar looked around at them. "One, you are wing mates. There should be no secrets between you as to your strengths and weaknesses, or we may all die out there on the hunt for Baikalan. Understood?"

"Yes, Master Emar," everyone murmured, but Jin noted the furtive looks sent her way.

"And two, you likely wondered why I brought your wing and not twenty battle-hardened wings on this mission. It's because right now, Jin is the only one who can kill Baikalan. If we come across him, then it's not numbers we need, it's a miracle." Emar looked at her. "Jin is our best chance for that miracle, and after last year, you are the best ones to fight alongside her. Any objections?"

All gave subtle headshakes, but Jin wondered whether anyone was masking their true emotions.

"Good. I know there's been friction and that you all consider blood bonding a terrible offense. But beyond this wall, if we do not stand together, then we will fall to Baikalan. Your ghosts can help you or trap you, so put aside any past grievances and trust each other."

Jin startled at his use of words. Did Emar know about her visions?

"You hold each other's lives in your hands," Emar continued. "So work together. You are dismissed; be ready to ride by sunrise."

As they filed out of the room, Jin still clutching her hand, Emar motioned for her to stay. Aadan cast them a frown, but Emar gave him a pointed look that made the rider bow out, shutting the door behind him.

"Blood bonding changes a rider," Emar said quietly when he had listened at the door to make sure the others were gone. "As I said, heightened senses. Your wing mates haven't noticed, but I do. Try not to make it obvious what smells you detest and which ones you . . . savor." The non-diseased side of his mouth lifted in a smile.

Heat rose in her, but she forced it down. "Did you have heightened senses?"

He grunted. "You haven't the faintest idea."

"What happens now?" she asked instead. "Does the empress know?"

He paused. "Yes. But no one else. I told your wing mates because their lives are at stake, and secrets between you only weaken you. Besides, knowing you have a rare power will give them confidence."

"But what of Rayshan's manifestation? Will this blood bonding affect that?"

Emar sighed and poured himself another cup of wine, then sat at the scarred desk. "You still don't know what his manifestation is?"

Jin shook her head. "No."

He nodded, though she thought she saw a flicker of disappointment. "Well, it will come. And when it does, take heed—it will be very powerful."

"You mean our blood bond makes it stronger?"

Emar shook his head. "Not stronger, as such. More like—you will enhance his power somehow."

"Was that how it was with you and Yalongma?"

Sadness crossed the man's face, but he nodded. "Yalongma was a black dragon, so he controlled air and raised storms, wind tunnels. When we blood bonded, I added precision to Yalongma's abilities."

"So you had better aim?" Jin asked, not sure she understood.

Emar smiled. "In a sense, yes. Together, we were able to compress air into invisible pellets and send them at great speed against our enemy. We could pierce armor and, of course, flesh. We would have made good assassins, given more time. Mengkhis Lai still bears scars from us."

"And what was Mengkhis Lai's blood-bonded power?" Jin asked. "What could he and Baikalan do?"

Her teacher poured himself another cup. "Baikalan had the power to turn himself and anyone he touched invisible, but Mengkhis Lai could turn others, and things, invisible." Seeing the look on her face, he added, "It doesn't sound formidable, but it was. And I hope you never witness him using it again. Whatever talent Rayshan has, I am sure you will learn to use it well."

Rayshan prowled at the edges of her mind. *If he was blood bonded, how is it that I never found him or the others in the Firesong?*

Good question. She posed it to Emar, who sighed.

"Another result of the blood bond is that once a dragon dies, his memories go with him and do not pass on within the Firesong." Emar paused. "I suppose it's the price a dragon pays for bonding closer to a rider and growing distant from his dragon kin."

She sensed that this final loss of his dragon, so that Yalongma did not even live on in the Firesong, had made his death even more painful. Rayshan, usually unsentimental about dragons and his own kind, silently keened at the thought of being forgotten by future generations.

She bowed. "May time heal your grief."

"And Jin," he added as she turned to leave, "I am sorry for the hand."

"About that . . ." Jin paused. "Any advice for the increased pain?"

"Yes," Emar said. "Avoid getting injured."

But his expression mirrored her own thoughts. Something told her that her wounds were just beginning.

CHAPTER 3

"Hail crown prince Wu Tai Shan, heir to the Dragon Throne and commander in chief of the Dragon Class."

A flurry of shuffling and low murmurs swept the room as he entered, his boots striding across the floor.

The group of twenty women in uniform plain robes looked decidedly awe-struck. He recognized none of them from court and suspected they had never set foot there. Though they were from noble families, he guessed they were all the last in a generous line of sisters, for most households would be loath to send their eldest or more beautiful daughters, who might bring influence via marriage, to a harsh and potentially short future as a dragonrider.

"Welcome to Dragon Class, noble ladies," he said. A few of them were already shifting nervously, clearly awkward at being in his presence. As court etiquette dictated, none looked at him directly.

"Dragon Class is not a court ritual. You do not need to avoid my gaze."

A few timidly glanced up, but many appeared unwilling to even do that. He couldn't help comparing them to Dragon Class's first female rider. Jin had hit Tai in the face at their first meeting, then robbed him for good measure.

"Our usual trainer, Emar Kul, is away on a short trip." Would it be short? He doubted it, but as per his mother's ruling, all news of Baikalan's escape and what the Dragon Class riders were actually doing in the north was to be kept under strict secrecy. "Therefore, I will be leading some of your initial training this week."

There were audible gasps and a titter. One offending girl stifled her mouth with a hand.

He summoned an easy smile. "I know all of you would prefer the old, cantankerous wisdom of master Emar Kul, but you'll have to settle for my unworthy leadership instead."

This cracked the tension, and many of the girls smothered laughter behind their linen sleeves.

"Your days will start at dawn, with some physical training, before you will take lessons in Dragon Class history, saddle care, and geography. Three months from now, we'll take you to the hatchery to see if any dragons bond with you. If you bond, you will stay. If not, you will go home, though anyone under twenty-five at the next dragon egg harvest may apply again." He gave an encouraging smile. "You've been shown your dormitories. I leave you in the capable hands of my assistant trainer, An Song."

The girls bowed, and he left, feeling like he'd done a job well but not sure it was the job he wanted.

❀

TAI'S PUNCH CONNECTED, ELICITING A SURPRISED GRUNT from his opponent before the prince arced a leg around, sending the man crashing.

"Are you losing on purpose?"

The royal training hall was hot this time of year, despite the floor-to-ceiling wooden shutters open to the north to catch any breeze. The teak floor already bore streaks of sweat where Tai and Chao, a burly northerner from the cavalry, were sparring.

Chao rose to his feet, his face twisting in embarrassment. "No, Your Highness."

"Then fight me. Just because I had my throat cut doesn't mean my head will come off if you punch me." He caught Chao's eyes flicker toward the scarf on his throat and sighed. His mother had ordered him to wear it always, but it was a stark reminder to everyone that he had almost died. Now everyone feared injuring him. Not to mention the scarf itched, especially with sweat running down him.

Not for the first time, he thought about how much

he missed Aadan. The Persian's absence took a toll on his well-being. Though Tai never told anyone everything, Aadan was the closest person to him other than his mother, and there were numerous things he now could not and did not want to discuss with the empress.

Chao rushed him, thick arms outstretched. Tai was ready, however, and lunged left before hooking the man's waist and pivoting so that his momentum brought them to the ground. There, Tai straddled him and locked his arm around Chao's neck.

Chao pounded a fist against the floor, signaling defeat.

Tai stood, dusted the sand from his forehead, and went to take a drink from the water cauldron. Although Aadan and Jin had only been gone for a few days, Tai felt as if it had been weeks. Aadan had taught Tai *koshti* in the first place when he was really supposed to be teaching him his mother tongue of Middle Persian. But Tai's talents did not include language, and he relied more on his charm for his role.

Chao moved toward the ring, but Tai shook his head. He wasn't in the mood to fight those who feared his mother. That was the good thing about Aadan. He had not held back and took Tai's orders to teach him koshti to heart.

The prince walked with his valet to his personal rooms, where his private staff dried him and helped him change into his royal yellow robes. They combed out his black hair and tied it expertly beneath his cap, then laid out palm-sized pots of green and chrysanthemum tea on the foyer tables for him as he came out, clean but decidedly grumpy.

Hu Ming, Tai's personal secretary, had arrived, his charcoal robes rustling as he approached. "Your Highness, I have your itinerary for the day."

Tai scanned it. There was an overview of Dragon Class weaponry, then a meeting with local nobles about a land dispute, and a meeting with the royal sculptor about a new piece his mother was having commissioned. He scanned it again, just to be sure. "What of the Dragon Class situation briefing? That was for today, was it not?"

Hu Ming shifted, his tone apologetic. "Your mother expressly said you were not to attend, Your Highness."

He looked up, surprised. "Then who is chairing the meeting?"

"She has appointed Marquis Sanjin to chair, Your Highness."

He bristled. Yet another sign his mother was slowly removing him from court duties. He knew she was using the pretense of giving him time to recover, but he also suspected that talk of her losing the Mandate of Heaven played a role.

Ever since the former War Minister Gao's coup, in which he had tried to kill Tai, whispers had risen about how the first female ruler of China had lost Heaven's goodwill. Though the empress had, in the regular monthly news briefings that went out to the prefectures, stressed Heaven's favor in granting her victory over the coup, whispers persisted that the coup's very existence signified great discontent amongst the powerful at court.

"Tell my mother I'd like to meet with her today." He scanned the paper with his itinerary, then put a finger on a line. "Here, ask her to make a short time for me after the sculpture showing."

Hu Ming bowed. "Certainly, Your Highness. The lady Meipin was going to visit as well. What shall I tell her?"

Tai sighed. It wasn't that he didn't like Meipin. She was pleasant enough, with court manners he sensed were as carefully cultivated as his own, but he didn't relish small talk and polite chatter today. He rubbed his temples. "Tell her there'd be nothing I'd love more than to spend the entire day with her, but I am obligated by my mother to attend to duties." It wasn't a whole lie. The last sentence held some truth.

He left to attend a meeting on the curriculum and dress codes for the new female recruits of Dragon Class. With the acceptance of women, they were going to have to re-organize the dormitories, design new rider uniforms, fit in separate bathing schedules, and, as he had himself raised, draft laws as to whether the riders could marry each other. This last issue proved thorny and quickly devolved into a shouting match amongst the gathered teachers and advisors.

He was almost grateful to go to the sculptor's meeting, but his heart sank when the small man lovingly unfolded the plans for the sculpture across a marble table in Tai's private foyer.

The drawing was a horrid, grand thing that left him speechless. It was a likeness of a royal warrior, astride a dragon and flying through clouds that curled around the dragon's legs. There were delicate scarves, like those worn by celestials, trailing from the warrior's armor. Tai kept in good physical shape, but this statue had muscles so large it was nothing short of laughable.

"This is meant to be me?" he said, inwardly wincing.

The sculptor's face fell. "His Highness does not like it?"

"It is a work of great talent," Tai assured him. "But it's not exactly true, is it?"

"Your Highness is very pleasing to the eye," the sculptor insisted. "The ladies of court all agree that no one compares."

"This prince is humble and undeserving of such praise," he said in the rote polite response. "But I was also referring to the dragon."

The sculptor frowned at the paper, smoothing out the section with the dragon's head. "Is it not large enough, Your Highness? I can paint it any color you wish. Black for nobility?"

"No, the dragon is impeccable. But I have never ridden a dragon."

The sculptor beamed, clearly relieved that he didn't

have to redesign anything. "But you are head of Dragon Class, and the empress was most clear: you must be seen riding a dragon."

His mother. Of course.

Tai was no stranger to compliments, but he drew the line at outright lies. His fear of heights had meant that he always rode in a carriage borne by a transport bronze, and though he didn't dwell on this, he didn't feel the need to hide it either. "Your work is exemplary, as always, Master Sculptor."

The list of issues he wished to address with his mother was growing long indeed.

As always, the empress was the picture of regal: dressed in gold robes over scarlet silks, her low bodice hugging a figure any woman in the empire would have envied. Prince Tai knew this was partly from the help of her personal army of mages, but her love of polo kept her in ideal form. The empress's forehead was decorated with an ornate crimson cut out of a lotus, one of the Buddhist's favorite motifs.

"Good morning, my son," the empress said, rising and coming down the steps from the desk in her large office, with floor-to-ceiling windows overlooking the palace. She glanced at his neck, covered now by his high collar. "Has the new balm helped?"

He nearly snorted. The long scar that ran from one

jaw to the other along his neck was a good half finger thick and still red despite the month that had passed since its close dance with a soldier's sword. The cut had not been deep, but the scar it left was surprisingly wicked due to the serrated edge of the blade that had made the wound. His doctors had assured him it would fade and soften with time, and the mages had worked on it as well, but Tai knew he was already being called "the Marked Prince."

"The balm is more for you than for me, I believe," Tai replied. It was a physical reminder of the coup, and he sensed that's why she hated seeing it.

She darted him a look. "There is no need to take that tone with your mother."

"I've had my neck sliced open. I think I've at least earned the right to be bitter."

The empress's face softened, and she strode up to him, placing a hand on his arm. "How many times must I say it? I had to call his bluff. I didn't think he was audacious enough to order your death right there."

Memories of the day surfaced, ones that still woke him at night, his scar burning, the roar of dragons crashing through the doors ringing in his ears. Gao, the war minister, had somehow brought the whole of the royal guard under his pay. All in order to take the empress's seals and, with them, the throne.

"But you took that risk and lost," he said. His mother had been the pillar of his world. Or so he thought.

"And no one regrets that decision more than I," the empress said. To her credit, she did have wet eyes and bit her lip. "You must forgive me, no matter how hard that is for you. Or we will be brought down even before Baikalan sets foot in this palace."

The thought gave him the shivers. Baikalan and Mengkhis Lai had attacked the palace once before, on the day of his birth. He had survived, but his father had not.

"Speaking of Baikalan, why was I not invited to the Dragon Class briefing?"

She turned and walked back up the steps to her desk, her back to him. "It's too soon for you to take on your more serious regular duties."

"It's been over a month, and I am fine."

"If you really wish to help with state affairs," she said, sitting down, "you can start by narrowing down our list of possible brides for you. Gao's coup and the Baikalan situation made me realize my foolishness in delaying the heir matter."

"You really think we are in danger?" Tai asked. "What did I miss in the briefing?"

"Nothing." She waved a hand and smiled reassuringly. "But it wouldn't hurt to have more allies."

"There are ways other than marriage."

"Much harder ways." She searched his face, eyes keen. "You are not interested in the dragonrider girl?"

Annoyance flickered in him. If rumors were weeds, this one seemed particularly hardy. *Perhaps*, a tiny voice inside whispered, *because there's a grain of truth to it.* "Well, she did save me when you couldn't. Or wouldn't. I'm unsure which one it was."

She looked as if she had been slapped, and Tai both regretted and relished his words. "But on the subject of marriage, I just don't see why we should give up one of our main points of leverage if we have other options." Where was Jin, anyway? He would have preferred to be with the Dragon Class, actively helping, rather than trapped in the palace, arguing with advisors about uniforms and the possible romantic liaisons between riders.

"Let me go and lead them," he said. "The head of Dragon Class hiding in his palace when Baikalan is free would seem cowardly and an admission that the Mandate of Heaven has left us."

The empress's face hardened. "Let them talk. There is no way I will risk you again, my son. If Baikalan or Mengkhis Lai got hold of you, the empire would be lost. I would be lost."

"But—"

The empress shook her head, the beads of her golden headdress clicking together. "You shall not leave the palace. Not until we know Baikalan's whereabouts."

A hard feat, Tai mused, given the dragon could turn invisible.

"You mean to make me a prisoner."

She leaned forward at her desk. "I mean to make you safe."

"You spoke of being a laughingstock," he said. "This will make me one."

"The Dragon Class will hopefully have Baikalan surrounded and recaptured soon. In the meantime, we mustn't take risks, my son, as my first one already cost me something precious: your trust."

Something in Tai squeezed at her words. It was true, he realized. He no longer fully trusted his mother, the one person in the world he had always looked to for the truth. And perhaps she did not fully trust him. There had been no lies between them. It was always them against the world, their empire to protect together. At least in that, he thought, she had not strayed. Her motto was clear: prioritize the throne. And in his critical moment, she did just that. But it hurt that she valued the throne more than she valued him.

"If you won't allow me to assist there, let me help you with the state work here. You always trusted me with diplomacy, yet for weeks, when I ask about our plans, you push me aside."

"I am doing so for your own good, my son," the empress said. "You were nearly killed. It takes time to recover from such shock."

"I'd recover best if I had distractions," he insisted. "Work distractions."

"You never took enough time to enjoy the princely life, my son," his mother said. "I deprived you, making you be my partner in all things because I had no emperor to rule with me. You should treat this as a well-deserved holiday, a chance to eat and rest and take on some leisure activities."

He couldn't believe his ears. "That's all I've done this last month. The empire's darkest hour in twenty years, and you want me to take on leisure activities?"

"That's exactly why I want you to do so," she replied. "You are safe within these palace walls. And you need the extra rest."

But as he returned to his rooms, her words chafed him more with each step. He questioned her sudden protectiveness, as she had always believed in toughening him through experience. She had been the one to insist he head Dragon Class when she discovered his fear of heights. In his fourth year, she found a tutor for him as he started to lisp. She insisted the man use a rod if needed to perfect the prince's speech. And just two years ago, when he had been grappling with the death of a woman he thought he loved, the empress had hired the empire's most famous courtesans to teach him the "arts of the bedchamber" to dispel his melancholy. He had learned the arts quickly. The melancholy, however, had taken longer to overcome.

Had his mother really become so frightened by his near-death that she was determined to coddle him? Or was she afraid of something else? Could she be worried other factions might gather around him to forcibly put him on the throne?

History had proven that was a popular tactic, even if he wouldn't dream of betraying his mother. And if that was the real reason she was keeping him sheltered from crucial political information, then it showed their mistrust was deeper than he thought.

Tai entered his rooms and tore the scarf from his neck, the air welcome on his scar. He sat down to look at his correspondence, which included letters from the Dragon Class provision master, details on possible new training, and a letter from the Ministry of Mages about a new Dragon Class mage appointee. But he finally put them all aside, unable to focus on anything but his growing sense that the foundations of his life were cracking.

CHAPTER 4

The guards seemed truly sorry to see the dragonriders go, and climbed to the crumbling wall ramparts to watch them fly northeast.

In the garrison courtyard, the three bronze dragons had grown to twice their sizes to better carry the eight mages from court, along with the grooms brought to tend the dragons. Emar climbed into one of the carriages and then gave the signal, and the dragons took to the sky.

Ezho's black dragon Turuchi smoothed the surrounding airflow to ease their flight. Jin rode toward the back, opposite and just behind Aadan and his silver dragon Wanli, who hovered on the edges of her mind until she reassured him her hand was fine.

As Emar had predicted, the wound still showed but was clearly improving even without mage help. The other riders had all looked at it incredulously.

"Well," Panshalar shrugged his large shoulders, "it does mean we should always let the lady go first into any battle. Take the brunt since she can't die."

She tossed him a poisonous look.

Even Aadan's curiosity had won out, it seemed, for he had examined her hand, touching the side of the wound until she hissed.

"Sorry," he said immediately, but despite the pain, she was the one to feel sorry when he let go.

The hand throbbed, but not nearly as much as it did last night. Up here, she could take her mind from it. She loved the feel of Rayshan's wings, the warm scales against her in the chill air. The countryside, seen from above, was not as barren as it seemed up close, but rather vast and free. They flew over tiny hamlets where smoke curled into the skies and rivers carved their way through lush plains and marsh.

Gradually, the land became less inhabited, until they flew over vast tracts with no permanent structures in sight. Once, they passed over a herd of animals that Jin thought were oxen but then realized they had the elegant curve of deer antlers.

Reindeer, Rayshan said.

And . . . herders? She could see a small band of people riding some of the reindeer.

"Chaakan," Emar explained when she asked. They had stopped for a quick relief at a stream that cut down a mountain, pooling in a stretch of grassland. "People of the reindeer. They wander these lands freely but are very different from the regular people of Khitan."

As they stood eating their rations of dried meats and plain buns, Panshalar elbowed Ezho. "Think this will help get us into the warrior banner when we apply?"

Ezho's mouth worked around a piece of meat before swallowing, "Hopefully. Imagine, all of our wing making it into the same banner?"

Jao and Panshalar nodded enthusiastically, but Jin glanced at Aadan. In their third year, Dragon Class graduates could apply for a banner of their choice, in which they would apprentice for a year before staying or being reassigned. Unlike her wing mates, however, Jin had no wish to join the warriors, and she knew Aadan felt the same.

"What do you say?" Panshalar elbowed Aadan next. "You're applying for the warrior banner, aren't you?"

Aadan smiled. "Actually, I had my sights on agriculture."

The others groaned, and Panshalar blinked as if stunned.

"Agriculture?" Ezho repeated, grinning. "Why?"

"I have my reasons," Aadan replied.

Good ones, Jin thought. He had confided his preference to her that night in the palace, how agriculture and food could win wars without fighting. The night they had kissed. The same night she had found out Prince Tai's assignment for Aadan to befriend her.

"You?" Panshalar turned to Jin. "You going to plant rice too?"

"There's nothing wrong with planting rice," Aadan retorted, finishing his dried meat and dusting his hands. "But that's not what dragonriders in the agriculture banner do."

"It's the end goal," Panshalar argued. "Make rain, take harmful metals out of soil. Perfect for retirement."

Jao snorted his laughter, but Aadan didn't take the bait.

"Jin," Ezho said, "you staying with us or joining Aadan?"

The question wasn't meant to be loaded, Jin knew, yet somehow it was. "I haven't decided." That wasn't quite true. Becoming a messenger would mean she could fly alone with Rayshan and travel.

More groans rose at her answer.

"Two pacifists in our wing," Panshalar lamented, then slapped Aadan on the arm. "You're contagious."

But Aadan wasn't paying him any mind, for his gaze locked on Jin, with an expression that almost looked wistful.

By dusk, they spied the torches of the Karahag fort in the distance, its walls glowing dusty plum in the sunset. The outpost squatted in the midst of low stone walls dotted with watchtowers. The northernmost post of the Khitan Kingdom, Karahag, was the last post before the vast wasteland that led to the barbarian tribes of the frozen tundra. A small affair, it nevertheless occupied a strategic part of the landscape.

As they flew in, Jin understood why they had built a post here. Mountains rose on either side, carving a narrow corridor through which anyone wanting to enter Khitan from the northeast would have to pass. The mountains were hospitable only to the craggiest of mountain goats, while humans and horses flirted with death and crevices that plunged several *li* deep.

Tall, crude mud-brick walls surrounded the fortress that marked the Khitan border with the northern tribes. Khitan flags flew on the turrets, along with the flag of the Tang Empire, as a welcome to them. The summer breeze played with the jagged ends of the banners, reminding Jin of teeth.

Morbid today, Rayshan commented.

I don't like anything to do with King Ulagan.

That is understandable, Rayshan replied.

She still hadn't forgotten her last encounter with Ulagan, when he had tried to have her executed for bonding with Rayshan. When the empress had refused but offered an additional dragon as a compromise, Ulagan had insisted Jin choose the egg, knowing she was loath to doom a dragon to his care.

The Dragon Class party circled first, bellowing several blasts to announce their arrival. Below them, the courtyard filled with a dozen or more soldiers, all looking up into the sky. The mages landed first, the giant bronzes touching down and gently placing the carriages on the ground. Soldiers dismounted and helped unstrap the carriages as the mages stepped out, led by Gu and a wide-eyed Yao Bing, and others hoisted the carriages to clear the area.

Her wing landed next, and Jin looked about her. The facilities were sparse, to say the least, and even at the height of summer, the place felt cool and windswept. Six watchtowers lined the northern wall, and one main building dominated the southern end of the fortress, its eaves curling at the ends.

The Khitan people were taller and more rugged compared to those in the south. Those who came forward now to take their luggage and usher them into the main building were broad shouldered and wore their hair shaved along the middle, leaving long braids down either side of their faces. They were dressed in thick robes lined with rabbit fur, and a ruddy-faced groom came forward to help Rayshan, his smile warm.

"King Ulagan is here and will welcome you shortly," a local Khitan person said. Judging from his clothes, he was a personal servant of the king. Dread began pooling in Jin at meeting Ulagan again. She disliked him almost as much as she had disliked Gao.

"Where are the bodies?" Emar asked.

The servant hesitated. "You wish to see them now?"

Emar nodded. "I doubt Baikalan's waiting for us to

go through niceties with the king before he attacks again."

They walked toward the northern tower, where an oversized curtain had been drawn across a frame.

The stench hit her like a hammer even from this distance. Only when they were behind the curtain did she allow herself to clap a hand over her nose. Jao and Ezho shielded their faces. Yao Bing, the young mage, seemed nauseous, and even Aadan's face turned green.

Lying there were six dragons: two golds, three blacks, and a bronze. Or at least what was left of them. All bore lacerations, some had entire limbs missing, and one gold's head had been nearly severed. Bone pushed through great gaps of flesh, and pools of blood had soaked into the ground beneath them. A cloud of crows screamed their indignation when Khitan servants came waving their arms and stamping. By the looks of the bodies, the crows had been feasting for some time.

Mage Gu Ben cleared his throat. "Didn't your mages cast a spell to deter the rot?"

One of the servants shrugged. "We've never had to perform such spells, nor on so many."

Aadan drew closer to a black dragon with an entire shoulder hacked open. "But what kind of dragon can take down a whole wing by himself?"

"Baikalan is a powerful one," Emar said. "He has strength beyond even the biggest bronzes. Though I had hoped that coming out of a magic-induced sleep, he would be weak." He turned to the servant. "And no one saw anything?"

"Master Emar!"

There was no mistaking the brash, booming voice. Jin turned to see a broad, dark-faced man striding toward them, his robes trimmed with fox fur and his boots lined with a fine weave.

"King Ulagan of Khitan," Master Emar said. "Thank you for receiving us and for your timely reports."

The king glanced at Jin before turning back to Emar and the others. "Welcome to Khitan, Master Emar. As you can see, we've had a bit of a bloodbath here."

"And where are the riders?" Emar asked.

"We sent their bodies home to their families," the king said. "Wanted to do right by them."

Emar's face darkened. "Did they all die then?"

"Every last one." The king shook his head. "One survived the attack, but he dropped like a stone the day after, good as beheaded. I questioned him as well as I could, but he wasn't making much sense."

"Do you remember what he said?" Emar asked.

The king shrugged. "It's all in the records if you'd like to see them. But what I want to know is what the empress intends to do now that Baikalan is loose and roaming, who knows where, in my country. I promised to keep the dragon, but only as long as the magic was in place, and she gave me her word that—"

"It's too soon to discuss such things," Emar said,

giving him a reprimanding glance. "Especially as we may want to discuss them in private."

The king looked around at the mages and the riders, nonplussed. "All I know is she promised to protect my kingdom if anything should happen, and I'd say it has. I can't have a rogue dragon killing off my people. If she wants my help, she'd better ask for it."

"All in due course," Emar insisted. "Has anyone been to the Well of Ice?"

The king of Khitan looked shocked. "Of course. First thing we did."

"And it's empty?" Emar pressed.

The king laughed. "Empty as an old man's threat. Besides, if you had seen the men and how destroyed they were, you wouldn't be wasting your time hiking up to the Well of Ice. Only one thing could have destroyed six dragons in the space it took my soldiers to fart."

"Even so, I'd like our Grand Master Gu Ben and his team to view the site themselves," Emar said. "Either the magic wore out, or Baikalan became more powerful than we realized. And we need to find out which it is."

The king spread his palms. "Of course. I am here to serve."

Emar squinted into the horizon. "Can we make the journey in the dark?"

The king grunted. "Only if you like to gamble. It's a

half day's flight through those narrow mountain passes."

Emar nodded. "Very well. We will leave tomorrow."

"As you wish," the king said.

Jin went to Rayshan to tell him there would be only one night's rest. Her stomach churned at what they would find at the Well of Ice, but just then, she caught sight of something that twisted her heart.

Opposite them, a servant was leading a dragon toward the fort's main gate, a chain around the beast's neck. She would have recognized the bronze dragon anywhere, although he was now much larger than when she had last seen him. She had, after all, chosen him out of the hatchery herself for the king of Khitan and watched him be bonded to the king despite her inner fury at having to do so. And here was the dragon, looking well-fed but with a wild mistrust in his eyes. Scars marked his hide.

Without thinking, she reached out with her mind. *By the heavens, what does he do to you?*

A painful buzz exploded in her head, making her break the bond immediately. The bronze snarled at her, revealing missing teeth. A fresh surge of anger scoured Jin, not just for his physical wounds but for the meaningless noise she had encountered in the dragon's mind, so different from Rayshan's.

"I must thank you again for Satu." King Ulagan and Emar had materialized next to her, and the king grinned at the repulsed look on her face. "He is a fine dragon, better than one I could have chosen."

"You mistreat him," Jin said, nails cutting her palm.

"Rider Jin," Emar grumbled a warning as the king's smile vanished.

"And you don't control your tongue when you should." Ulagan scowled. "He is my dragon, and I suggest you and your wing focus on finding the worst dragon out there, for you have bigger problems than how I treat my property."

Jin was about to say something back, but Rayshan gave her a warning buzz in her head. A sentiment echoed in Emar's stern look.

The king and Emar moved away, speaking of the preparations for the morning. Jin scowled at the king's back and noticed another figure, a young girl of sixteen or so, standing near a cattle pen by the fort's western wall. The girl looked different from everyone else in that her robes were finer, and she wore a delicately woven hat with gold fringe over thick black hair. As they drew closer, Jin noticed a familiar slant to the girl's mouth, the cut of her small nose, though the eyes were lighter than Ulagan's. She must be Ulagan's daughter.

They walked into a round yurt, the carpets laid out with elaborate designs of deer, birds, and wolves. A central brazier in the ground had an entire sheep on its spit, tended by a group of women.

Servants showed them to cushions ranged along the

perimeter, and Panshalar, Jao, Aadan, and Ezho all took seats on the left where indicated. Jin was about to join them when Ulagan's voice boomed out.

"The most favored rider in the Tang Empire will come sit in the place of honor, on my left."

Jin hesitated, a cold knot in her stomach. Ulagan had no love for her or her dragon, and an invitation to sit next to him was like an invitation to drink poison. Upon Ulagan's insistent wave of the hand, she bowed, walked over, and lowered herself to the cushion next to him, Emar flanking his other side.

"Welcome, Riders, and let us show you some Khitan hospitality before we get down to business," Ulagan said. "Here, we only conduct business after sharing meat and tea."

A servant came and offered a tray with cups of steaming fermented mare's milk. She offered it first to the king, then to Emar, and then to Jin, who took the last cup. Jin would have preferred water or even weak black tea instead of liquor, but rejecting hospitality was unthinkable.

She drank and noticed the king's daughter walk through a flap at the yurt's side. The girl had a pronounced limp, though whether from injury or disease, Jin wasn't sure. The girl silently took a seat behind her father, and Ulagan motioned toward her.

"My daughter, Nomu, the only daughter in a long line of sons," Ulagan said proudly. Jin wondered where these sons were, as she saw no sign of them. Had the king of Khitan left them at home in the capital? "A warm welcome to our riders. May we be successful in finding Baikalan and re-imprisoning him."

Everyone drank, and women immediately refilled their cups.

"How did he escape exactly?" Emar asked. "The report was vague."

The king's expression darkened. "How should I know? My agreement with the empress was simply to keep watch and allow the Well to be placed within my lands. I didn't say I would be responsible for keeping him there. That's why you are here, dear Emar."

The part of Emar's face that was unaffected by the white disease twitched. "But surely you have some theories. How did you know he escaped, for instance?"

"The Well is empty!" Ulagan exclaimed as if the answer was obvious.

"So you examined the Well?"

"Of course! And found nothing to indicate who had let him out. The dragon had destroyed all tracks."

"But it had to be a mage," Emar said smoothly. "Only a mage could break the spells binding Baikalan. Have you questioned your mages?"

Ulagan knocked back another cup of tea. "I don't make mage business my business."

Jin hid her doubts in her cup. Ulagan was a man who claimed to know all, even when he knew nothing. To admit a shortage in his expertise was unlike him. Perhaps he was worried about the empress's wrath at losing Baikalan, which would make sense. Would the empress protect him from Baikalan now that the dragon was free? What web of politics was being spun here?

"But now that Baikalan is out, where do you think he's gone?" Ulagan said. "Straight to Mengkhis?"

"I wouldn't know," Emar answered, watching his cup being refilled.

Ulagan guffawed. "Come, a dragon will go straight to its rider. But my question is, is it possible for Baikalan to find him?"

"You know as well as I that Mengkhis Lai's whereabouts are secret."

"Precisely!" Ulagan slapped a thigh with one large palm. "Is there any danger of Baikalan finding that out, Master Emar? I hear only some know of Mengkhis's exact location. Should we be worried?"

"There is an invisible dragon loose, King Ulagan, and our riders have been slain," Emar said. "We should all be worried."

Ulagan glanced at Jin. "Rumors are Emar here knows where Mengkhis is buried." He turned back to Emar. "Is it true?"

"It's true there are rumors," Emar replied. "But I suggest we focus on our current problems first."

Ulagan gave a sly smile. "The empress has always trusted you. You grew up together, no?"

Jin glanced from Ulagan to Emar, surprised. She had never heard of Emar's childhood or the empress's.

"I was in her household," Emar answered, putting down his empty cup.

Ulagan motioned for a servant to refill their cups and took a large bite out of a haunch of mutton, which he chewed as he gesticulated. "But you and she have *yuan fen*, intertwined fates. If there's anyone she'd tell Mengkhis's location, it'd be you, am I right?"

"Why is this so important to you?" Emar asked.

Ulagan's smile faded. "Because if there's a dragon out there trying to find Mengkhis and you know Mengkhis's whereabouts, then I don't want to take you right to him, do I?"

Emar regarded him for a moment. "I thought the Well is empty."

"It is." Ulagan raised his cup, and his daughter came with her half walk, half shuffle to replenish his wine. "But who knows if the dragon might return?" The girl turned and made her way to Emar, and Ulagan's mouth turned sullen. "My daughter Nomu here is beautiful, is she not? She'd make a fine wife for a prince, but it seems your empress is holding out for better."

Emar sipped his drink. "I don't make imperial marriage my business."

Ulagan threw his head back and roared his laughter. "Well said. We heard all sorts of wild rumors up here, even those about this female rider being married to the prince." His look at Jin was more of a leer than a glance. "That prince is filial, I'll give him that. Will drink his own piss if his mother just asks."

Jin bristled. Tai might be arrogant and a flirt, but he didn't deserve that insult. Rayshan sent a warning through their bond.

Don't lose yourself, Jin. Don't give him the satisfaction.

Jin leaned on Rayshan's strength and forced her heart rate to slow, pushing the anger down to a safe level. Since the blood bonding, her emotions had also grown wilder, harder to harness.

She looked across the fire toward Aadan and froze. Beyond the far cushions, standing just next to Aadan in the shadows, was Minister Gao, a disturbing smirk on his face. But then he was gone, his form disappearing like ash in the flame, his smile the last to disappear.

She noticed Aadan watching her intently and turned away, hoping he couldn't tell how shaken she was. She didn't need him, or anyone, thinking she was losing her mind. Ulagan was deep in conversation with Emar and Grand Master Gu Ben, while Yao Bing seemed engrossed in animated debate with the younger Khitan mages.

She rose and murmured excuses before rushing from the yurt, grateful for the fresh night air.

You saw him again? Rayshan murmured over their bond.

Yes. It is happening more frequently. What's going on?

Not sure. I also have seen dragons appearing and then disappearing. But I don't know what the visions mean.

Rayshan, I'm going mad.

No, he growled. *I felt it too.*

Then perhaps we're both going mad together.

Well, at least we'll have company. But his words held no comfort. Something was very wrong with her. And she couldn't help but believe that maybe the blood bond was slowly destroying her from the inside out.

Like it did Mengkhis Lai.

CHAPTER 5

As expected, Tai found his mother at her private temple, with a few maids-in-waiting, her household servants, and half a dozen monks.

He lit the obligatory incense one of the maids held out, bowed three times to the gently smiling Buddha, and then placed the smoldering sticks in the urn of ash and knelt on the cushioned knee stool next to his mother.

She didn't open her eyes, but the wrinkling of her brows told him she knew he was there. She continued with her prayers, her mouth moving silently. The monks chanted softly in one corner, their beads whispering through their fingers as they kept time. Tai glanced at the walls, where snarling demons with tusks and rolling eyes gleefully stirred cauldrons full of tormented souls. Tai had always found it ironic to try and find peace in a place adorned with graphic scenes of misery.

"I thought I might find you here." He had worked his most charming smile on his mother's lady-in-waiting, who knew all the empress's movements. It had been short work finding out all his mother's upcoming meetings under the pretense of arranging a surprise boat picnic.

His mother clapped her hands together and bowed three times to the great gold statue above them. When she straightened, she gazed up at the Buddha. She had commissioned it in Tai's birth year, and now its placid gold face glowed in the candlelight that burned even in the day. Like many of the city's most prominent Buddhas, the face bore a remarkable resemblance to his mother.

The empress had, from the time of her ascension, ordered gold statues of the deity built in her likeness at all the temples. Tai had never seen the exact official figures, but he knew the sum was staggering. The empress had always told him it was money well spent to make the people venerate her. Statesmanship, she had told him, was just as much about image as it was about actual ruling.

"Is something on your mind, my son?" she asked, turning a thoughtful look on him.

He shrugged, casual. "I heard you might be meeting Marquis Sanjin here. I was simply curious to sit in."

"You have a knack for ferreting information. Who told you?"

"A good politician never reveals his sources." He brushed stray incense ash from his robe. "What has Sanjin found out?"

She hesitated, then sighed, resigned. "Gao's graft was deeper than we suspected."

"How deep?" Tai shifted on his knees to better look at her.

"That's what I am about to find out."

A servant entered, followed by a tall, thin man with a smooth, unblemished face and lips that stretched above a sharp chin. He wore the all-black silk robes of his high status. The servant announced Marquis Sanjin, then retreated.

"Peace upon your morning, Your Majesty." Sanjin bowed low, betraying no surprise at Tai's presence. Tai had known Marquis Sanjin all his life, and his mother had told Tai he owed his life to the Royal Veil. But even so, Tai found him difficult to warm to, for despite the calm, benign exterior, Tai always sensed a core of ice. He respected the man who headed the imperial police, but had heard unbelievable accounts of methods used in the euphemistically named "tea rooms."

"I'm afraid I have much to report, and none of it is pleasing," the marquis said.

"Flowery words won't cure ailments," the empress said, standing and turning to face the marquis. "What is the greater picture?"

Sanjin glanced at Tai, but at the empress's nod, continued. "The imperial accountants have now gone through over half of Minister Gao's finances and books, but it seems each leads to others. It appears he and his connections have pilfered significant sums from the war treasury to fund his own schemes. I have traced some of the money to private soldiers, including those who participated in the coup. He also paid for certain weapons and supplies, while other funds went to bribing officials, it seems."

"Names?" the empress asked.

"I will have a list soon," Sanjin promised. "But all signs, Your Majesty, point to our armed forces and our war treasury being severely depleted."

Tai thought on this, incredulous. Just when they needed their army to fight Baikalan, they discovered it punctured with holes. It was almost like Gao was laughing at them from beyond the grave.

His mother echoed his own question, "How did this happen?"

Sanjin's look turned sour. "He bribed many of the accountants, Your Majesty. They were in Gao's employ and helped him fix the records so that we paid to outfit the imperial army, but no supplies actually arrived. They instead went to Gao's personal coffers through a private arms supplier."

"Let me guess, one of Gao's relatives," Tai said. The man had relations with nearly all the wealthy and influential families of the empire, as his family tree was wide and its roots deep.

Sanjin nodded. "Precisely. I don't yet have the final tally of how much he stole, Your Majesty, but it was exorbitant."

His mother's expression didn't change, but Tai knew she was masking her rage. As she hid many things, he thought wryly.

"I want you to investigate every department," the empress said to Sanjin. "Put together accountants loyal to us and comb through all the main ledgers. The Ministries of Works, Rites, Personnel, audit them all. Make sure there are no other ministers or government officials who are following Gao's path. My son will make sure you have full access to the Dragon Class accounts as well." He finally heard the fury break through. "This makes us a laughingstock, having our money stolen by our own people. A rat in the nest."

A rat she had been willing to let kill her son, Tai thought, the scar on his neck twitching.

Sanjin bowed. "I have already started that process, Your Majesty. We will find how deep the rot goes."

"And I expect you to remember the wise saying that a great man does not shy away from poison when dealing with weeds."

Tai caught the glance between his mother and Sanjin.

"I agree. Now is not the time for a soft touch, Your

Majesty," Sanjin said. "A plucked weed grows back nine leaves."

"But we will hold trials," Tai said firmly.

Sanjin regarded him. "Of course." He bowed.

"Have you had news from the riders in Khitan?" Tai asked.

Sanjin folded his hands behind his back. "They sent a message from the Beitou post of the Great Wall, saying they were about to enter Khitan territory. I expect another message in a day or so."

"Notify me when you hear," the empress said.

"Us," Tai cut in. "Please notify us."

Sanjin bowed once more. "Of course, Your Highness."

The empress turned to leave, but Tai decided he would push his luck. He wasn't sure when he would next be able to surprise Sanjin and his mother by dropping into their meetings, and he was curious as to whom his new superior in the military would be.

"Have you decided on a new Minister of War, Your Majesty?"

His question made both of them pause, and once more they shared a look that made Tai wonder how many conversations they deliberately excluded him from.

Days after the traitor Gao's death, Tai had pushed for Emar to be named Minister of War, but his mentor had shot down his proposal in less time than the old man took to knock back a cup of baijiu.

"I'm a rider, or at least half of one, and will be until I'm in my grave," Emar had muttered, continuing to amend a list of supplies for the trip to Khitan. "I'll not stay in court in silks and repulse everyone with my white disease."

His mother had seemed unsurprised by the refusal, saying she had expected as much and she, therefore, favored new blood. Her sights had landed on Li Shan, the military administrator for Dunhuang. Tai had never met him but knew from history books the man's skills in war strategy. Tai's father had banished Li Shan to a remote post after a drunken argument, but Empress Wu wanted his family reinstated.

"Li Shan refused the post," his mother said.

Tai frowned. "On what grounds?"

His mother turned to Sanjin. "How did he phrase it?"

"He said he is a frail old man unworthy of even a sliver of Your Majesty's generosity," Sanjin replied. "My guess is that old grudges run deep."

The empress pursed her lips. "A general would never refuse my appointment if I was a man."

"Emar refused," Tai pointed out.

"That's different," the empress said, icy. "Emar would have refused me if I was the Jade Emperor himself."

"Is Your Majesty sure she doesn't wish me to persuade Li Shan to reconsider?"

Tai caught Sanjin's meaning and felt a chill at the

man's ability to speak of torture with such calm. His mother had always waved away his questions about the throne's policing methods, arguing that wolves who didn't use their teeth were destined to live as dogs.

"No," his mother said in answer to Sanjin. "An unwilling servant is the worst burden of all. I will think of alternatives."

As they left the temple and Tai parted ways with the empress and Sanjin, he heard the head of the Royal Veil murmur to his mother.

"Do not take too long, Your Majesty. There are those saying that Heaven's favor is no longer with you, and not having a War Minister makes hungry men hungrier." Sanjin's voice dropped in warning. "As they say, the longer the night, the wilder the dreams."

CHAPTER 6

The morning after their arrival in Khitan dawned crisp, with curls of smoke rising from the morning kitchens as the horses stamped their hooves and the soldiers gathered to make the trip north through the winding mountain pass.

Jin cinched the saddle on Rayshan, taking over from the groom who had brushed him down the night before.

Ready for this? she asked.

As ready as one can be to face an invisible dragon.

She looked at her wing mates preparing to ride. Each of their dragons called out to her, and she mentally greeted them—even Jao's dragon, who, like his rider, was quiet and reticent with her.

I still don't understand this whole etiquette thing, where the dragons aren't telling their riders I can speak to them?

It's complicated, Rayshan replied, coiling his tail. *A*

blood bond is between dragon and rider, and only to be judged or punished by the Dragon Queen. For those who leave the dragon's ancestral home of Nine Claw Mountain, the bond with our rider is sacred.

She spied Aadan and Emar consulting each other some distance away. Emar patted Aadan's shoulder and then began making his way to the dragons readying to depart.

Ulagan's soldiers were forming into groups. There were about two dozen, and another dozen mages. Ulagan had explained that he had sent a battalion of soldiers to the site earlier in the week, as he didn't want to take any risks with Baikalan. This way, magic at least would be on their side in case the escaped dragon returned. Everyone wore thick winter robes in anticipation of the Well of Ice, and dogs snapped at the heels excitedly, eager for the trip.

You're on edge.

She thought on it. *Something about Ulagan's soldiers seems odd.*

Perhaps you don't like them because they're all Ulagan's men.

She had to admit that was a possibility. What was hovering at the back of her mind?

Jin had no time to think on it further, for Emar was motioning everyone in the wing to gather.

"We fly in formation. No one goes too far ahead. Jin, I want you to hang back. Ezho and Panshalar, you take the front. The bronze dragons will make up the middle."

"Shouldn't Jin go first?" Panshalar asked. "She's the one who can't die." Aadan gave him a cool glance, but the giant shrugged. "It's true."

Emar's look never faltered. "If Baikalan really does come back, I expect him to sneak up behind us, not come from the front."

Panshalar nodded in understanding, while Ezho looked disappointed that he wasn't leading the group due to his skill.

"And Aadan?" Jin asked before she thought better of it. Aadan glanced at her, eyes questioning. *So you do care?* he seemed to be saying. She looked away, hiding her thoughts.

"Aadan stays behind," Emar said. "I want him to be here to examine the bodies and talk to the healers. Now, if there are no more questions, let's fly!"

Jin shoved aside her unease that Aadan wouldn't be with them, then mounted. He would be safer here anyway, she told herself.

The king of Khitan frowned, glancing at Aadan thoughtfully. "Master Emar, do you not trust my own top healers who examined the dragons' bodies?"

Emar grunted. "It's protocol, King Ulagan, nothing more."

Ulagan smiled tightly. "In that case, I'll assign an assistant." He motioned for a servant and gave a few curt commands in the Khitan tongue, then clambered onto his gold dragon, a hulking, scarred thing she thought she heard him call Shatang.

The bronze that Jin had been forced to choose for Ulagan had a carriage harnessed to him. These were the only dragons the north had, a gift from the empress of China to the king for keeping Baikalan in the Well of Ice. A part of Jin hoped that the dragons might be withdrawn now that the king had inadvertently let Baikalan escape.

But she knew that was wishful thinking.

Catching her look, the king grinned. "I'm thinking the empress might gift me a third dragon if we recapture Baikalan."

Jin's insides writhed, but Rayshan sent a calming hum through the bond and jerked his head.

The bronzes from Dragon Class expanded to triple their sizes before the Khitan soldiers squeezed into the carriages attached to them. The mages stood at regular intervals around the dragons and chanted several verses, walking first one way and then another, in a spell to make the carriages lighter and, therefore, easier to carry. She had seen this trick a few times before—once when she had stolen Rayshan's egg and another few times in the capital when she had seen the mages working on the boats of rich merchants who shipped goods through the city's canals.

Once the carriages were lightened, the mages, including Yao Bing and Grand Master Gu Ben, climbed in with Emar, and the doors closed. The king gave the signal to fly, and the convoy took to the air. Ezho led on Turuchi to ensure smoother, faster flying. Panshalar went next on his gold dragon Bayan, and Jao's bronze, Nakkalan, took a carriage full of mages into the air. Jin flew last, chancing a look behind her. She saw Aadan watching them from a turret, while just beyond him in the paddock was Wanli.

The dragon told her to fly safely.

Jin faced forward again, watching the dragons in front. Satu, the king's bronze, flew steadily, wings pumping as the carriage attached to him swayed occasionally in flight. The king rode his gold dragon alongside.

They flew through towering mountains on either side, once in a while disturbing a goat, climbing higher into the mountains before breaking through to the other side and seeing a long, undulating plain.

Here, the weather changed abruptly, and Jin sensed that it was magic induced. The temperature dropped to an abnormal low for summer, and a few *li* later, dustings of snow appeared on the ground, followed by a gentle flurry of snowflakes that settled against Jin's hair and along the dragons' ridges. Still, they flew on, though Jin could tell the bronzes were tiring. Bronzes could not keep their size and strength for hours on end without exhausting themselves, and they would likely need a full night's slumber soon.

Jin smelled snow, wet, and the crackle of something else in the air. What was it? Something about the smell of this place, of the people and dragons around her, wasn't right.

They flew into the snow flurries, and Jin shivered. She wondered if the blood bond made her feel cold more.

No, it helps against the chill, Rayshan said.

So my shivering is nerves then.

Undoubtedly.

This wasn't reassuring. They stopped at a small valley to rest, the bronze dragons panting from exertion. The Khitan soldiers came out of their carriages to stretch their legs, passing around bottles of liquor amongst themselves and the dragonriders. Panshalar took a generous swig and then handed it to Ezho, who grimaced.

"It warms the insides. You'll need it as it gets colder near the Well of Ice," Ulagan commented, slapping a flask into Emar's chest.

The older man took it and sniffed.

"If you'd prefer your watery southern fare, I have some of that too," Ulagan said.

Emar pushed the flask back. "I brought my own."

Ulagan shrugged and pocketed it. "Suit yourself."

They remounted.

"How much further?" Emar asked.

Ulagan consulted one of his mages. "A few hours at most. We will reach it by the hour of the horse and then camp there tonight."

Jin wasn't sure she wanted to camp near Baikalan's

prison, empty or not. She climbed up on Rayshan, watching the others prepare to leave. Most had drawn their fur coats tight against the cold, the robes held fast by thick sashes.

As they flew, the snow worsened until a soft layer blanketed them, numbing her hands. At some unseen signal, Ulagan's gold began to descend. Jin followed as the dragons in front of her spiraled down to a snow-covered indent in the ground, where Khitan soldiers on horseback waited. There were about a hundred of them, with evidence of a campsite behind them.

This is one battalion? Jin thought in surprise. It looked like more.

He's right to be cautious of Baikalan, Rayshan replied.

There didn't seem to be much marking this spot, however, and Jin wondered whether the Well of Ice was hidden or still a distance away.

Emar apparently thought the same, for when he exited the carriage and came to Ulagan, he was scowling at the landscape, as well as the line of soldiers who had not, Jin noticed, dismounted to pay their respects to their king.

"What are we doing here?"

"You wanted to visit Baikalan's Well of Ice. This is it," Ulagan said. The soldiers from Karahag were piling out of the dragon Satu's carriage, along with the Khitan mages. The imperial mages, including Yao Bing and his master, stepped out of Jao's carriage, pulling their hoods over their faces.

Jin looked around. She couldn't see a well, much less anything that resembled a hole or cave large enough to shelter a dragon.

"This?" Emar looked about. "This is undisturbed ground."

Ulagan's mages had fanned out and were busy brushing the snow from the perimeters of a space roughly the width of five dragons nose to tail. Grand Master Gu Ben paced along the perimeter, Yao Bing shadowing him closely while the other imperial mages walked to the middle of the area, testing the ground.

Ulagan held out his arms, smiling, and a distinct chill that had nothing to do with the weather slithered down Jin's back. "The Well lies beneath us."

A whistling filled the air, just as a rain of arrows thudded into the bronze dragons and their riders. Jin watched, uncomprehending, as the slain bronzes crumpled to the ground, blood marring the churned snow.

She whirled. The mounted Khitans were nocking another round to their bows as the Khitan riders' horses broke into a ring, surrounding the newcomers. Jin and her companions drew their weapons as Ulagan's soldiers drew their spears, leveling them at the riders and Emar. Yao Bing and his master slowed, then stopped as several Khitan mages encircled them.

And that's when Jin noticed it.

The Khitan spear points were bone. None of Ulagan's men carried the tang of metal—they wore sashes for belts and had bone-tipped weapons and lace-up leather shoes. No one wore jewelry or helmets. Even the horse saddles were pure felt and bridles made of leather.

"What is this?" Emar's face paled so that even the good side seemed to match the diseased side. "Where is Baikalan?"

"Safely below," Ulagan said. "But today, we free him."

And then everything seemed to happen at once.

The Khitan soldiers loosed a volley of ivory blades. Panshalar doubled over with a blade in the shoulder, while Ezho sank to one knee, a gushing wound in his thigh. Jao screamed and reached for his sword, but the blade flew from his hand to land by the king's gold dragon, and soldiers pounced on Jao. A group of Khitans pulled ropes over Nakkalan's muzzle before he could breathe flame. The king's bronze threw his giant bulk against Turuchi, Ezho's dragon, and the two locked jaws on each other's throats at the same time, eyes venomous. Jin moved to leap on Rayshan, but a burning sensation shot through her veins, crumpling her.

"Not so fast, girl," Ulagan said, still grinning. His gold dragon was eyeing them intently, mouth open. At her confused look, the king laughed. "Ah, Emar, you haven't taught your students about all the powers a gold has?" He turned back to Jin. "I don't know the science of it, but it appears that people have metals in their bodies. All a gold dragon needs to do is pull, and it warps you."

Jin gasped. What was happening inside her? In Rayshan? She felt ill, and not just from the sight of her Dragon Class colleagues lying dead and peppered with arrows. Nor was it from seeing Bayan with his wings pinioned to the ground, thrashing against the ropes around his jaws.

No, this was something else, as if the strength had bled out of her body, and nausea was a living thing gripping her.

"Stop!" Emar shouted. "How many people did you kill to practice this?"

"I lost count, but it was worth it." Ulagan walked over to stand over Jin as she slipped from Rayshan's back and into the snow. "My Shatang can draw the iron right out of you." Rayshan swayed, snarling against the gold's pull, but was unable to free himself. "I would like to kill you slowly, as you took my jade from me, but unfortunately, I don't have the time. So quick it is." He motioned for one of the soldiers, who jogged forward and handed him a spear.

"Ulagan," Emar said, striding forward before soldiers pressed their spear points to him. "You are mad if you think you can free Baikalan and control him."

"Oh, I don't dream of controlling Baikalan," Ulagan said. "You will."

Jin's mind reeled. She retched, and then, at a motion

from Ulagan, the gold closed his mouth, and she lay there, gasping as her head spun and her body regained its feeling.

"You, Emar, know the location of Mengkhis Lai, and I think Baikalan will be very happy to cooperate if it means regaining his rider." Ulagan turned back to Panshalar and Ezho, who were swaying.

The liquor. Jin cursed. Of course, the liquor that they had drunk because they refused the northern wine. Ulagan had counted on the riders preferring their local brew. She looked over at Grand Master Gu Ben and Yao Bing. The youth was trying to support his master, who had slumped to the ground.

"Ulagan," Emar snapped, "think logically. This will never work, and you cannot kill dragonriders. It is taboo, against the Dragon Queen's rules."

Ulagan shrugged. "Those are China's rules. And you, Master Emar, are no longer in China."

Jin tried to use the distraction to grab the dagger from her belt, but it flew from her grasp and landed at the gold dragon's claws.

"Good boy, Shatang," Ulagan said. *Sha-tang.* The name sounded exactly like "sand pool," but now Jin was sure it had another meaning: *sha* for "kill" and Tang for the Tang dynasty. Jin would have laughed if she didn't fear descending into hysteria. Turning back to Jin, Ulagan stepped on her wrist. "Tie her. Mages, begin the ritual. And kill the Tang mages."

Soldiers came forward to bind her, and though

Rayshan rose to her defense, another wave of nausea felled them as the gold dragon yanked the metals in their bodies. She vaguely heard screaming as Yao Bing fell to the snow, his blood pooling in the surrounding footprints and his eyes already glassy.

Jao's and Panshalar's dragons roared in their fight against Shatang's power. But she knew they were outmatched. Jao's Nakkalan was exhausted from having flown at triple size, while Panshalar's gold only knew how to draw on external metals, none of which the enemy was wearing.

Ulagan pulled Jin to her feet once her arms were tied. Her head was still spinning from both Shatang's power and the death all around her. She could barely tell up from down, but she stumbled through the snow as Ulagan pulled her along, her rage building. The mages had uncovered five oblong stone markers at five points of the perimeter and had taken up places, hands at the ready.

Jin tried not to look at the blood-spattered snow and the bodies of all the mages, including Yao Bing's, sprawled at awkward angles where they had fallen. The young mage would never pester her with questions again. Grand Master Gu Ben, all of them—in all her thieving days, she had never witnessed such sudden and casual taking of life.

"You don't fear the empress's wrath?" Jin spat out.

Ulagan shrugged. "No."

"If you don't fear her, you should fear me."

His chest shook with mirth. "The day I fear a woman is the day I am no longer fit to live."

The Khitan mages began chanting, and Jin could feel an energy, something ancient and dark, humming around them. It seeped into her bones, and the gold had given up on her and Rayshan, clearly satisfied that they were both too crippled to do any harm.

The soldiers brought Emar, Jao, Ezho, and Panshalar to kneel at Ulagan's feet, both Ezho and Panshalar grimacing at their wounds, and Ulagan motioned again at one of the soldiers. They hastened over with a bone-tipped spear.

"I will give you all a chance to swear allegiance to me," Ulagan said. "Swear your loyalty, and I will spare you."

Jin looked at Ezho, Jao, and Panshalar. Ezho stoically kept a brave face, but Panshalar looked frightened, and Jao was pale with anger more than fear. She smelled the sweat and terror and didn't blame them. The same odors enshrouded her.

"You'll kill us anyway," Emar spat.

"They'll swear allegiance," Jin said. The four men looked at her, dumbfounded. But she mustn't let them die. Who would warn Aadan? "Spare them and kill me. That's what you really want, isn't it?"

Ulagan looked at her and shrugged. "I suppose you're right." He lowered the spear, then frowned. "But on second thought, how far can I trust an allegiance sworn at sword point?" He motioned to the soldiers.

"Take the old man. Tie the others out there to the center of the circle. Let them be our offering to Baikalan."

"No!" Jin screamed. She tried to get to her feet, but pain shot through her anew. The dragon Shatang was only obeying his master, but at that moment, she envisioned driving a dagger through the dragon's chest. However, this would not kill Ulagan like it would a regular rider, she knew, for his bond with his dragons was mage-forged. Unlike hers and Rayshan's, it did not bind the king and his dragon in life and death.

Ulagan yanked her by the hair. "You should never have taken my jade, girl. But now that you have, know this: Minister Gao promised me lands, promised me much better conditions for keeping Baikalan here. Your killing Gao . . . well, let's say not everyone here welcomed that news."

"You are a fool with a fool's hand, Ulagan," Emar said. "The empress has much more power than you do, and you have nowhere to hide."

Ulagan snorted. "Let her bring her fight." He pushed Jin until she was back in the snow, her mouth full of blood and ice, her insides seething from the gold dragon's force. "Now, say goodbye, Rider Jin."

She twisted around to stand up and fight but caught sight of Emar, who was silently mouthing the words, "Stay down!"

And then there was a breathtaking pain in her chest. She looked down at the blood-smeared spearhead protruding from her ribs. Fire seared her back, her lungs, her flesh, her very mind. She thought she'd go blind with agony. A roar filled her ears—Rayshan's cry, enraged and powerless. Several soldiers had pinioned his and the other dragons' wings to the ground with spears.

The chanting reached a crescendo, and the ground beneath her quivered and swayed. With a crack that sounded like lightning, the snow caved in right beneath Jao, Panshalar, and Ezho, and they disappeared along with Turuchi, Nakkalan, and Bayan. The imploding snow swallowed their screams.

The Well of Ice had opened. Her vision went white.

Stay with me, Rayshan said. *You are alive. You are alive.*

But why can't I feel anything? she cried, her vision blurring.

The white nothingness around her gave way to a shadowy jade-colored head emerging from the lip of the snow, followed by claws. Impossibly large claws.

Baikalan, someone hissed in her head, and then all dissolved into white.

CHAPTER 7

*A*adan stared at the laceration, willing his mind to focus. This was doubly difficult given the stench, which was only partially alleviated by the scented scarf he had wrapped three times around his nose and mouth.

The courtyard was nearly deserted, with only a few soldiers on the outer wall, plus the resident leather-worker who seemed to have planted himself permanently in a nearby portcullis, hammering nails into shoes.

Aadan ran a hand over the stubble that had grown in just one night and then looked from one dragon body to another. All lacerated.

"The rider of the gold one was the kindest."

He looked up to see a girl of roughly sixteen in a fur-trimmed hat standing there, her hair arranged in neat but simple plaits. The king's daughter, he remembered. She had been sitting behind Jin last night. Which was possibly the only reason he remembered her so well, he admitted to himself. He'd been trying not to steal looks at Jin, with a woeful success rate.

"Did anyone see them die? Or see Baikalan?"

The girl paused for a moment, then shook her head. "No one heard anything. It was after the mid-summer festival. Everyone had much to drink that night."

Aadan nodded, then turned back to the bodies.

"I didn't think girls rode dragons until I saw it for myself." She paused. "Is it true they are taking women recruits now?"

Aadan turned away from the bodies, seeing that the child was determined to interrupt him. "Yes, this winter will mark the first intake." All because Jin had the defiance to steal a dragon, bond with him, and persevere through Dragon Class. He had never met anyone with such grit, and as an exiled prince, that was saying much. The thought of his status as the exiled heir to his father's throne brought back memories of his last argument with his father, but the girl cut into his thoughts again.

"The Dragon Class probably wouldn't take me because of my leg."

She seemed to wait for Aadan to contradict her, but lying was not one of Aadan's skills.

"My father will send me off for marriage soon anyway," she said. "But I'd rather live Rider Jin's life."

The girl couldn't be more than sixteen, perhaps

even fourteen. And though many girls married at that age, Aadan personally didn't approve. He had seen his fair share of girls who seemed to lose something of themselves when they married at young ages.

"Satu doesn't seem to mind my leg."

"Satu?"

"My father's bronze dragon. He lets me climb on his back when he is resting. Though my father, of course, scolds me for it." Her brow creased. "You won't tell him, will you?"

Aadan shook his head. "I will not."

She grinned, the smile so childlike he again felt a flash of anger at Ulagan for sending her to marry at this age. She limped away, and Aadan turned back to the task at hand. He had no way of helping her. The fates were decided. However, he might be able to do something here, figure out how Baikalan had managed to kill all six riders and dragons with no one noticing.

Baikalan was a large dragon, true. But for all dragons to die . . .

He peered closer at the wounds. What was it about them that bothered him? Crows had already eaten away at many wounds, but some of the original cuts were still intact. These were straight-edged, with no jagged ends, the kind of slices made when a fishmonger gutted flesh. He checked each dragon's wounds, then consulted the scrolls the examiner had provided.

The records noted deep gashes, but from what Aadan had seen, they were not from claws. Claws made jagged wounds, and during a struggle, they would rip at the edges as the victim thrashed. These looked smooth, as if the dragon had conveniently stood still while the enemy wreaked havoc.

Aadan pondered this, something uneasy working into his thoughts. He called to Wanli, asking his dragon to pull the water out of the body before him. As a silver, Wanli could draw water from the air, plants, and even flesh. Wanli stirred and obliged, but then stopped, telling Aadan that something in the fluids of the bodies felt different.

Aadan took the scrolls and headed toward the yurt to find his appointed assistant. As he passed the leatherworker, he noticed that another man had appeared next to him, and they were deep in conversation. One of them looked up at him, his eyes following.

Aadan walked across the wide courtyard to the yurt where he knew his assigned assistant was attending to cattle arrangements. He drew the flap aside and entered to see the wraith-thin assistant arguing with another of Ulagan's men. The assistant immediately came to Aadan's side.

"Where is the healer here?" Aadan pointed to the scroll. "I'd like to speak to Ganchu. He examined the bodies, yes?"

The assistant read the name at the bottom of the scroll, his mustache moving as his eyes squinted. "Yes, he did. But he is away. I can answer any questions."

Aadan regarded him. "If you didn't do the examination, how can you answer my questions?"

"I have some knowledge of the process, and I read the scrolls," the assistant said. "Ganchu is at another posting and won't be back for several days."

"Did he test for poison?"

The assistant looked surprised. "Is there any need? Those wounds are so great, they couldn't possibly have died from poison."

"But they didn't die fighting. Why?" Aadan argued.

The assistant nodded. "I see. I'll make sure to send a message to Ganchu."

"Do you not have other healers who can test for such things?" Aadan asked.

The assistant shook his head. "Not that I know of, but let me inquire." His eyes darted over to a water clock in the corner. "I will make sure to have an answer for you by the noon meal."

Aadan glanced at the water clock as well. How long did it take to see if there was a healer in a small fort? Something about the assistant's smile didn't fit, and as he left the yurt, he saw the leatherworker and his companion still glancing over at him as if they had been waiting for him to leave.

He was, for the first time, distinctly aware that he was the only dragonrider present at the fort. The other riders would be back tomorrow night at the earliest. He looked into the sky, then around at the fort. He caught one of the guards looking away as if he didn't want to be observed watching.

Something's wrong, Wanli, he said to his dragon.

Wanli questioned him with a hum.

I don't know what, but we need to leave. We're being watched. He had noticed that the two leatherworkers had daggers at their belts, and not the leatherworking kind. The guards on the wall, similarly, always gazed in instead of out, as if any threat was inside. He had the sneaking suspicion he was more prisoner than guest.

He mentally tallied what he had on him—two daggers strapped to his leg leathers, his Dragon Class seal, and some coins. His winter coat, long sword, and bow and arrows were in his yurt. He decided he could do without his supplies and opted to head toward the latrines at the southwestern edge of the fortress. As he turned a corner, he caught the leatherworker standing up as if to follow.

The previous riders stationed here had not died the way Ulagan described. Baikalan had not killed them, and whoever had killed them had used poison as an aid. There was a lie here, and though Aadan didn't know the whole of it, he knew enough to recognize danger.

Which meant he was not the only one in it.

Jin.

He cursed, hoping she and the other riders and Emar were safe. He went to the latrines and pulled the canvas flap closed behind him, leaving his boots where they would be visible from under the covering.

In his bare feet, he looped back around the walls and over to Wanli's pen. He could see the assistant out in the courtyard now, speaking with one of the guards and looking distinctly worried. The assistant nodded and moved away while the guard went back to his post.

Aadan crept forward, keeping his head down and ears primed. *Wanli, are you ready?*

The dragon snorted gently, and Aadan followed his bond around the side of the wall until he was in the pasture. There, a guard shifted from one foot to the other, worrying at a scab on his hand.

On my cue, Aadan said, looking around. A shout sounded from near the latrine. Clearly the guards had discovered his shoes, but no Aadan.

Now!

Wanli unfurled his wings and pummeled the guards at the pasture gate with a bracing spray of water. They flew into the air, landing on their backs and rolling before spluttering and scrambling for their feet.

Aadan sprinted toward Wanli, his legs and arms pumping. He was almost there, but he could hear the soldiers already on their feet and giving chase.

Wanli's warning sounded in his head, and Aadan crouched, narrowly missing another blast of water that shot past him and hit its target. He kept running and then leapt the last arm's length, his bare feet finding purchase against the scales. His dragon waited one heartbeat, two, for him to settle before launching from the ground, his silver wings beating back the last attacker who tried to grab onto Wanli's claw.

Aadan had ridden bareback only a few times, but he was grateful for that little practice now. Shouts rose from the ramparts, and archers lined up, taking aim.

Without waiting for Aadan's word, Wanli rained down fire, immolating several Khitan soldiers and sending others scattering for the turret's cover. Aadan clung as Wanli took them high, a flurry of arrows skimming just a hand's breadth below.

At his dragon's question, Aadan answered, *North. Toward the Well of Ice.*

CHAPTER 8

She was drowning.

Water was flowing around her, and she could hear her heartbeat, along with the rush of water. Grit was in her mouth because she'd been rolling in water. She was going to die here.

She was back in the cage, back in the rushing river that wanted to suck her to her death. Water was filling her mouth, her nose, burning its way into her and numbing her limbs. And then hands were pulling her out.

Haitao, the head of the Red Crows thieving clan, was sitting next to her on the bank.

You survived because you're a survivor. You have none of my blood but all of my grit. Because I made you what you are.

He smiled and leaned forward, but something was wrong with his head. It was sliding forward until it fell at her feet, and she was looking at a bloody stump of neck.

Merciful blackness consumed her again. Why did her body ache so much? Several sharp things pressed against her, gouging her back. Something stank. Was it her? The stench of oil and fat and smoke seemed inescapable.

She tried to open her eyes but hadn't the strength. Something huffed, like some great slouching beast.

She forced her eyes open and stared at a wall of fur. Matted fur that reeked. She grimaced and reached for Rayshan but heard nothing. This only panicked her until the darkness swallowed her again.

JIN WOKE, AWARE SHE WAS NO LONGER MOVING. SHE HAD been so used to the rocking and bumping that now that it stopped, she had woken. She took a deep breath, but the act made her eyes water in pain.

Where was she? She tried to sit up, but that only sent fire splintering through her once more, this time so wicked that the tears flowed freely down her face. She lay there, trying to adjust her eyes.

You are awake.

Rayshan? Her relief was palpable. *Where are you? Where am I?*

Near. I am near. She heard her own relief echoed in his words. *We are somewhere to the east of the Well of Ice.*

Emar? What of—

I don't know. Regain your strength. I will tell you what I know later.

Jin managed to turn her head and look around her. She was in some sort of conical tent, with a hole in the roof through which stars peered down at her. The same stench of oil, fat, and smoke lay heavy in the tent, though now it mingled with juniper, leather, and the heavy aromas of something cooking over a fire.

A huffing startled her near her head, and then something wet pressed into her neck. She didn't have the strength to bat it away and thought to herself, *Is this how it ends?*

The tent flap opened, and a woman with a leathery, wizened face entered. She wore her hair in two plaits looped on themselves so that they formed great hoops on her drooping breasts. She clucked and waved her arms, and to Jin's shock, she saw the great horned silhouette of a reindeer step out of the shadows.

The woman waved again, giving the beast a loving smack on the rump. The animal lowed in protest but, at another smack, trotted out of the tent, shaking its antlers in disapproval.

The woman came and sat cross-legged next to Jin, examining her. She then smiled, revealing a perfect row of brilliant white teeth. The woman looked ninety if not a hundred, yet even with only the fire for illumination, Jin discerned the once beautiful lines in her cheekbones and the delicate slant of her eyes.

"*Idiht?*"

Jin frowned.

The woman tried again, but Jin only managed a weak sigh past her lips. The woman nodded once, clucked again, and then mimed eating.

Jin's stomach responded to the idea of food with gusto, but at the same time, the thought of sitting up made her sick.

The woman pushed an arm under her and pulled her to a sitting position with surprising strength. The room spun, and her chest ached horribly, but amazingly, Jin didn't faint.

The woman took a bowl from the fire and sprinkled something in it, then held it out to Jin. She was loath to drink anything after Ulagan's display. What if these people were part of his force?

I don't think so, Rayshan said. *They came and bandaged you and took you with them and freed me.*

Where are you? she asked again.

Close. I cannot come near, as their reindeer grow skittish.

Reindeer. She remembered the people they had flown over on their way here, the Chaakan. She looked around her again, noting the reindeer skins, the cups made of horn, the bowls of bone, and plates with what looked like lumpy white cheese on the floor nearby.

How long have I been asleep?

A week or so.

A week. Nausea reared its head again, and the

woman pressed the bowl into her hands, motioning for her to eat.

She obeyed. It was mushy, like meal, and completely unappetizing, but Jin suddenly realized how famished she was. She ate the rest without complaint and then tentatively held out the bowl. The woman refilled it from a pot on the fire, then smiled that dazzling smile again as Jin wolfed it down.

The woman reached forward and pulled back Jin's shirt, which was also of deer leather. She revealed a mound of what looked like black earth packed with fat and a foul-smelling mash of herbs on Jin's side. The woman gently pulled on the poultice, easing the edges from Jin's skin, and even in the dim firelight, Jin could see that her wound had closed over. Though it was still puckered and red, it was clean and would likely heal like her hand.

"*Chi aztai baina*," the woman said, patting the wound there. She pulled out a packet of herbs from near Jin's pillow and then, with water and fat, reapplied a layer before pressing a cloth over it and motioning for Jin to lie down.

"My wing mates?" she asked, but at the puzzled look on the woman's face, she racked her head for a way to show her meaning. She held up four fingers, then pointed to herself. "There were four of us. Where are the others?"

The woman shook her head and took the empty bowl, departing.

When I woke, there was nothing but a gaping hole where they had been. Everything had closed over them.

Emar? Jin asked, heart heavy.

No sign of him or Ulagan. My guess is he didn't know we wouldn't simply die together there.

And Baikalan has escaped.

Appears so.

Why would Ulagan release him? Jin still couldn't make sense of what had happened. *How can Ulagan think that Baikalan will listen to him?*

It seems that Ulagan is counting on Mengkhis's goodwill once he brings Baikalan to Mengkhis.

Jin digested this. *He has more confidence than any fool has a right to.*

Possibly. But that doesn't change the fact that he has Emar and Baikalan, and who knows what he will do next?

Jin shuddered, her body shaking with the knowledge that things were very bad. She tried lifting her arm, but the effort made her break out in a sweat.

You're lucky. We'd both be dead if not for the blood bond.

She thought back to Emar's words: "Stay down." Had he known what was coming? Had he tried to protect her by letting Ulagan think she was dead? She was the only one who could play that game, and perhaps he had made sure that she would have a spear through her but then live to save them.

The tears stormed her then, tears of rage at Ulagan and tears of sorrow for her wing mates. Were Panshalar, Jao, and Ezho dead? There was little chance they had survived, but maybe there was a pocket of air in the cave that would save them. Maybe Panshalar's dragon drew enough metal to get them out, or maybe Ezho's black Turuchi used the air in the earth to push them out. Maybe . . . maybe . . . If only she could stand and fly, she'd go to them. But her body wouldn't obey, no matter how she tried, and the effort drained her.

Jin slipped back into sleep.

A SEA LAPPING AGAINST A SHORE. WAVE UPON GENTLE wave came to the beach, and she looked out at a horizon stained orange with sunset. But the orange grew to red, and she realized that it wasn't the sky that was red, but the sea itself. She looked down at something, tapping her toe, thinking to brush away a crab, but instead she found a bloated face near her foot, the eyes staring up at her. She stumbled back, losing her balance as she fell to the sand.

Only, the sand wasn't sand.

It was another body, and another, until she realized that she was on a beach covered by bodies, and the ocean itself was a sea of bodies, all bobbing against each other like engorged boats, with no escape. She was drowning—

Jin.

HER EYES FLEW OPEN, AND SHE TOOK DEEP LUNGSFUL OF air. Morning air, not salt air. Air carrying scents of firewood, leather, tea, and wet fur. Morning light seeped in from the doorway, where the antlered head of the reindeer was poking in, his eyes regarding her reproachfully.

"Did I take your bed?" she asked.

She wondered if the deer slept in the tents. As if in answer, he walked in like a landlord, found a spot near her bedding, and then unceremoniously buckled his knees and lay down, settling his rump squarely on one of her legs.

"Get off!" she cried, but the beast looked at her with cool contempt. It turned away, deliberately ignoring her.

A child of ten or so entered, his hair pulled back into a cropped ponytail. He shouted something when he saw Jin awake, and soon, a whole gaggle of children came to stare.

Clearly she, and not the reindeer, was the oddity.

A sound of whooshing came from outside, and the children scattered, giggling and squealing. The old woman entered, this time carrying a steaming bowl of dumplings and hot milk.

Again, Jin found the dumplings lumpy and oily, and the milk so strong it nearly stuck in her throat, but hunger won out. Her stomach growled as if it might eat the reindeer. Seeming to sense her thoughts, the beast stood and walked out, tail flashing in alarmed white.

The woman took Jin's wrist in her hands and checked her pulse, then checked her bandages. She motioned for Jin to sit up, and with her help, Jin just managed it. Then she hooked an arm under Jin's shoulder and pulled her to her feet.

The unexpected move made Jin nauseous, but she forced herself to stay standing. The woman spoke a few words, pointing outdoors and taking deep breaths. Yes, Jin thought. Fresh air would do her good.

She hobbled with the woman until they were outside, and the light set her head throbbing. The sun was already high over a blindingly green valley speckled with scarlet poppies, blue daisies, and yolk-colored flowers that Jin couldn't name.

A smattering of yurts similar to the one she had exited stood in a loose semi-circle, each twenty paces apart, with a glittering lake beyond. Jin estimated roughly fifteen yurts in all, some with banners flapping in the breeze. Smoke rose from most of them, and children darted in between the tents, chasing reindeer of various sizes, while others squatted in the dirt, sorting berries or playing a game with stones. Women with flowing braids like the old woman's called out to their children, and a man smoked a long pipe in a doorway while another seemed to be fixing a bone knife.

It was a scene of a peaceful, ordinary day living out on the northern plains, but what cheered Jin the most was the smudge up in the sky in the distance. She would recognize the dip and glide of Rayshan's wings anywhere.

Seeing her look, the old woman pointed and nodded. Jin's heart swelled with relief, for though she could hear him, it was reassuring to see him. Her world readjusted a little more at the sight of her dragon.

The woman led her to one of the reindeer and began to milk it. When there was a bowl full, the old woman motioned for Jin to help churn it in a leather bag strapped to a foldable wooden rack, and Jin obliged. Though she wanted to go to Rayshan, she knew her legs weren't up for it.

She sat and stirred the milk, her thoughts churning with it. Had that been the woman's intention all along? To sit her down and work her body and her mind?

If Ulagan had killed the riders, then he truly didn't care what the empress thought or did. And though Jin would stake her life that the man held a grudge like a miser hoarded gold, she sensed his actions were not just about her taking Rayshan. There was something deeper, and until she knew what that was, she couldn't know his next move. He would find Mengkhis, and then what?

But what if they went directly to the capital to take the empress? If none of the riders had escaped, then no one would be the wiser as to their fates, and she didn't put it past Ulagan to send fake correspondence back from the mages to buy time before alerting the court to their deaths.

Her skin prickled. What of Aadan? Ulagan had been reluctant to leave any riders behind, and now she knew why. But did that mean Aadan had been killed at the fort? The thought he might be dead made her churn the milk with such vehemence that the woman took the leather bag from her and had a young girl come escort Jin back to the yurt.

As the woman waved away Jin's apologies, Jin fought down the lump in her throat. Was she the only one left alive from her wing? A sourness filled her mouth at the memory of Emar's words: "Jin's our best chance at a miracle."

But if they were dead, it was because Ulagan had wanted Rayshan back. She was no miracle.

She was a death sentence.

CHAPTER 9

Tai grew increasingly restless as the days passed.

He buried himself in what tasks he could: overseeing the Dragon Class dormitory changes; approving the curriculum and orders for weaponry, leathers, and saddles; and the hiring of new instructors, tasks which kept him busy until his candles had burned down to puddles in their holders.

Outdoors, he rode his horse, a fine Ferghana steed from Bactria named Leiyu. A gift from his mother, Leiyu was her undisguised attempt to buy his forgiveness, and despite his resistance, he had grown fond of the horse. He mastered all the obstacle courses he set for Leiyu, sparred with Chao, threw himself into archery practice, and dove into books on ancient history and biographies of previous emperors. Yet still, he felt trapped and idle, especially as no other news had come from Khitan, and his mother's staff had become much coyer about revealing her schedule. Which meant he was sure he had missed a few meetings between her and Sanjin.

So when his valet delivered the official notice from the imperial household that the renovations at the royal pools were now complete, he had a servant fetch him towels and a robe and set off.

The royal pool was located between his own and his mother's suites in an ornate building called the Palace of Eternal Springs. Smooth marble flooring had replaced the former chipped slabs, while lifelike animals of various hues covered every pillar. A dozen porcelain pots full of lotuses lined the walls, their heady perfume filling the air. The pool now had a waterfall at one end that flowed off a lip of granite into the main baths. A round, sunken basin lined in gleaming jade tiles steamed in one corner, the *kang* beneath it keeping the water hot.

He was happy to find the premises deserted. His distant cousins, aunts, and uncles had clearly not been as eager to test out the waters as he was. He stripped down to his under trousers, loose silk pants with slits in the sides, and jumped in, the water warm but still cool enough to heighten his senses. He swam with long strokes. His mother had brought him into this very pool when he was first learning to swim.

He remembered her voice even now. "Your father

fed his mind and neglected his body. Don't make the same mistake."

"Your Highness has an excellent physique."

Tai stopped swimming and turned in the water to find a plump—or, if he was honest, overweight—man in blue robes and gray trousers standing at the pool's edge. The man had a long braid bound up in a bun, fleshy cheeks, and a flat nose over a mouth that seemed to stretch into a smile of its own accord, as if this was its natural state. Even when not smiling, the eyes twinkled with a secret joke that gave him an irresistible affability.

"Prince Tai." The man bowed low, hands in his sleeves. "I am honored to be in your presence and have been looking forward to this. Friends well met are a joy indeed."

"Friends do not intrude on others while they are swimming," Tai remarked.

"Ah! I apologize." The man beamed. "I like to look to the future, and in the future, we are close friends."

"Your honorable name?"

"Situ Han, Your Highness!" The man bowed again, face still split in the widest of smiles. "I am the new mage assigned to Dragon Class."

New mage? Something clicked in Tai's memory. "Oh yes, the letter about the Ministry assigning someone else. What was wrong with our last one?" He remembered the last one, a quiet and serious sort but a very good mage. Tai wasn't sure why the man had resigned.

"He's passed, that's what's wrong," mage Situ Han said cheerfully.

"Grief must bow before fate," Tai said the traditional words of condolence. "Why was I not notified?"

"Oh, not passed as in deceased," the mage said, chuckling. "He passed the exams for higher appointment, as the Ministry determined his calling was elsewhere."

Tai regarded Situ Han for a moment, gauging, keeping his features polite but wondering at how such a humorous man had risen so high in a ministry known for valuing austerity. "And do you have experience with dragons?" Tai remembered one mage who had been so noxious about being around the beasts that Tai had to fire the man, as his negativity proved infectious.

"Can't say I do, Your Highness," Situ Han said. "But I do have great experience with princes, and that's why I'm here."

"Oh?" Tai raised an eyebrow. "Well, I travel with the dragons, so you'll need aptitude with both."

The man chuckled. "So I hear, though I also notice you haven't been traveling with dragons much of late." The man had cheek.

"I have had more duties at home."

"Of course." The mage pulled out a pouch of melon

seeds. "Do you mind? I find it always helps to chat over refreshments."

Before Tai could refuse, the man took off his shoes, sat down, and put his legs in the water. He happily cracked one seed between his teeth, then, looking around, expertly flicked the shells into the nearest pot of lotuses. Tai would have been irked by the man's treating his pool like some corner teahouse, except it was strangely endearing.

"I represent the Ministry, and I'm here less to look after the dragons and more because we agree you could use a . . ." he spat out a shell from his mouth and flicked it ". . . well, ally, frankly."

"Ally?"

"Yes, ally. Friend. Helpmate, whatever you prefer to term me would be an honor, Your Highness. The Ministry would like to form a deeper relationship with the man who will be emperor."

Tai kept his smile broad, though he gauged the man's reaction with a keen eye. "So, Grand Master Gu Ben sent you?"

Situ Han bowed. "The one and the same."

"I see. But may the empress live ten thousand years. She is not acceding the throne."

The man flashed another smile and cracked another seed. "Of course. I don't mean that your mother is going to fall dead. That would be most unfortunate. As I said, I look to the future, and you are the future."

Tai approached the edge of the pool. "Judging by my

mother's age and health, the far future. You'd be wise to understand that I have no interest in shortening it."

Situ Han looked unperturbed and instead simply waved a plump hand. "You mistake me. I mean no disrespect. But here, let me leave you with a little reading." He drew out a scroll and cast about for a place to put it as if just noticing that water and paper did not go well together. He pushed it back in his sleeve. "I'll leave it with your valet. I've been told you're not just good looks and a pretty voice."

Tai managed a polite smile.

Situ Han stood and tapped the scroll. "I highly suggest you read this, and in the meantime, I assume you'll want me to start with certain inventories in the Dragon Class mage supplies, followed by routines. I notice that there is not much regular mage work conducted. We should rectify that."

Tai raised an eyebrow. The other mages had certainly not been so meticulous.

"Oh, one last thing, Your Highness," the man said, brushing melon seeds off his robe, catching them with one deft movement, and carefully depositing them in the lotus pot. "I would be willing to teach you magic. If you'd like."

It took Tai a moment to realize that the man was serious. "I do not have your dedication to the mysteries. I am rather attached, not just physically, to my manhood."

The man grinned again, glancing down into the

water toward Tai's groin. "Oh, I understand, Your Highness. It's a fine set." At Tai's expression, Situ Han shrugged. "Servants will always talk, Your Highness."

Clearly, his mother's maids were not the only ones with loose tongues.

"But rest assured we would never ask the Son of Heaven to remove his tools for enjoying the clouds and rain, so to speak," the mage continued. "That would be most inconvenient for you, not to mention short-sighted. We'd be willing to make an exception for you, Your Highness. Think about it."

He held a hand toward the steaming hot pool, and his lips barely seemed to move before the steam shrank away and the water crackled as it solidified into ice.

"Mage powers are quite useful." Situ Han beamed. "See? I'm also not just a handsome face and pretty voice, Your Highness."

"I would never presume so," Tai replied.

As the man retreated, humming a tune to himself, Tai wondered what exactly mage Situ Han was, and whose agenda he served.

CHAPTER 10

On the third day, Jin felt strong enough to walk out of the village and head toward Rayshan's circling silhouette. He trumpeted in welcome as she drew near.

Once she had trekked a reasonable distance from the smattering of yurts, Rayshan sped toward her and landed. She had never been so grateful to see his scaled head and leathery wings, to hug his broad nose in her arms and let the thrum of the bond vibrate through her core.

You feel well, though you look terrible.

She grimaced. *Thank you.*

Aadan isn't here to see you, so it doesn't matter.

Her stomach plummeted at the mention of Aadan, and a flutter of contrition came across the bond.

I am sorry. I spoke without thinking.

Do you know where he might be?

Rayshan stretched his wings. *Hopefully on his way back to Changan.*

Preferably with Ulagan's head, Jin added.

Are you fully recovered?

I believe so, Jin lied. She was grateful to talk about her own wounds rather than imagine Aadan imprisoned, hurt, or worse. *Ten days to recover from a spear through the ribs. That's not bad. Though it hurt like the eight levels of hell.*

Rayshan cocked his head, ears flat and eyes narrowed. He wasn't fooled. *Are you well enough to ride?*

She had serious doubts, but she also missed riding so much that she nodded anyway. Rayshan growled but knelt and waited patiently while she scrambled onto him, wincing. It took a long time, and Jin was thankful that Rayshan made no complaints.

When she was astride, he took to the sky, but gently, and the air brushed her face, bringing the scent of winds and smoke and rain and cloud. Mixed in was Rayshan's blend of musk and sunbaked rock, the damp earthiness that lined his scales. They rode higher, and though her limbs pained her, she didn't speak out, the tears streaming down her face tears of emotional pain instead.

Sensing them, Rayshan landed, even though Jin wanted to stay airborne forever.

She rubbed her eyes, smothering the sob that threatened her.

Vengeance will come, Rayshan comforted her. *Get better first.*

And so she did. Until she was physically strong enough to ride long distances and defend herself, she could not find Emar and the others—*if* they were alive—much less make it back to Changan.

Over the next two days, she tried to drive out thoughts of her wing mates by focusing on healing, and silently encouraging her body to strengthen. Every day she ate all she was offered in an attempt to seal the wound in her side.

By the fifth day, she was able to change the bandage herself with the strips of cloth and the foul-smelling medicine the old woman had left for her. She was in the middle of pulling her shirt over the new covering when she heard screams and the thunder of hooves, followed by bellows from the reindeer.

Rushing as much as her wound allowed, she yanked the flap aside. A dozen Chaakan on horseback were fanning out along the huts, yelling and brandishing swords. Women grabbed their children and ran for shelter while men came rushing with wooden clubs and any other weapons at hand. A group of attackers had circled the reindeer and were whooping as they slapped at flanks and rushed at the bleating calves.

Jin had been a thief long enough to recognize robbery when she saw it. And her injury could go to the eight levels of hell. She was not about to let the old woman and her people lose their livelihoods.

Rayshan! To me!

She was striding, then running, only remembering that she was empty-handed when she reached the first attacker on horseback. He had a flat nose and heavy brows, under which he glared at Jin. He sliced his sword down, but she was ready, dodging and whipping out one arm to grip his wrist. A quick twist made him drop his sword, before her other hand latched to the back of his belt. She yanked, her blood bond strength clearly surprising her opponent, and he came off the horse and crashed onto her.

Her wound burned anew as a fist found her ribs, making her scream. Her attacker readied another blow, but then giant green jaws closed over him to the waist, the bones crunching like gravel as Rayshan tossed him to one side. The mangled body landed in a heap, unmoving. Jin pulled herself to her feet, half aided by a well-timed nudge from Rayshan's tail.

Seeing Rayshan, the thieves froze, momentarily disoriented. But then one of their group gave a piercing whoop, and the party converged once more on the reindeer.

The thieves began driving the animals away from the yurts at a breakneck pace. Some of the Chaakan men gave chase on foot, while mothers wiped their faces as they held their children close.

Jin cursed beneath her breath and pulled herself onto Rayshan.

Cut them off. We'll drive them back here.

Rayshan took to the sky, and it was only a few wing beats before their shadow covered the raiding party and the reindeer below. Rayshan roared a warning, which made the raiders whip their horses faster.

Do they honestly think I can't fly faster than a horse can run? Rayshan commented drily. He banked so that they turned in the air and came low, skimming the ground straight at the reindeer. The panicked beasts immediately turned tail and began running north, bellowing their fear as Rayshan and Jin bore down on them.

Flame?

Jin had no sympathy for the thieves despite having been one herself. All her frustration and anger over the past few days, her helplessness over not having saved Emar, Yao Bing, her wing mates, Aadan—it all burned like some fire that needed release. She had a chance to defend the Chaakan who had taken her in, repay the woman who had found her near death and mended her.

Something in Jin wanted to watch all these men turn to cinder, but doing so would also kill their horses.

Warning fire.

Rayshan angled his head and spewed flames just over the riders' heads, singeing hair and spurring the horses into a terrified run in opposite directions.

One reared on its hind legs just as a lick of fire rolled past, catching its mane. The horse fell sideways, crushing the flames and its rider beneath it. It scrabbled to its legs and bolted, the rider bouncing lifelessly behind. The others turned and galloped after it, abandoning the reindeer who had thundered off to the north, their hooves clicking in alarm.

Are you alright?

I think my wound's ripped open again, but I'll be fine.

Rayshan swung his head toward the herd, then lifted his snout and flared his nostrils. *Let us get you back so you can heal.*

We can't just leave the reindeer.

Rayshan spread his wings. *Don't worry, the others are coming.*

Despite this, Jin waited until the silhouettes appeared on the horizon and the women had come. Their voices filled the air as they sang to the reindeer, soothing them and coaxing them back.

Only when one of the women gave Jin a nod did Jin deem that she and Rayshan were no longer needed. She leaned forward and held on to his ridge as he flew her back to the village and landed near the yurt.

Women and children crowded around as soon as she had dismounted and Rayshan had backed away, while the old woman clucked over Jin's freshly bleeding wound. Rayshan circled into the sky, a safe distance away, so the Chaakan could bring their reindeer back.

The old woman shooed everyone out of the yurt and stoked the fire, giving Jin worried looks. Though she was sure the woman had different reasons for worrying, Jin, too, felt uneasy.

We will have to leave, healed or no.

There was no arguing with Rayshan's statement. The thieves would talk, and once word leaked that these people had been defended by a jade dragon, all of Ulagan's forces would be hunting for Jin. And possibly for the Chaakan people. Perhaps she should have let the thieves take the reindeer.

"You must leave," Jin told the old woman as she came to dress her wound. But as always, the woman simply nodded in a polite imitation of understanding her. With her fingers, Jin mimed two legs walking and gestured to indicate the village. "All of you. You must leave. Go somewhere far."

The woman silently dressed Jin's wound, then brought a bowl of soup. Jin heard the telltale clicking of hooves, then a snuffling at the doorway, and the woolly head of a reindeer poked in. The old woman said something to it, making it low at her in answer before retreating.

Let's leave tomorrow, Jin said. *The sooner we go, the safer these people will be.*

Are you strong enough?

I have to be. The thought of Ulagan's men destroying these people sickened her. *We'll leave an obvious trail so that Ulagan follows us, not them.*

THE NEXT MORNING, JIN FORCED HERSELF TO RISE AT dawn. She used a blanket from the bed to pack water, some dry foods, and a knife. She had explained to the woman that she needed to leave, to which the woman had said nothing, simply watching her.

When she exited the yurt, however, she found a small gathering of Chaakan had come out of their homes. The people drifted toward her and pressed items into her hands or into her blanket: a lump of reindeer cheese, a pair of shoes, a bone knife, a water skin.

Their gratitude showed in their eyes, and Jin wished she had a way to thank them. But what did she have? Anything distinctive of hers would only prove to Ulagan that they had sheltered her.

And so she walked on, nodding in thanks with each gift that she tried to give back but that they gently insisted she take.

Only when she had crested the hill by the lake and left the last yurts' outlines behind did she hear the beat of wings, the shadow that signaled Rayshan. He landed before her and bent his head to her.

They will be fine. I have left prints and feces a quarter day's horse ride south from here. Ulagan's men should think we are heading to Changan.

Good thinking. She readied herself to mount, then squinted. *What are those? Eagles?*

Rayshan swung his head around, then gave a disbelieving snort. *No, it's Wanli! And . . .*

But by now, Jin could see for herself. Wanli's silver scales and white-flecked wings caught the sunlight, while next to him, Jao and Panshalar banked on Nakkalan and Bayan. They flew down low, skimming the grass, until they pulled up to Jin and landed.

She tried to run toward them, but the wound in her side protested, and she fell.

Aadan vaulted off Wanli's saddle in an instant and pulled her up but then just as quickly let go.

"Jao! Panshalar!" She almost hugged them, and the giant actually slapped her on her back, sending her crashing back to her knees.

"Oh! Sorry," he said, bending and helping her up with one meaty hand. "Just—it's good to see you."

She looked around at their faces. "Emar? Where's Ezho?"

Their grim looks made her heart squeeze.

"We were buried in Baikalan's cave afterward," Panshalar said, "and only Nakkalan's expanding saved us from being crushed."

"But Ezho . . ." Jao said, before his lips formed a tight line. "We couldn't revive him."

Jin's heart twisted. Ezho. Gone? "What of his dragon?"

"Turuchi flew off. We didn't know where," Panshalar muttered. "Wouldn't come back."

To find a place to die, Rayshan answered, melancholy.

Jin wanted to sit down but, out of pride, stayed standing. "And Ulagan?"

Aadan shook his head. "Not sure. We came to find you as soon as possible, and now that we have, I think our safest bet is to return to Changan as quickly as possible. If all the mages died, as Jao and Panshalar said, then no one in the capital knows what happened."

"But what of Emar?" Jin said. "We have to find him."

"We don't know if he's alive," Aadan argued. "And we're outnumbered. Emar wouldn't want us to risk more lives. He'd want the empress alerted."

Jin wrestled with the truth of this.

"As next in seniority, I'm wing leader now." Aadan paused, the title clearly still unfamiliar to him. "And I am responsible for getting you all home."

"You came to look for me though," Jin argued. "Why not Emar?"

"You're not in Ulagan's clutches where we have to fight Baikalan to get to you," Aadan retorted.

"Can you fly?" Jao asked.

Jin still felt torn about leaving Emar, but she knew Aadan was right. They couldn't possibly fight Ulagan and Baikalan combined, and if the empire didn't know Ulagan's plans, then everyone there was in danger. Was she ready to fly? She would have to be. A thought occurred to her.

"Aadan, what languages do you speak again?"

He frowned. "Why?"

She told them about the raid. "Ulagan's going to know I was here," she said. "If there's a way to tell these people to flee, we have to warn them."

Aadan nodded. "I can try."

"The dragons should stay here," Jin said. "Otherwise they'll frighten the reindeer."

After telling the dragons their plan, Jin led the riders back to the village. Jin noticed Aadan's boots. "Those are Yao Bing's."

The Persian's face hardened. "Long story. I had to leave Karahag barefoot. Yao Bing's shoes fit." He glanced at her. "We buried him. And the others."

She nodded, looking ahead and ignoring the threat of tears. As they neared the tents, children converged and swooped upon them all like locusts, eager to ogle their leathers and yell questions at them.

"I think it's Khitan," Jin explained. "Can you—"

"*Chini dharma ken bey?*"

The riders glanced at Aadan, who shrugged. "The language is close to Turkic."

The children started yelling all at once, delighted that Aadan spoke their tongue.

"Good. Now you can thank the matron for me," Jin said. "And tell her the reindeer should be made into meat."

Aadan frowned. "I don't think they ever eat the meat. The reindeer are sacred."

"And how do you know so much?"

"I read."

Jin scowled at his tone but felt grudging admiration. She had spent a week here, having to make signs for where to relieve herself or for more food or to ask for a clean bandage, when Aadan communicated so easily.

Are you always attracted to the clever ones? Rayshan asked.

I'd rather not have that conversation now.

The old woman came out of her tent when they approached and flashed that impossibly brilliant smile. Aadan bowed low to her, Jao and Panshalar hesitantly following suit.

Aadan spoke a few words, and the old woman smiled, delighted. She answered, and Aadan turned to Jin.

"She says you are welcome to stay here for the rest of your life, as you are a sacred entity."

Jin was puzzled. "I helped them. But that doesn't make me sacred."

Aadan asked again but looked confused. "I don't quite understand. She says something about you being a flame? Do you know what that is?"

Jin shook her head. "No."

The woman spoke again.

"Flame of the dead, I think she's saying," Aadan said, his brow arched in concentration. "Though some of the words can have multiple meanings, I don't understand."

Jin frowned. "Perhaps it's their name for someone who returns from the dead. They found me with what should have been a fatal wound, and I lived. I think she's a spiritual leader here."

Aadan nodded. "Yes, she's the shaman of the tribe."

"Please thank her for taking care of me," Jin said, "but let her know she must leave because Ulagan and his forces will try to find me."

Aadan turned back to the woman, his words flowing from him with ease. How did one man have so many talents?

"She says she knows, and you will always have a home here and be known as the Dragon Flame."

Jin felt a sudden surge of gratitude toward the woman and wanted to give her something, anything. These people had fed her, nursed her back to health, and dealt with her dragon when she was beyond dead. But she had nothing to give them. What could she give?

"Please tell them I owe them my life, and I will always be indebted."

Aadan spoke, but the woman waved a hand, then answered.

"She says it is they who owe you."

Jin shook her head. "Scaring the thieves was easy with Rayshan."

"She says . . ." Aadan listened again. "She says they owe you not just for that."

"Then for what?" Jin asked.

Aadan spoke again and listened to the woman's reply. "She says she owes you for finding her husband."

Jin looked at the woman, baffled. "I don't know what she's talking about."

Panshalar shrugged. "Maybe it's a local expression that means something completely different. The saying, 'Hold your horses,' doesn't mean to actually hold horses."

Jao tossed him a smirk. "Right. Finding a husband actually means to do the laundry."

"Why not?" Panshalar protested, indignant.

The old woman insisted on giving all of them supplies and packed them a satchel each with dried jerky, cheeses, barley patties, and packets of tea and powdered milk.

They said their goodbyes, the children walking with them out of the village until their mothers called them back.

The four dragons were waiting for them where they had landed, impatient to be off.

"Are you well enough to ride?" Aadan asked Jin as they mounted. The concern in his voice made her heart hitch.

"I'll have to be," Jin answered, reminded of her conversation with Rayshan.

As they rose into the air, she reprimanded the dragon. *So much for not being seen in this state by Aadan.*

A chuckle sounded in her head.

But it was not Rayshan. It was Wanli.

CHAPTER 11

They avoided the south, deliberately flying north over what they guessed were uninhabited lands dominated by nomadic peoples like the Chaakan rather than the Khitan.

Aadan, Jin knew, had studied maps all his life, and he and Wanli made sure they were staying to the outer borders of Khitan as they flew.

Panshalar had argued for following the coast, but Jin and Aadan had vetoed the idea. Following the ocean meant they would have to land on the coast for rest, and there was too much risk of Khitan ports or hamlets discovering them and reporting their whereabouts to Ulagan.

And so they flew north despite the necessary backtracking, around the perimeters, flying by night just to be safe and finding shelter during the day. They took turns keeping watch, and Jin volunteered for extra shifts, as her blood bond meant she needed less sleep.

But if she was honest with herself, it was also because she dreaded her dreams. She saw Emar's face, the look in his eyes as he told her to stay down, and she dreamed of Ezho. The others described how they had said prayers and offered food before they left, but a fist-sized lump of sadness refused to leave her chest.

Ezho had been the least hostile of her wing mates when she had first arrived in Dragon Class and, in the end, had fought at her side against Gao during the attempted coup. One day as they camped, she thought she saw him, alive and well, standing before her as the others slept, but then he was gone. She pushed thoughts of insanity from her mind.

They ate sparingly of the rations the Chaakan woman had given them, and the others even stopped eating it, simply watching her while she ate her share.

"How can you stomach that stuff?" Panshalar rubbed the back of his hand across his nose. "Even I don't eat it, and I'll eat anything."

Aadan chewed on it thoughtfully, pulling a piece out of his mouth and examining it critically. "It's like reindeer hoof ground into powder and then made into a cake."

"Actually, that's close." Jin had watched the old woman grind bones from a marmot they'd trapped and make it into a paste with milk and reindeer cheese.

Panshalar grimaced. "I can't wait to be back in Han territory. I'm wasting away."

Though even wasted away Panshalar stood two heads above her, Jin agreed. Panshalar had to tighten his belt, and his leathers had begun to hang on him. Circles had formed under his eyes, making her wonder if he was ill.

Her answer came when Jin woke at their resting site one day to the faint sound of pained moans. Panshalar was missing.

Jin rose and went searching for him, apprehensive. She and Rayshan found him with Bayan a little way down the hill from where they had camped, sitting opposite his dragon and murmuring to him.

"What are you doing?"

Panshalar whipped around guiltily. Bayan raised his golden head and lashed his tail.

"Nothing—just—"

Jin glanced from the dragon to Panshalar, who had beads of sweat on his brow. "Just what, exactly?"

Panshalar glanced at his dragon, then said with a touch of defiance, "We're manipulating metal."

It dawned on her that Panshalar's weight loss was not only from their terrible diet. "On yourself?"

"There's no one else." The northerner looked down, his voice quiet. "And after what happened in Khitan, I just keep thinking, if Bayan and I had known how to draw metal like that other gold dragon, maybe—well, maybe we could have done something."

How had she not realized her wing mates might be carrying their own guilt, seeing the dead in their own way? She sat down next to him, still a little dumbfounded. "Can't you practice on other things? The rocks and soil?"

"It's different when it's in a body. The metals don't . . ." he flexed his fingers, as if trying to explain with his hands ". . . move the same way. Don't know why. But it requires practice on an actual person. Or animal, I suppose."

Jin thought on this. "There's a reason Emar didn't teach you that."

Panshalar's shoulders hunched, miserable. "And he sure suffered for it."

"But you can't practice on yourself or us. You're weakening yourself." She paused. "It's clearly unhealthy for you. You have to stop."

Bayan huffed, his tail whipping, and Jin heard his agreement.

Panshalar didn't answer, but he was likely thinking the same thing: how many people had King Ulagan killed to allow his dragon the power to draw metals from living things?

"Do you think Wanli could draw the water out of someone in the same way?" Panshalar asked. "Kill them by drying them out?"

Jin nodded. "And perhaps Turuchi could have killed someone by sucking the air out of their lungs. But that's not what we use their powers for." She stood and scanned the landscape. "I have a better idea for how to use Bayan's skills."

❁

TOGETHER, PANSHALAR AND BAYAN TRACKED DOWN A dried lake nearby with mineral and metal deposits. As per Jin's hunch, they found deer tracks from herds that frequented the lake to eat salt and other minerals, and from there it was short work to track down a meal. When they brought back a doe to the other two men, Jao was clearly eager, while Aadan's face was a storm cloud.

"You left? Without word?" he said tightly.

"We didn't go far," Jin argued.

"That's not the point!" Aadan shot back. "We stick together. There's to be no wandering off without telling me."

"Yes, Nursemaid Aadan," Panshalar snickered, which earned him a dirty look from Aadan and a smothered grin from Jao.

Once they'd given the dragons their portions, there was only a leg to share between the four of them. The men ate raw so as not to create smoke that might draw enemies, but Jin found the texture repulsive, no matter how much her stomach growled in protest.

Panshalar shrugged at her disgusted look. "Raw meat is a delicacy amongst some in the north. This is much preferable to the Chaakan food."

128

Jin shook her head and wandered away in search of fresh air.

After some time, Aadan joined her, and she wondered if he was about to lecture her again on disappearing. They hadn't had any time without the other men, for even though Aadan had lost his books in the flight from the fort, he still seemed absorbed in a hundred and one things that took him away from wherever they camped—food gathering, scouting, checking weather conditions and covering any tracks or other traces of their presence.

"You haven't been the same since you returned from the Singing Sands."

"Blood bonding changes you."

He shook his head. "I'm not talking about the blood bond. It's something else. You . . . seem haunted."

A chill worked its way down her neck. Though she didn't want to admit it, Aadan seemed to know exactly what ailed her.

"I've seen a lot of deaths lately," she said.

"We all have," he said.

"But I see the ones who have died."

"That's natural."

"No," she said, suddenly angry that he was trying to normalize something that was so wrong. She wanted him to see, wanted the benefit of his knowledge. Perhaps he could explain it, convince her that it was simply a stage of grief like Panshalar trying to manipulate metal as a way to regain some semblance of control over his life. "The dead appear, and they are so real, I cannot tell them from actual people, except that I know they have died."

He frowned. "When do you see them?"

"There's no rhyme or reason," she said, frustrated. "At night, during the day."

"So not just in dreams."

"No!"

He held up his palms. "Don't get angry. I'm just trying to understand."

She forced out a breath. He was right. There was no need to take it out on him. "I myself don't understand."

"Is it always people you know?"

She nodded.

"Then it might be something you're . . ." he seemed to search carefully for the right words, "thinking through. We all deal with loss differently. And as you said, you've seen a lot of death in a short time." He regarded her quietly.

"You think I'm losing my mind?" she said, fearful.

"Not at all. I'm glad you confided in me." Aadan cocked his head. "But I do wonder why you didn't say so sooner. I'm not the enemy. I remember how you nearly bit my hand off the first time I helped you."

Aadan had warned her on her first night in Dragon Class that the men in the dorm were about to jump on her, and she had turned on him in anger. "I was right though, wasn't I? You were helping me so I would trust you?" At his wounded look, she regretted her words.

"I swear by the Wise Lord that I wasn't even thinking of my promise to Prince Tai when I helped you," he said quietly. "I dislike mismatched fights, so I was on your side."

As they walked back toward the cave to prepare for the night's flight, he glanced at her. "You don't speak much of your upbringing."

"It doesn't make for happy conversation."

"Clearly, if you grew up thinking no one would ever help you voluntarily." He paused. "Someone betrayed you?"

Jin tensed. "Not exactly."

When she lapsed into silence, he raised an eyebrow. "Sharing your past doesn't make us lovers, you know."

Her face heated. She was being infantile. "True. Why don't you tell me something about your childhood then."

"Fine," he said, stopping to pull a pebble from his boot. "I grew up with three sisters."

She stopped next to him, surprised. "You've never mentioned them."

His smile was pained. "They died during the plague year about ten years ago."

Jin's heart clenched for him. "May your grief cease with time," she said automatically, but felt the traditional phrase was lacking. Over ten years had passed, and she could tell from his face, from her own experience, that grief never fully ceased. "To lose three children . . ."

"It devastated my parents," Aadan agreed. "But we all try to make meaning out of the most painful events. My father saw it as a sign that the Wise Lord had taken his daughters, all so he could focus his attention on me."

Jin sensed the layers of pressure in Aadan's voice. "Because you are the exiled heir, and this was a sign you were meant to return and take back Persia?"

"Yes." He paused. "Though I often think the Wise Lord could have conveyed his intent by other means." He drew a deep breath, then turned and began walking again.

She followed silently for a moment. "Haitao."

Aadan turned. "What?"

"Haitao. He was my father—or at least as much of a father as I ever had. Trained me to be a thief but taught me to trust no one, that those who show kindness only want something from you, even if it's just to feel good about themselves. He went to great lengths to prove it and punished me when he sensed I trusted anyone too much."

Jin told him of the time she and Lu had stolen a pouch of coins from a merchant. Lu had persuaded her to pocket one, that no one would know. She had, and then Haitao had taken her to the courtyard, pulled the telltale coin from her pocket, and caned her, turning her back into a patchwork of black and blue.

That night, Lu had snuck to her room with medicine and explained that Haitao had forced him to do it to teach her a lesson. She demanded he leave, so he sat outside her door all that night and whispered stories to her to distract her from the pain, not stopping until she had fallen asleep. The next night she let him tend her back with salve.

"I knew I could trust Lu from then on," she finished. "And we remained close, ironically because Haitao tried to break us."

"I see why you distrust people," Aadan said. "Men. And me. Especially me."

His voice carried hurt, and though she berated herself for it, she said, "In your position, I would have done the same." She remembered the betrayal she had felt, learning he had been on orders from Prince Tai to befriend her, perhaps more, but only for the purpose of monitoring her. It had cut because she had overcome so much to think of Aadan as not just a friend, but something more.

He looked down, frowning. "The terrible thing is I didn't want to do it, and yet I did. I didn't have the strength to say no." He turned to her, his face earnest in the fading sunlight. "I will never do that again."

She wanted to lean against him, to believe in what he said, no matter what the demons inside her hissed about it being a lie. It was a good lie, one she'd like to believe.

And his scent. She needed space, if only to clear her

mind, but his hand caught hers. "I want you to trust me again, Jin."

"I do too," she said softly, "but the problem is, I have no idea how." She slipped her hand away and walked back to the others.

CHAPTER 12

The clinking of armor mingled with the sound of trumpets and drums as the soldiers fell into file and began their drills. Swords glittered in the late summer light, and halberds clashed under the infantry's fluttering blue and red banners.

From where Tai and the empress stood on the balcony overlooking the Courtyard of Eternal Peace, the troops looked impressive. Their movements were in unison, orderly, and disciplined.

But it was an illusion.

The spears broke more often than Tai would have liked, and the swords, he knew upon closer examination, were of lower quality than in previous years. The metal was of a lower grade, and the smiths who had made the most recent batches lacked the skill of those ten years ago.

Likewise, he noticed a difference in the horses.

These animals were smaller and had less stamina, and their necks were shorter, a sure sign of a lesser breeding. Whereas when he had first become commander in chief of Dragon Class, almost all the cavalry stables had housed the best Ferghana horses, these now were clearly stock from local, inferior breeders. They might hold their own in battle, but they were a far cry from the tall, long-legged steeds from Bactria that a previous emperor had worked so hard to secure.

"The leech," the empress muttered next to him. Though not a military woman, even his mother could see, now that the troops were being displayed before the ruler, where corners had been cut and money had been secretly bled away.

Tai nodded. "The troops are well trained at least, but they are not well equipped." He was glad he had come. Not that his mother could have prevented him from attending, for the Dragon Class would also be drilling today.

The empress shook her head. "We will need an ocean of gold to bring the arms back to what they were."

"Taxes?" Tai suggested. "Though the nobles will be restless if given more taxes to bear."

The empress frowned. "Entitled and overfed, all of them. But you are right, they will whine about not having as many serving girls or a little less Maru wine at the winter festivities, and possibly stir discontent."

"You could ask the monasteries," Tai said. "They

have been beneficiaries of your generosity for years. It is time they gave back."

"It's important now more than ever to appear strong, or the enemies will gather, and the people will worry. Worried people topple governments, my son."

Tai stared at her. "Those statues are made of gold. Five of them might mean the difference between our armies winning or losing whatever is coming our way."

She shook her head. "As I said, image counts for much."

He stifled his disagreement with difficulty. Was this due to a recent meeting between her and the head monks of the city? He watched in silence for a moment as the infantry filed out of the courtyard and gongs signaled a changeover. Three dragon squadrons circled overhead and began flight maneuvers, displaying aerial tactics. Assistants hurried to line up straw targets at various points in the courtyard.

"So, if not taxes, what is your solution?" Tai asked, though he suspected he knew.

"We must find an ally via marriage."

"I agree. Who are you marrying, Mother?"

She sighed. "There is a time for jests, my son."

"I am sorry. I simply thought of broadening our options. Given that your first priority is always the throne."

The empress shot him a dangerous look. "Would you like a stepfather who will strip me of my power and force a child on me that will then take your place?"

He watched a black dragon swoop and spout flame, squarely hitting one of the straw targets and destroying it within seconds. "I don't think there's a man alive who could do that to you against your will. In fact, mightn't you marry him, take his assets, and then have him killed?"

She looked at him as if he were a stranger. "Do you really think I would do that?"

"No," he said quietly. And it was true. But he was no longer sure whether he thought that because she was above murder, or simply because it would actually be a highly complex feat to pull off. He sighed. "Very well. You're thinking of Meipin?"

She drew a breath, and he had the feeling she was grateful to change the subject back. "An alliance with Meipin would solve many of our problems, especially the financial ones." The empress watched as a whole line of dragons followed the black's lead, and one after another, the targets burst into flame. "Her family has always been loyal to us. She's beautiful, witty, and knows court expectations. I thought you would find all those things attractive."

Tai searched his mother's face, but her expression remained clear. Deep down, though, she must have also been thinking of Peilah—the favorite daughter of a prominent trade official. Tai had found her irresistible for a time, but then she had died. Some said by his mother's hand, and though he had never believed those rumors, he found his firm beliefs weakening.

"My wanting to find other options has nothing to do with Lady Meipin's charms," Tai said. "Only with choosing the best option for the empire." Was this true? Just a year ago, he would have discussed his marriage objectively, without a thought to his own wants, because he had believed in the throne above all. But now?

The empress appeared to take him at his word, however, tapping her gold-painted nails thoughtfully. The flaming straw targets had been replaced with fresh ones, along with a rack laden with weapons. "What other options? We could indebt ourselves to another country, I suppose. Most would only be too happy to have the ruler of China beg for their mercy and help."

"We have allies who would be grateful for our protection," Tai countered. "They would ally with us."

The empress scoffed. "And why do you think they need protection, my son? Because they are small and weak. They can't help us against the likes of Baikalan or Mengkhis. If you are going to suggest alternatives, Tai, make them realistic ones at least."

A line of gold dragons had formed a circle above and now took turns swooping. On their descent, they used their powers to pluck a weapon from the rack and hurl it toward a target.

"Of course," his mother continued, "we can pursue an alliance elsewhere. I considered Champa, but there are rumors the king is enamored with some dancer and has problems of his own. His army has suffered for it, and the crown prince squanders whatever he can. Marrying them would only inherit a bellyful of debt." She frowned, lips pursed. "What of the Caliphate?"

"Medina?" Tai tried not to show his distaste. His marrying a princess of Aadan's enemy would definitely drive a wedge between them. Throne above all, but Tai still valued his friendships. "It's far away. Getting them to send us an army or relying on their help would be risky."

The empress continued to drum her gold-painted nails against the balustrade. A dozen rings covered her fingers, all of them ornate except one small one that was a simple gold. "Parhae then? That would keep King Ulagan in his place."

Tai nodded, unenthusiastic. "Better than Nihhon. That would appear aggressive." The island kingdoms on the far side of Parhae were rich and powerful, but it might send a message to Parhae that they would be squeezed from both sides. A small and frightened enemy, Tai knew from history, often proved dangerous.

The empress sighed. "I can't help sense resistance in you, my son. You can have any concubine you like, have your pick of the courtesans, but you can't marry whomever you want. You do know that, don't you?"

"Of course," he replied. "Besides, there's no one who has my heart more than you."

She gave him a sharp look, and for a moment, he pitied her the glimmer of gratitude there, as if she genuinely wanted that to be true but suspected he was simply playing with her emotions. "It's good you inherited my charm."

Tai smiled, but inside, her question had made him think. If he could marry anyone, who would he choose? Hazel eyes and hair entered his mind, but he dismissed it.

When the Dragon Class review ended, they returned to the empress's quarters and found Sanjin waiting. Tai caught the letter he tried to discreetly hide in his sleeve, along with its Khitan seal. The head of the Royal Veil darted a look at the empress.

"I am the commanding officer of Dragon Class, am I not?" Tai looked to his mother. "If there is news of my riders, I deserve to know."

His mother nodded. "You are right. Speak, Sanjin."

"Your Majesty." Sanjin bowed. "I have received another message from the Dragon Class mages in Khitan."

"You don't look pleased," Tai commented.

Sanjin hesitated. "Simply wary."

The empress let a servant take her coat off her shoulders, revealing the gold-and-red silk dress she had underneath. "What do they say? Have they found Baikalan?"

"It's more what they don't say, Your Majesty." Sanjin paused. "We have a certain set of phrases that are to be included in each letter. And the missive I received has none of them."

Tai frowned. "You think it's not from our mages."

"That's correct. I think someone impersonating our people wrote these letters."

"The Khitans are intercepting the mail?" the empress asked.

"Or worse," Tai said, his gut twisting. "Our mages cannot write back."

"Because they are dead," the empress continued his thought.

"There's no hard evidence of that," Sanjin said. "But it means something is not right in Khitan."

Tai began to pace. "And what of our messenger? He must have received the mail from our mages directly?"

Sanjin shook his head. "I asked that, Your Highness. Apparently, he was told that all our mages had left for the Well of Ice, but they had provided this letter before leaving."

"Where the inexplicable happens, there must be a demon," the empress murmured, citing an old proverb. "Ulagan is hiding something."

"Yes," Sanjin agreed. "The question is what. And why now, when Baikalan has escaped?"

"Unless . . ." the empress's eyes narrowed as she trailed off, and all three of them stiffened at the thought that Ulagan had something to do with Baikalan's release. "He's either a fool or a monster, to unleash this."

"Possibly both," Sanjin said, grim. "But we can't rule out that Baikalan is helping him."

Tai's first instinct was to demand he himself leave with a squad of dragons for Khitan. But the tactician in him knew that was folly—sending the crown prince into a possible trap would likely be playing into Khitan's hands. "And how do we find that out? Along with Ulagan's plan?"

"I will ask amongst our network and see if I can find out. But that will take time."

Which we may not have, Tai thought to himself. *Only Emar or Jin's wing can tell us what Ulagan is planning.*

"In the meantime," Sanjin continued, "I suggest we continue as if nothing is wrong, or we will alert Ulagan and make things worse."

"So we wait and see." Tai tried to keep the frustration out of his voice, and he looked out the window over the imperial city spread out in the afternoon light. The thought that Aadan and Jin might be dead, or injured, or simply in Ulagan's clutches would haunt him now, and the thought of sitting by and doing nothing was already weighing on him.

"Does he have the means to attack the capital directly?" the empress asked sharply.

"Normally, no," Sanjin replied. "But if Baikalan were to aid him . . ."

"I will ready the Dragon Class," Tai said. "If Khitan is planning an attack on the capital, we can meet him prepared." He gave his mother a long look. "But in order to do so, you need to keep me informed," Tai said, "which means I need to be included on all discussions involving the enemy and Emar's group."

The empress hesitated, then nodded. "Very well. But you are not to leave the palace."

"Your Majesty, I think—"

"If there is a chance that Baikalan and the Khitans are coming for us, then you will stay within these walls," his mother said, fierce. "I will place guards around your quarters if I have to, but you do not leave this palace, do you understand?"

He seethed, but sensed he should satisfy himself with the victory of regaining access to intelligence, and leave the battle over his freedom for another day. "Yes, Your Majesty."

CHAPTER 13

Jin sat cross-legged, needled by not just the sun climbing higher but also by the scents where they had bedded down at dawn beneath a rock outcropping. She smelled juniper and peony mixed with pine, goat droppings, and even the faint tinge of smoke from a forest fire on the horizon. She was practicing how to close down her senses, but with minimal success.

Panshalar's loud snoring didn't help her focus either. She glanced over at her other wing mates. Jao was curled against his dragon, whose nostrils flared gently in sleep. But Wanli was stretched out, along with Aadan, who was cradled in the crook of his foreleg, his legs stretched and crossed at the ankles, his head leaning back and his face serene.

Jin resented his untroubled slumber. Aadan seemed able to sleep anywhere, anytime, when sleep eluded her even when it was her shift to rest. No matter how she tossed or how she buried her face in her arm, she couldn't escape seeing Ezho and Turuchi disappearing into the snow, the blood pooling under the young mage Yao Bing.

And then, when she tried to think of other things, happier things, Aadan's sandalwood scent overwhelmed her, sending her mind spinning in a completely opposite direction, until she felt like one of those toy tumblers, that, when pushed, bowed one way and then another.

She stood and walked gingerly around the sleeping men, out from under the overhang. Up this high, on these mountains, they had counted that no wayward farmers or herders would find them, but one never knew. She surveyed the horizon and reached out to Rayshan.

Anything?

Shhh . . . I'm hunting it.

She fell silent. Since Rayshan and she didn't need as much sleep, she had volunteered to keep watch first, which also helped avoid bad dreams.

Rayshan's emotions fluttered at her across the bond.

How did Emar stand it? A lump rose at the thought of Emar, and whether he was still alive. *How did he stand his senses being overwhelmed like this?* She reached out a hand, every hair on her skin responding to the light as she rotated her forearm in the sun. She smelled the water in the leaves, the crackle of a distant thunderstorm. If she really focused, she could hear all the heartbeats of the dragons and riders asleep behind her. Only one wasn't asleep. One was . . .

"Everything alright?"

She turned to see Aadan walking over, pulling his curly hair into a topknot with both hands. "Sorry if I woke you."

"I wasn't asleep, actually."

She raised an eyebrow. "Why pretend?"

He shrugged. "To fit in."

She fought a smile. Aadan had a knack for fitting into any situation and with anyone, like a willow. It was another quality she liked about him, that she found familiar because as a thief, she had always done the same. They stood in silence, looking over the landscape for a while, and as the breeze shifted, making the scent of sandalwood flood her senses, she stepped away.

"You always do that when I'm within arm's length," Aadan sighed. "Am I repulsive now?"

She shook her head. "It's not that."

"Then what?" he asked. "If it's about my orders from Prince Tai, I can't undo what happened, only—"

"I know you did what you had to. It's not that."

Aadan sighed. "Emar said it was best for wing mates not to have secrets. He wasn't just talking about the blood bond."

She looked at him, surprised. "He threw a knife at

me, remember? To prove the point. It was all about the blood bond."

"True. But before that, he'd taken me aside and given me a big talk about how secrets destroy you from the inside out."

She frowned. "What secret are you hiding?"

He regarded her, gauging. "I can't tell if you really don't know or you just enjoy the torture?"

She tried to ignore his proximity. Why couldn't the man eat more mutton so he smelled sour, like Panshalar?

A flurry of beating wings broke off her reply as Rayshan landed lightly next to them, a wild boar in his mouth. He dropped it and shook out his wings.

Dinner, he said, then regarded the pair with a shrewd eye. *Should I have stayed away?*

No, you came back just in time.

They took out their knives and began work, Jin offering a haunch to Rayshan.

I've eaten, he said, and promptly began sniffing around the shrub for a hidden place to bed down. Food always made dragons sleepy. When he hesitated over two spots and then finally chose one and curled down, Jin found herself alone again with Aadan.

They worked in silence for a while, pulling the hide off the boar and then dividing the carcass into portions they could carry.

"I hope there's enough for all of us," Aadan said.

"Between your appetite and Panshalar's, Rayshan will need to be bringing down herds."

She pelted a piece of boar skin at him, which he dodged.

"Don't play with our food," he scolded.

A laugh rose in her, and in trying to cut it off, she gave an undignified half snort, half cough instead.

"What was that?" Aadan asked, cocking an eyebrow.

"Nothing. A laugh, but then . . . does it matter?" she asked, defensive.

He grinned, pushing an escaped curl from his eyes. "That was the ugliest sound in the world. Yet . . . I'm going to try my best to make you do it again."

The air was suddenly too warm, and she avoided his eyes, focusing instead on the boar.

They continued like this for a few moments in silence, and Jin was grateful Aadan didn't press her to look up. She found it hard enough being around him and not wishing for more.

When they had finished, they began cleaning up the evidence of the boar, scuffing dirt over the offal and blood.

"Jao and Panshalar told me how Ulagan put a spear through you," Aadan said softly. "And how you tried to save them by offering your own life."

She shrugged. "I can't die, so it was the natural thing to do."

"I'm sorry I wasn't there."

She looked up and caught the anger in his face. "I'm

not. You might have been killed as well. And then, who would be here to eat marmot bone cake and boar with me?"

He snorted. "How did you survive on just marmot and whatever else the Chaakan eat?"

"That wasn't as bad as the waking dreams." She paused. "I think about Emar, whether he's alive."

Aadan nodded, eyes clouded. "Me too."

"Ulagan killed them all, without hesitation, like they were bugs, not people." She swallowed past the disbelief and anger in her throat. "I can't stop seeing Ezho's face, Yao Bing's . . ."

He moved as if to hold her, but then seemed to stop himself. Part of Jin was glad, but a greater part wished he hadn't.

"You remember that time we read about Mengkhis Lai?" she said instead. "About how his power made him lose his mind?"

Aadan frowned, clearly confused as to what he saw as a change of subject. "Yes."

Jin glanced at Rayshan to assure herself he was asleep. She didn't want him to hear, because if she was losing her mind, then Rayshan would be affected too. "What if I'm on the same path? What if I'm . . . hallucinating those who've died?"

Aadan bent to tie a knot in the boar's skin, which they were using to carry the meat. "From what I've seen, seeing dead people doesn't make you Mengkhis. Mengkhis enjoyed having power over people and craved more. He enjoyed death for cruelty's sake. I don't see you doing that. You've become an inspiration to women joining Dragon Class, but you don't sing from the rooftops about it."

"Maybe that's because my madness has just started," Jin said, her throat tightening.

"You need to see the positive sometimes, not just the negative," Aadan said. He wiped his hands on the boar hide. "You're not anything like Mengkhis Lai."

"How do you know?"

"I just do." He paused. "Even if you don't."

They picked their way down to the river nearby. Jin dipped her arms in, the cold water flowing over her, numbing her, taking the blood and offal from her fingers. Aadan scrubbed his face and beard, and Jin hoped that the water might wash off his sandalwood scent as well. But water, it seemed, only changed his natural odor, enhancing it rather than erasing it.

He looked over and frowned. "Do I have something in my beard?"

She quickly looked away, conscious she had been staring. "No," she said too quickly, then stood, wiping her hands on her clothes and about to move away. But Aadan was somehow standing right before her, blocking her.

"Emar told me not to keep secrets, Jin, and he's right," Aadan said. A heavy pause followed. "The hardest part of all this has actually not been Ulagan or escaping Khitan."

"What then?" she asked, viciously ordering her pulse to slow. Rayshan was stirring in response. She knew she should move away but found herself lingering.

He was so close now she could see the water beads in his beard, which had grown since they'd left the fort. It was black as night, but the sunlight made the edges look almost purple.

"It's been the pretending."

"What pretending?" she said, suspicion creeping in.

He shook his head. "You misunderstand me. The pretending that I don't feel anything, that I don't wish you'd talk to me every time you walk by. Pretending that you can look through me and it doesn't cut."

A glow ignited in her. His hand was on hers, and he leaned in close.

"By the Wise Lord, I needed to say that," he murmured.

She pulled back, and her heart twisted at the wounded look on his face. "This isn't a good idea. You don't know me, Aadan. You don't know—many things."

"Then tell me."

She struggled, debating. "I found something out last year," she said, her voice thick. Was she really about to tell him? What would he think of her? But she couldn't lie about this, not to him. And if he wouldn't end it because of her being the first female dragonrider, then her bloodline would deter him. "This year. With Gao. When he had me imprisoned before the test, when he told me to never come back, he told me my background. He showed me a document of my birth."

Aadan frowned. "So?"

"It's a prison birth document, Aadan," she said. "I'm likely the child of a murderer." She had lost the document along with her leathers, but every detail had been etched into her memory. "My mother was a woman named Lan Ming, and she was imprisoned for killing her husband. I was born in a prison and sold on her execution day."

Aadan absorbed this. "That's a very tragic story. But—"

"You don't want to be involved with someone with that kind of bloodline," Jin said. Even in the smallest village, no one wanted the child of a criminal to marry into the family. Such a match would invite disaster into the home, not to mention the poisoning of one's offspring with tainted blood and bad luck. Having been a thief would have been stain enough, but the child of an executed criminal was nearly untouchable, especially for someone of noble birth. She found Aadan almost irresistible, but she couldn't bring that to anyone's family, much less his.

"How do you know this is true?"

His question gave her pause. It wasn't ironclad, but Gao had numerous resources at his disposal, and she doubted he would have left any shred of evidence unexplored. "There's a very good chance it is."

"There's also an equally, if not greater chance, that

it's not," Aadan said. He still held her hand and squeezed it, pulling her closer. "Besides, it doesn't matter."

"How can you say it doesn't matter?" she argued.

"Because it wouldn't change how I feel."

"But it means there's no future," she insisted.

"You've already made Dragon Class into a meritocracy," he said. "Surely rewriting China's three thousand years of traditions would be easy."

"Did you just make a jest?"

He shrugged. "Did you like it?"

"I can't decide."

"Then see if you like this." He kissed her, and she felt as if she was back in that amazing moment from that night before his betrayal, the sense that the world had fallen away and there was nothing but him, the cool water in his beard, and the scent of sandalwood flooding her senses.

He pulled away, his expression turning sheepish as he glanced over her head toward where the dragons lay. "I accidentally woke Wanli."

"What is he saying?"

"It's not repeatable."

She allowed herself to touch his cheek. A fierce, wild hope flickered in her that birth, class, station, their roles as dragonriders—they could overcome all of it. "Don't celebrate too soon. If you don't like pretending, what are you going to tell the others?"

"Maybe I'll try the truth." He leaned in again, and

heat rose in her until Aadan's arms locked around her waist and viciously yanked her to the ground.

A bone-shattering roar ripped the air as flames burst around them and trees lit up like torches.

Jin recognized that roar.

Baikalan.

CHAPTER 14

They rolled, the heat searing them on all sides. Jin was on fire—her hair had caught sparks, and Aadan was slapping down the flames with his arm.

She had no time to assess the damage, for Baikalan was descending on them, green jaws open and talons outstretched, so large and mighty it took Jin's breath away, for she had never seen a jade besides Rayshan. They rolled in opposite directions, and Baikalan's claws churned up earth as if it were water. He prowled in a tight circle around them, yellow eyes hard, his open mouth showing teeth the length of her longest finger.

A flash of green and a blaze of heat cut across Baikalan's path, and Rayshan stood shielding Aadan and Jin.

Are you both alright?

Yes! she called to the others. *Wanli, Nakkalan, where are you?*

Aadan rushed for the knife he had dropped while dressing the boar, but Baikalan blew another blast of fire, singeing the earth and making Aadan stop in his tracks.

You are blood bonded, Baikalan snarled in her head. *Did they send you like they sent the others?*

Emar. He was talking about Emar and his wing, Jin realized. *Where is Emar?* Jin demanded. *Please let him be alive!*

Come with me, and I will show you, Baikalan answered.

Wanli landed behind him, jaws open and ready to spray water.

I will let them go if you come with me, child, Baikalan said. *Otherwise, I kill them all.*

"What is he saying?" Aadan snapped. "Tell me!"

"He says he'll call off the soldiers if I go with him," Jin answered.

"Not a chance," Aadan said, striding forward and vaulting onto Wanli's back.

Ah, love makes tigers out of lambs, Baikalan hissed. He swiped a tail at Wanli, who blasted a spray of water at the large jade. But Baikalan disappeared, and the water hit nothing but air.

Then Jin was flying, smashing into a nearby boulder. She heard something crack but forced herself to get up—Aadan's knife lay on the ground just an arm's length away.

Wanli! Again!

Wanli kept spraying water around them until Baikalan's shape showed like a glistening outline against the sun, water droplets etching the impossibly large beast and his wings. Jin dove for Aadan's knife. She grasped its handle, turned, aimed, and threw before the dragon's outline evaporated.

The shriek told her she hit home, but the rage burning her mind told her Baikalan's hatred toward her had doubled. The pain was enough to puncture Baikalan's concentration, and he flickered into visibility, blood staining the chest area near his right foreleg.

He wheeled in the air, faltered and righted himself, then began flying away. Ignoring the pain along her neck, she sprinted to Rayshan and leaped up to grasp the saddle.

Go! Go now! We have to finish him.

Rayshan gave chase at blistering speed. But the older dragon was faster and drawing away. Rayshan put in a burst of energy, closing the gap.

Jin sensed Wanli and Aadan flying behind her.

Hurry!

I am!

They gained on the other jade, and Jin was gratified to see that Baikalan seemed to be tiring. The wound was taking its toll, and he hadn't bothered to take out the blade, no doubt worried it would do more damage out than in. The blood was flowing thick, and hope flickered in Jin. Perhaps she had delivered a fatal blow.

Just as Rayshan was about to snap his jaws around the jade's tail, the dragon turned upside down, folded his wings tightly around himself, and dived.

He hurtled toward the plains below like an arrow, and Rayshan was hard-pressed to follow, even though he himself knew the move.

And then Baikalan vanished, dagger and all.

No!

Though she had seen him appear in midair, Jin was still shocked by his sudden disappearance, as if he never was.

Rayshan only just managed to pull himself up from the ground, but clipped a foreleg as he did so. Pain seared through Jin, mirroring Rayshan's. He flapped his wings and made an ungainly landing, Wanli joining him and Aadan leaping off to come to their aid.

"We can follow the blood," Aadan said, pointing.

"I'll follow," she said. "You go back and make sure Jao and Panshalar are alright. Wanli said they were outnumbered."

Aadan hesitated, then touched her face. "Be careful."

She nodded and watched him leap back on Wanli before checking on Rayshan. *Are you badly hurt?*

A scrape. He sniffed the air. *Rain.*

She swore under her breath. Rain would wash away the blood, and at the rate the dragon was flying, the blood droplets would likely be far apart.

Her fears were confirmed as they rose into the sky and the clouds gave way so that the smell of wet grass and soaked earth drowned out the scent of blood.

Perhaps your aim was true, Rayshan comforted her.

One can always hope, she replied, raging at the rain slicking her damaged hair and prickling the burned flesh at her neck. *Or perhaps,* she corrected herself bitterly, *one can* only *hope.*

CHAPTER 15

In the days leading up to the trial, Prince Tai wondered if it was possible to literally drown in paperwork. How could so many of the officials have been in Gao's pocket? It was astounding and sobering. Clearly, many had been unhappy enough with their lot to accept bribes and favors from Gao.

What had motivated them?

It was not a lack of pay, for their salaries had all been generous. Had they been afraid of Gao? Or worse, was it really what his mother often feared, that deep down no one could stomach a woman on the throne?

He rubbed at his eyes, the papers and details starting to swim. He needed to know them thoroughly, though, if he was going to sit in on the trial in a week's time and listen to the testimony and advise his mother on judgment. Nothing toppled an empire more quickly, he believed, than an unfair justice system.

A servant announced the mage Situ Han, and moments later, the mage entered, tossing a package on Tai's desk.

Tai looked over at the item wrapped in oilcloth and string, then up at mage Situ Han's beaming face.

"Your Highness, may I present you with a gift."

"What is the special occasion?"

The man's broad face split into a grin. "You'll see."

Tai unwrapped the package, and a rough purple robe of silk and linen fell out. It was new looking but clearly second-hand, with the emblem of a raven on the left chest. "A mage's robes?"

Situ Han chuckled. "Oh, it's much more than that. It's a pass to leave the palace."

Tai frowned. "I don't understand."

The mage pulled out a bun from his sleeve and took a generous bite, then settled into the seat next to Tai instead of opposite him. The prince still marveled at the man's presumption. "I sense you'd like a change of scene. I thought I might offer you a chance to do so. As my apprentice."

Tai sighed. "I told you I'm not interested in mage lessons, though thank you for the offer."

Mage Situ Han wasn't put out in the slightest. "Oh, you'd just be pretending to be my apprentice. Princes can't leave the palace. But mages can."

Tai glanced at him, assessing. Did Situ Han somehow know about his last conversation with his mother? How she had forbidden him from leaving the palace? "Assuming I'd care to be your lackey, where would you take me?"

Mage Situ Han chuckled. "That's a surprise."

Tai cocked his head. "You know, this sounds like an elaborate scheme to kidnap the prince and hold the empire for ransom. I'd be a gullible man to simply don a robe and follow you out."

The mage finished his bun and swallowed. "Or you'd be a faithful disciple of Lao Tse."

Tai had spent his fair share of time memorizing the Taoist sage's writings, as all princes had to, but he was still lost as to Mage Situ's meaning. His confusion must have shown, for Situ smiled indulgently.

"If you want to govern the people, you must place yourself below them," mage Situ Han said. "In this palace, you live above them. Ride with me through the city. You'll find it worth your time."

Tai wavered, but the mage had kindled a small flame of longing in Tai, one he now couldn't put out. He hadn't left the palace in a month. More. For a prince who had regularly traveled on diplomatic trips and who enjoyed the world beyond these walls, the days had grown dry. He longed to leave, if only to escape the constant worries over what was happening in Khitan. Yes, the risk of kidnapping was valid, but was he really going to live in fear until Baikalan was captured?

"Very well. When do we leave?"

The mage beamed, wiping his fingers on his belly. "I find the present is always best."

"Instability stalks us! Who knows what famine and drought lurk next season? Who dares predict what calamity heaven brings?"

Tai scowled beneath his mage's hood, careful to keep his face averted and his eyes on the rotund figure before him as he and mage Situ Han rode through the crowded Changan North Road, which ran parallel to the Avenue of Vermillion Birds. This street was narrower than that main avenue and much more crowded. They had been riding for half an hour now, and this must have been the fifth such disaster-monger they had passed.

"Some say that the feared Mengkhis Lai has broken free and rides for the city now on his cursed dragon!"

He hated rumors. His life and his mother's life had been dictated by rumors, and they had a way of seeping into his destiny like water through clay. Rumor, his mother had repeatedly counseled him, could kill him faster than any assassin's blade if he let it take root.

The rumor that he was illegitimate had dogged him from a young age, for though he looked nothing like his father, his good looks from his mother and the fact that all princes suffered such gossip made this easy to dismiss.

Then, there was the rumor that the empress had killed Peilah. This rumor had always been easy to brush aside . . . until now. He had always believed his mother in all things, for it was them against the world. But now that his mother had shown how much she tried to control him, he had doubts.

Peilah had been unlike any other girl he knew—brash, bold, like a comet on a dark night. She had made it known she would court the crown prince and had been obscenely brazen about it. He learned the secrets of the girls at court, how this one had a lumpy mole she didn't want anyone to know about, and that one snored as loud as a panda in rut.

Peilah had been the one to teach him the most about court manners despite all the elite tutelage he had received. And he had flowered.

"You have the face of a god," she had said. "You shouldn't be afraid to flaunt it." And she had shown him what heights wit could reach. Her poetry made him laugh and cry and snicker by turns, some of it kind, others scathing of the girls at court, and yet others poking fun at her many admirers. She encouraged him to ride his horse in continuous games of polo until its legs gave out. He accepted her dare to drink with her until the room spun and their stomachs heaved, and she had challenged him to crush toads underfoot with her. All actions that now shamed him.

His face still burned at the memory of that clear, starry night in summer when she had devised the prank of replacing the wine in the horse master's flask with horse piss. They had stayed to witness the horse master's spluttering rage when he took a swig. Then they had run laughing back to her quarters and fallen on top of each other in the fountain, her snickering and him cursing at the weight of his robes as they clung to him, pulling him into the water. She had regained her feet first, standing up sopping wet while her light silk gown hugged her like skin.

The world had frozen for a moment. Even while her hair hung in disheveled ropes down her shoulders, she was breathtaking, her beauty able to make fish forget how to swim and birds how to fly, as the poets said. He saw more then than she had ever revealed, and though he was no stranger to desire, having been surrounded by the empire's most beautiful women all his life, he had never known the feeling to be so all-consuming.

Then, she was taking off her garments and going to get dry ones, and he was watching her walk away. He pulled himself out of the fountain and followed, closing the gap between them in a few strides. He didn't know what gave him so much confidence when she normally took the lead, but he was kissing her, and she was responding. Thoughts fled him, and he knew what it was like to be lost on a wave, but then she was pushing back against him, and he knew he had transgressed.

"That is for marriage," she had whispered, eyes wide

and lips wet. "Make me your empress, and every night will be like this."

He had pulled back, ashamed and awkward. He stuttered an apology for pushing himself on her, but she laughed outright at this, and this unexpectedly crushed him. For he had lost himself, whereas she hadn't.

The steady drone of chanting drew him out of his thoughts. They had entered the southeastern quarter of the city, and Tai urged his horse to follow mage Situ Han's across the Second Ring Road that ran in a semi-circle from the city's northwest down past the palace before cutting to the city's eastern gate, the Gate of Spring Light. At this hour, the road teemed with horse carriages, sedans, camels, and donkey carts bearing foodstuffs and wares for the two main markets.

"There, Apprentice," Han Situ called over his shoulder. "The Temple of Original Dharma."

Tai made his way across the wide ring road and looked at the temple's visible roof tiles. He knew of the place from studying Changan's geography and Buddhist history, but he had never visited. Seeing it for the first time, he understood how it awed residents, pilgrims, and dignitaries alike.

Five towering pagodas rose from the temple, one at each corner and one, the tallest, in the very heart. The gold tiles glimmered in the sun, and vendors crowded the streets adjoining the temple, offering visitors all sorts of religious merchandise: incense, prayer beads and wheels, silk scarves, and fruits for offering to Buddha. Horses and pedestrians wove around sedan chairs born by servants in fine and not-so-fine garb. But as they made their way to the main entrance, mage Situ Han motioned for Tai to dismount.

"We'll leave the horses here," he said, handing a coin to one of the many grooms who plied a trade at the temple entrance.

Tai set off for the main gate, but mage Situ Han pointed. "We're going another way, Apprentice."

Curious, Tai followed him around the corner.

Here, the street was filled with a wholly different sort of visitor from those at the main gate. Some had missing limbs, and others suffered ailments that affected their movements and sight. Still others clearly looked like they simply suffered daily from lack of food, while hardened eyes stared out of gaunt faces.

Mage Situ Han made his sedate way through the crowd, and Tai followed, hesitant.

"The monasteries must provide good meals," he said in a low voice. "The amount of money donated from the palace ensures enough for all."

Mage Situ Han nodded vigorously. "Oh yes, there is plenty for all."

His tone held a hint of irony, and Tai's unease grew. A side door opened, and everyone stirred, jostling for the closest spots. Two plump monks in saffron brown robes, one with a bulbous nose and the other with a birthmark on his cheek, stood before the crowd and motioned for order.

The crowd immediately sank into quiet, and the monk with a birthmark spoke.

"Everyone will be allowed inside shortly to partake in the food. But first, let us offer prayers for our Celestial Ruler, Empress Wu of the Celestial Light, reincarnation of the Bodhisattva himself."

Reincarnation of the Bodhisattva? Tai glanced at Mage Situ, but the mage was still looking at the monk with undivided attention.

". . . ill will and fury at our own suffering," the monk was saying. "But where does suffering come from? It comes from want and from our own actions in the past. We reap our own karma, and only by doing good can we advance in the next life to better things." He paused for effect, and the crowd shuffled, restless. "Therefore, do not resent your lot in life, no matter how wretched, for know that you brought this on yourself by deeds you don't even remember. Those who are above you in station are above you because of their good deeds in the past and are now exalted. Do not rail against them, for there is no virtue in hatred. Rather, work to raise yourself so that you may return to the next life better and more enlightened. Follow the example of the Celestial Empress, and you, too, will know comfort and freedom from want."

Tai cast a look about him, taking in the dull faces lined with hunger and worry, and swallowed his disgust. The monks were blaming these people for their own suffering and asking them to be grateful for it? And yet everyone stood in deadened silence, eyes on the monks.

"Now let us pray." The monk led them in a quick chant, which everyone followed, and then the monks stood aside and ushered the visitors in through the open door behind them.

Those who came out clutched small packets of leaf-wrapped rice, which they devoured and fought over like hounds. Some grains fell to the ground but were quickly scooped up by children who shoved the rice, dirt and all, into their mouths. Some who were not quick enough received a cuff for stealing from the adults, and Tai felt sickened.

"This is what they give to eat? There must be vegetables and fruits at least." Stricter Buddhist doctrine deplored meat, but the monks at the palace never seemed to be thinner for it.

Mage Situ Han shrugged. "You can ask them. Perhaps there has been a delay in the delivery of other foodstuffs?" He paused. "A delay of roughly the last fifteen-odd years."

The crowd was dispersing now, and the monks were encouraging those lingering and those who had come too late to move on.

"Come," mage Situ Han said. "We can't visit the temple and not see its most famous draw, the Statue of Benevolent Mercy."

Tai followed the mage into the courtyard and joined a line of devout citizens buying incense and waiting their turn to kneel at the main pagoda. Inside, Tai had to crane his neck to see the top of the great gold statue. Though carved from a single block of wood, the statue towered above everyone, the long ears hanging to the shoulders and the face of the Buddha decidedly female, with more than a passing resemblance to his mother.

"Plated in real gold," Mage Situ murmured as he handed Tai some incense. "A scraping of one of the fingernails alone would feed several families for a year."

"Have some tried to steal the gold then?" Tai asked.

Mage Situ made several bows, then placed the incense stick in the urn along with the thousands of others there. Several women were praying intently, their eyes squeezed shut and their hands working wooden prayer beads with undivided devotion.

"They have, and ended up tortured." Mage Situ raised an eyebrow. "The monks don't take stealing lightly, and it seems that they are more than happy to see punishment meted out in this life rather than in the next."

Tai placed his smoldering incense in the urn. "You show me all this to turn me against my mother."

Mage Situ Han looked offended. "I think you are too clever to turn. No, I show you this to give you the freedom to choose." They began walking out of the temple and back into the streets, where Tai noticed the gaunt faces, the barefoot children with dull, desperate eyes hunting the streets for scraps. One boy, no older than five, emerged from the temple door with a bun in his hand, when a swarm of older children descended on him. Before Tai could reach them, the gang had run off with the bun, leaving the boy in the street with scraped hands and a bleeding mouth.

"Here," Tai said, pulling the boy to his feet. He searched his pockets, but as he was wearing mage robes that weren't even his, he didn't have any coin on him. "Situ, give the boy what you have."

The mage hesitated, then pulled a few *fei* from the purse at his waist and held it out.

The boy eyed him with suspicion, but then took the coins and ran without a backward glance, as if afraid they would change their minds.

"Those same children will find him and beat him for it," Situ Han remarked.

"Hopefully not before he's bought something and eaten it," Tai muttered.

They began walking back to the temple's front entrance.

"I think the monks of this foreign religion are a parasite on this land, but I must give them credit," Situ said. "They have a wonderful story in their Buddha: a prince so moved by his people that he gave up his palace and his wife to study the nature of suffering. How can anyone not love a god like that?"

"You want me to follow the steps of Buddha?"

"Not at all. My comforts and the new courtyard in the palace are very agreeable. I wouldn't want to have to give them up because the head of Dragon Class abdicated."

He spied a vendor selling pastries and, with a deft motion, produced two coins that he dropped into the vendor's hand before sweeping up the food.

"I'd offer you some, but a prince must keep in good form," he said, shoving a pastry into his mouth. He swallowed it, then waved a crumb-studded finger. "The problem with the Ministry of Mages is that we don't have a good origin story. And people love a good origin story. We don't stand for good or evil because magic isn't good or evil. It just is. Those people you saw all believe in a better life because they think they'll be reincarnated as the powerful or rich, whereas we mages simply know death for what it is: the opposite of being."

"That's very cheering."

"My point exactly," mage Situ Han said, licking his fingers and promptly buying a box of glutinous rice cakes dotted with red beans. "Even if it's the truth, it's not a recipe for converts, is it? And as you can see, the monks and monasteries like this one are offering the people promises of reincarnation, but at the expense of the empire. You are in a unique position to do something about it."

"You're grooming me to be your puppet ruler, are

you?" Tai was no stranger to others wanting to control him.

Mage Situ grunted around a mouthful of rice cake, then motioned at the groom to bring their horses. "Remember, whoever controls the puppet has to be the one doing all the paperwork and sitting in on all the meetings. I'm not cut out for that. I just want to go to the feasts."

They mounted their horses and turned them toward the palace.

"But I do think you have the ability to make a fine emperor on your own, one who can change things." His smile returned, wide as ever. "You just need a little magic and a few friends in your corner."

"What makes you think I have no friends?"

"Princes don't have friends, Your Highness. They have allies."

Tai studied Mage Situ. The man now seemed utterly uninterested in Tai, wholly preoccupied with working something out from between his teeth. A large finger prodded within his gums, and Tai wondered at how he, the crown prince, was out in the streets with this revolting yet strangely charismatic man.

"But if you have no need for more friends, will you accept my offer to teach you magic, at least?"

Tai watched the man flick the food from his finger into the street. The sight made him reluctant to accept anything. "It's a kind offer, but I don't think I will."

The mage gave him an offended look. "Your Highness, here I am offering you my warm cheek, and you give me your cold buttock in return. This is a unique offer. The first, as far as I know."

Tai searched for a threat in the mage's words but could find none, especially as Situ Han's face broke into a gleeful smile. A vendor was serving up bowls of pungent bean curd and calling out to passersby.

"Ah! Fermented tofu! I can never resist. How much, brother?" Situ Han goaded his horse forward, leaving Tai behind with only his misgivings for company.

CHAPTER 16

*J*in returned to find a dozen of Ulagan's soldiers lying dead in the dirt. The remainder had fled when Aadan returned, realizing they couldn't fight a third dragon and live.

Panshalar had a broken leg that made him unable to ride unaided. Jao had fared better, though he now boasted an arrow wound in the shoulder, and Nakkalan had several cuts along his belly. Aadan helped her wash the wounds and then use leaves as a compress, making Jin wish she'd paid more attention in her healing classes. Her neck had blackened and blistered, and she used a knife to shave off the burned hair before applying cold water and a bandage.

If only they were back at lessons now. Theory and physical training were preferable to the last weeks, where their lives hung in the balance.

Aadan fashioned a splint from the stiff boots of a

dead Khitan soldier, fixing Panshalar's injured leg to it. He then took the stirrups from the saddle of one of the Khitan horses, devised a sling, and tied Panshalar to Bayan's saddle. Panshalar's face gleamed with sweat, but he didn't complain, and they decided they would fly immediately.

When they had rested at a river's fork just half a day from where they estimated the Great Wall's easternmost end to be, they found Panshalar had already lost consciousness, slumped like a bag of rice in his sling.

His dragon Bayan's worry seeped into Jin's mind, and she did her best to comfort him. *We'll get him to a doctor as soon as we can.*

They decided to fly straight south to the sea in order to cross into the Tang Empire sooner instead of circling northwest to hug the border. It was a risky move but one they favored due to time. They couldn't risk Panshalar's wound becoming infected or healing the wrong way. And so, as the grasslands gave way to rockier steppes, they banked south and west, flying by night to avoid detection.

Though Jin kept her ears and eyes out for any signs of Ulagan's army, she spied none. If he was mobilizing a large force, then there were no signs of it in the occasional towns they passed, which seemed to slumber at night just as usual.

Jin wasn't sure whether to be unsettled by this. Had she really killed Baikalan? Had his death meant that Ulagan suffered an irreparable blow?

They flew over remnants of the Great Wall, huge swathes already crumbling into ruins by the seashore after years of neglect. But all that, Jin thought grimly, might change.

They drew closer to a coastline as sunlight leaked over the horizon. This was to be their last night flight, for now that they were over the border and into safe territory, they could fly by day again. Assuming Panshalar could fly.

I'll miss it, Rayshan said. *Night flights allow you to be close to the stars and fly with less effort, as it's cooler.*

But we don't have to hide, Jin replied.

Like you don't have to hide your emotions for Aadan anymore, Rayshan said lightly.

Jin gripped Rayshan more tightly. *You were asleep!*

True, he laughed. *But you should know better than that by now. Wanli is overjoyed, says he hasn't seen Aadan this content in ages.*

And you? she asked.

I am a dragon. If my rider is happy, I am happy.

They landed near a coastal village. As they dismounted, Jin saw it was an abandoned one. Houses and shops lay in disrepair, their roofs sagging or, in many cases, completely caved in. The streets were only discernable as mere outlines now, with grass and trees reclaiming the avenues.

Her senses flickered like a lamp in a draft, and Rayshan's ears flattened.

"This is not a good place," Jin said to her wing mates.

Panshalar looked around, eyes bright with pain. He seemed to have lost weight even in the two days since the attack. "What's wrong with it, besides there being no doctors and song houses?"

"It's . . ." Jin tried to put a word to it. "It's dead."

Aadan was watching her keenly. "It's Jimo."

"Jimo?" Jao asked. "Never heard of it."

"It's only in rare books like *Horrors in the Age of Chaos*. Jimo used to be a bustling port city until Mengkhis arrived."

Jin's skin prickled. There were energies and invisible eddies of . . . something all around them, and she knew Rayshan felt it too. His tail whipped the ground, and his nostrils flared.

"Mengkhis killed everyone here in one of the most famous massacres of the time," Aadan said.

"Then why haven't we learned about it?" Jao said.

Aadan looked away over the waves.

"It's like Emar said," Jin answered. "The books skip much of history, don't they? How do you know about it?"

"I found a copy of *Horrors in the Age of Chaos*," Aadan answered. "When I asked my father, he confirmed it."

"My parents said nothing," Jao replied, still skeptical.

"Most Han families didn't," Aadan said. "They far

prefer the official approach of keeping silent on such things."

Jin shivered. "I don't like this place. I say we leave."

Aadan glanced at Panshalar. "I'm not sure we're able."

Panshalar groaned. "We've been flying all night, and my leg is in agony. Just a few hours, please. If everyone here is dead, then there's no danger to us, am I right? Besides, we're back in Tang lands."

Jao shrugged. "He has a point. And he's not the only one tired of leaves, berries, and raw meat."

Jin sighed, torn. "Alright. I'll find some firewood." Now that they were back on the empire's soil, they could risk a fire again. Even if Ulagan's forces came over the border, the remaining structures in Jimo offered the riders some cover.

She and Rayshan escaped to the fringes of the town, grateful for space on their own. What she wanted to say she wanted to discuss only with Rayshan, without being overheard by the other dragons.

What if our blood bond has connected us to the dead or cursed us? she said. *I can't explain why we have these visions unless the blood bond did something to us. As Emar said, it often kills riders. What if it's making us hallucinate?*

Rayshan huffed. *I've been trying to look into the Firesong to see what this is, but I can't find anything about blood bonding creating visions.* She heard him growl in thought. *And as Emar said, there are no blood-bonded dragon memories at all.*

Is it harder to see what is further in time? Jin asked.

Rayshan hummed. *Yes. The further something is in the past, the harder it is to grasp. Baikalan's memories are the most recent, so I see those most clearly. Beyond him, another jade, but he died young. It's hard to see what his life and memories are like. And the memories of jades are easier for me to access.*

If only there was someone we could ask, Jin said bitterly. *I should have told Emar about the visions. Or even if I were back at the palace, I could go to the prince's library and see if I could find anything.*

She was drowning in questions and running out of places to look for answers.

A SEA, LAPPING AGAINST A SHORE.

Wave upon gentle wave brushing the beach. She had been here before. The horizon bleeding with sunset. She looked down at the crab tickling her toe, thinking to brush it away, but instead, she found a bloated face near her foot, the eyes staring up at her.

She stumbled back, falling to the sand. Only the sand wasn't sand. She knew what she would see before she looked, but she couldn't help it. Another body, and another, that familiar beach covered by bodies, and the ocean itself was a sea of bodies, all bobbing against each other, trapping her. She was drowning again—

JIN SAT UP, EYES ADJUSTING TO THE DARKNESS AND THE stars above, the scent of crabs and sand and blood still in her nostrils. She had returned to the other riders, who had found shelter in a crumbling stone inn outside the main village. Only she had refused to sleep within walls, and chose to stay with Rayshan in the inn courtyard.

Rayshan?

I saw it too.

Was it a dream?

He shifted against her, and she was grateful for his warmth. A chill wind had come in from the ocean, smelling of metal.

Perhaps. Though it didn't feel like a dream. It felt like . . . a memory.

The Firesong?

Yes. Perhaps a memory of Baikalan's. I'm not sure.

It would not be the first time they had seen the infamous dragon's memories. Jin remembered how Rayshan had learned a signature dive through the air. *Have you seen it before? I have.*

Yes, he answered. *Once.*

Do you think it's of Jimo? Of here?

Could very well be. He paused. *I think we should revisit it.*

She shuddered. *What? Why?*

If it's Baikalan's memory, then it may prove useful. The

more we know about him, the better, if we are to find him. Besides, if he's the only blood-bonded dragon alive, then he's also the only blood-bonded dragon whose memories we have access to. That makes them valuable.

Though the thought of seeing that beach and those bodies sickened her, she had to agree that Rayshan had a point. She splayed her hand on Rayshan's shoulder, feeling the smooth scales beneath her. *I'm ready.*

That strange haze rose around her, signaling her entry into the Firesong. Indistinct shapes floated past, remnants of memories and people and other dragons. The haze pressed in on her, heavier and harder until she thought it would crush her, when suddenly the haze of the Firesong cleared. She stood outside a tavern, her throat parched and her clothes dusty.

She noted she was dressed in a man's clothes, but didn't have time to figure this out, for someone was opening the tavern door, and then she was entering.

A long room had wooden tables crowded along one side, with patrons enjoying clay jars of wine and kettles of tea. The second story had a grand plaque on it announcing this to be the Gold Carp Inn. A few patrons looked up, clearly interested in the dragonrider clothes—for Jin dimly recognized that she was in dragonrider leathers—but otherwise, business carried on while the proprietor at the main bar wiped down cups.

A man's voice, low and rugged. "A cup of *shaoshing,* please."

At the proprietor's reaction Jin realized she had been the one to speak. But before she could make sense of this, the proprietor had leaned forward, elbows on the bar.

"Certainly, esteemed rider," he said with a wide smile. He pursed his lips, made a guttural sound deep in his chest, and spat a glob of spittle on Jin's shoe. The proprietor looked at Jin, his smile replaced with open loathing. "My father fought your kind in the Northern Campaign. I won't serve you or any of your sort here."

Chuckles rose around Jin, and she saw a few of the patrons raise their cups in support of the proprietor's words.

"If you're parched, go drink the sea!" someone called out, eliciting laughs and a table pounding.

A hot rage flowed through Jin to the point where her limbs shook, and the sound of her hammering blood almost drowned out the derisive cries of the patrons. She vaguely sensed she was walking out of the tavern, felt the cobblestones under her boots, and all the time, a roar was building in her, demanding her surrender. It was a force refusing to be denied, and she didn't even want to fight it. It won, crashing over her like the waves she saw dimly through rage-shrouded eyes.

And then she was flying, wings pumping beneath her. But it was not Rayshan.

Baikalan.

He shimmered beneath her like light, and as they

passed over the village, no one looked at them. Jin realized that he was invisible, and she was too.

They soared above the town, and screams broke through the night. Women ran into the streets, shrieking, and men came running.

What is happening? Jin thought. She could see no injuries, but then she saw someone kneeling in the street in what looked like an attempt to feel the air.

"My son! I can't see my son!"

Children's frightened wails arose, and another woman cradled what appeared to be an empty blanket.

Could he—had he turned the children invisible? Jin thought in growing horror. What had Emar said? That a blood-bonded rider enhanced or focused their dragon's ability. Baikalan could turn invisible, and Mengkhis could not only do the same, but make others unseen as well.

She was circling the town square, then descending on the tavern where she—or Mengkhis, rather—had been insulted. She jumped down and strode into the tavern, where the proprietor was calling for a doctor while plates and jars crashed to the ground. Patrons milled about, confounded at things that moved on their own, at invisible hands that clutched and bodiless voices that cried out for help.

The proprietor caught sight of Mengkhis, and his face crumpled with hatred. "This is you, isn't it?"

"Drink the sea, and I will give you back your children." Mengkhis's voice was calm.

The proprietor paled. "What?"

"Every man over eighteen in this city will drink the sea until I say stop, and you will see your children again. Otherwise, they stay this way forever."

The proprietor looked to his wife and then to what Jin took to be his child. His voice quavered, but he replied, "Very well."

Jin tried to cry out, but nothing came. Instead, she found herself on a beach, looking at the sands where thousands of men stood facing the dark waves while women crowded the city edges, wailing.

"Drink!"

Jin recognized the voice as Mengkhis's, coming from her own mouth. She spied the proprietor of the tavern, standing ankle-deep in surf, as he knelt and brought a handful of seawater to his mouth. Those behind him looked to the city, where Baikalan circled above the gathered women and invisible children, discernable from hats that had no heads, jackets without bodies, and the way mothers clutched unseen hands.

"You will stop when I say stop," Jin heard herself growl, and the men kept scooping water into their mouths, grimacing as they swallowed. One woman came running down the sand, and before Jin could shout a warning, Baikalan had opened his mouth. A blast of flame engulfed the woman, followed by a heart-rending child's scream from the city's edge.

Some of the men turned, stumbling away from the

water and fleeing toward the women, but Baikalan quickly breathed flame on them as well. Jin cried out, tried to run, but her feet seemed trapped in the sand, with no ability to even move, much less change the outcome. Everything swayed and melted together for a moment until she was looking out at a sea floating with the swollen bodies of thousands of men. This scene was familiar, for she had dreamed it. Only it was no dream.

Women and children came stumbling onto the sands, pulling bodies from the sea in a desperate search for husbands, brothers, fathers.

Bile burned in Jin's throat. But something sickened her even more than the sight of the destruction and horror that Mengkhis had wrought: the deep sense of satisfaction that hummed through her veins.

She was a monster.

And it felt wonderful.

CHAPTER 17

The morning of the trial for those involved in Gao's embezzlement carried the promise of rain, and Tai decided boots would be best. He had slept poorly, plagued by nightmares where he found Aadan and Jin standing by the Temple of Original Dharma, their limbs missing.

He rose hours before the trial and had his valet dress him, then looked over the morning bulletins. His mother was doing a fine job of keeping any hints about the new threats on the border out of the official announcements sent to the prefectures. Instead, there was news about new temples, more road works that would benefit the merchants, safety measures to be put in place for the reduction of crime.

Tai noted there was no mention of the money flowing to the monasteries nor any new taxes for the richest landowners. Instead, there was a long list of those to be tried, along with flowery paragraphs stressing the fact that lawbreakers would be punished.

He ate a hurried breakfast of stewed rice with spiced quail egg and water chestnuts, then headed to the Hall of Justice, only to find the place empty. He was early, but that didn't explain why there were no guards or signs of a hearing. He sent a servant to inquire with the clerks, and the servant returned to inform him that the trial had been moved to the Courtyard of Eternal Peace.

"Why has the trial moved to an outdoor area?" Tai asked.

The servant bowed low. "I do not know, Your Highness. They didn't say."

"And why was I not informed?"

"The clerks said it was a last-minute decision, and they sent a message this morning."

Tai went through his messages meticulously each day. He would not have missed a note of this import. Anger and unease dogged him as he mounted Leiyu and rode to the Courtyard of Eternal Peace with his personal guard.

He heard wings and looked up. Three golds, a silver, and a black flew overhead, their riders low on their backs. The wind from their passage blew Tai's robes as he strode forward, his disquiet mounting.

He rode through the palace yards until he reached the Courtyard of Eternal Peace, one of the largest courtyards in the palace. It was a grand space, with enough room for over a thousand people to gather, and had been expanded when his mother had taken the throne.

By the time he arrived, he heard the murmuring of a large crowd. The guards bowed deep and stood aside, one of them guiding him to his mother. There had been no seat placed next to her, and he recognized her smile for what it was: a ruse to hide her surprise.

"Welcome, my son. We had a delay with your chair."

"Forgetfulness is in the air, it seems," he replied. "First, someone forgot to send me a message about the location change, and now they have forgotten the crown prince's seat."

Servants hastened forward with a wide chair with carved dragons for arms and placed it next to the empress.

"Don't make a fuss," she said. "Mistakes happen."

Tai sat down, unconvinced. The five dragons he had seen winging overhead were now sitting on specially designed perches overlooking the courtyard, steam hissing from their nostrils and their talons scraping the stone perches.

"What is this?" he asked. "Why is the trial here?" He saw none of the court's senior judges, nor any telltale benches or desks for witnesses and magistrates.

"It was the only space large enough for the occasion," she said grimly.

"How will you hear all the testimony from up here?" he said, dreading the answer.

"I won't be hearing any testimony. They all confessed."

A drum was rolled in on large wheels that rumbled, and a messenger followed behind, holding mallets twice the size of his fists. He began beating the drum in a regular rhythm, and gates on the far end opened.

Guards marched in, accompanying a long line of people dressed in prisoner robes. The guards all carried spears and wore helmets with the imperial crest. It took several minutes for the prisoners to fill the square, but by the time the drumbeats had died down, there were a hundred or more people standing in lines of ten in the courtyard.

A somber mood descended on the spectators who stood behind silk ropes along the walls. Tai recognized various officials and saw Meipin not far away from her uncle, Minister Wei. Everyone waited, tense.

Sanjin stood and strode to the front of the dais that held the empress's throne and Tai's seat. He made his voice loud enough for all to hear.

"You have all been found treasonous to the empress and the throne. You have blatantly stolen monetary assets and accepted bribes in exchange for actions detrimental to the Dragon Throne. It is, therefore, the royal decree that you shall die here today. By her infinite mercy, the empress shall allow you to inflict your own death by a gift of poison. Those who do not submit will be beheaded."

Tai's gut churned. Death, even by one's own hand,

was usually reserved for generals who had shown cowardice or those who had aggrieved the throne. It was not for bribery, even at this scale. He looked at his mother and realized this was no trial. This was a straight execution disguised as mercy.

"Mother, what are you doing?"

"What must be done," she said calmly. "Even if it's upsetting."

"Upsetting?" he hissed. "It makes no sense! You will create more enemies and drive anyone with a grudge against us into hiding!"

She turned to level a calculating stare at him. "On second thought, I am glad you are here, my son. It's good to see what you must do as a ruler. For one day, you will have to sit here and kill a hundred, perhaps a thousand, of your own people."

"I would find another way," he said.

"I'm sure you would. This is why you are not ready to rule," the empress said. "You do not understand that too often, there is no other way. Besides, you are too focused on the dying, when the most important people are the living."

She gestured, and he noticed for the first time the members of the audience, who looked particularly terrified. He recognized the head of the record keepers, Chen Feimin, as well as several secretaries in the Treasury. They looked ashen as the executioners examined their swords and the guards commanded the first row of prisoners to kneel.

"Sometimes, my son," the empress said, and he thought he detected sadness, "it is necessary to kill the chicken to teach the monkey."

He was familiar with the old saying, but it did nothing to prepare him to watch the slaughter.

"Salute your empress!" the prison guard barked.

As one, the first line of prisoners recited in unison, "May you live ten thousand years! If the empress chooses that I should die, then I should die!"

The executioners strode forward, one with a blade and one with a tray of cups. The first few took the cups and drank, but as they writhed upon the ground, fear rippled through the remaining prisoners, and their hands shook too much to take the poison.

Tai wanted to close his eyes but knew that wasn't an option. Everyone would be watching the Marked Prince, comparing him to his mother, perhaps already noting his disapproval.

The executioner with the blade strode forward and, with a mighty swing, severed the next prisoner's head from his body. The prisoner slumped forward, blood wetting the stones. The next prisoner followed suit, and another. Tai watched, queasy yet knowing that speaking out would not save these people. Sanjin would kill them later, perhaps in a worse way. Any protest he made here would simply weaken the throne, publicly showing his division with his mother.

One prisoner panicked and lurched to his feet,

stumbling as he pushed through the line of kneeling prisoners to make a break for the entry.

The dragon nearest him, a gold, opened his jaws, and a rolling wave of fire enveloped the escapee, along with a few of the unfortunate prisoners next to him. A scream rose from the victim, but was soon swallowed by the flames. A swarm of servants came forward with buckets of water to put out the stray sparks that had leaped onto the courtyard walls.

Several sobs now racked the line of prisoners, and several of the spectators had averted their faces or closed their eyes in prayer.

The executioner continued down the row, unperturbed by this interruption, then onto the third, pausing at intervals where a servant hurried forward to offer a jar of water. Once he'd quenched his thirst, the executioner carried on.

Tai turned to leave, unable to bear any more, but his mother's golden nails dug into his arm.

"Now that you're here, see it through. You cannot be ruler without watching the executions you order."

"I did not order this," he said, cold. "And it surprises me that you could."

Her voice came out fierce. "I would do this every day of every year, my son, if it meant never having to see you with a sword at your throat again. To see that scene every night in my sleep." Her eyes were dry. "You underestimate my will as an empress, but you haven't the slightest idea what I am capable of as a mother."

"Killing them will not give us an army," he protested.

"No," she replied. "That will come with a marriage to the Parhae princess." At his look, she continued, "I have sent an envoy. Hopefully, we can reach a bridal agreement soon."

He swallowed, his throat dry with fury. "You sent an envoy without telling me?"

"Yes. Time was of the essence, especially as we need allies, not just Meipin's wealth." She paused, apparently interpreting his silence as acceptance. "I knew you'd agree with me."

Death. Marriage. Life choices he had no control over. He had never felt so insignificant, so much a spectator to his own existence.

And with this thought came the desire to reclaim his life, to stand by his words and prove that an iron fist and a cruel hand were not the only options. He didn't even know where he was headed, didn't remember mounting Leiyu or riding through the palace until he was standing before the Dragon Class barracks, staring at the door to mage Situ Han's private apartments. He didn't remember pounding on the door, but he must have, for mage Situ Han's broad face appeared.

"I accept," he said, before the mage could speak. "I want to learn magic."

The man nodded, his expression serious for once. "Come inside."

CHAPTER 18

After Jimo and three days traveling in deserted valleys and steppe lands, Aadan said that they should reach a Dragon Class outpost in half a day's time. From there, they would send a fresh dragon to Changan with news of Ulagan's betrayal, as well as their return. Not to mention, find a doctor.

Despite Jin's best efforts, Panshalar's leg was beginning to swell, which everyone knew was a bad sign.

The plan made sense, but it didn't mean that Jin didn't wish to tear straight back to Khitan herself and find Emar now that her wing mates were safe. But as Aadan had said, looking for Emar now would be like fishing for a needle in the ocean, assuming he was even alive. Given that his dragon had died years ago at the claws of a blood-bonded dragon, Emar was truly on borrowed time.

And so, that evening, as night crept over the land,

they readied themselves to fly the last distance to the outpost. The stars blinked in the sky, and the moon bloomed into existence as the light faded. Jin mounted Rayshan. They rose into the air, flying until the moon was high. Close to midnight, Aadan made the signal to land.

She peered through the clouds and saw a flicker of torchlight below. As they approached, she spied the silver-and-crimson Dragon Class banners flying over a small garrison.

With a surge of relief, the riders banked and touched down, eliciting a shout from the guard walls.

"Who walks there?" a reedy voice called out, and as the dragons came into the light, the guard hastened to call for the gate to be pulled up.

Jin and her wing entered a small garrison. From her geography lessons, Jin knew there were over a hundred such posts across the empire to give sanctuary to traveling riders and their dragons. Each outpost usually had two permanent riders from the messenger banner, officially titled the Banner of Communications, along with a wing of five from the warrior banner. In a paddock toward the back, Jin spotted a black and a bronze curled next to each other and heard their inquisitive thoughts as they noticed the newcomers.

A stout man with a flowing white beard exited the garrison's main building, pulling on his Dragon Class seal and wrapping a robe about himself. His hair was in disarray.

"Riders, this is late to be—" He stopped short at the sight of Jin and Rayshan. "By heavens, you're not . . ."

"This unworthy rider is rider Wang Kway Jin." She motioned to Aadan, who folded one hand over a fist in the traditional greeting.

"Aadan Sassan, wing leader."

"Honored," the stout man said, bowing quickly. "This unworthy man is Lieutenant Cho. By heavens, what are you lot doing all the way out here?"

"You haven't heard the news then?" Aadan asked. "About the attack?"

Lieutenant Cho shook his head.

"We also need a doctor," Jin said, indicating Panshalar, whom Jao was helping down from his dragon.

Aadan gave Lieutenant Cho details of their return from Khitan, while Jao fielded the grooms who came out, rubbing sleep from their eyes as they prepared to care for the dragons.

When Aadan had finished, the man nodded. "By heavens, and I was to retire to the fields after this winter." He motioned them forward. "Come, let's get you fed. I'll see to sending a fresh rider ahead to alert the palace."

Jin could have ridden further, but she knew her wing mates were beyond exhausted and eager for a real meal that wasn't half-raw meat or caked in reindeer fat. They followed Panshalar as he was led to a nearby room, where a bleary-eyed man in cotton robes and a disheveled bun appeared to tend to the injured leg. Only when he shooed them out did they leave and follow Lieutenant Cho into the garrison's mess hall.

Smoke and aromas of that night's dinner lingered in the small space, and someone roused the cook. Plates of cold pickled eggs, noodles, and marinated cabbage were put before them, along with slabs of bean curd drenched in a salted soy paste and scallions.

As they ate, a servant came around to pour hot tea into cups for them while the garrison leader watched them with interest.

"We haven't had any word out of Khitan for some time. We were wondering what happened, by heavens."

"The king of Khitan is rebelling," Jao said before Aadan shot him a look.

"What?" Jao said defensively, but the garrison leader had latched onto the word.

"Rebelling? Against the empire?"

"This news is really for the empress's ears," Aadan said.

The garrison leader looked affronted. "I'm the one on the border here. You don't want to share what's going on so I can protect my men?"

"Tell your men to be on alert, and we appreciate your messenger letting the empress know we are alive. But we must get our message to the empress directly."

Aadan's voice was polite, but Jin didn't think the garrison leader was fooled. Aadan feared passing on any sensitive details about Ulagan's actions to a messenger from one of the outer posts, who might have Khitan relatives or connections.

The garrison leader still looked ruffled. "Very well. You won't be traveling tonight, I take it, given your wing mate's condition?"

Aadan shook his head. "First light, if we can manage."

"I'll see to supplies and send one of the messengers on tonight. You'll want some rations along the way, along with new clothes, won't you?" The Lieutenant darted a glance at Jin, who was still in her Chaakan clothing.

She dipped her head. "I'd be grateful."

"We don't have women's clothes," he remarked, looking like he regretted the offer.

"A smaller man's clothes will do," she said.

They finished up their meal and were shown to their rooms. Jin was both grateful and disappointed when she was led to a separate room on the second floor. At least she wouldn't have to lie awake smelling sandalwood. The garrison leader showed her a tile-lined bathing room on the lower floor where a small stove kept water warm, with buckets and towels for riders.

"There's no lock, I'm afraid," Lieutenant Cho said, seeing her examine the door. "Not necessary, given it's only men."

"I'll be quick."

He nodded, clearly eager to leave her.

Jin peeled off her clothing, then ladled water from the basin and poured it over herself, letting the tepid water clean away the grit and grime. The small bucket was nothing like the palace baths, but she had never been so grateful. And though the water stung her partially healed burn, she relished feeling the remnants of reindeer fat, butter, and sage smoke leave her.

She found a jar of soap balls and used one to make a paste for her hair, rubbing it in and then rinsing, holding her head to one side to keep the soap out of her burn. She combed out her hair and plaited it, then reached for the clean tunic and pants the garrison had provided. Just then, the door swung open, and Aadan walked in.

She snatched the nearest piece of clothing and wrapped it around herself, the water soaking into the fabric and making it cling.

"Sorry, I didn't—"

"I'm done, anyway." There was an awkward pause as he made no move, and his eyes narrowed.

"Your ribs . . ."

Jin glanced down to where the spear had pierced her. "It looks worse than it feels."

He looked pained, but retreated out the door. She quickly dried and changed into her clothes, which were now wet, but there was no help for it. She walked out and found Aadan standing outside.

"There's no lock," she offered.

"So I gathered." His gaze wandered to her neck. "How is your burn?"

"Better."

He reached out to touch her, but at her glance around the courtyard, he lowered his hand and gave her a smile instead. "Good night."

She hurried away, pushing back at Rayshan's amused snort in her head.

But all the way up the staircase and to her room, sandalwood followed her. When she opened the door to her bedchamber, she found a small jar wrapped in paper on her bed.

She unwrapped it and noticed writing on the back.

An ointment from the doctor. Use it, or I'll apply it myself. Aadan.

She smiled, sitting on a chipped stool. The scent of sandalwood still clung to the jar, but then it became so strong that she realized it must be coming from elsewhere. There was the sound of a footfall outside her door, a pause before they continued on.

Jin hesitated a moment, then pocketed the salve and opened the door. A light shone at the end of the hall. Following it, she entered a room cramped with bookshelves, the walls peeling and the scrolls dusty. There was only one seat, a long bench pushed up against a window, where Aadan sat with an open scroll in his lap.

"It's a bit late to be reading, isn't it?" She sat down

on the opposite end of the bench and reached out to check his scroll.

"Couldn't sleep."

"Even after a bath?"

He hesitated. "Especially after a bath."

"Thank you for the ointment." She pulled it from her pocket.

"Did you use it?" At her hesitation, he motioned, and she handed over the jar. "Turn around."

She did as he asked, sitting with her back to him while he opened the jar, and then his fingers were on her neck. She expected pain in the wound, but instead, there was a cooling sensation. His fingers were gentle.

When he had finished, his hand lingered for a moment on her shoulder before she reluctantly moved away and turned to face him. She glanced over at the scroll he had put down.

He tried to hide it, but when she looked indignant, he gave in and watched her read the title.

"'Simplified Handbook of Laws for Dragonriders?'" she read. "No wonder you look embarrassed. This is what you read for pleasure?" At his expression, she frowned. "What's wrong?"

"Nothing, just . . ." He gazed at her for a moment. "Once we are back in the capital, I don't know what will happen. It looks like we're going to war."

She pulled at a thread on the trousers, twisting it. She had never known war, but she supposed he was right. A foreign king didn't kill your riders and behead your dragons without some dire consequences. "Are you afraid?"

"I wouldn't be human if I wasn't," he replied. "But part of me wishes . . ."

"What?"

"Part of me wishes we could just stay here."

"In this rat-forsaken place?" She looked around her at the musty books, the peeling paint on the walls, and the chipped table between them.

He smiled. "Not necessarily here. Just away from the capital. Somewhere Wanli and I could work on irrigation systems, and you and Rayshan could join the local messenger banner. That's the banner you'd choose, right?"

She remembered that conversation they'd had, the night that seemed years ago and yet was only a couple of months gone. His remembering her words touched her more than she expected. "Yes."

"Messengers don't get promoted as easily. Why be a messenger? Some would say you could join any banner."

She rubbed a seam in her rider leathers, trying to find the words. "I'd never been outside Kwannay Province before I met Rayshan. The world is so much bigger than I thought. And in my life as a thief, I saw fancy people and exotic riches passing through, but I was always in the same place." She paused, remembering. "And everything about my life felt fixed, stuck somehow: I would remain in Kwannay, working for Haitao until I died an early death." She swallowed. The memory of Lu, how he had dreamed of becoming unstuck from Haitao's clutches, wedged a lump in her throat. "Flying to all corners of the empire, maybe to other countries, feels like freedom. Just me and Rayshan." She frowned, a new thought occurring to her.

"What's the matter?" Aadan asked.

"I still don't know what Rayshan's ability is. What if it turns out to be something that means I can't join a banner?"

Aadan shook his head. "I've never heard of that. Don't worry, it will come."

"I hope it's something powerful to use against Ulagan," she said, anger and bitterness returning. "Like making the earth split open."

"How about spontaneous combustion?"

"Useful, but easily gets out of control."

"True." He smiled. "I read of one jade who could speak to animals."

"That sounds better. I'd have Ulagan torn apart by dogs."

He cocked his head. "Are you usually so vengeful?"

"I don't know," she said honestly. She shuddered at the memory of how it felt to be Mengkhis, how vengeance had made her blood sing. "I'm becoming a lot of things lately." She glanced at him. "Does it bother you?"

"Nothing about you bothers me." He paused, his smile slipping.

"Except?"

"Nothing," he said, but it was too late.

Jin debated leaving it alone, but couldn't. "Tell me. Except what?"

He sighed, looking away. "Except that you won't give us a chance."

She stiffened. "It's not me who won't give us a chance. There are rules."

"Then tell me," Aadan said quietly, "if there were no rules, no expectations of us, would we be together?"

"What's the point of asking that question?" she asked, anger lacing her. "There are always rules. There's no point imagining there aren't."

"There's every point," he replied, suddenly also heated. "I'm asking you now, if the empress gave her blessing, would you still say we had no future?"

The question took her by surprise. "I don't know," she retorted. "But why is this about me? What of your winning back Persia? Your father certainly has expectations of your future, and they don't include irrigation systems."

His face closed, and she realized she had delivered a hard punch of reality. "I'm sorry. That was . . . unkind."

"No," Aadan said quietly. "You're right. But the truth is, I can't give him what he wants."

"You'll find a way," Jin said. "You once said that you believed in taking Persia without a fight, and I know—"

Aadan shook his head. "I'm not talking about whether I can win back Persia. I'm talking about whether I can be who he wants." At her questioning look, he continued. "He's groomed me to be a Persian prince, but I'm only Persian on the outside. I was born in China, raised in China. I can explain every classic Persian poem, and I know the *Book of Kings* by heart, I can hold my own in a *koshti* fight, but I've never set foot outside the empire. How can a place I've never seen be my home? How can I rule over such a place? And now . . ." His shoulders tensed.

"Now what?"

"The Persian community is growing restless," Aadan said, pinching the bridge of his nose. "They tire of being guests in a foreign land, and now that I'm nearing the end of Dragon Class training, there are louder and louder grumblings about why I am not planning my triumphant return."

Jin leaned in, but resisted the urge to take his hand. "I don't have answers for them," Jin said, "but as for being Persian or Chinese, maybe you don't have to choose. I gave up choosing whether I was Chinese or huren a long time ago."

He regarded her for a moment, his eyes shifting from pale green to emerald in the lamplight. "So what do you say you are, when people ask?"

"No one's cared to ask."

"Well I care," he said softly, "and I'm asking."

Jin's heart and breath tripped at his tone. "I'd say . . . I'm me."

"Yes." He placed a hand on her cheek, and she put hers over it without thinking. "Yes, you are."

She closed her eyes, willing him to stay silent and simply have this moment where choices didn't exist.

"I can't pretend I don't care, Jin. Can you?"

She kept her eyes closed, wishing with everything she had that she didn't have to say what she was about to.

"No," she answered, opening her eyes and forcing herself to brave his gaze. She couldn't speak above a whisper, the words she had to say like splinters in her skin. "But if we pretend there's a future, then we're lying to ourselves. Yes, I broke rules, but doing it meant I killed many people and scarred others. Is that what you want?" She hurried on, before he could say something that would make her throw every last scrap of caution to the wind and simply plunge into the unknown with him. "And you're the wing leader now. How will it look for you if you're . . . with me?"

Aadan kept his eyes locked on hers. "I'm willing to figure it out."

"At what cost?" she said softly. "Do you even know how many ways the empress and others could crush us?"

He searched her face. "Is that really what you fear?"

What was he saying? "Of course, isn't that fear big enough?"

Aadan leaned back, regarding her. "No. Not to me. I think certain things are worth fighting for." He stood. "Even if you don't."

With that, he turned and walked out.

You said the right thing, she told herself. Deluding themselves would lead straight to disaster. But then why did she feel ashamed, as if she had broken something good and fragile?

CHAPTER 19

"You're harnessing magic, Your Highness. Not passing a turd."

The mage's humor was starting to grate on Tai. Mage Situ Han stood to one side, savoring a bean-paste bun as if it were the last in the empire.

"You can't do tai chi with that posture, much less harness magic," mage Situ Han said. He finished his bun and wiped his fingers, then came and joined Tai in his movements.

Noticing Tai's look, the mage slapped his ample belly. "One day, you, too, can have this fine physique. Now focus, Your Highness."

Tai sighed but tried to do as the mage instructed.

"Now the elements all form a harmonious whole, and when you slow your breathing and follow the rhythm of your *mai*—" he reached out and tapped Tai's wrist to indicate his pulse "—you will find it. But you cannot sense the elements when you are not in tune with your mai."

Tai breathed in, then out, concentrating on his chest rising and falling beneath the loose cotton tunic. He tried to clear everything from his mind as he renewed the seemingly endless circle the mage had drawn out for him in charcoal on the ground. He had been walking, one foot carefully in front of the other, along this circle hundreds of times, with the pace and stance that Situ had shown him.

"Attune yourself to your mai. That's the first step in being able to move in harmony with the Way." The mage began to walk, and Tai had to admire how the corpulent man seemed to transform once he began walking the circle that was considered the basic building block of practicing magic. His body became supple and exuded power, his feet were sure, and the belly that normally seemed like nothing more than the mark of a glutton now seemed part of a powerful whole, reminding Tai of a rhinoceros the king of Aksum had once sent as tribute.

Now, the mage motioned for Tai to follow.

"When your mind has attuned, you will find that you can make something lighter or heavier." Mage Situ Han set out a portable brass scale in the middle of the circle, the arms shaped like curled clouds. He placed a feather in one dish and a gold ingot in the other. "I want you to make this ingot weightless so that the feather arm comes down."

Tai had been doing this walking exercise for their last three lessons and had made no visible progress whatsoever. He had to tamp down his impatience, for Situ Han always insisted that magic came not to the impatient hand. But it was hard not to think he was wasting his time.

And why *was* he wasting his time with this?

Had this all been just a silly, impetuous idea born of his frustration? The desire to do something, anything, to be active? To fight back against his mother's sudden cutting him off from political matters and making him a prince in name only?

Yes. It was all of those, and he would not apologize. He would not simply sit by, and if he could master magic, that was something he would use. If only to never again have a sword drawn across his throat.

A sharp rap came on his shoulder, and he startled.

"Your mind is not empty, Your Highness," the mage chided in a sing-song voice.

"And neither is your mouth," Tai replied in a perfect mimicry of his tone.

"Well, these buns are from the best bakery in the East Market. They're famous," the mage said around the food. "Empty your mind, feel the elements around you, and make this ingot lighter than a feather."

Tai let out a breath and redoubled his efforts, placing one foot before the other in rhythmic steps. Empty the mind. Breathe nothingness in, breathe everything out. He thought of a blank space, like a piece of paper, and held to it.

A clinking of metal sounded, and he opened his eyes to look at the scales. Immediately, the ingot shot back down, the feather taking flight and then drifting to rest on the floor.

"Aha!" the mage cried. "You did it. For a brief moment, this ingot weighed less than the feather."

Tai grinned, triumphant.

"Ah, proud of yourself, are you?" the mage said, wiping his mouth on his sleeve.

"There are napkins available," Tai pointed out. "Those aren't simply decorative."

"Careful now," the mage said. "Your charm is slipping." He replaced the ingot and the feather. "Did you read the scroll I left you?"

Tai couldn't recall what the mage was referring to for a moment but then remembered. "No. I haven't had a chance."

The mage raised one bushy eyebrow. "A prince with no official duties, and you didn't get time? Very well, I'll just tell you the gist then. There is a legend foretold amongst the mages. Sit down. We might as well be comfortable."

"You want me to read a fairy tale?" Tai asked, taking a seat on a nearby chair where a teapot huddled on a ceramic warmer next to two cups.

"Shh, Your Highness, and listen." The mage settled opposite him. "This legend foretells an emperor, a great emperor who will come to the throne. Now this fore-telling lies in the writings of a great mage, the one who served the first emperor. He and the emperor were quite fond of predictions, you see, and the mage became skilled at foretelling events. Anyway, this mage foretold that one day, a Mage Emperor would sit on the Dragon Throne. This Mage Emperor would marry the daughter of the dragon, and together, they would usher in one thousand years of peace and prosperity and make China the greatest nation in the world. As you can imagine, the Ministry of Rites and Mages would like to see this legend come true."

Tai poured his tea and sipped. "Well, clearly, I am that Mage Emperor."

"Yes, our thoughts exactly."

Tai put down his tea. "I was jesting."

"I am not. You have it in you."

Tai glanced at the scales with the ingot and the feather. "I don't seem to have much talent for it. You said yourself, you've never seen a student take longer than I to change an item's weight."

Mage Situ Han regarded him with a serious look. "Do you know what talent is worth, Your Highness?"

"I think you're about to enlighten me."

Mage Situ Han let out a long, unhurried belch. "That's what it's worth. A bellyful of gas. Nothing. Less than the spit I eject onto the floor in the morning."

Tai raised an eyebrow. "That's very vivid."

"People overvalue talent, Your Highness. If I had a

fei for every talented person who walked in wanting to be a mage, I'd buy myself ten singing girls, one for every day of the week. Three for the holidays."

Tai didn't bother asking what a castrated man wanted to do with singing girls.

"But what is worth everything in heaven is what's here—" the mage tapped Tai's chest, then his head "—and here."

"Heart and wits?"

Mage Situ Han shook his head. "Heart, yes. Wits, well, wits are useful. But you need to be able to fall seven times and rise eight. And you, Prince Tai, have that ability. You've failed more at this task than anyone I know, and yet here you are, trying again."

"I think that's the first time someone has been able to tell me I am talentless while making it sound like a compliment," Tai said. "Have you considered a career in government?"

Situ Han shrugged. "It would be disastrous. Everyone would be jealous of my rakish looks and ways with women. Now, back to work."

"One more question." Tai paused. "Why are you training me in this? If you're planning another coup, I can tell you right now you are wasting your time. I will not overthrow my mother."

Situ Han shook his head. "Do I look like a traitor? No one is suggesting a coup. I am simply trying to do my duty of preparing the next in line, for when the time comes. May Her Majesty live ten thousand years."

Tai tried to find a sliver of truth or lie in the mage's words, but that affable face was as open and honest as ever. He had to admire the man, for if he was hiding ulterior motives, Tai could not catch even a whiff of them.

"I believe in the legend," the mage said quietly. "Or perhaps I'm a fool with much hope. I hope for a time of peace because as young as I look, I am actually a fair deal older than you, and I remember the age of chaos. I do not need my grandchildren to see that. Ever."

"You cannot have grandchildren," Tai pointed out.

The mage shrugged. "Other people's grandchildren. Is it so hard to believe that some amongst us, even those who have no children, would wish for peace for other living beings?" He looked Tai in the eye, no hint of humor in his deep brown eyes now, no smile on the thick lips that reminded Tai of a carp.

"Then perhaps we should get back to lessons," Tai said.

"One of the smartest things you've said," mage Situ Han agreed.

As the days passed, Tai trained while the palace prepared for the Festival of Sevens. Maids cleaned every hallway and replaced all the carpets, took down lanterns and repaired them with new silk screens, washed and aired curtains, and scrubbed the floors.

Ornate ceramic pots of lilies, peonies, plum trees, orchids, and carnations appeared in courtyards, and great teams of workers came to prune the gardens and clean the fishponds.

Tai tried to talk his mother out of holding the Festival of Sevens to honor the cowherd and the weaving girl, as it seemed a frivolous festival given the current uncertainty around Khitan. But his mother insisted it was important to keep up appearances, to let no one suspect there was any danger on the doorstep, much less that they were worried.

Moreover, the mass executions had cast a strange pall over the palace. Everyone seemed more industrious, but Tai noticed that people didn't look him in the eye as often. While some might have taken this for respect, Tai didn't like not being able to read a person's face.

Dragon Class's own accountant was clearly at great pains to keep him updated with the meticulous records, eager to show that everything was above board. But Tai wondered at what his mother had driven beneath the surface and what the palace said behind closed doors.

"We are spending money we don't have," Tai told her. "Pretty fireworks when what we need are weapons, and boots, and men." He paused. "I saw the prices. What do these fireworks do to cost so much? Sing and dance?"

His mother sighed. "There has been a shortage of

fireworks lately, as the merchants have reported a surge in demand from overseas. But a festival without fireworks would be no festival at all."

And so Tai watched as carriages laden with boxes of firecrackers rolled in, along with foods and exotic animals, some for the table and some for the grounds. Everywhere he looked, money flowed out of the palace, and Tai couldn't help the morbid thought that it was like their lifeblood was seeping away, being squandered when it should be focused on Dragon Class and finding Baikalan.

This also provided little comfort to him, for though he enjoyed seeing the riders train and ride their dragons, visiting and speaking with the recruits only reminded him of Aadan. And Jin. And the deafening silence around their current whereabouts that threatened to drive him mad.

Therefore, when mage Situ Han asked him what he thought about the report from the Fulian Dragon Class garrison, Tai frowned in confusion.

"The garrison where the returned riders landed after coming from Khitan," mage Situ Han said, raising one eyebrow. "Has Your Highness not heard?"

"No," Prince Tai was forced to admit, resentment against his mother kindling. How had the mage known the latest news from Aadan and Jin, yet the commander in chief of Dragon Class had not?

"Ah," Situ Han said, taking a casual tone to help save face for Prince Tai. "Perhaps the empress is waiting for the right moment. Apparently, the king of Khitan killed the dragons stationed there and lured our riders there to release Baikalan. Perhaps it is not my place to—"

"Emar?" Tai demanded.

"Held by the king," mage Situ Han said. "But the riders are on their way back to Changan as we speak. And they killed Grand Master Gu Ben as well, so now there will be much infighting as to his replacement, which, if you ask me . . ."

But Prince Tai was barely listening, his scar starting to itch. He barely registered to thank mage Situ Han and didn't bother changing his robes before striding out of his apartments and making straight for the empress's quarters. He was relieved to hear Jin and Aadan were safe, but Emar was like an uncle to him, having taught him everything he knew about Dragon Class. He burst in on his mother, who was meeting with Sanjin.

Both of them looked at him, surprised at his intrusion. His mother wore an elaborate headdress with gold and ivory tassels that hung down to her cheekbones, with phoenixes made of jade and silver rising from the elaborate hairstyle she'd chosen today. A trio of tailors was measuring out lengths of silks for the empress's Festival of Sevens gown, while Sanjin wore his usual attire, streamlined and austere.

"Your Highness." Tai bowed, keeping his anger in check. "I understand there has been news from the riders and of Emar."

"Tailor, you may go. We will finish this later."

The tailor bowed, and his assistants gathered their boxes of thread, scissors, and silk, then departed.

"I was about to summon you," his mother said smoothly.

"When did the message arrive?"

"This morning." At his dark look, she added, "I simply wished to consult Sanjin before alerting you."

"The gall is extraordinary, Your Highness," Sanjin said to Tai, who knew the marquis was attempting to break the tension. "I am guessing Ulagan thinks he can harness Mengkhis Lai."

"How?" Tai asked.

"He has Emar," the empress said simply. "He will seek out Mengkhis. Though how he thinks he can fight his way through China, I don't know."

"Then what?" Tai asked. How else would Ulagan get to Champa?

She glanced at Sanjin. "Would he go by sea?"

Sanjin shook his head. "Not without boats. And where would Khitan acquire boats?"

"He could buy them," Tai said. "We should inquire with the boat merchants, see who has been commissioning boats and where those have gone to."

Sanjin nodded. "I have already started looking into that, Your Highness. In the meantime, I also took the liberty of arranging some reinforcements to the walls. Just in case."

The empress nodded, and Tai noticed her twisting her ring. "Leave us, Sanjin."

"Your Majesty, I'd like to—"

"I said leave us," the empress said, sharper this time. Sanjin bowed and retreated.

The empress stood for a while, silent, and Tai sensed she needed a moment to gather herself. When she finally turned to him, he was surprised to find her eyes teary.

"I am sorry I did not tell you when the messenger arrived. This news has been so much worse than what I feared. I feared Baikalan's escape, but the fact that Ulagan is determined to seek out Mengkhis?" She shook her head, the beads in her headdress clicking. "I worry we are dealing with a madman. And a madman cannot be reasoned with. I need to crush Ulagan, my son," she said. "And I will."

"It used to be we," Tai said. "You involved me. Now you treat me like a child."

"Because you are my child!" the empress shouted.

Tai looked at her, stunned. He could not remember the last time she had actually shouted at him. She was strict, unbending, sometimes unflinching in her discipline, but she never shouted. Such behavior was to lose control, and his mother valued control almost above the throne.

"When you have your own children, you will understand," she said, voice taut. "I will protect you and do what I think best for you. And I expect your obedience."

"Your Majesty," he said, keeping his voice even, "I am your son, yes, but I am also your commander in chief of Dragon Class, as well as someone who cares about Emar. I deserve to be informed."

He thought her stony expression cracked at the mention of Emar. "Very well," she said stiffly, clearly wrestling her emotions. "Now I must ask you to leave. The tailors are returning, and I still have multiple gowns to fit."

Tai bowed and left. As he walked back to his apartments, he wondered at his mother's feelings for Emar. He knew they went far, that he had worked as a stable boy in her household when she was growing up, and the empress's father had treated Emar as the son he never had. But when Tai had asked whether this meant he should address Emar as uncle, his mother had firmly dismissed the suggestion. Tai's grandfather, who had died before he was born, was a dragonrider in a house long renowned for dragonriders even though they had been at the bottom of the nobility—some even whispered they had dropped below the line of nobility to be little more than commoners since their fortunes had suffered at one of their ancestors' gambling habits and never fully recovered.

But then his mother had been plucked from her home because of her breathtaking beauty and sent to court. And the rest, as he had heard it, was the stuff of legend. His father had seen her and fallen instantly in love and made her his concubine. The move had not pleased the emperor's wife and favored concubine, but they had died childless within five years, and his father had made his mother empress.

He recalled questioning his mother once after Emar had referred to the empress as "Little Zhao."

She had honed in on his question like a hawk on a hare. "If you're asking whether he shared my bed, the answer is never."

He remembered his relief at the time, for his mother's romantic dealings would only throw more doubt upon his own origins. Even if it was impossible for Tai to be Emar's son, given Emar was a huren, the empress's enemies would have pounced on any chance to paint her as a woman who had many lovers, hence throwing suspicion on any offspring.

Rumors. How he hated them.

CHAPTER 20

*J*in hadn't expected the sense of homecoming that flooded her at the first sight of Changan's outer walls. The heart of the empire took up so many li it seemed to stretch to infinity, even from this high up.

The capital was divided into wards, and five canals linked the city from north to south. Barges laden with goods, tributes, foods, tradespeople, and servants moved along these waterways, and the city teemed with the sounds and smells of over a million souls. Jin found it hard to imagine a larger city in the world.

People looked into the sky as the dragons winged overhead. They flew well above the allotted marker line for flying, making sure to stay a good few hundred *mi* above the city buildings. They drew near to the imperial palace, itself a city with vermillion walls wide as boulevards, gold-tiled towers rising above the audience halls and government buildings. Snarling mythical animals adorned each corner, warding against evil spirits.

Not that they'd do much against Baikalan, Jin thought grimly.

Rayshan huffed. *With any luck, Baikalan is dead.*

They circled and then banked to the north, where the Dragon City and the Blood Oval lay. Here was the landing arena for dragons, along with roosting perches, and as they descended, grooms gathered below, eager to take the dragons and hear their news.

"Come," the head groom said. "We will help you freshen yourselves, and then the empress and Sanjin will want to see you."

ONCE THEY HAD WASHED THEIR FACES AND PULLED THEIR hair into a semblance of decent grooming, servants led them through numerous wings of the palace and into the royal audience hall. Jin and her wing mates waited on their knees.

Before long, a herald announced Her Imperial Celestial Empress, Empress Wu, and her son, Crown Prince Tai.

The riders gave the expected greeting of, "Ten thousand years, may the empress live ten thousand years."

"Rise," the empress said as she ascended her throne and sat. Jin stood with her wing mates. The empress was as breathtaking as ever, though Jin thought she saw heavier makeup than usual beneath her eyes. And Prince Tai, Jin couldn't help but notice, looked like he might even win a competition against his mother in the looks department. She had forgotten how regal and classically good-looking he was.

"Welcome back, Riders," the empress said. "We read the message that the king of Khitan has turned against us. Let us hear it from you. Is this true?"

Aadan and Jin glanced at each other, but it was Aadan who spoke. "It is, Your Majesty. He tried to kill the entire wing, and then he released Baikalan. Our being told to come was a decoy to get Emar out to Khitan."

The empress's voice was tight. "And is it true he intends to find Mengkhis Lai and release him as well?"

"Yes, Your Majesty," Jin said.

A hush fell on the group, and Jin glanced behind her. Marquis Sanjin had entered. His very presence still made her shift on her feet, ready to flee. Every thief and criminal knew Marquis Sanjin and the dark joke about his name: the word Sanjin was a homonym for "three pounds." That was all that was left, it was rumored, of anyone he interrogated.

The head of the Royal Veil now motioned to the servants, who bowed and closed the doors. This news would spread panic through the palace, something Jin was sure Sanjin and the empress wanted to avoid.

"Did he say how he would do this?" Sanjin asked.

Jin shook her head. "Only that he was obviously angry at being insulted by a woman on the throne, and he meant to topple it."

The empress's face hardened. "I'm glad I put Gao's people to death. I'll have to make sure the executioner keeps his sword honed. You have done well, and Sanjin will call a meeting of the ministries while we decide what to do."

A quiver worked its way from Rayshan's bond. Out of the corner of her eye, Jin saw a girl of eighteen or nineteen step out of nowhere. One moment, the corner of the room had been empty, and the next, she was walking toward them—a woman with a breathtakingly beautiful face but shrewd, mean eyes.

Jin inhaled sharply but realized she wasn't the only one. Tai had stepped forward, his expression incredulous.

"Peilah?"

Jin looked at Tai, perplexed. He could see this girl? Then she noticed that everyone seemed able to see her.

The newcomer smiled, but it was a wicked smile that transformed a beautiful face into an eerie one.

The empress's skin had turned as white as the finest porcelain, and Aadan looked like he was witnessing a walking tree.

The girl strode forward until she was directly before the throne. "You killed me, but I'll wreck you, you demonic fox!"

Gasps filled the room as the girl rushed the stairs, and the clerks fell back as the guards drew swords.

Tai reached out to grab the girl's arm, but his hand went through her. She turned her glare on him then and opened her mouth, but suddenly she was softening, crumbling from the head down until she was nothing but gray dust on the floor. Tai stood there, looking as if he was rooted, while Jin pulled deep breaths, her insides cold.

"What was that?" the empress's high-pitched shout broke through Jin's shock, and she saw from Sanjin's expression that he had read the truth on her face. In two strides he was across the room and beside Jin, regarding the pile of ash.

"Everyone but Rider Jin, get out," Sanjin commanded. "Riders, clerks, everyone. Now!"

His words startled all into action, and the scribes and attendants were only too happy to leave a room where they had seen a ghost. No one wanted to be there anymore, except for Aadan, whose eyes never left Jin before he reluctantly followed the others toward the door.

"And if anyone speaks of this," Sanjin continued, voice oily, "I will have your tongue carved out."

Though Jin thought it impossible, the silence thickened. Sanjin and empty threats went together like snow in July.

Once the room had cleared and the doors were relocked, Sanjin stalked around Jin, who stood still, fear coiling in her at being the sole object of attention. Both Tai and the empress had their eyes locked on her.

"I demand an explanation," the empress said. "If this is your method of a sick jest, I will have you boiled alive."

Sanjin bowed. "Your Majesty, I don't believe this was a jest." Turning back to Jin, he asked, "How did you summon her?"

"I—I didn't," Jin said.

"Has this happened before?"

Jin hesitated. Every word she said could land her in the tea rooms.

"Since when?" Sanjin snapped.

"Since . . . since the geography test."

"And was it always like this?"

She swallowed past her fear. "They disappear into ash. But this is the first time other people have seen what I've seen."

"If you are lying," he said evenly, "I have ways of squeezing the truth from you." Sanjin studied her face. "Do you know what you are?"

"A rider, Marquis Sanjin."

He flashed her a humorless smile. "Let me rephrase. Do you know what your dragon is?"

Jin looked at him.

"Your dragon is a flame."

Jin frowned. Why did that sound familiar? And then she remembered. The Chaakan shaman had called her a flame, Aadan said. But what did that—

"She can summon the dead?" Tai asked slowly.

"That's not possible," the empress said. "Flames are a myth."

Summon the dead. What were they saying?

Sanjin turned. "Your Majesty, unless we were all hallucinating the same thing at the same time, it is the only possible explanation. Now, judging that this has only started happening since Jin joined Dragon Class, my guess is that Rayshan has manifested."

Jin's thoughts whirled, and she reached out to Rayshan. *Is this possible?* She raced through her memories, examining each one. She had first seen the dead in the palace a few days after they arrived back.

No, Rayshan said. *That wasn't the first time. The first time was the Singing Sands.*

She cast back and remembered: how she had seen Lu, who had told her to find the strength to stand and fight back against Gao. She looked at Prince Tai and had a sudden memory of dancing with him the night she had asked for the key to the library. And he had leaned in close to whisper in her ear that Baikalan, the last jade the empire had known, had manifested only when his rider Mengkhis was near death.

I was near death, and you summoned Lu, Jin realized.

Rayshan hummed. *I hadn't realized that's what I was doing, but it's possible.* His confusion was almost as complete as hers.

"But then how do I summon, why—"

Sanjin held up a hand. "I cannot provide many answers because I do not know them."

"Then who does?" the empress demanded. "I refuse to have a palace full of the dead." Her eyes narrowed. "My naysayers and enemies will be celebrating if they catch wind of this. The dead coming back to life is an ill omen. The worst of omens."

Jin's stomach fell. There was no arguing that. To have the dead walk amongst the living was an abomination, a sure sign that the Mandate of Heaven had ceased. Those who had witnessed tonight's events would likely start wondering if Heaven had declared that a female ruler was against the natural order.

Sanjin turned to the empress. "We will keep this a secret, but this may also be a useful tool." He turned back to Jin. "You continue to be full of surprises. I have someone I would like you to meet."

The empress glared at Jin as if furious for her very existence. Jin couldn't quite blame her. She had, after all, in the space of a year, challenged the status quo within Dragon Class, and now Rayshan had manifested a very unusual and undesirable skill.

You should have just stuck to invisibility or traveling instantly.

Rayshan growled in reply. *Look where invisibility took Baikalan.*

He wasn't wrong. But summoning the dead . . .

Before she fully understood what was happening,

Sanjin was leading her out of the chambers and ordering his guards to take her to Meipin's quarters.

"She is not to leave, understood?"

Jin knew it was pointless to argue about being jailed. She had little strength or will to leave the suites anyway, even to seek out Aadan, for she was bone weary and famished and couldn't remember a time when her thoughts had been in more turmoil.

eipin's suites lay on the west side of the imperial palace. The noblewoman was already there when the soldiers arrived to deposit Jin, and unabashedly hugged the dragonrider before hooking an arm through hers and leading her inside the rooms. The familiar ponds were full of koi, the lanterns were lit, the shrubbery was meticulously trimmed, and the table was set with the finest foods.

"You have much to tell me, I imagine," she said, glancing at Jin's hair and face. "The court can talk of nothing but what actually happened in the north." Her voice lowered. "Not to mention—is it true you saw Peilah?"

"Word travels quickly. Who is she?"

Or was, she corrected herself. How had she seen someone she didn't even know? Unease clawed her as she tried to fight the sense that she had absolutely no control over Rayshan's manifested power or her own.

"I'll explain later. Tell me, what happened up north?"

"Nothing good," Jin said. "Almost all of it bloody."

Ahlu was standing in the doorway and bowed low. "Welcome home, Lady Jin."

Was she home? She supposed she was. And though the soldiers standing guard outside reminded her that she was, for now, also a prisoner, this was about as close to a home as she had now. She sat in the dining room while Ahlu poured them Maru wine. Apparently, Meipin was still drinking the best.

"And Baikalan?"

Jin filled Meipin in as much as she could. She trusted Meipin not to spread gossip. She would ration and siphon the information, though partly for her own purposes of advancing women in government: Meipin harbored the secret ambition of seeing girls like herself in male-only quarters such as the Secretariat.

"My, and I thought my days trying to get women into the Treasury here were full of harrowing events," Meipin said. "And what of this . . . of what happened tonight?"

Jin paused, trying to think how to explain the ridiculous to Meipin. "Sanjin thinks I—or rather Rayshan, can summon the dead." She frowned. "Who was that girl? And why did she say the empress had killed her?"

Meipin pursed her lips as she poured more wine and took a delicate sip. "That was Peilah." She paused, then, seeing Jin's expectant look, continued. "Peilah died two years ago. Many think the empress had a hand in it."

"Why?" Jin asked. "Why would she kill her?"

Meipin tapped her cup and sighed. "Peilah didn't exactly make friends. She was shrewish and displayed her ambitions for power like a peacock displays its tail. It didn't help that Prince Tai was infatuated with her, to the point of being an embarrassing puppy dog. It reached the empress's ears, and many believe she had Peilah poisoned." At Jin's look, Meipin waved a hand. "To be honest, no one but her family cares, given that she was an unpleasant wretch of a human being." Meipin grimaced and glanced around as if the girl might appear. "I shouldn't speak ill of the dead, but I'm not saying anything Peilah didn't already know."

Jin swallowed. "The empress would really do that? Put her to death?"

Meipin nodded. "I think it wasn't so much the prince's infatuation as that Peilah wouldn't settle for the position of concubine. She wanted to be empress and was working to make the prince hand it to her. The prince hasn't been interested in anyone since." She smirked and gave Jin a sideways glance. "Well, almost."

Jin sighed, exasperated. "I know what you're hinting, and you're mistaken. Besides . . ."

Meipin raised an eyebrow. "You were about to admit something, I can tell!"

Jin hoped her face wasn't betraying her. "No."

Meipin's eyes narrowed, and her mouth curved. "Did something happen with that Persian?" Jin's face must have given her away, for Meipin squealed and pointed a peach-colored fingernail at her. "Ah! It did!"

"Nothing happened!" Jin protested but knew Meipin wasn't convinced. "I just hope no one executes me for being able to see the dead."

It was Meipin's turn to scoff. "You're hard to kill, and also, they'll potentially lose a jade. Far better to think of ways to use you."

She glanced at Ahlu, who came to refill the wine pitcher. "No, no, any more, and I'll never wake tomorrow." She rose and hugged Jin once more, her smooth, fleshy arms light yet reassuring.

"Welcome back. It is good to see you."

Jin smiled. "And you." She meant it. If one didn't count the Chaakan people, she had not been around female company for what seemed a lifetime, much less female company she could readily speak to.

THE SUMMONS FROM THE EMPRESS CAME EARLY THE next morning, though it didn't matter, as Jin had not slept at all.

After the shock and chaos of the day's events had

worn away, the realization that Gao had not been an illusion had hit her like a fist, driving away all thoughts of sleep. She saw Gao in every shadow, heard his voice in the gongs that sounded out the hours. Had she killed him, or instead given him eternal life? She could have sworn she had heard him laughing in the dark, his last words before she killed him scurrying in her mind like mice: *You are like your mother, nothing more than a common murderer.*

Jin had only just dressed when Ahlu came to announce the messenger. He bowed low, one hand over his fist.

"The empress asks that you attend her, Rider," the messenger said.

Jin's heart hammered. She reached out to Rayshan.

The empress wants me. I shall come by as soon as I can.

She could almost hear Rayshan thrashing his tail. *Very well.*

Jin followed the messenger outside to where two horses awaited, and mounted. She had never been very good on horseback, but now that she rode a dragon, the whole thing felt even stranger to her, like riding a toy horse instead of a real one.

They passed through the long outdoor corridors and courtyards that led north to the imperial private quarters. Everywhere, she saw evidence of the festivities being prepared: halls were being swept, courtyards tidied, and new paint applied to the garden pagodas.

When they reached the empress's quarters, Jin

wondered if the woman had also passed a sleepless night, for she was in the same robes, as if she hadn't changed or closed her eyes. Jin knelt until the empress bade her rise, then stood in silence, waiting. The empress didn't say anything for some time.

"When I was a young girl, my father brought an impoverished huren and his mother into our household," Empress Wu said. "He was an odd choice for a stable hand, being a huren and having no gift for obedience, but my father insisted he would prove his worth." She paused, as if expecting Jin to interrupt, but Jin kept silent. "He had a gift with horses as if he could speak to them, and the wildest of them would bend to his will given time. Everyone told my father he was wasting his money on this boy, but my father disagreed. He said the boy showed promise, and he might even one day be a dragonrider, something none of his girls could become." She turned to Jin. "My father had only daughters, ten of them, in fact, and no sons to follow in his footsteps to become a dragonrider. He was always ashamed, and though he prayed for a boy, it seemed Heaven delighted in cheating him, and none of his concubines bore sons who lived."

Jin sensed the empress's resentment toward her father, a man who sounded as if he saw no value in his girls simply because they would never carry on the dragon-riding tradition. Why was the empress telling her this?

"In the end, my father was proven right. Emar went

with the initiates to choose a dragon. Yalongma chose him, and he became one of the best we had."

"I thought all dragonriders had to be noble, Your Highness," she said. She still wasn't sure why the empress had chosen to tell her this story of Emar, but curiosity overcame her.

"They do," the empress replied. "My father adopted Emar as his son and gave him the title of duke at his death."

"So Emar is your brother?" Jin asked, astounded.

"In title, yes. He was a gamble, but he was invaluable." She turned to Jin. "I tell you this because I am trying to gauge whether you are another Emar, or a snake that I should behead."

Jin stayed silent, willing herself not to flinch under the empress's gaze, which had cooled.

"That little trick you pulled last night, do you have any idea how harmful that could have been? Could still be?"

"I am sorry, Your Majesty," Jin replied, bowing. "I do not yet control whatever it is."

"And that is exactly the problem," the empress said. "But first, do we even want to control it? Is it something we even wish to exist?" Her silks rustled as she moved closer to Jin, examining her. "I have made many mistakes in my life by allowing certain . . . anomalies to exist."

"You mean ordering Emar's blood bonding, Your Majesty?" Jin had to ask.

The empress regarded her. "He told you."

Jin nodded.

"That was a mistake. But a necessary one. And now I'm paying the price." She stopped, as if worried she had admitted too much, then turned. "And that is why I don't know what to do about you. You saved my son, and me, from Gao. And I thank you for it. But this manifestation of your dragon's, your blood bond . . . it could destroy me. Destroy the throne. And as you know, I cannot kill you. So what would you advise me to do?"

"I don't fancy the option of being buried like Mengkhis Lai," Jin said.

"Then think of a solution, because I don't see many."

Jin hesitated, unsure what to say. She instinctively reached out to Rayshan.

Like loves like. Make her see herself in you.

Jin took a breath. "Some would say a woman on the throne is an ill omen, but you have turned that into a good omen."

The empress raised a thin eyebrow. "Have I? I think I have merely convinced some that I am as competent as a man, if not more so. I have to kill more people, win more battles, than any other emperor. But no one sees my sex as a benefit."

"What if I can prove that Rayshan's summoning the dead is such a benefit?"

The empress regarded her thoughtfully. "That would be a start, though I don't know how you will persuade an empire that raising the dead is a good thing."

Jin didn't have an answer. Yet. After she had discovered that her hallucinations were in fact real, she herself was horrified at this new power, and lay awake in cold fear of Gao's reappearance.

"I will speak to Sanjin," the empress said, interrupting Jin's thoughts. "But make no mistake that I can give you a life of pure and absolute pain, bury you as I did Baikalan if you do not obey me. I can't afford to be sentimental about people, even those who have saved me."

Jin bristled at this but forced herself to say, "I understand, Your Majesty."

"I will allow Sanjin to have you until after the Moon Festival to see if we can harness this ability of yours and Rayshan's." She paused. "Show me you can control it, and I will allow you to remain in Dragon Class. But I cannot have you letting the dead appear whenever they wish, making accusations and endangering my throne."

Jin swallowed. She knew the threat behind the words. Would the empress have her imprisoned like Baikalan? Exile, she knew, would be too risky for the empress. When she had disappeared during the geography test, one of the empress's greatest fears was that she would go to a rival kingdom and offer her services there.

If she couldn't serve the empire and she couldn't

remain in Dragon Class, then that left something worse than death.

SANJIN DIDN'T TELL HER WHERE THEY WERE GOING. Instead, he simply instructed her to follow the other dragons in the convoy, who had gathered at the Blood Oval for departure. Prince Tai was there, consulting with Sanjin and a Dragon Class official. She caught him looking her way, but at her glance, he turned back to his conversation. She mounted Rayshan, who asked about her meeting with the empress.

We have two months to convince the empress this ability is essential and a good thing.

Rayshan huffed. *She certainly knows how to set deadlines.*

Everyone figures the king of Khitan will be moving by then. They can't have us falling into the wrong hands, and if they can't use us either, then . . .

Rayshan snapped at a passing bird. *We'll have to make use of our two months.*

Agreed. If only to control this so that I can stop seeing Gao every day. She shivered involuntarily, shaking off the fear that stalked her every time she saw anyone vaguely resembling Gao.

Aadan and her wing had come out to say goodbye, but in front of Sanjin they hadn't been able to speak freely, much less have any privacy.

Before long, Sanjin gave the signal to depart, and the dragons took to the air. She watched Aadan and the others disappear from sight below as she and Sanjin's people ascended into the sky, skimming under the low cloud cover and heading west. They aimed for the western hills, a cluster of small rumples in the landscape that Jin knew housed some of the nobles' summer retreats. Lakes dotted the terrain, along with thick copses of firs and pines.

They flew for a little over an hour before the riders banked and headed toward a large, sprawling country estate. As they landed, Jin saw the sign of the Royal Veil everywhere: the character for "Zheng," or "righteousness," was carved in plaques on the doors, arranged as a mosaic in the courtyard, and painted on various walls.

"My summer home," Sanjin explained after he had exited from a carriage. "We will be safe here."

Safe from what? Jin asked Rayshan.

Rayshan hummed back, also not reassured. Could word of her and Rayshan's abilities have leaked out despite Sanjin's threats? In her home province, Jin had once seen a crowd storm a house where a woman was accused of being a fox demon and causing the outbreak of a pestilence. The crowd had beaten her to death in the streets, with the police appearing late enough to be ineffectual. And though more people fell ill in the weeks following the woman's death, no one seemed to spare two thoughts for having killed an innocent person.

Hopefully people wouldn't be so rash as to storm the Royal Veil's home and face a dragon?

Jin oversaw Rayshan's stabling in an attached paddock with the other dragons, then followed Sanjin's servant. He led her to what appeared to be Sanjin's private rooms, which had been laid out for tea. The sight sent a shiver down her, for tea rooms were the euphemism for where the Royal Veil interrogated his victims.

"Sit," he said, gesturing to a chair next to him at his desk. Another chair sat opposite him.

"Are we expecting someone else, Marquis Sanjin?"

"Yes, our guest should be arriving at—ah, sounds like she is here."

She heard muffled shouting, what sounded like a curse and someone running, then a cuffing.

Jin looked over at Sanjin, but he seemed perfectly composed as he poured three cups of tea.

The doors burst open, and guards with swords at their belts entered, each holding the arm of a woman who was still thrashing to get away.

She looked roughly fifty, with raven and silver hair that had largely escaped from her braid. Her robes were cheap but clean and well fitted. It was her face, however, that bore signs of a hard life. Scars criss-crossed one cheek, their fine lines almost beautiful in their precision, like a snowflake.

At the sight of Sanjin, she stilled, dread in her eyes.

"Sit, Lady Yuli."

The woman's eyes narrowed as she took in Jin, then him. "I didn't do it."

Sanjin raised an eyebrow. "Do what?"

"Whatever it is I'm accused of."

"You misunderstood my invitation," Sanjin said. "Despite the setting, this is not a tea room session."

The woman shuddered at the mere mention, and Jin couldn't blame her.

"Then what?" the woman spat, her voice quivering.

Sanjin gestured for her to sit. "Please."

Casting the guards suspicious looks, the woman sat on the edge as if the chair itself was poisoned.

"Lady Yuli and I go back quite a ways," Sanjin explained. "We are good friends."

Jin highly doubted that from the look in Yuli's eyes and supposed the Royal Veil had no friends.

"Lady Yuli, I would like to introduce you to Wang Kway Jin. Perhaps you have heard of her."

"Why would I have heard of her?" The woman tossed Jin a wary look.

"Because she is the empire's first female dragonrider."

Yuli shrugged. "Congratulations. But nothing to do with me."

"True. However, I believe her dragon is a flame."

"A flame?" Yuli asked. "You mean a death flame? That's impossible."

"Why impossible?" Sanjin countered.

"Because . . ." Yuli trailed off as if the answer was obvious. "Because animals can't be flames."

"It seems you are, once again, mistaken in your assumptions."

Yuli flushed. "What makes you think she's not the flame?"

"Deduction," Sanjin said. "Which I believe is one of your weak areas, so I won't waste time on explanations. Suffice it to say, I want you to teach her everything you know. See whether she can harness her dragon's flame to control their summoning of the dead."

Yuli's eyes flew back to Jin. "You think she can control a flame?"

Before Jin could answer, Sanjin said, "The dragon has the power. They summoned someone who looked as much like flesh and blood as you or me. Everyone there thought the dead had come back to life."

Yuli's mouth opened, then shut again, as if she had so many questions crowded there that none could find their way out.

"I believe you have only ever been able to manifest them as phantoms, am I right?" Sanjin asked.

"Yes, Marquis. Though I didn't have the power of a dragon behind me," Yuli retorted defensively.

"Well, now you do," Sanjin said. "I want you to teach Jin how to control it, and I want her to be able to summon someone at will."

"I can do that."

"By the end of the moon festival."

Yuli's face paled. "That's impossible."

"That's the time I can offer."

"And if I can't?"

Sanjin sipped his tea. "Then I'm afraid your pardon will be revoked."

Yuli ground her teeth. "So I don't have a choice."

"One can always choose death," Sanjin said. "I just find that most people prefer life."

CHAPTER 22

The polo ponies thundered down the field, chasing the bright red bamboo ball flying its way toward the far goal.

From the sidelines, Tai watched his mother, her hair in a topknot and her riding breeches billowing as she jerked her mare around and dove into the fray, trying to get a clear hit. The other ladies were just as competitive, and in the distance, Tai spied Meipin goad her own gelding forward, cheeks flushed and eyes bright with the thrill of competition.

Someone hit the ball with great force, sending it flying overhead. It arced toward the sidelines where Tai was standing. He caught it in one hand, making the players whistle and clap.

"Toss it in!" his mother called.

"Certainly," he shouted back. "As soon as you give me a few moments of your time."

She kept her smile but murmured something to the other players and cantered over. She dismounted, handing her reins to a waiting groom. Tai tossed the ball back in amongst the players, and the horses converged on it, sending it soaring toward the far goalpost.

"I need to ask you," he said without preamble, "did you have anything to do with Peilah's death?"

The empress sighed, as if she had expected this. "Tai, the culprit was found. He—"

Tai shook his head. "I know the court case. I need to hear it from you."

The empress didn't say anything for a moment, but simply wiped mud from her cheek with the back of her hand.

"Did you?" Tai pressed.

"The important question is really whether you'll believe me if I say no."

"Answer me. Please."

She held his gaze. "No." Her tone sharpened to a blade's edge. "I know how taken you were, but she had more enemies than a dragon has scales. You want the truth? The truth was that I didn't have to kill her. There was a long line of willing volunteers."

He digested this. His mother was an excellent liar; he just wasn't sure anymore how much she lied to him. "Then why did she say you killed her?" he asked.

His mother shifted the polo mallet in her hand. "Her mother likely told her it was me as she lay dying.

But there is no way she or her mother could have known who poisoned her. You are going to have to decide whether you trust me, my son. Do you?"

The Tai before the coup would have told her the truth, that he wasn't sure and had his doubts. And then they would have worked through it together. But instead, he found himself answering, "Of course I trust you."

And as he walked away, the lie burned in him like a curse.

TAI ROLLED UP THE SCROLL AS HE DRESSED FOR THE Festival of Sevens.

He had read it multiple times since he'd first opened it after his initial lessons with mage Situ Han. The legend of a Mage Emperor was described like a fairy tale, complete with pictures of what the writer thought a peaceful empire would look like and what the Mage Emperor would be—tall, smooth-faced, and good-looking, his robes flowing with power. The woman was depicted as beautiful and elegant, with her hair drawn in a simple hairstyle and her face turned modestly away from the man's, though her hands held a baby dragon.

Tai didn't believe much in fortune-telling, for all his mother's quiet superstitions and the monks' insistence that the future could be divined from the smoke in incense or the cracked bones of sheep. But Situ Han seemed such a practical man of reality. It intrigued Tai that he could have such faith in this story.

How anyone could go from having no magic to being a Mage Emperor seemed far-fetched. Even more far-fetched, perhaps, was the foretelling of his marriage to the Princess of Dragons. Who was this person? The only female even remotely connected to dragons now was Jin—and perhaps the new recruits to Dragon Class.

And then, once this ridiculous thought lodged itself, it wouldn't leave. What if he was meant to be an emperor, and Jin was meant to rule with him? She certainly had achieved fame and made the impact that would allow people to follow her and like her, for he knew she had won allies as well as enemies during her time at Dragon Class. Conservatives like Gao had—and did—despise her, it was true, but it was impossible to miss the admiration in the new girl recruits, the whispers in the corridors of how Jin had exposed the fundamental lie peddled within Dragon Class and at court: that dragons didn't bond to girls.

He had to admit the idea of marriage to Jin didn't displease him, which in itself was lunacy given he knew her even less than he had known Peilah, or even Meipin. Yet he found himself playing out an imaginary conversation where Jin confessed to having been attracted to him since she had stolen Rayshan from his inn chambers. She had rarely shown any signs of affection only because she had feared creating rumors.

At this, his short-lived fantasy faltered. Jin was not easily intimidated, and certainly not by rumors. But, he argued with himself, he had charmed enough women in his life to recognize that Jin wasn't completely immune to him—the telltale way her nose wrinkled when she held back a smile at something he said. A man could always hope, and this particular hope was like Maru wine: it seemed to only strengthen with time.

He stepped into his robes and submitted to the servant who did his hair, then entered his foyer where his entourage bowed low, ready to escort him. Mage Situ Han was there, and he bowed as well, though his eyes crinkled.

"I'll try not to outshine you," the corpulent mage whispered as they left the suites.

Tai smiled. "That would be kind of you. I don't take competition lightly."

"I hear some of the Dragon Class female recruits will be there," Situ Han remarked as they walked toward the main courtyard in the Pavilion of a Thousand Blessings, where the Festival of Sevens was to take place.

"Yes, try to behave."

The mage chuckled. "I am thinking of you. Do any strike you as the foretold Princess of Dragons?"

"No," Tai replied. "Are you sure the foretelling

didn't have any other clues? Name, parents, date of birth? A telltale mole would be helpful."

"Laugh all you wish," Situ Han murmured. "The foretelling will come true, you'll see. And I already have my bets placed on a certain woman."

Tai cast him a sharp look, but before he could ask further they had reached the hallway leading to the Festival, where the sounds of drums and flutes greeted them.

A flurry of fanfare announced the prince's arrival, and immediately, guests swarmed him, edging him away from the mage. Tai donned his smiles and his charm, peppered everyone with compliments, and remembered to address each by name.

Lanterns blazed from the roof eaves, swaying in the late summer breeze that gave welcome relief to the heat of the seventh month.

The women of the palace were out in force, dressed in their finest silks and gossamer gowns, the heat allowing them to wear low cuts, sheer scarves, and sometimes even sheer skirts over silk slippers. Everyone had taken great care with their hair, coiling it into elaborate designs or piling it in the long flopped-over bun style with strips of jeweled ribbons.

The kitchens had also clearly been busy, preparing heaping platters of sweetened nut cakes, palm-sized biscuits glazed in honey and almonds, and fried dough sticks studded with dried fruits and peanuts. The sky gave the empress good face, the clouds having been chased on to other parts of the empire, leaving a clear view of the heavens.

Some had brought out fine cows decorated with gold tassels in honor of the cowherd, while many of the girls were showing off their latest weaving designs. Sogdian acrobats in flimsy silk garments moved amongst the crowd, showing off tumbles, flips, dances, and hoop throwing. Several fortunetellers and match-makers drifted amongst the crowds, offering to tell futures and divine love matching for couples, while exotic animals like peacocks and lion cubs strolled the grounds, their necks dripping with precious stone necklaces.

As crown prince, Tai was expected to move amongst all the guests, show his face, and judge the annual weaving competition. The ceremony of Double Seven, the Festival of the Seventh on the Seventh, was an extravagant affair where men pursued their love interests, girls flirted with admirers, and everyone drank and ate until the stars had melted into dawn.

But Tai's heart was not in it this year, perhaps because mage Situ Han had distracted him with talk of this Princess of Dragons. He also couldn't help recall a previous festival where Jin had broken tradition to invite him to dance, and he wished she was here.

His collar felt stifling, but he knew it would incense his mother to see his scar visible. So he ignored it, smiling and drawing on his deepest charms. He was gratified to see it was still working. Several courtiers and girls had that basking-in-the-sun expression as he spoke and smiled. He made sure to look them in the eye and bow just enough to convey his undivided attention. He composed poetry on the spot to praise the weaving made by the Rites Minister's daughter, then listened attentively as a forestry official tried to convince him of the value of changing all the palace chopsticks to lacquer instead of silver to save them polishing.

As the night deepened, he wondered how much longer he could politely extricate himself from dry conversations. If Aadan had been here, he would have had someone to talk to. But Aadan, he knew, had requested special leave to visit his father. Tai caught sight of Meipin with a gaggle of friends, playing a *pipa*, and was almost grateful to glide over to her. She was familiar, at least, and their games of flirtation were so entrenched that it was like second nature.

"Your Highness!" she purred, ever ladylike. "You honor us with your presence, though my weaving is unworthy of your attention."

"Nothing you ever do is worth less than a thousand poems of praise, Lady Meipin," Tai admonished, donning a mock look of reproach.

"The prince's tongue is even sweeter than the cakes." Meipin giggled.

"But not as sweet as the works that all of you ladies have presented here," he said, casting a look at the woven fabrics. They were, to be honest, all highly skilled in their needlework, but he found them uniformly dull. If they hadn't woven scenes of the moon over water, then it was the tried-and-true pattern of the cowherd serenading his weaver fairy in the sky. In some, there were magpies who formed the bridge to help the lovers meet, and in others, the fairy was wiping tears that were falling as rain to the earth. He had seen these a thousand times and would see them a thousand more.

"I will have a hard time judging the winner," he said truthfully.

"You are too kind," Meipin said. "Perhaps you would be willing to help me set a lantern afloat on the water?"

He offered an arm, which she took, and they strolled down to the canal that had been built in the gardens, Meipin's maid Ahlu following discreetly behind. Several other people were already standing on the banks or kneeling down, putting their paper lanterns onto the water. Others were pointing up at the sky, where the stars were already starting to appear.

"You and your mother are under much stress, I'm sure," Meipin said in a low voice.

"All the more reason to be at fun events like this," he replied, keeping his voice light while stealing a glance at Meipin. Though they had grown up together, they had never really had conversations outside their carefully prescribed court flirtations.

She made a sound of disagreement. "Your Highness

looks pre-occupied. Are you missing the company of a certain dragonrider?"

Was her smile mischievous or coy? She could have just been referring to his friendship with Aadan, which was well-known. He gave her an admonishing look. "What man could wish for any other company when in your presence?"

Meipin's smooth face was completely guileless. "Oh? My mistake, I thought something was worrying Your Highness."

"The only worry tonight is you not enjoying the festivities. My mother has gone to great expense, you know."

As if on cue, a chorus of exclamations rose as the main braziers in the gardens were doused with a great hissing of steam. A loud boom sounded, before a crackle of fireworks lit up the sky, drawing gasps and applause. Clouds of silver, red, and pale gold sparkled above in a glittering display before drifting away on the night wind. Once the smoke had cleared, everyone stood admiring the cowherd and weaver fairy stars burning bright in the heavens, a bridge of stardust forming a path between them.

"What a beautiful and well-fated couple you make," a voice broke in at Tai's elbow. They turned to see one of the matchmakers at their side, his broad face split in an obsequious smile, his hands already reaching out to seize Meipin's fingers.

"Shall we see whether this enchanting lady loves

you, sir?"

The man was so inebriated that he hadn't recognized the crown prince, Tai realized. Meipin looked embarrassed, but the matchmaker quickly pulled a small rock from seemingly nowhere and pressed it into Meipin's hand.

He deftly closed her fingers over it and said in a voice of mystery, "Behold, if your true love is near, it will glow red, I swear it!"

"Careful of what you promise," Tai said, "or you will break this humble boy's heart!"

The man shook his head vigorously. "Never, sir, never! My love tokens always tell the truth! Look!" He pulled open Meipin's hand to reveal the rock, which now did actually glow as if a fire had been lit within.

"You see!" the man crowed in triumph. "The lady loves you, sir, with a love pure and true." The matchmaker pulled another stone from his pocket and reached out for Tai's hand. "Your turn, esteemed sir. Here is a stone, and it won't lie. It will glow if this lady is your true love."

Tai had no desire to hold the stone, but the matchmaker pressed it into his hand, and Tai silently willed the matchmaker to be the fraud that he was. For then, the stone would glow, and Lady Meipin wouldn't lose face.

At the matchmaker's gesture, Tai opened his palm. The man's wine-flushed cheeks paled at the sight of the stone lying unchanged in Tai's hand.

"Clearly, the love is one way," Meipin said, giving Tai an accusing pout.

"Or these stones are defective," Tai said smoothly, glancing at the matchmaker.

"My stones always work!" To the man's credit, he looked genuinely surprised.

"Perhaps you should test it on someone else," Tai suggested, holding out the stone.

The matchmaker shook his head. "No, keep it, a gift from me to you as my apologies for the night."

He bowed low as Tai pocketed the token, smiled at Meipin and held out an arm for her to walk on with him. "A fun party trick, but clearly, he needs more practice."

"Clearly," Meipin murmured, squeezing his arm. She looked up at the stars. "Ah, well, the stars are beautiful, and even if you don't love me, I think we both understand that people of our station have to marry for many reasons, and none of them are for love."

"Lady Meipin," he said, "you must not heed a fraudster peddling stones."

Her look of reprimand was only half mocking. "I know I am not your first choice in marriage, Your Highness. But I believe in being friends with one's spouse, even if there can be no love."

He shot a glance at her, trying to sense the meaning behind the words. Did she know about the bridal proposal to Parhae? Ahlu stood at a discreet distance and gave no sign of hearing their conversation.

"I am not a naïve girl, Your Highness," she murmured. "We have grown up together, but I know enough to sense when someone has no . . . fire for another. And I like you. You are witty and a good man at heart, as far as men go. But I doubt that we will ever love each other with the passion that the cowherd had for his weaver girl."

He looked up at the stars again. "Stranger things have happened."

"Perhaps," she murmured. "But I am one to make the best of things. If everyone brings kindling, the fire will burn bright, as they say. If I were to become empress, I would be a friend to you, not a foe. And I can be a powerful friend." At his expression, she continued, "I overhear many things my uncle mentions, which includes news about Gao's embezzlement, and dealings in the north." She smiled at his flicker of surprise, but the flirtation was gone. "Along with our family's wealth, I could be a great source of information for you. I don't know if such things are of interest to His Highness, but if they are not, I will stop my silly chatter."

Tai appraised Meipin as if seeing her for the first time. The beautiful nobleman's daughter, who had been groomed as his potential empress, had always seemed like a fine enough person, but he now understood that her persona was carefully cultivated—perhaps as carefully cultivated as his own. He reprimanded himself for his own stupidity.

"I never find the Lady Meipin's chatter silly," he murmured. "But why do you tell me this? For better favor in being chosen?"

She smiled. "As I said, Your Highness, we have little choice in who we marry. If I only wanted to become empress, I would be sitting with your mother, not you."

He smiled to mask how close to home she had hit. His future, his past, his present—his mother controlled it all, and certainly more than he had ever thought possible. He was beginning to understand how little his words or feelings mattered.

She put on a conciliatory face. "But that's why I am speaking to you. I loathe the thought of marrying a reluctant husband. If we are to share our lives, then I think it's best we play on the same polo team, don't you agree?"

"I think the Lady Meipin has wisdom beyond even the wisest men at court."

She slipped her arm back through his. "Your flattery always sounds the nicest, Your Highness. Now, shall we light that lantern and make a wish?"

They had reached the canal's bank, where servants handed out bamboo and paper lanterns to partygoers. He took one, while Meipin took another.

"To love," Meipin said, smiling wistfully. "Of all kinds."

She bent down to set her lantern afloat. It spun lazily as it joined the others drifting in the current, bellies aglow with wishes.

Tai lit his candle, placed it inside the lantern, and then pushed it gently away, watching it disappear into a flotilla of indistinguishable hopes. He was glad Meipin didn't ask what he had wished for, because he wasn't sure he had an answer.

He could do worse than to marry Meipin, he knew. She was generous, graceful, and from a powerful and learned family. And as he had just found out, much smarter than he or anyone gave her credit for. Would the empress still favor Meipin if she knew that her money came with a sharp mind? Perhaps he would keep that secret, for in this sea of courtiers, he was beginning to appreciate Meipin's point: he needed his empress to be his friend, and his only. But he had always hoped for more.

As they climbed back up the banks and rejoined the main festivities, Tai spied a servant with a pallid face, his robe bearing the insignia of the messenger banner, hurrying across the grounds toward his mother's royal tent.

He watched for a moment, wondering what message the servant bore. Meipin followed his gaze.

"Hopefully not bad news," she commented.

Before long, the empress came sweeping out of the tent, her expression somber. The servant followed, along with a few of his mother's closest maid servants, and they wove through the crowds toward the northern gate, where the empress's quarters lay.

His mother would never retreat this early from an

imperial festival unless something was gravely wrong. Tai excused himself from Meipin, who bowed, and then headed toward his mother's quarters, heart tight.

Tai found his mother standing by the window in her private audience chamber, her face ashen, her arms tucked into the sheer sleeves of her tailor-made gown.

"You should be at the festival," she remarked.

"So should you," he said. "What is wrong?"

She hesitated, then gestured toward a teak box sitting on the table. "Parhae sent their reply to my suggestion of a royal marriage."

Tai approached the box slowly, wondering what could have made his mother so apprehensive.

He reached out and lifted the lid on its brass hinge.

A head stared back at him, the eyes still open. He covered his mouth, for despite the heavy perfume in the box, the contents still reeked.

He closed the lid and turned back to his mother, trying not to breathe. "Who is this?"

"The envoy I sent with our proposal," the empress said, her voice quiet with fury. "Along with a note to say that he has married Ulagan's daughter."

Tai had a memory from his last trip to Khitan, where a quiet girl with a favored leg watched him with wide, curious eyes. Tai's dislike of Ulagan only intensified at the thought of the daughter, hardly more than a child, being wedded to a man three times her age.

"He is punishing us," Tai said. The Parhae king had made no secret of his desire to put one of his daughters on the throne by arranging a marriage to Tai, but the empress had been loath to promise her son to anyone in order to keep that choice title free as long as possible. It seemed the royal families had run out of patience. "The negotiations must have started some time ago."

"And now we know where Ulagan is getting his ships," the empress said. "Parhae will provide them."

Tai cursed. That made sense. As a coastal kingdom, Parhae had numerous long-distance ships. In all honesty, they were far more formidable than the Tang Empire's, and were certainly capable of traveling the great distance to the southern kingdom of Champa, where Mengkhis Lai was. This way, they would avoid traveling through Tang territory.

"We are most definitely at war then." Though there had been skirmishes, with rebellions along the borders where certain Parhae cities had resisted Tang influence and where Dragon Class had been deployed to restore the peace, the rulers had managed to avoid outright war: Parhae due to its inferior strength, the empress due to the inevitable drain on resources and money. She had no desire to subjugate another kingdom that she would have to keep in line. Now, however, things were more complicated.

"We are in a worse situation than I thought, and Meipin's wealth won't buy us the defenses we need immediately," his mother said. "It may be best we seek another ally. Persia perhaps, or Tibet, to buy their loyalty." She turned, biting her lip in thought. "I will send a letter to Nihhon. A marriage with them will keep them on our side, at least."

"That doesn't solve our financial issues," Tai pointed out.

"Let us make sure our enemies can't multiply like rats, and then we will figure out our funds."

"We may need to fight two fires at once," Tai said. "What of taxing the monasteries? They are sitting on enough wealth to purchase a kingdom. If they are seen to be giving back, they may even grow their popularity." After his visit to the temple, he kept his ears open to general opinions on the temples. Through his valet and secretary, he had heard that the middle class grumbled about how the monks at the hundreds of temples around the city had profited from alms. Not to mention that they drained funds from many wealthy families, claiming good works for the temples would help followers avoid hell and reincarnation.

"The monks are a pillar," the empress said. "Everyone is so intent on whether I am a man or woman, they've forgotten I'm also human. The monks are the only ones who seem to remember that and support me regardless of my sex. If I were to take their money, they would turn on me."

"Not if you do it diplomatically," Tai said.

The empress laughed, but it was sharp and bitter. "You cannot charm every snake, my son."

CHAPTER 23

The early autumn air had lost the heavy heat of summer, but the season's lingering cicadas still droned in the willow trees lining the lake. Jin sat on the upper banks with Rayshan lying nearby, his tail slithering lazily through the grass.

Opposite her, Yuli sat cross-legged, her sharp eyes studying Rayshan with interest.

"Drawing the dead is easy. It's something that Rayshan will do naturally, like breathing. He is like a candle, and the dead will find him like moths find light." Yuli held up a finger. "Manifesting the dead, however, takes power. Which clearly he has. Very powerful flames can manifest someone's image, but manifesting someone physically?" Her eyes narrowed. "That is another level, one that is almost of legend, it is so rare. Manifesting who you want, when you want, is also part of the control that comes with being a flame."

"How long have you been a flame?" Jin asked.

"Since I was a child," Yuli replied. "Now stop asking irrelevant questions. You're wasting time." She drew a breath. "Let me feel what you feel when you become a flame. Tell your dragon to flare."

"To flare?"

"Yes," Yuli said impatiently. "You mean he doesn't even know how to control it?"

Do you know how to control it? Jin asked him.

Sometimes, Rayshan said, a little defensively. *It happens most when I sleep, but occasionally it happens when I react strongly to something.*

"He can't control it," Jin said. Rayshan slapped her arm with his tail in reprimand. *What? If we want to really harness this thing, we might as well be honest,* Jin told Rayshan.

Rayshan grumbled his reluctant agreement.

Yuli sighed. "It's like controlled breathing. You breathe all the time without thinking. It's a natural function. But really think about it and control it, and you can control anything. It's about understanding your flow of chi. You know what chi is?"

"Of course," Jin said. Even those not in medicine knew of the life force that flowed through every living thing, the pulse of energy that gave breath.

"Very well." Yuli motioned for Jin to hold out her hands. Jin did so, and Yuli clasped them in her own. Jin was surprised at how warm they were, how strong they were compared to the woman's ruined face and bamboo-thin frame.

"Feel your own chi in you. You have to be able to listen to it and identify it, pick it out from the fabric of all the other chi around you," Yuli said. "Listen. Feel."

Jin took a deep breath and stilled her heart, shutting down her hearing and other senses, until all she heard were three heartbeats: hers, Rayshan's, and Yuli's, which she was surprised was steadier and slower than either hers or Rayshan's.

"Good. You are listening. Now listen to my words. Manifesting the dead is like turning ash back into a tree, or making the exact same pot of water from released steam."

Jin frowned. *That already sounds impossible.*

"Nothing is created, nothing is destroyed," Yuli continued, her rough fingers rubbing circles in Jin's palms until Jin felt a tingling heat. "But life force is the most magical energy in the world and, therefore, hardest to reform into what it once was at a single moment in time."

The energy in Jin's palm grew warmer, almost humming in Jin's ears.

"It takes concentration," Yuli continued softly, "an immense power, to draw those exact life fibers back together once death has scattered them. Rayshan is the raw flame, but you focus his power."

The energy in Jin's hand seemed to burst into a translucent flame, a wild explosion of heat. Jin instinctively pulled away, but Yuli's grip on her hand was firm, and Jin stared at the little bonfire of energy in her hands.

"You two are like a kettle and its spout," Yuli said, leaning close over the miniature storm of energy. "He is the wind, but you are the sail. You decide when, where, and how much to fill the sail so that you go where you wish."

The flame thinned into a needle, then rounded into a ball, then flattened like rolled dough.

"Remember, girl," Yuli continued, her fingers continuing to rub Jin's hands, "you can't change the wind's direction or demand it subside. So you respect its power and work with it, not against it. Control your chi, slow it down."

Jin let her heartbeat slow further, siphoning out the sounds of the forest and the surrounding smells.

"Now tell your dragon to flare," Yuli commanded. "I found it helps to think of something that makes you salivate. Something you like to eat, perhaps. Something happy."

Think of oranges, Jin told Rayshan.

Immediately, a light glow came from Rayshan. The energy around them shifted subtly, and Yuli grinned. "Yes! That's it. You are flaring, see? I can feel the chi change around you. Now more. See if you can make your flare brighter."

Think of a whole crate of oranges.

Rayshan's glow flickered, then burst forth in a

bright, warm glow that seemed to light up the surrounding forest.

"Ah, good, here they come. Do you see them?" Yuli asked eagerly.

Jin saw three figures in the swaying willows on the edges of the lake. She didn't recognize them, but one was a thin girl with a long braid and a sallow face, while the other two were portly teenagers with wide eyes and pinched mouths.

"Good, let them go," Yuli said, and Rayshan's flare subsided. The figures dissolved into ash and carpeted the grassy floor. "That was good."

"Who were those people?" Jin asked.

"No idea," Yuli said dismissively. "You must understand—when you flare, you draw in anyone. It's whoever senses it and comes. Now, let's flare a few times just so Rayshan can get used to this ability."

They tried it again, with Rayshan thinking of different happy memories that seemed to dictate how strong he flared. Hatching and meeting Jin for the first time. Flying for the first time. Winning the contest at Ice Beard Mountain. Yuli made them identify and remember these memories, growing their flare strength until they were drawing the dead faster, with more figures appearing every time. Jin noticed Rayshan's strength flagging, along with her own.

Yuli called a break halfway through the day and ordered the supervising soldiers, who were never too far away, to bring meals. "Enough to feed five," she snapped at them. "Flaring is hard work."

Rayshan picked unenthusiastically at the goat carcass that had been brought for him.

Eat now. I'll ask to take you hunting later. This cheered him, and his appetite returned.

Jin found Yuli's prediction true. When the plates of roast fowl, lotus-leaf-wrapped rice, and steamed vegetables arrived, it was all she could do to keep from wolfing every last morsel. Yuli had no hesitations, resting her bowl rim against her mouth and hurriedly shoveling rice in with her chopsticks, along with generous portions of the roast quail and vegetables. She downed it all with tea and motioned at Jin.

"Don't be shy. You should drain Sanjin of whatever expenses you can. You know he'll repay himself with the flesh off your back anyway."

A silence fell, for Jin sensed Yuli was being literal.

"How did you come to be arrested?" Jin asked, swallowing a mouthful of seaweed and wood ear mushroom.

Yuli scowled. "I blackmailed him. Or at least I tried to."

The food turned cold in Jin's stomach. And she sometimes thought she had mud for brains. "You blackmailed the Royal Veil?"

"He wasn't the Royal Veil then," Yuli said, her scowl deepening. "He was a local magistrate. An innocent man he'd put to death appeared to me. I told Sanjin I'd tell the authorities using this dead person as a witness."

"And so he punished you?"

She nodded. "And you want to know the best part?" Yuli paused, slurping her cup of tea dry. "When he refused to pay my fee, I went to the higher-ups and told them. I thought at least if I couldn't get rich, I could do the right thing." She laughed then, the sound so bitter it was painful against Jin's ear. "And they refused to lift a finger, refused to give the family a pardon so they would at least be able to earn an honest living without the stink of criminal on their family name." Yuli indicated her cheek. "And Sanjin gave me a new face to remind me what happens to those who question him."

Jin was silent. Stories of Sanjin's cruelty were not new to her. Every thief in Gaozhou knew of the man's tactics and feared ever meeting him or his staff in the tea rooms. But somehow, today, the story struck her doubly hard. Perhaps because of what she knew about her own past. She was possibly the daughter of a murderer, and if so, the same stigma that applied to that family would apply to her, never to be erased even in the face of evidence.

She had seen the effects of a criminal record on a family—businesses died, people refused to let their daughters marry into a family where someone had been arrested. Many had ended up on the streets after their businesses failed, selling off their children to singing houses or thief gangs. It sickened her to think that someone in Sanjin's position not only refused to recognize his own mistakes, but tormented others for them.

"What do you think of your hero now?" Yuli asked.

"He's not my hero," Jin replied.

"No, I suppose he's no one's hero," Yuli said. "But if you're valuable to him, you're about as privileged as it gets." She slurped the last of her rice from her bowl and washed it down with a helping of tea. "Enough about the suffering of the living. Let's get back to those who are fortunate enough to be dead."

THEY SPENT THE AFTERNOON TRYING TO FOCUS ON giving the dead form.

"Phantasms," Yuli spat. "Any flame can bring forth phantasms of the dead. But to bring them back with a body, with flesh, blood, something you can touch—now that takes power." She chewed on her lip. "Power most people don't have. I've only seen it once, and only fleeting, for a few heartbeats. Nearly killed the person, it did. But if you had the power of a dragon . . ." her eyes gleamed ". . . then you may change everything."

Yuli had Jin concentrate more on her chi, and on Rayshan's, visualizing herself as a funnel.

"Let's try to use someone familiar to you. That will be easier," Yuli said. "A mother? Father?"

Jin shook her head. "I didn't know my parents."

Yuli looked impatient. "Well, think of someone."

"I had a brother. Of sorts." Jin's voice tightened at the thought of Lu.

"He'll do," Yuli said briskly. "Now, think of every detail of how he looked. His face, hair, everything you can remember. Try to call him to you. Call him to you, and manifesting him will be easier."

Jin took a shuddering breath, not sure she wanted to see Lu. The guilt at her involvement in his death still pained her like a blow, and the sight of him standing before her just might break her. When she'd last seen him, she'd thought him a hallucination, but now, knowing she had really seen his spirit made it different.

"Ah, there is pain there. That is good," Yuli said. "Pull on that pain. He will hear your call."

Jin put a hand on Rayshan and felt him flare. Everything around them faded and blurred, then pinpricks of light were flowing around her, rushing toward Rayshan and coalescing.

A shape formed, watery at the edges, but then she recognized Lu's wide frame, his square face.

"Jin."

"Hold on to it," Yuli said. "Flare harder."

Can you flare more? Jin asked Rayshan.

Rayshan answered with a blast of light.

"Jin, you don't need saving again, do you?" Lu's tone was teasing but tinged with worry.

Jin's eyes filled with tears.

"Focus!" Yuli snapped. "Don't bend to the emotion.

Just let it flow through you. Don't try to make him say what you want him to say, or let your emotions cloud it. Just let him come through. Can you see the little pieces of him?"

Now that Yuli said it, Jin could see little motes around Lu, like shining fireflies. She tried to grasp them, to focus on them, but they danced out of her reach.

"Don't grab them, invite them," Yuli said.

"How?" Jin said, frustrated. "What's the difference?"

"You don't know the difference between grabbing and inviting?" Yuli scoffed. "Come now. Show the pieces of him that you are inviting them. Flare harder, Rayshan! This takes power, power only a dragon has!"

Jin repeated her words to Rayshan, who rumbled in his chest, but his flare grew brighter, and Lu slowly solidified.

"It's working!" Jin breathed. She could almost feel Lu filling out before her, his outline clearer against the background of the willows.

Yuli reached out, unsure, then placed her hand on Lu's shoulder, where it stayed—a solid hand upon a solid shoulder.

"You did it," Yuli breathed. "You manifested the dead!"

And then the flare died in Rayshan, and exhaustion soaked Jin like a thunderstorm. Lu crumbled to dust, his look of confusion the last thing Jin saw before dizziness took hold and she crashed to the ground.

CHAPTER 24

When Tai found Aadan waiting for him at his chambers, suggesting they have a bout of koshti, Tai couldn't have been more relieved. A sparring session with a friend was exactly what he needed to release his energy after a frustrating lesson with mage Situ Han, where he hadn't been able to make a pebble float in a glass of water, no matter how many measured circles he'd walked.

Even mage Situ Han seemed to have reached the end of his tether by the hour of the goat, his interest in Tai moving ever more toward the platter of lotus paste buns he had ordered to be brought.

Tai knew Aadan must have something he wanted to discuss, but Tai didn't mind. Anything to get his frustrations out.

"I've missed our sparring," Tai said.

Aadan nodded. "As have I. I hope you haven't become too soft in my absence?"

Tai grinned. "We'll find out."

They stripped down to their trousers and circled each other, then began trying to bring each other down. Tai was indeed rusty, and Aadan gave no quarter.

"No practicing, Your Highness?"

"Not with anyone brave enough to land a blow."

After half an hour of tackles and throws, Aadan called a break, and they retreated to the watering jug.

"You are different," Aadan said, taking a drink.

"In what way?"

Aadan glanced at him. "Just something has changed in you. Your energy."

Tai considered telling him about Situ Han and his magic lessons. But the whole thing seemed slightly treasonous and far-fetched, so he decided against it. Besides, he didn't want to get into explanations about the prophecy of a Mage Emperor and a Princess of Dragons, even if the whole thing was false.

"How is your father?" Tai asked instead, remembering Aadan had missed the Festival of Sevens.

"The same," Aadan answered. Tai had known Aadan and his family as long as he could remember. The old Persian had never stopped thinking about his rightful throne and homeland. "He'd like to offer the empress his help."

Tai kept his face free of skepticism. "That is much

appreciated. We need help from wherever we can get it. What did he have in mind?"

Aadan swallowed, and Tai knew the Persian had seen through him. "He has no army, true. But with only a few of the empire's squadrons from Dragon Class, we could defeat the Caliphate and have Persia back under our control. Throw our weight behind your mother."

Tai nodded. "I am sure you're right. But I suppose there's the law to get around."

"You mean not allowing Dragon Class to fight foreign wars?" Aadan said. "Surely these are exceptional circumstances."

He wasn't wrong.

"Tell me, if you were on the throne, would you break that rule?" Aadan asked.

Tai started. It seemed everyone was asking him what he would do once he was ruler, and the question was beginning to nettle him.

"I would do what needed to be done to win us allies. But whether going to Persia is the best choice, I really can't say. It's risky and involves two steps instead of one."

Aadan smiled. "Marriage does what war can't, as my mother says. Well then, who are you considering?"

Tai grimaced. "Parhae sent our envoy back without his body. There was no letter, but I interpret that as a no."

Aadan's eyes widened. "By the Wise Lord, the dogs have grown audacious."

"Very." Tai hadn't realized how many people resented his mother being on the throne. There were always the naysayers at home, but his mother had been empress since his birth. He had never experienced an emperor's rule, which meant he was only just appreciating what an anomaly his mother was. Her enemies here and abroad remembered the time of emperors and longed to reinstate that tradition.

"Then Champa?"

"They have problems of their own, and their army is no rich prize either," Tai said.

"What of Lady Meipin?" Aadan said. "Your mother always favored her."

"That's one option," Tai replied, non-committal. If one couldn't marry for love, a friend was better than a stranger, he supposed. "Or there's Nihhon, now that Parhae is lost."

Aadan nodded. "Well, I've heard the women there are very beautiful."

Tai snorted. "I don't want beauty. The last beautiful woman in my life . . . well, you know that disaster well."

"True. She was . . . not good for you," Aadan regarded Tai curiously. "So if not beauty, what do you want?"

"I'm in line for the Dragon Throne. What I want in a bride is irrelevant," Tai replied, keeping any tinge of bitterness out of his voice. The motto of throne above all grew less comfortable by the day since Gao's coup, and suddenly the future stretched before him in a long, painful series of joyless political calculations and sacrifices. "Speaking of wants, I sense you have something on your chest. Something besides sending Dragon Class to Persia."

His friend looked startled but didn't deny it as he brushed the water from his beard. "You're right."

Tai waited, letting Aadan find the words.

"I have a theoretical question for you."

Tai noted the forced casualness. "Theoretical? Careful, Aadan, you are becoming a true politician."

Aadan snorted, then seemed to turn a shade redder than their exercise warranted. "I was looking into the laws of Dragon Class. Article fifty-seven section nine states that Dragon Class riders may only marry those assigned them by the throne and need the head of Dragon Class's blessing."

Tai leaned against a pillar, arms crossed. "You have indeed been studious. And which noble lady is lucky enough to have your eye?"

"It's only theoretical," Aadan insisted. "If a woman was not of noble birth, would it be within your power to bend the rules?"

"And has this woman agreed?" Tai asked. "Theoretically."

Aadan cleared his throat. "Let's say yes."

"I'd have to know who this woman is. I can't in good conscience let a friend marry a heartbreaker, can I?"

Aadan laughed. "She isn't heartless."

"I thought this was theoretical."

"It is."

"Well, then . . ." Tai considered his words ". . . it would be up to my discretion, according to the law. Theoretically, of course."

Aadan nodded, seemingly encouraged by this.

Tai had known after the last Dragon Class geography test that Aadan harbored feelings for Jin, and even then, it had sparked a very sharp-clawed demon in him. He had hoped it would leave on its own, but he was learning that this particular demon intended to take up residence.

"While we're on the subject of marriage, I have a theoretical question for you," Tai said, pushing himself off the pillar.

"Certainly, Your Highness."

"I've been in heated debate with all the conservative advisers regarding the new laws we'll have to draft now that we have women in Dragon Class," Tai said, pulling his undershirt over his head. "Should we permit dragonriders to have relations with each other? Possibly even intermarry?"

A telltale mask fell over Aadan's features, and he seemed very busy knotting the inner sash of his undershirt. "It's a good question."

"And what would you advise?"

Aadan drew a breath. "I don't see why not."

"You don't?" Tai feigned surprise. "Mightn't it—complicate things?"

"True. So you're going to vote against it?"

"I haven't decided," Tai said, leaning an elbow on one knee. "I was hoping for some wisdom from an impartial friend."

The Persian sighed, then looked over with a regretful smile. "I'm afraid I can't say, Your Highness. I'm not impartial."

❀

AFTER PARTING WITH AADAN, TAI TRIED NOT TO TAKE out his pent-up frustrations on mage Situ Han and the lessons that followed, but failed.

His mother keeping him prisoner gave him a feeling of impotence that made him livid, and Aadan's conversation only made him more irate and miserable at the same time. He tried to tell himself it was simply jealousy that Aadan had the freedom to pursue whomever he chose. It had nothing to do with his friend's close relationship with Jin, a relationship that Tai didn't know much about and couldn't hope to replicate. Were they close? How close exactly?

There was nothing he could do about that, so he forced his thoughts back to the task at hand. The mage had explained to him that lightening something in water was far harder than in air, but this did little to ease his frustration. The mage suggested they work on heat and cold instead.

As he tried to focus on the walking circles he

performed around the cup of water, unsuccessfully trying for days to turn it to ice, he wrestled with the notion that he was powerless on all sides: with his mother, with his personal life, with magic.

"Your Highness is thinking of something else," mage Situ Han said, pelting him with a bun.

Anger flared in him. No one even considered touching the crown prince without permission, much less flinging food at him. He noted the oil stain the bun had left on his shoulder. How dare this man?

"Careful I don't have you flogged for disrespect," Tai said, brittle.

Mage Situ Han lifted a bushy brow. "Oh ho, like mother, like son, is it? My apologies, Prince Tai. I hadn't realized I had worn through your invincible charm barrier so soon. What bothers you today?"

Tai took a deep breath, berating himself for letting the mage get under his skin. "I apologize. I sometimes feel the burden of my station and let myself slip."

Mage Situ Han nodded, his voice thick with false sympathy. "Ah, yes, the burden of your station. Well, no one says you have to bear it, Your Highness. You can walk out of this palace and never look back."

Tai leveled him with a contemptuous frown. "You and I both know that's impossible."

"Impossible?" mage Situ Han chortled. "Reversing time is impossible. Making wood from ash is impossible. You escaping your mother and becoming a common hermit in the mountains? Very possible." He spread his fleshy hands. "In fact, I can help you devise a plan if that's what you'd like. Go and wander the mountains like some melodramatic poet. Or you could find good employ somewhere with the skills you have. At the very least, your looks mean you'd make a fine plaything for some rich noble who'd be eager to pay you to warm his bed."

Despite himself, Tai's mouth fell open.

"No one is forcing you to stay here and be prince, Your Highness," mage Situ Han said quietly. "You can walk away and never come back. Or you can stop pitying yourself, accept my instruction, and become a great emperor. A great Mage Emperor. All you need is a little magic."

"You don't think I can do that on my own, then?" Tai countered. Did his voice sound as peevish to Situ Han as it did to him?

"Of course you can," mage Situ Han said. "But a wise emperor will accept any advantage they can earn. And in uncertain times where we may have to face the likes of Mengkhis Lai again, you may be grateful for some mage skills." He paused and leaned back. "So, shall I make inquiries about available hermit huts, or shall we continue?"

Tai sighed inwardly. He turned back to the cup of water, focusing on his mai and clearing his mind as mage Situ Han had taught him, then began the familiar walking circle for what seemed the thousandth time.

He raged at it as he walked, but the water remained as liquid as ever.

"Try again," mage Situ Han instructed.

And so he walked another circle.

Again.

And again.

And again.

CHAPTER 25

*A*fter her collapse upon summoning Lu, Yuli gave Jin the rest of the day off, but called her back to training the following dawn with renewed vigor. It was as if Yuli's fire had been stoked, and Jin reminded herself that she had no time for rest, no matter her exhaustion. Her and Rayshan's survival at court depended on controlling their flare.

Jin trained with Rayshan day after day, focusing her chi as Yuli taught her, then calling Lu forth. Every day, she managed to manifest him more and more until he actually began to tease her.

"Aha! Good," Yuli said. "You are calling the life force forward that gave him his personality. That is truly manifesting."

But no matter how hard she tried, she couldn't manifest anyone else. She refused to try Haitao, knowing that she would only have to fight harder against the pain of his accusations. She would die before conjuring Gao. Jin became aware of how many people she disliked.

At one point, Yuli summoned someone from her past, but Rayshan could not make them manifest beyond a certain point.

"You have to take the final step, Jin," Yuli said. "I cannot harness Rayshan's power, as only you are bonded to him."

And so Jin tried harder. And ate more. Yuli kept ordering, day after day, more food to fuel their sessions, and never did a servant raise a complaint. Instead, they brought double what Yuli asked for, and Jin was surprised that they managed to eat it all. Yuli didn't seem to plump by even a single *liang*. Jin had the unpleasant thought that she was feeding the dead, that all the food simply went through her and Rayshan and into the souls who sought them out. It was like they were bottomless pits, mouthpieces for famished ghosts who could never be satiated.

Sanjin seemed to disappear for days at a time, and sometimes Jin thought she and Yuli practically had the run of the place. But even so, she often found herself too exhausted to explore, falling into deep sleep at the end of the day and even sometimes trying not to nod off during the lunch hour. Yuli, for her part, feared Sanjin so much that she never tried to escape. Jin had the feeling that the freedom was illusory anyway, as servants hovered in every hallway and outside every door, their soft shoes eerily silent.

On one of Sanjin's returns, he left a package wrapped in silk on her bed. She opened it to find several books on the theory of "human flames" and summoning the dead.

"These books are banned," Sanjin warned her the next day. "Take care you don't let others see you with them."

"Thank you," she said, surprised that Sanjin would let her have them.

Despite her exhaustion, she read through them each night. Most of it was anecdotes of flames who had summoned the dead, powerful shamans and others who had conjured the deceased, in the belief that appeasing ghosts could ease famines and disease. Occasionally she curled up next to Rayshan in the dragon stables, a structure built on solid wood pillars as high as regular roofs.

Most people who see the dead deny it, apparently.

He snorted. *You did, too, remember?*

Yes, well, I had very good reasons to believe I was losing my wits.

I will tell you when that happens.

Rayshan, she asked hesitantly, *why don't you ever want to summon the dead? Is there no one you would want to see?*

Who would I summon? His voice carried amusement.

We dragons don't form the attachments you do. We are solitary creatures.

Jin thought about what she knew of dragons, of Nine Claw Mountain, where the Dragon Queen lived, and where she chose the one hundred eggs that would be given to the Tang Empire. *Even the ones who are not chosen to serve the Tang Empire, the ones who stay in Nine Claw Mountain, don't form attachments either?*

Rayshan raised one eyelid. *In that sense I and the others in Dragon Class are lucky. We experience bonds that those in Nine Claw Mountain never will. Dragons mate, yes, but we don't mate for life. We don't look after our young. We are self-sufficient, or we die.*

I still say dragon ways are brutal.

Which is why I'm glad I was placed on the mountainside and entered Dragon Class.

What about the Firesong? You enter the Firesong to commune with other dragons.

We visit the past to survive, not for sentimental reasons. Perhaps it's easiest if you think of it as a dragon's library, there for everyone to use and learn from, but not because we are attached to everyone else there or want to revisit memories.

She had never thought of it like that, but it made sense. And it made Rayshan even more precious to her, for it made her realize that she was all he had.

Autumn deepened, and the Moon Festival drew near, along with the deadline for Jin and Rayshan to prove their control over their flare. The marquis informed Jin that he would be returning to the city to spend the night of the holiday with his family but instructed Jin and Yuli to continue training, for unless she could manifest Lu for more than a few heartbeats, she would have failed.

For her part, Jin couldn't help but despise the holiday.

Remember, you do have family, Rayshan said, nudging her with his nose. They were in the hunting grounds behind Sanjin's house, where the marquis kept an endless supply of deer and wild boar. Rayshan had fed and was now wading into a large lake to scatter fish with his tail.

Jin looked up at him, smiling. *Of course. You are the best family I could ask for. It's just . . .*

Moon Festivals at the Red Crows' headquarters had been a time of great celebration, where Haitao pulled out the stops and let the wine and food flow freely—or at least as freely as someone of Haitao's discipline would allow, once they had done their pocket-picking. For festivals meant drunk people in the darkened alleys who had purses to lose, and crowded streets were the Buddha's gift to thieves.

But after they had stolen their quotas and handed their takings to Haitao's wiry accountant, they would gather in the courtyard in the early hours of the morning with a precious few moments to pass moon cakes around, each filled with lotus paste and delicious, rich egg yolks as round as the moon itself. And though no one had blood ties, for that night and New Year's, everyone put aside their squabbles and suspicions, their jealousies and their dislike of each other, and pretended they were a normal family celebrating autumn.

Jin was unprepared for the loneliness that swept her. Last year, she had merely been alone during the Moon Festival. But this year, she knew everyone in her thief clan was dead.

Jin left Rayshan to return to her quarters and see if she could convince the skeleton staff there to draw up a meal. Yuli drifted in shortly after as dusk settled, cradling a bottle of wine.

"Can't celebrate alone, can I?" The woman's gruff tone, Jin sensed, was a bandage over loneliness and fear.

Jin laid out what furniture she could. Just as she had moved a round table under a willow, the doors flew open, and a familiar voice cried out to the clapping of hands.

"Happy Mid-Autumn Festival, Jin!"

Meipin swept in with a swirl of silk and chiffon in complementing layers of peach, chestnut, and pale green. Silver rabbits and hairpins carved into moons adorned her elaborate hair in honor of the festival, and a scarlet paper cutting of a crescent sat between her brows.

Ahlu and a retinue of servants followed, each dressed luxuriously and each with rabbit- or moon-shaped jewelry in their ears and hair pieces.

"Meipin? What are you doing here?"

"I knew the marquis would keep you imprisoned over the holidays, and I thought I'd come visit," she said. She glanced at Yuli, and Jin thought it a testament to her diplomacy that she didn't flinch at the woman's scars. "I'm not intruding?"

"Of course not," Jin said, quietly elated. She turned. "This is Yuli, my . . . teacher."

"Honored." Meipin dipped her head. "This unworthy woman is Wei Meipin."

Jin went to find more chairs but discovered that Ahlu and the servants had already wordlessly raided the rooms and brought out what stools and tables they could find.

Meipin had brought delicacies in hot baskets, cold noodles in fine soups, dumplings with skins so delicate Jin thought she would see through them, and a feast of dishes that included wine-soaked chicken, braised pig trotter, whole duck roasted in honey, and baskets of steamed crabs along with glutinous rice overflowing with chestnuts and pieces of salted egg.

Bowls and chopsticks were found, along with wine cups, and soon, the whole party of women were seated and laughing. Meipin had brought her stringed *pipa* with her and sang songs on it, substituting more and more words as the night deepened so that the lyrics became bawdy and the laughter that followed grew ever more raucous.

Jin had not relaxed like this for a long time. The only thing missing, she felt with a pang, was Aadan.

"I know that look." Meipin tuned the pegs on her pipa as the surrounding women began bringing out great platters of moon cakes and melon seeds. "A certain rider had to go home to his family. Besides, this was a bit of a last-minute idea."

Jin looked around at the feast and guests, incredulous. "This was last minute?"

Meipin shrugged modestly. "I know how to make things happen."

"Thank you," Jin said sincerely.

Meipin grinned. "The palace is dull without you. I'd rather be here than over there." She arched one finely blackened eyebrow. "And to be honest, I think a certain prince feels the same way, so his loss."

Jin made a face. "You and your rumor-mongering. I shall be there at your hundred-day ceremony to toast the son you have with Prince Tai."

It was Meipin's turn to make a face. "A beautiful son we would make, I am sure, but I don't look forward to it. It'll ruin my figure."

Jin smiled, then asked, "What does go on back at court? Has there been news of Emar?" She had been away so long and so engrossed in training that she knew nothing of what was happening in Parhae or with Ulagan.

Meipin hit a chord on her pipa and pursed her lips. "No one knows if Emar's still alive. But my uncle thinks there's a good chance he is. My uncle says Mengkhis would likely wish to kill Emar personally, and Ulagan probably knows that."

"Where is Ulagan now?" Jin asked, voice tight.

"Best guess is off the edge of Bohai still," Meipin said. "There have been reports of attacks along the coast, an invisible monster eating the village livestock."

"Do people know it's Baikalan?"

Meipin shook her head. "No one is allowed to speak of it. All the messages are coded. I only know because my uncle lets me sit in on his briefings."

Jin's throat closed. She thought back to Jimo and the destruction she had seen there, and her heart went out to the villages being attacked by something the empress wouldn't explain to them or let them understand. If they knew, then they at least had a chance to defend themselves.

"How goes the training here?" Meipin asked, glancing at Yuli. Jin's teacher was in an intense game of chess, surrounded by onlookers whispering amongst each other as to the best moves.

Jin sighed. "I don't know. I am making progress, but then sometimes I wonder if my ability will help anyone."

"Of course it will," Meipin said. "You can start by

bringing back my second cousin." At Jin's confused look, she added, "He helped ban women from the only calligraphy academy that allowed female students."

Jin frowned. "And you'd want me to bring him back?"

"Absolutely," Meipin said, as if this should be obvious. "I want to tell him to his face that he's a son of a turtle and see his expression when I say I've made the academy headmaster lift the ban."

Jin stared at her for a moment, then both of them burst out laughing.

"Trust me, you have a powerful gift," Meipin said.

Jin took a breath. "An unusual gift."

"Then it suits you, girl rider Wang Kway Jin. You are nothing if not unusual."

"That's not a compliment."

Meipin plucked a chord, making a reproachful sound. "If someone gifts you a horse, ride it, don't complain of its teeth."

Jin smiled.

A cheer rose from the chess corner, where Yuli had apparently won her game and was collecting the winnings. Meipin strummed the pipa again, striking up the melancholy tune "Farewell" by the poet Du Mu. Drunken applause broke out from the guests as they drifted over and found seats. Meipin called out to Ahlu to join in, and after much encouragement, the servant's voice rose in answer to Meipin's.

My feelings are many, yet I show none,
The wine is sweet, yet no smile can I summon.
So warm, the candle, unlike our goodbye,
And in tears we dissolve, till sun kisses sky.

Jin's heart continued to sting long after the last mournful note had faded.

THOUGH JIN WISHED MEIPIN COULD STAY LONGER, SHE knew her friend had her own parents to see back in Changan, and she reluctantly farewelled her the morning after the Moon Festival.

"Whatever goal Sanjin has set for you, finish it soon so you can come back," Meipin said sternly, hugging her. "It's not good for my social status to have you so far away."

Jin grinned at the joke. She had, when she first met Meipin, resisted her friendship because of suspicions that Meipin simply wanted to use the novel female rider as a talking piece or tool to advance women. Jin now knew she had been wrong.

Sanjin ordered Jin and Yuli to train harder than ever, dropping by to watch with an impassive face that always made Yuli falter in her instructions. In the final week of their training, Yuli was clearly as exhausted as Jin. "If you can hold a manifestation for one minute, you will be the strongest flame in the empire.

"Don't focus only on the physical. Sometimes it's a feeling, a personality trait that made them who they are," Yuli said. "Focus on that, and they will build themselves around it, like a skeleton."

"Is that what you do?"

Yuli shrugged. "Well, I've never been able to do it, remember. But my mother did. And she always said, 'Think of the person's essence. If you had to reduce them to one word, what would it be?'"

Jin thought on this, the one word that described Lu. She thought back to all their childhood memories together—of him pulling her from the river, tending her wounds, telling her his dreams of opening a tavern, lying to Haitao and saying that he had killed that thief, not Jin, in order to save her from Haitao's wrath and put his own plan in motion.

Hope.

Lu had always hoped that he would change his fate, and others'. He had always believed that there was a better life for him—and for her—out there. He had insisted she hope when she had stopped doing so at a very young age.

She drew a breath. *Let's try again.*

Rayshan rumbled his response and flared.

Jin focused on the hope that Lu had given her, buoying her. Lu flickered into vision before her, and she reached out to touch him. He was solid, his shoulder firm and his head towering over hers, with that familiar sweep of hair and that grin.

"I could get used to being alive again," he said.

She laughed, tears springing to her eyes.

"But then you'd have to quit dragon riding and come mind an inn with me," he said.

Yuli poked him hard in the arm.

Lu grabbed her by the wrist, eliciting a slap from Yuli, but Jin managed to separate them. "No hitting! And no slapping the dead, it's disrespectful."

"Too true," Lu agreed. "Are you going to eat that?"

He bit into the orange she had brought for Rayshan, but then shook his head in disappointment. "It's not the same." He tossed it to Rayshan, who snapped it in one bite. "Thank you for saving Jin."

Rayshan whipped his tail in response and said to Jin, *I didn't even know I was doing it.*

"So, Jin the dragonrider," Lu said, smiling. "It suits you."

"It's not what I could have expected or imagined," she replied.

"No. All from that heist at the viceroy's."

Jin turned to Yuli. "Could you give us a few moments?" A persistent ache was twisting its way from her head down her neck, and she knew she had little time.

Yuli frowned, clearly worried their deadline was closing.

"We have manifested Lu, for over a minute now. I think Sanjin will let you keep your pardon," she said. "Please. Just a few moments."

Yuli nodded and busied herself with the remainder of the food as Jin and Lu walked toward the bamboo grove.

As they walked, they reminisced over old times and talked about what could have been, about Haitao's death and those of their clan: Mole and Fox and Mikang.

"Will you bring them back too?"

Jin twisted the thread on her cloak. "I hadn't thought about it. This is all new."

He nodded. "Want my advice?"

"No," she said.

"Good, here it is. Don't bring them back. And perhaps you shouldn't bring me back again either."

She looked at him, surprised. "Why not? I'd keep you here forever if I could."

He smiled but then indicated her temple. "You have new lines on your face. This has cost you. Manifesting the past—there's likely a reason it's a dark art, Jin."

Jin shook her head as if she could fight the exhaustion that was creeping on her. "I'd take a thousand wrinkles."

"What if every line was a year of your life?" Lu said quietly.

"I can't die," Jin said. "After Rayshan brought you back that first time, I—I changed. I can't die by normal means."

Lu regarded her, surprised. "You're serious. Well, I suppose some would say that's a blessing. Even more reason to live your life, ride your dragon." He looked over at Rayshan, who was flaring gently as he lay against the grass. "Because what's the point of always flying the skies of yesterday, when you can be flying those of today?"

"I didn't think I'd miss our past," she admitted.

"Me neither," Lu said, then grimaced. "Your present life must truly be terrible."

She laughed, and the tears overcame her. She sniffled as she wiped at her eyes.

"Look," Lu said, putting his hands on her shoulders, "if you need me, little sister, you'll always find me. But I'd rather live on as a memory than return as a recreation of myself."

He stepped back. Even as she tried to fight, she could feel him crumbling, feel his life force slipping from her and scattering. And though she knew he was right, that she shouldn't cling to the past, so many of the answers she sought lay buried with the dead.

CHAPTER 26

Sanjin didn't display any emotion at Yuli's excited report about Jin's progress. Instead, the next day he ordered Jin and Rayshan to follow him to a large training yard on the west side of the compound, where racks of weapons lined the walls, and a light layer of sand covered the floor.

"Where's Yuli?" Jin asked as Rayshan flared his nostrils and took in the surroundings. A heavy smell of sweat, wood, and sand permeated the courtyard, as if ingrained.

"I want to see if you and Rayshan can flare and summon the dead on your own without her," he said. She reached out to Rayshan when Sanjin held up a hand. "She tells me you aren't capable of manifesting more than two people at a time. Is that true?"

Jin nodded. They had tried once, after she had summoned Lu, but doubling the effort had meant only phantasms appeared, rather than flesh-and-blood versions.

"Very well," Sanjin said. "Then find someone specific. A general from Parhae."

Jin looked at Rayshan and relayed the message, then asked the question in both her and her dragon's minds. "Did you know him?"

Sanjin shook his head. "But his reputation was great."

What would happen if she failed to summon who Sanjin sought? "We haven't yet tried to reach someone we do not know."

"Then it's good we're trying now, isn't it?" the marquis said tersely.

Very well, Rayshan said. *Let's start with a name.*

"His name?"

"Admiral Chang Ren. From what I understand, a giant of a man. Missing an eye from a campaign against Nihhon."

Jin drew a breath. Name, appearance. It was less than what she and Rayshan had in the past, and she hoped it would work. She placed her hand on Rayshan, and he flared, bright and strong. The surrounding courtyard darkened and blurred at the edges, and everything seemed to hum with life.

Motes swirled and danced, converging on Rayshan, but she knew none were who she sought. She sifted through, searching, rejecting those that came. Some were more forceful than others, but she had grown more adept at avoiding their grasp.

He doesn't want to be found.

Rayshan's comment made sense. Parhae. She thought of the little she'd learned during their history classes, and wished she had Aadan's skill for retaining facts. She remembered some city names, maps of the sea by Parhae's coast, and the motes around her scattered, drawn away, while others flooded in. Jin focused, picturing a one-eyed giant, someone who sailed and lived at sea, being an admiral.

It seemed Rayshan's flare would go out, but suddenly, she saw a cluster of motes forming, shaping into a torso and then into a man. She funneled all her energy into this cluster, and Rayshan, sensing her attention, flared even harder.

A man stood before Sanjin in the training ground, his expression one of suspicious bewilderment.

Sanjin, however, smiled. "Admiral Chang Ren, I presume?"

The man turned to look at Sanjin. "Are we in Han lands?"

"You're in China, and I am head of the Royal Veil," Sanjin said. "I have need of you and your expertise."

Rayshan growled. His flare was weakening, and Sanjin seemed to sense it.

"Why would I offer anything to Han scum?" the general spat.

"Because you died at the battle at the Parhae border due to some very poor choices on your leader's part,"

Sanjin said. "Commander Guling has excellent taste in ship décor but a poor grasp of geography, no?"

The general's face soured. "You are telling me I am dead?"

Jin felt a stab of sympathy for the man.

"Unfortunately, yes," Sanjin said. "But on the positive side, we will be engaging Parhae and your good General Guling again. I'd like to know what tactics they tend to use at sea."

"I'll not sell out my country," admiral Chang Ren growled.

"The king of Parhae is about to unleash Mengkhis Lai," Jin cut in, eliciting a cold stare from Sanjin. But she didn't care. That ache had started again, signaling that her strength was flagging and, with it, their time. "Do you know what he will do to Parhae if he is freed?"

The admiral scowled. "You lie."

"I wish she did," Sanjin said. "Being female, Rider Jin is prone to believe that men might wish to do good by the world. But I urge you to think about how Guling treated you."

Chang Ren spat once again. "Freeing Mengkhis Lai would be a fool's goal. If it's expertise you want, then you'll have it. The navy is well trained but has few ships. They'll try to move by night, if possible, under stealth to gain the advantage. I've told you about all I know. And if I've found you've lied to me—"

But Rayshan gave a puff of breath, and his flare

died. Chang Ren collapsed into the sand, his ash mingling with the grains there at Jin's feet.

"Well done," Sanjin said crisply. "I think I can convince the empress to keep you both." He turned to leave the training grounds.

Anger welled in Jin. "We're not a puppy."

The marquis stopped and turned, walking back to her. Jin refused to flinch.

"True," Sanjin agreed. "You're not nearly as well trained, and you're far larger. Otherwise, I think it best you don't think too highly of yourself. You are a useful tool, and as long as you are useful, you will have a place in the empire and the comforts it brings. Don't make the empress or me think that you're more trouble than you're worth." Anger coursed through her, and he held her gaze as if deliberately allowing her time to calm herself. "I feel like we are becoming friends, and I don't want to have to show you the extensive arsenal I keep for my enemies. Are we friends?"

Jin didn't answer, and Rayshan bared his teeth.

"I suppose that will do," he said. "Every friendship has rocky patches. Now, we'll be returning immediately to the palace."

He turned once more to go, and this time Jin and Rayshan followed.

"With Yuli?" Jin asked.

"Yuli is gone," he said without looking at her.

Jin stared. "What do you mean, gone?"

"I dismissed her. Her services are no longer needed."

"Is she safe?" Jin demanded.

Sanjin stopped walking and turned to face her. "Not that it's your right to question me," he answered coolly. "But, yes, she is safe. And has been well rewarded."

"With coin?" Jin asked.

"Something better," Sanjin answered. "Her life."

Jin bristled at this and made to argue, but Sanjin cut her off.

"You can find her in her usual quarter in the eastern temple district if you don't believe me. But that's for your own time. Right now you're on mine." With that, he swept past the archway leading to the grounds, calling for servants to attend to Jin and Rayshan.

She returned to her room to find her few belongings packed into the carriage attached to a great bronze dragon waiting in the main courtyard. The same riders who had escorted them here would escort them back to the palace, she saw. Jin mounted Rayshan, who stretched his wings appreciatively.

It has been too long since we've flown, he complained.

Lu's words came back to her, and she felt a pang. *Yes, it's true.*

For during the last two months, while they had practiced their flaring, Rayshan could barely focus on anything else. Yuli had hinted that one day, he might not need his full concentration while flaring and would even learn to fly while flaring. But until they had practiced many more hours, flaring would require Rayshan's full attention while he stood still or even lay down.

They flew through the autumn countryside, the grass now blazing with yellows and reds. The harvests were being taken in, and everywhere, there were signs of preparation for winter.

At one point, Rayshan broke rank to do a stomach-churning loop in the air, which unsettled the other dragons but made Jin's heart roar with joy.

THEY RETURNED TO CHANGAN AND LANDED IN THE Blood Oval to the welcome of several of the students. They flooded out of the dorms to greet the arrivals, some even hailing Jin, and she saw a few female recruits lining the banisters of the second floor, craning their necks for a glimpse of her.

Aadan was there, and Jin's heart lurched at the grin that lit his face when he saw her, even though he quickly suppressed it. She wondered if she'd ever tire of that look, of knowing that he smiled for her. And though she still smarted from their argument, she couldn't deny she had missed him.

Go, Rayshan harrumphed knowingly. *I'll wait for you.*

She worked her way through the students until she

reached Aadan. They stood, trying not to drink each other in, and failing.

"You've missed much," he said stiffly. His voice lowered and seemed to catch. "And been missed."

She searched his eyes, and even she couldn't mistake the tender hunger there. For a moment, the future didn't matter, just the now. "I've missed you too."

His smile warmed her, but then he frowned. "You look . . . tired."

She knew he was referring to the lines of her face. "It's been a strange couple of months."

"Indeed. Come to the mess hall. We can make the excuse you need something to eat before the meeting."

"What meeting?"

"A strategy meeting on the offensive against Ulagan." His face darkened. "And Parhae as well. You heard they joined forces?"

"He means to sail his troops down and free Mengkhis?" Somehow, through all this training, she had managed to keep the king of Khitan and his plans at the back of her mind. But now, being back here, it pulled everything to the fore again. She was only being trained so she could help defeat Baikalan and King Ulagan.

Well, if she could sink a sword into the man who had tried to kill her, she'd be happy to do it.

She went to Dragon City with Rayshan, removing his saddle and making sure his quarters were clean before hurrying back to the mess hall to meet Aadan.

They piled their plates with stewed pork and black beans, and for a while she let herself enjoy the peace of just being near him again.

A memory surfaced of how Emar had shown her this mess hall a year ago when she had entered as a hunched-over, quiet and scared girl who had had the audacity to bond to a dragon and now found herself in a man's world. And she had been astounded at the fact that food was here for all, generous meals provided to the Dragon Class initiates who would defend the empire.

Then, it had all seemed like some far-flung impossibility.

Now, she was being called upon to do exactly that, to defend the empire, while other girls, new to this space, jostled in the doorways or just out of sight to catch a glimpse of Jin, still apparently too shy to join her at the table.

And Emar . . . she pushed the thought away. Imagining whether Emar was even still alive made her ill.

Jao and Panshalar joined them soon afterward. Jin noted that Panshalar had regained much of his weight and seemed almost as strong as before the attack. Jao stayed quiet as per usual for much of the time, but then curiosity won out.

"How was Marquis Sanjin's summer home? I hear he takes the best of the Royal Veil to train there."

Jin swallowed a mouthful of shredded potato, then heaped pickled cucumber and diced eel into her bowl.

"He's rich, if that is your question. But I didn't see much of it."

"You can't have been working as hard as us," Panshalar said. "The training for this upcoming war has been brutal. I can't walk without pain."

"That's from your injury, you melon," Jao replied. "The rest of us are fine."

"You weren't so fine in the pool," Aadan said lightly, clasping several slices of duck egg with his chopsticks. "Could barely keep up."

Jin dropped the morsel she had been about to eat and quickly speared it in her bowl. "You're training in the pool?"

Panshalar nodded. "The prince has ordered daily swimming lessons. In case we fall into the sea."

Aadan smiled reassuringly. "You will be fine. You learn quickly."

Her doubts reached Rayshan, however, for he stirred in her mind.

Do not be anxious. If the men can do it, so can you.

They never had to fight their way out of a submerged cage.

Even more proof that you are tougher.

"Jin, you know where the pools are, right?" Aadan was looking at her in a way that made her realize she had missed his question the first time.

She nodded. "I'll find it. There's something I have to do first."

CHAPTER 27

When Jin arrived at the war room for the meeting and finished her formal bows to the empress, she looked around her at the gathering of military men, along with the war hero Oyang Kang. She had only met him once when she had first arrived at Dragon Class, but since then, she had heard—and read—the stories of his and his black dragon's prowess on the field.

Sanjin and Prince Tai were both there, along with a short man with a chest wide as a wine vat and a face that reminded her of riverboat workers who plied the canals. A large map was stretched on an ornate wooden rack, showing Tang China, the Bohai Sea, Parhae, and Nihhon in various colors.

"I was saying to Commander Oyang that we'd like him and Commander in chief Zheng to take over the offensive as soon as possible," the empress said. "We have word that the Khitan king is amassing at the port of Anshi with ships from Parhae."

Jin looked over at Zheng. A naval commander in chief. That explained the weathered face.

Oyang Kang nodded. "Yes, it's quite a force. We narrowly escaped an attack on the way back."

"No sign of Emar?" the empress asked.

Oyang Kang shook his head. "He's likely dead by now."

The empress's lips tightened. "He might not be. They may keep him alive to let Mengkhis do the deed."

The mention of Mengkhis was enough to chill any other warm thoughts in the room.

"Do we have enough dragons and riders to take down the ships?" Tai asked.

Oyang Kang shrugged. "It depends on the ships. Only a quarter of our dragons are military. The rest have not seen real battle. Even the messengers are not experienced against armed ships."

"And because it's a sea operation," Sanjin added. "Our dragons cannot land."

Jin reached out to Rayshan. They had never been over large bodies of water, it was true.

Our wings make it difficult to get to the surface, though not impossible.

"How many seaworthy vessels do we have that can act as dragon carriers or landing docks?" Sanjin pressed.

Commander in chief Zheng's voice was quiet for such a thickset man. "Two at most."

Two? Jin was no naval expert, but that sounded paltry, and she thought she detected a whiff of rebuke in Zheng's voice.

"That's not nearly enough," Tai said. "Can our navy repel the Parhae ships unaided by Dragon Class?"

Again, the commander's voice was soft, his expression admirably devoid of any blame. "Under normal circumstances, yes. But the enemy has an invisible dragon in the skies. We cannot fight Baikalan and the Parhae forces, I am afraid."

"Can Jin provide us with an army?" the empress asked Sanjin.

Zheng cleared his throat. "Aren't such things dark arts, Your Majesty?"

"Dark times call for dark arts," the empress replied curtly. "Now, Marquis, can she or can she not summon an army?"

Sanjin didn't even glance at Jin before shaking his head. She resented being treated like a disappointing pet dog, but kept silent. "So far, it seems she is capable of summoning and giving substance to one person, but not several."

The empress hissed in frustration.

"Your Majesty," Tai said, "it seems our problem is not a lack of soldiers. Our problem is a lack of ships."

"I did summon one of the more senior Parhae generals, Your Majesty," Jin said, grateful for Tai's defence. "And he did give us advice as to how Parhae now favors moving their ships." She glanced at the commander in chief. "He said that the navy prefers to travel at night to avoid detection and outright combat."

Sanjin nodded. "If that's the case, they will try to slip by the Bohai neck and into open sea under the cover of night."

Commander Zheng frowned. "You're suggesting attacking at night?"

"It might work to our advantage," Tai said. He walked to the map and pointed at a spot in the Bohai where a protrusion from Tang lands reached out and almost met a similar protrusion from Parhae. "This neck of the peninsulas allows our dragons to travel less distance by sea. If we surprise the enemy at night, make it a quick operation, then we won't have a protracted fight where we risk losing our dragons due to fatigue or injury that sees them fall into the water. For once they do, we will be hard-pressed to rescue them."

"Your thoughts, Commander Zheng?" the empress asked.

"Any plan that relies less on the few sea hawk warships we have," Zheng said, "the better."

"Marquis Sanjin," Tai said, "it would be prudent to see if we can confirm that the Parhae navy will indeed sail by night. Do we know how many ships Parhae is readying?"

"My informants say a third of their force is in port,

Your Highness," Sanjin said. "So twelve warships in total."

Tai turned to Oyang. "How many wings would you need to take on twelve warships?"

Oyang thought on it. "A smaller force might be best, as we will be able to move in and out faster if time is an issue. I would say we need two squads, one to fight the ships and another to deal with Baikalan, for I am sure he will be our greater threat."

Jin added this up in her head. Two squads meant thirty dragons, which would have been more than enough for twelve ships. Except, of course, that they had to contend with Baikalan.

"You shall have them," the empress said.

AFTER THE MEETING, JIN HEADED STRAIGHT TOWARD THE Halls of Justice.

Are you sure you want to do this? Rayshan asked.

Yes.

Your birth does not define you.

No, but our past feeds our present.

Aadan already told you he didn't care about your birth, didn't he?

I sometimes dislike that you know me so well. Rayshan had touched on one hope: that if Gao had been wrong about her, then at least she wouldn't have to worry about bringing shame to Aadan. *But I want to know for myself.*

Rayshan sighed. *Human folly. I won't pretend to understand it. But I will support you if this is what you want.*

She made her way to the courtyard and showed her Dragon Class seal, remembering the day last year when Emar had first given it to her. The guard looked at her curiously but ushered her in. When she reached the clerk, a bent man with papery skin and a beard cut in a neat square looked up at her as if she must be lost.

"This is the Records Office, Rider," he said.

"Yes, I know. I'm looking up a record. Of a criminal."

He frowned, then wrote out on a piece of paper a series of words and a number. He held it out. "Down the hall, follow the signs for criminal justice records."

She took the paper and read it, then followed his directions. Lanterns glowed even during the day, and the place smelled of paper, ink, wood, and dust. She entered a wide room at the end of the hall, where a clerk in a pressed blue robe motioned for her to sit in a chair and wait. She saw no one else in line but sat obediently.

After a long time, the clerk looked up. The surprise on his face showed he hadn't realized she was female.

"Oh, Rider Jin."

Jin started. She wasn't used to others knowing her

name, and she hadn't the faintest idea who this person was.

"What can this humble servant do for you?"

She held out her piece of paper. "I'm looking for court records from the Year of Chaos. Criminal records of a woman by the name of Lan Ming."

"Anything else? Crime? Punishment?" the clerk asked. At her lost look, he explained, "Everything gets recorded here, and the more information I have, the better chance I have of finding it. You have a year, that's good. Crime would give me another start."

"She was executed for murdering her husband."

"Ah." The clerk cleared his throat and stared at the paper. "That's helpful. I'll see what I can find. I'll need at least three days to check; we do have so many records."

She hid her disappointment. "Of course. I'll come back in three days."

"I'll send you a message," the clerk suggested. "It will save you a trip back."

She nodded. "Thank you."

"Peace upon your evening, Rider Jin."

She left him scratching out a note on a cream-colored piece of paper and wondered at the smell she sensed as she exited. The clerk smelled of fear, which struck her as odd.

CHAPTER 28

The Dragon City pools were a large building in the southeast of the complex, consisting of three pools on three different levels, with the highest one flowing into the second and the second flowing into the third. The floors were of the smoothest marble, while mosaics of leaping fish and boats with multi-colored banners covered the walls, so vivid that Jin almost expected them to sail off into the water.

Jin walked in, her leathers conspicuous in a room where everyone had stripped down to their inner cotton trousers. Aadan stood a head taller than the others, and she tried to avert her eyes.

The hollering began almost immediately, and for a moment, she regretted going to the records office first instead of seeking out the swimming instructor. But she hoped that the men's reactions would help with her proposal.

The swimming instructor, Master Xi, was a giant of a man with a thick goatee and a body that seemed as wide as Jin was tall. He frowned down at her. "You expecting to ride a dragon here?"

Jin bowed, trying to ignore the looks of the other riders. She noticed three who had been close with Madu, Gao's nephew and another firm opponent of her entering Dragon Class last year. Aadan, Jao and Panshalar, she saw, were glaring warnings at the others.

"Master, I know the basics of swimming, but I'd like your permission to train at a different time, alone."

The man's lip curled. "No one advised me I was to be a private trainer for a coddled princess. I was told you're a rider, so you'll train like a rider. There's a spare pair of trousers in the basket there—" he pointed toward a reed basket on a bench, "and you can cover your *mantou* with your inner garment."

Snickers erupted around them, and Master Xi barked for silence.

Jin's cheeks burned. She was less insulted by his slur about her breasts than she was by his insinuation that she wanted special treatment due to her character flaws, and not the men's. She bowed and stalked toward the private bathing quarters, snatching a pair of trousers on her way.

When she returned in the loose cotton trousers, with their slits up the thighs, and her strapless under-bodice, she was relieved that most of the riders were already in the water. She quickly found Aadan, Jao, and Panshalar and slid in next to them, trying to ignore the leers, as well as the cold panic that coiled in her belly at being in the water. At least it was shallow enough so she could stand.

"Like last lesson, I want to see you swim to the end and back," the instructor barked, crossing his meaty arms. "Rider Jin, you have missed multiple lessons. Can you put your face in the water? No? Aadan, your job is to make sure she can swim to the other side by the end of class."

When the instructor had moved away to bark at another rider's technique, Aadan turned to her.

"Ignore them," Aadan said, pushing the wet hair off his face. "Here, let's practice by the wall before you try swimming on your own."

She nodded, though the feel of the water was enough to make her prickle with fear. She had always enjoyed submerging her head in baths, but this was different. The cold of the water and the depth seemed to take her right back to that terrifying day in the river.

"I won't let anything happen to you," Aadan reassured her. He motioned with his arms. "Like this: one, then the other."

She mimicked him, slicing the water with her arms.

"Good, but keep your fingers together like this." He reached forward and closed his fingers around hers. His touch sent a jolt through her. "You're creating a paddle."

They practiced a few more times, and Jin had the impression that Aadan was trying to avoid looking at her bare arms and shoulders. "Think you can manage to try swimming the length of the pool?"

She took a deep breath. The end of the pool was several lengths of a dragon. She shook her head.

"Take your time," Aadan said.

They tried small distances. But even by the end of class, Jin couldn't swim the whole way without panic seizing her like a dragon's jaws, and she would make an undignified scramble for the side of the pool.

"Save yourself some time and let her sink, Persian!" one of Madu's cronies called out. His laughter was cut short by Panshalar's fist hitting his jaw.

"Sorry, brother," Panshalar said, rubbing his knuckles. "A slip of the hand."

Jao nodded to Jin in quiet encouragement. She felt a stab of gratitude for them. Could these really be the same people who had ridiculed her on her first day in Dragon Class?

"It's not about strength, Rider," Master Xi said, standing over her after her fifth try. "It's about technique. You'd better hope you improve, or you'll be turtle fodder if you fall over the Bohai Sea."

As they all pulled themselves from the pool to head to the changing quarters, Aadan gave Jin an encouraging glance, but she saw the sullen condescension from some of the other riders, particularly the one Panshalar had hit.

A wave of frustration rolled over her, and even Rayshan's comforting hums in her head couldn't dispel it. She could summon the dead, but she couldn't do a simple thing that others found easy.

Everyone has different mountains to climb. You will climb this in your own way, Rayshan told her.

Yes, well, I'm running out of time for this one.

"RIDER JIN, I HAVE BEEN LOOKING FOR YOU."

She turned to see Oyang Kang leaning in the cave entry. She had come here to be with Rayshan and tend to his scales, claws, and teeth, as well as work past the frustration of her humiliating swimming lessons. After a week, her panic in the water had only deepened, fueling more jibes from riders outside her wing.

Out of official dress, Oyang Kang looked just like she remembered him the first time she had seen him, striding into the mess hall. Only this time, he didn't have his entourage, and his hair wasn't as windswept but combed hurriedly into a bun and wrapped with blue silk. He wore trousers under the usual rider leathers, and the scar across his eyebrow stood out after a full summer's sun.

"You found me, Rider Oyang," Jin said.

He strode into the cave, gazing at Rayshan in admiration. "A jade. Incredible. I have heard much about you, each story more astounding than the last. Especially this one that you are a flame."

"Rayshan, not I," Jin corrected him. "I am merely the vessel."

Oyang smiled. "Modesty. Wonderful in women and heroes."

She tensed, unsure where this was going. She didn't like not knowing another's agenda.

He chuckled. "You are becoming quite the legend. Your stories are being retold. I hear of girls asking to join Dragon Class. It is refreshing, inspiring even. I don't think even I have been able to inspire such interest in Dragon Class."

Jin shrugged. "I don't seek it out."

"No, I imagine you don't," Oyang said. "But here we are, two heroes."

"I wouldn't call myself that."

"It doesn't matter what you call yourself. Others call you a hero," Oyang said. "A lot to live up to."

"For now, I'll settle for just living, Rider Oyang," Jin said. "Did you come find me to offer me advice on heroism?"

He chuckled again and uncrossed his arms. One hand reached back to rub his neck in an almost self-conscious gesture. "No, I actually came to ask a favor."

Jin waited.

"I wondered whether Rayshan—you—could help me communicate with someone."

She cursed under her breath. She should have

predicted that people would come to her for this. Meipin had joked of it, but others would surely, like Oyang Kang, have real requests. Was this her future, being sought out as some Lady Yuli? "I'm not sure I'm the right one. I mean, I'm not sure that's what I'm—"

"Please," Oyang said, voice soft. "I lost a brother in Parhae, and I just want to see him again."

Lu's warning flashed in her mind, and she asked Rayshan for his thoughts.

If we give in to him, what's to stop us from doing this for everyone?

Jin thought on it. There was no rule against using Rayshan's gift for private purposes, but she didn't want everyone running to her to do the same.

"Please, for a fellow rider. I will only ask this once."

"Rider Oyang, it is not my place to advise you, but I don't think you should do this."

He stood there, clearly trying to think of what to say. A voice spoke in Jin's mind. The voice told her that Oyang had not been himself and was being eaten by guilt.

Oyang's dragon was speaking to her, from where she didn't know. But one thing was clear: he was begging her. She had a feeling she was going to regret what she was about to say.

"I will on one condition. That you do not tell others of it."

Oyang Kang nodded, placing one hand over a fist. "I swear it. No one will hear of it."

"Very well."

She sat, and the voice in her head gave thanks.

Don't thank me yet.

She bade Oyang to sit as well. She took a deep breath, remembering Lady Yuli's instructions.

"When you think of your brother, what is the one emotion that comes to mind? The one thing about him?"

Oyang sat still for a while, then said, "Timidity."

Jin nodded and reached out to Rayshan. *Ready to flare?*

Rayshan curled his tail around himself and lowered his neck, where Jin placed her hand. He glowed with that special light that wasn't light but that shone all the same when she looked around at the now darkened, blurred surroundings.

She visualized Oyang Kang's face, as that was the closest image she had to his brother. Energy and soul dust moved about them, forming and shattering. She sifted through them, pushing back at those who wanted entry but who she instinctively knew was not the one she sought.

At Oyang's intake of breath, she looked over and saw a stocky man, a little shorter than Oyang, standing before them in the cave.

Oyang tentatively rose to his feet, his face disbelieving. He reached out and placed a hand on the other man's arm. Feeling the solid flesh beneath his hands seemed to unleash something in Oyang, and he pulled his brother into a tight embrace.

The other brother hesitantly put his arms around Oyang, who stood there, rocking him.

"I thought I'd never see you again," Oyang said.

"Where am I?"

Jin was about to answer, but Oyang cut in.

"That's not important right now. I wanted to see you, to say that I should never have taken you to Parhae. It was my fault. Do you forgive me?"

The younger brother looked confused, then said, "I remember marching into that border city. We were outnumbered. But then, I don't remember anything after passing the gates and meeting a contingent inside. What happened?"

He looked from Oyang to Jin to the surroundings. "This is not Parhae. Where are we? Are Mother and Father nearby?"

Oyang frowned. "No, they're—we're not home, Brother, this is the capital. I have little time. I need to know you forgive me."

"Forgive you?" his brother asked. "For what?"

"For . . ." Oyang hesitated. "Do you not remember?"

The brother seemed to sense the truth in Oyang's face. "Did I . . . did I die? Am I dead?" He looked from Oyang to Jin in disbelief.

Oyang's face contorted. "Oh, my brother, I am so sorry. I only knew when they brought your body . . ."

"But this, how is this—" The brother looked at his

hands and then looked at Jin, and Jin felt a stab of pity for the man. What was it like to not know one had died? To have no sense of time and space?

"You have but moments," Oyang said. "Less. Jin and Rayshan are flames, and—"

"Flames?" Oyang's brother said, clearly more at a loss than before.

"It's hard to explain," Oyang said. "Do you forgive me?"

At this, his brother's expression changed, as if something had just fallen into place. "You said battle would be good for me. I didn't want to go. You insisted."

Oyang's face twitched. "I did, and I was wrong."

"Well, I told you, didn't I?" his brother said. "Mother told you. But you were the hero of the family, and I had to follow your footsteps, didn't I?"

The man's voice was rising, the tears in it and the hysteria spiraling as the words poured from him. "Father's hero, Kang fought this, Kang overcame that. Why can't you be more like your brother, little Oyang? Why can't you be a rider too? Why do you spend all your time carving toys for children when you could bring honor to the family? Well, have I brought honor, older brother? Am I honorable now in death?"

Each sentence seemed to hammer a white-hot nail in Oyang, his shoulders slumped and his face thinning with each word. "I am sorry, I am sorry, Brother. You need to forgive me . . ."

"No," the brother hissed, "I do not need to forgive you. Not now. Not ever. And I hope you rot in your guilt as I am rotting on the fields of Parhae."

And before he could say another word, Oyang's brother crumbled to ash, the wind picking up the remnants and blowing away the gray-and-white cloud until it disappeared into the night.

Jin's head was cracking, her limbs going slack with exhaustion, and she could tell through Rayshan's bond that his flare had died. She wanted nothing but a day's sleep.

Oyang, she noticed, looked as if his brother had taken part of the life from him. His eyes were dull and fearful, his once broad shoulders seemed to have slackened and narrowed, and there was a bend to his spine that hadn't been there. He looked stunned and wounded, like an animal that had been shot but not killed.

"Are you alright?" Jin asked, tentative.

For a while Oyang simply opened his mouth a few times, before finally looking over, as if only just noticing her. He ran a hand over his face. "I don't know."

"I am sorry," Jin said. "A close friend warned me to not reach into the past and recall the dead without very good reason."

Oyang didn't answer for a moment but instead gazed out into the distance. "I didn't call a retreat."

"I'm sorry?"

"In Parhae," he said softly. "I didn't call a retreat. And I should have. I should have, but I thought we could have a hero's victory, take it all quickly and surely, and that there would be songs about us. And there will be songs. But none for my brother."

An invisible weight seemed to crush the breath out of him. As he left, thanking her again, Jin saw not a hero, but a straw man, dry and brittle.

CHAPTER 29

*J*in ran her finger along the scrolls, mouthing the words to herself. She picked out three that seemed promising and took them back to the table where the others sat in a haphazard pile, then sank onto a rosewood chair and began to read.

Occult Practices of the Barbarian North described tribes much like the Chaakan, where shamans summoned the dead and used cracked bones to predict the future. These shamans seemed to possess the gift at random, where each generation had one flame, but these flames did not necessarily come from the same family. The writers' tones were dismissive and condescending, which made her question everything they claimed as true.

By nightfall, her eyes began to water. She lit one of

the lanterns and gazed again at the luxurious library around her. The vast room was paneled in teak, with south- and north-facing latticed windows to keep the worst of the heat out in summers. Ornate copper braziers, each as tall as she was, stood guard in the corners, their carved dragon mouths glowing from the coals within. The shelves were neatly lined with rows upon rows of books and scrolls, organized by subject and then by title.

She always found peace here, or at least a semblance of it, for it was Prince Tai's private library, and she had the key, kept on a necklace she wore so she wouldn't lose it. She came mostly for the wealth of information, but she also knew that she welcomed the safety from prying eyes, as her return had sparked a new wave of people who wanted to come by her and Meipin's chambers to ask for favors, talk to the female dragonrider, or simply gawk.

Several of the new recruits had been brought to see her, but she had to admit she was too shy to field their questions for long and she disliked being the center of attention. As a thief, she was used to moving unseen and unheard amongst the shadows, dismissed as a street urchin. Even when she had dressed as a noble and attended elaborate parties, she had been playing a part. Meeting these recruits as herself, as Jin the dragonrider, made her feel exposed.

Even Aadan's company hadn't felt quite right of

late. He had seemed more on edge, and when she asked him what was wrong, he complained of increasing pressure from his father and the Persian community to raise forces and retake Persia. Though Jin didn't even know if the empress would allow Aadan to leave Dragon Class, his father's ambitions were certainly another reason they had no future.

She sighed and pulled another volume to her, determined to banish thoughts of insurmountable barriers between her and Aadan. She found nothing about dragons being flames, and soon, she'd have to admit to herself that she'd need to try her luck at the main library. But then she'd have to mingle with the other initiates and Dragon Class riders, and they'd all see her taking books about flames.

"I was hoping I'd find you here."

She looked up. Prince Tai pulled out a chair as she hastily stood and bowed.

"Good evening, Your Highness."

"Are you really going to do that every time?" he asked with an amused smile. "You saved my life. I think we can dispense with formality."

Jin sat back down, casting a glance over her books. Prince Tai picked one up and read the title. "'Witchcraft of the Northern Tribes and Shamanism.' Hmm. Haven't read that one."

"I doubt many have, Your Highness. Thank you again for letting me access your library."

He smiled, putting the book down as his eyes

lingered on the key sitting just under her collarbone. "My pleasure. Finding what you're after?"

"Not really, no," she admitted.

He gave her a look of mock hurt. "I offer you the best library in the kingdom and it's not enough?"

"It's a wonderful library. But it's missing some key books."

"Such as?"

"Books on Mengkhis Lai, for starters," she said. "There are one or two, yes, but nothing about the massacre at Jimo or other events that most people don't know about."

He appraised her thoughtfully. "Almost all those books were banned and burned."

"How can you fight an enemy you do not know?" Jin protested.

He leaned back in his chair. "You do have a habit of coming up with some very good questions. I suppose the prevailing logic was that we had vanquished the enemy, so we had no need for books about him."

She caught the frown in his tone. "You don't agree with that policy?"

He hesitated. "Not that it matters, but, no. I don't."

She looked at him curiously, seeing him in a new light. "How does what you think not matter?"

"Why?" He broke into a smile, leaning forward. "Does it matter to you?"

Why did he make everything sound like a flirtation?

Worse, he made it sound so sincere. And worse still, it made her like him.

"How do you feel about summoning the dead?" he asked.

Jin took a breath, thinking. "I can do it better now. Rayshan and I have honed our focus."

"I didn't ask how well you did it. I meant, how do you feel about it?" He shifted in his seat, eyes searching hers. "It's not a gift one asks for, is it?"

"No," she answered. "Truth is, Your Highness, it makes me feel a little like—an oddity."

He raised an eyebrow. "I thought you'd be used to that by now."

"An even odder oddity, then. It's . . . eerie, being a candle for the dead."

He shrugged. "Death suits some people much more than life. Some of my favorite people are dead."

She laughed, and an intense, breathless expression came over his face. A thought bloomed, making her recoil at her own naiveté. "Why are you here, Your Highness?"

His smile was almost boyish. "Because I enjoy your company."

Don't fall for it. "Is Your Highness here because he wishes to summon someone?"

His surprise looked so genuine that for a moment, Jin doubted her own instincts. "Is that why you think I'm here?"

"I thought you might have wanted to summon . . . Peilah."

He flinched, and the warmth fled from his eyes. "No, I don't wish to summon Peilah. Now or ever. She is the past, and that's where she should stay."

She heard a world of emotions in his voice and remembered Meipin's words. The man before her now did not resemble an infatuated puppy, but a hardened soul who had seen personal pain and tragedy. She remembered what he had confided to her that night at the Spring Festival ball, of how his father had been killed on the night of his birth, with Mengkhis Lai laying siege to the palace. He had every right to want answers from the dead.

She was about to apologize for her suggestion, when he stood abruptly.

"I didn't come to summon Peilah, or my father, or anyone else. I didn't come here for your or your dragon's abilities." He stopped, as if unsure whether to continue. "I came here for you. Good evening, Rider Jin."

Guilt cut through her. She could have been more tactful in bringing up such a sensitive subject. Perhaps he still loved Peilah, and given the rumors about his mother's involvement, he likely wrestled his own demons about her death. She sighed, knowing there was no hope of continuing her research now.

Jin was still thinking about Prince Tai on her way back to her apartments when she noticed a flurry of activity in the Blood Oval, where riders milled in groups of heated discussion. She detoured toward the Oval and almost immediately ran into Jao and Panshalar.

"Where have you been?" Jao demanded.

"In the library. What's happened?"

"Haven't you heard?" Panshalar demanded, then shook his head. "Emar's alive, and here."

Relief, warm and heady, rose in Jin. "Where? How?"

"We're bringing his things to his quarters," Jao said. "Here." He handed her a box that Jin could tell was Emar's personal opium pipe, given the smell. She started toward Emar's quarters just outside the Blood Oval when Panshalar's shout called her back.

"The empress gave him new quarters, near the imperial apartments."

She turned and followed Panshalar and Jao out. Bo Tan, another recruit, held the handle of a stacked basket of food. He fell into step with her, his eagerness to be friendly both awkward and amusing for Jin. She had saved his life on Ice Beard Mountain and helped him pass their first test, and he had never forgotten that favor.

"Did you hear what happened?" Bo Tan said after a quick greeting. "Emar escaped! Escaped Baikalan, imagine!"

"How?" Jin asked.

Bo Tan shrugged. "No one knows for sure, but I'm hoping Master Emar himself tells us."

"I heard they found him on a beach," Panshalar commented as they crossed a vast courtyard flanked by rows of snarling stone lions.

"What, like some fish?" Jao scoffed. "Unlikely."

When they arrived at the quarters, they found the gates guarded by armed men and a crowd of Dragon Class riders, all bearing gifts and waiting to pay their respects. Everyone was being turned away, however, with a thin-faced man Jin recognized as Emar's personal valet politely thanking everyone for their kindness and entrusting their offerings to him. Jin's heart dropped at not being able to see Emar.

When Jin approached with the opium box, the valet was about to take it when he eyed Jin and held up a hand. "Rider Wang Kway Jin, my master asked to see you if you came."

She looked in surprise at Panshalar and Jao, but at the valet's insistent gesture, she picked up the opium box again and followed the valet in, the guards closing the doors behind them.

Inside was a luxurious courtyard filled with straight-backed pines and stone dragons whose backs served as benches. All sounds of the riders outside were muffled in here, and the thick scent of incense, opium, and ginger wafted on the air.

The valet led her up stone steps into a hallway that branched off to either side, with another courtyard ahead. She followed him through this courtyard to another set of doors, which the valet pushed open before bowing low. Emar lay on a wide canopied bed swathed in blue silk, half a dozen pillows propping him up and a smoking table on the mattress next to him.

"Master Emar, rider Wang Kway Jin wishes to call upon you."

Her heart lurched at the sight of him, for though even when she had met him, he had looked like a ruin of a man, what with his whitened flesh and dead eye, he had been robust compared to now. The blankets dwarfed his emaciated frame. The good side of his face looked sallow and empty, like a sack of rice that had slowly bled its contents.

"Clearly, I look awful."

Jin tried to rearrange her expression, but the old man waved a hand toward a nearby stool, and Jin sat.

"You have my opium box, I take it?" he asked the valet.

The valet stepped forward. "The doctor says you are only to have a small amount."

"I've survived Baikalan twice," Emar grunted. "I'll do what I want in the time I have left."

The valet's mouth twisted, but he obediently took the box from Jin and began preparing a pipe.

"Master Emar," Jin said. "It is good to see you. I wanted to come find you, after, but . . ." There were no words, so she stopped. "I am sorry."

The man looked at her as if perplexed. "And what

would that have accomplished? You are not strong enough to take on Baikalan." He paused. "Though is it true? That Rayshan has manifested?"

Jin nodded. "He is a flame."

"Hmm. And I thought life held no more surprises for me."

The valet held out the pipe and helped Emar sit up more. The man's hair hung in a loose braid down his back, and his shoulders hunched, but his hand clutching the pipe seemed strong and determined. He drew on the opium and let the smoke out in a thick cloud.

"How did you escape, Master Emar?" Jin asked.

"A story for another day," he said. "But let's just say I followed Sun Tze's rule to make the enemy think I was weak when I was strong."

Jin swallowed. "They won't be able to find Mengkhis Lai now, will they?"

Emar scowled. "I gave them a false lead as part of my escape. But it's only a matter of time before they find out." He took another few draws on his pipe, then turned to her. "I hear you have been looking through records."

Jin frowned. How had he known? "A personal matter."

"A criminal matter?" he asked, sucking on the pipe.

Jin didn't see the point of denying it, as Emar clearly already suspected. "It seems I am the daughter of an executed criminal."

"Therefore?"

"Therefore—" Jin paused. "Therefore, I am stained."

"You were a thief who stole a dragon, remember," Emar reminded her. "That's a treason that could have had you put in the mines or executed."

"I didn't know I was stealing a dragon. This is different."

"Don't judge too harshly," Emar growled.

"A woman killing her husband? Dooming her own child?" The anger seeped through, and Jin berated herself. What had she expected? Her secret dream that her parents had been good people forced to give her up was just that, a dream. She had never had reason to believe it true, and yet it still somehow hurt whenever that dream was pierced.

"She didn't doom you," Emar said. "You're alive, aren't you?"

Jin kept quiet.

"I knew a woman once," her teacher said, voice soft. "She was married to a man who loved her. But then the man was sent into war when he was not suited for war."

Jin looked up. "Did he die?"

"In the sense that the breath left his body?" Emar shook his head. "No. But the man who returned was not the man she had married. He was a demon. He had been hollowed out, and in the place of flesh and blood, he had been filled with pain. And to ease his own pain, he inflicted it on others. Day after day. But that's the thing about pain and anger. It doesn't leave you when you pour it into others. It's just a well that keeps refilling. She tried to leave once, but he found her. And so she bore it for years until she couldn't."

Jin swallowed. She was no stranger to violence, or to violence in the name of love. Hadn't Haitao, her surrogate father of sorts, always argued that he lashed her to make her stronger? But Emar's story drew her in. "What did she do?"

Emar took another tug on the pipe, then held it out to the valet to be refilled. The valet silently obeyed.

"One night, after he had beaten her until she had barely a tooth left in her skull and had crushed the bones of her hand under his foot, she waited until he fell asleep. And once he was, she slit his throat. Like a pig. To the law, she was a murderer, but to the man and her son, she was a goddess of mercy."

"Who was she?" Jin asked, though she suspected she knew.

"My mother," Emar said. "A kind man took us in afterward and vouched to the police that she had taken her son and fled an attacker in the night, hence her injuries."

"The empress's father," Jin guessed.

Emar nodded, glancing at her. "What did she tell you?"

"That her father adopted you so you could join the Dragon Class." Jin thought on his words, a growing chord of empathy forming in her.

Was her past similar to Emar's? Had they both come from women running from the men in their lives? Ever since she had read the birth document of a child born to a murderer, with her name scrawled over the top, she had lived with the fear that she was of terrible blood, a tainted monster. Worse than what Haitao had made her. But if a man like Emar could have a violent father and criminal mother, perhaps her worry over her own origins was unfounded. "Does anyone else know? About your parents?"

"No," Emar said shortly, as if the admission pained him. "Not even the empress."

Jin dipped her head. "I will not speak of it to anyone."

"I know you won't." He shifted on his pillows, leaning forward until the earthy, sugary scent of poppy resin surrounded her. "I tell you this because once you let your past decide who you are and what you can do, you have lost. And Ulagan and Baikalan know that. You understand me, Rider?"

"Yes, Master Emar," she answered, though she knew it was easier said than done. And as she left, she thought of Master Haitao, her clan boss. He had never let her forget her past, reminding her always that he had saved her from the streets and that she was an unwanted child. Her past was the very reason for who she was, why she was, and what she would never become. Yet Master Emar might be right. He had not let his past define him, and hadn't she broken out of her past by becoming a dragonrider?

Emar was right. Perhaps her birth and who her parents were didn't matter. Perhaps all that mattered was the future, and defeating Ulagan.

CHAPTER 30

When Jin walked to the pools the next day, tying the drawstring of her trousers, she slowed as she noticed the figure standing before all the riders.

"You're late, Rider Jin," Prince Tai said, turning at the sound of her footfalls.

She bowed. "My apologies, Your Highness."

Jin took a place next to Jao, as Aadan stood on the far side, and it would have looked conspicuous for her to seek him out. "Where's Master Xi?" she whispered.

"Sick," Jao answered.

"And the prince is substituting?" Jin asked, incredulous.

"Everyone in. I want to see you swim two lengths without stopping," Prince Tai commanded. "Extra points if you can do a length without breathing."

Jin's heart sank. She noticed Aadan's worried frown

and tried to keep a brave face as she dutifully slid into the water behind the others. This was going to be very humiliating. Somehow, losing face in front of Prince Tai seemed a true low.

Don't punish yourself with such thoughts, Rayshan admonished. *Just do your best.*

She swam behind the others, keeping her face out of the water, but it was still no use. The memory of that day in the river, of the rushing water in her nose, her mouth, the cold, the absolute cold, terrified her and froze her limbs.

"Rider Jin."

She glanced over and found the prince looking down at her. Everyone else, she saw, had already made it to the other side.

"Are you alright?"

"Yes," she said firmly. "Swimming is not my strength."

He turned to the other students. "All of you swim four lengths underwater." When they had all started their exercise, he turned back to Jin. "This is your twelfth lesson, is it not?"

It was the thirteenth, but she didn't fancy emphasizing her lack of progress.

The prince undid his sash and began disrobing. "I will have a chat with Master Xi about his teaching methods, but in the meantime, we have to hasten your progress."

Prince Tai stripped down to his under trousers, a

finer weave than those worn by everyone else, but the same clothing, nonetheless. She wouldn't stare. She wasn't staring. By the eight levels of hell, she was staring. Jin wasn't sure whether the heat she felt was from seeing a royal person's naked torso, for such displays were generally forbidden to non-royals, or just that she had not expected any teacher to actually enter the pool.

"That's not necessary, Your—"

But he had already jumped in next to her. "You fear the water, don't you?"

She was about to deny it, but then, at the clear disbelief in his expression, she opted for the truth. "Yes. I nearly drowned once."

"And that's why you dislike putting your face in water. That's when you panic."

Her silence spoke for her.

By now, several of the students had finished their swims and were muttering to each other at the sight of the prince in the pool. Jin scowled in shame at having to accept the prince's help in this way, especially in front of Aadan. Master Xi and Aadan hadn't been able to teach her to swim, and now a third person would try?

Tai turned to them. "Who here knows how to swim on one's back?" A few raised their arms, though Aadan wasn't one of them. "Good." Tai nodded. "Please demonstrate, and then I want you to break into groups, four to each of the three who know the technique."

Aadan gave Jin another inscrutable glance but then joined the others.

Tai turned back to Jin. "Fortunately, there's a way to swim without putting one's face in the water." He tapped his shoulder. "Lie back and put your head here, and relax your body."

She hesitated.

"Do you need me to make it an order?"

Jin flushed, then did as he asked, turning to stand facing away from him. She cautiously leaned back until her head rested on his shoulder.

"Good, now arms out."

She did as he asked and felt his hands lifting her arms to either side of her on the water's surface. His palms were surprisingly callused for someone who lived in luxury.

"Don't look at your feet. Look up at the ceiling. And breathe."

She tilted her face up, her forehead just below his chin, and breathed in as he asked. He smelled of candles, clove, and the agarwood that reminded her of Buddhist temples. A very different smell from Aadan, whose sandalwood was foreign and exotic.

"Good. Just relax and keep looking up. You won't sink."

The ceiling above, she noticed for the first time, was painted a deep blue and white to mimic the sky. His hands beneath her arms moved to the small of her back.

"See? Relax, and your body floats."

Amazement flooded her. She really was floating, and it took no effort, unlike when she had to put her head in the water. Here, gazing up, she could put aside the memories of not being able to breathe in that river.

"That's all for today, everyone," the prince called. "Good work, and Master Xi will be back for your next lesson."

Jin moved with everyone else toward the pool's side to get out, but Tai's voice stopped her. "Everyone but Jin. You will need extra lessons."

She frowned as the prince walked through the water to stand next to her, her eyes at the level of his scar. "Your Highness is generous, but I'm sure I can figure out the rest myself."

"As the saying goes, the stupid bird must learn to fly first."

Anger sparked in her. "You're calling me a stupid bird?"

"Forget your pride. This is a matter of making sure you can survive if you fall into the sea." He pulled himself out of the pool in one smooth motion, water running off his arms and legs. "I expect you back at this pool later today."

From the corner of her eye, she noticed Aadan hanging back, letting the others file to the bathing areas while he gathered his towel. "I have training at the Oval today, Your Highness."

"I will see you are excused," the prince said, holding

one hand down to her while the other slicked the hair back from his face. "I've seen you fight. You don't need more time in the Oval. You need more time in the water if you are going to attack Ulagan's ships."

She grasped his hand and allowed him to pull her up out of the pool. Did she imagine it, or did he pull her a little closer to himself than necessary? She became painfully aware of the soaked trousers clinging to her legs.

"I'll see you today at the hour of the horse," he said.

He walked away, pulling his towel to himself as he went, nodding to Aadan as he passed.

SHE DIDN'T SEE AADAN AGAIN UNTIL THE BELL AFTER lessons, when he strode up to her in the hallway and asked why she wasn't headed toward the Oval. When she explained that Prince Tai had ordered her to do swim lessons instead, a strange look crossed his face.

"I'll talk to him. I can teach you."

"You didn't raise your hand that you know how to swim on your back. I need to learn that to survive."

This was, she knew, paramount, despite what her injured pride said.

Aadan nodded, then looked around. When the last rider had left the hall, he reached into his coat pocket. "Here, I have a gift for you."

She stared at him, uncomprehending. Only two

people had ever given her a gift. Prince Tai had given her a saddle when her old one had been shredded. And Meipin had given her a picture of her home city, but the piece had only made her strangely homesick.

Aadan pulled out a palm-sized package wrapped in an orange-colored silk scarf and pressed it into her hand. "This is usually given at the Persian New Year, but I thought you could use some now."

She looked down, the smell of the roasted pistachios, almonds, and raisins inside reaching her even before she undid the silk knot.

"They're from the Persian market," Aadan explained. "It's called problem-solving nuts. It's traditional that if you make a wish and then eat them, your wish will come true."

She looked up at him, and the hesitant anticipation in his light green eyes made her chest tighten. "This . . ."

"It's not much, I know," he said in a rush, then took a breath, as if calming his nerves. "But I thought you could use some wish granting right now. I can't help you with the swimming, but maybe this can."

"Thank you," she said, the words feeling inadequate.

A gong sounded from the Oval, and Aadan glanced over. "I'd best go. Good luck!"

She watched him leave, and though a light rain started on her way to the pools, she didn't feel the cold at all.

ONLY WHEN SHE WAS STRIPPING DOWN IN THE CHANGE rooms at the hour of the horse did some of her apprehension return.

We'll both feel better knowing you can handle yourself if you fall into the sea, Rayshan said.

True. But this is humiliating, Jin replied.

Humility creates an excellent environment for learning, Rayshan pointed out. *Besides, are you sure it's only humiliation you were feeling? Because I thought I sensed—*

Oh, please stop, she sighed, as she changed into a new pair of under trousers she had brought.

Why are you humans so ashamed of such things? Rayshan asked with genuine curiosity. *We dragons regard physical desire as just a natural phenomenon. It's like being ashamed of one's color or need to eat.*

And how do you know what the traditions of attraction are with dragons? Jin asked. *You haven't even—*She stopped midway through pulling off her inner jacket. *Wait, what is your mating cycle?* Their dragon lessons had focused on care and prevention of disease and bugs, but had remained absolutely silent on this topic.

My first breeding season will occur in a year or two, Rayshan said lightly.

But there are no female dragons here. What will you—

"Rider Jin! You're not sneaking out on your lesson, I trust?" the prince's voice called from outside the dressing rooms.

She checked the sundial on the floor of the bathing

quarters, a skylight serving to both warm the room and tell the hour. Curse it. She was late.

A conversation for another time, Rayshan said, chuckling. *Swim well.*

She hurriedly folded her clothes and then stepped out to meet Prince Tai. He was already down to his trousers, the slits along both sides showing his thighs, his hands clasped behind his back. A valet stood at a discreet distance.

Tai looked as if he was suppressing a smile. "I thought perhaps you had decided to make a run for it."

"As you said, if I'm going to fight Ulagan, then I'm going to need to know how to swim."

While being distracted, Rayshan added.

Yes, you're very distracting, she shot back.

Prince Tai's gaze caught for a moment on the stretch of her abdomen where the trousers and bodice didn't quite meet, and he frowned. "I'll ask the Dragon Class tailors to work on appropriate swim clothing for female dragonriders since they will be training with the men." He gestured to the pool. "After you."

She slid in, but the prince went in head first, coming up with wet hair. She wondered if he was deliberately humiliating her with his grace in the water.

He tapped his shoulder, and she leaned her head back against him, her body floating to the surface. Jin tried focusing her chi the way Yuli had taught her, to calm herself. After a moment, however, she realized that the erratic heartbeat she sensed wasn't her own, but Prince Tai's. Perhaps he regretted taking on this task, for he surely had more pressing responsibilities. And was possibly still upset about their conversation in the library.

"Try to loosen yourself," he said. "Tension and water do not go well together."

She took a deep breath, willing herself to relax.

"You cannot die, and yet you still fear the water?" he asked after a moment.

She bolted up, staring at him. "Her Majesty told you?"

He sighed. "Actually, she didn't. I noticed all the blood bonding books had been taken from the library when you left for Khitan."

"Perhaps I was researching Mengkhis Lai, Your Highness," she countered.

"I watch most Dragon Class training sessions," he said. "You're faster, lighter on your feet. You continue training after sunset when most people can't see."

Jin crossed her arms. She had protection of sorts from the empress, but that didn't mean Prince Tai couldn't make her miserable in his own way. "What are you going to do?"

He massaged one shoulder, his gaze sweeping the pool. "I had planned on teaching you to swim. But if you'd rather not, I have a reputation for being one of the best poets at court."

She hoped he would interpret her shudder as

caused by the cold. Aadan had long ago given up on her appreciating poetry. "Let's swim."

"Very well." He looked as if he was fighting a smile. Once her head was back on his shoulder, he cleared his throat. "You didn't answer my question."

"I think I fear the water more now that I can't die," she answered after a pause, eyes on the ceiling. "If I sink, I will be underwater forever. I don't know whether I die over and over or whether I simply exist. But either way, an eternity in water being alive is worse than death, isn't it?"

"I don't know," he answered. "Both sound preferable to some of the minister meetings I've had to listen to."

"Do you make light of everything, Your Highness?"

"I find making light helps me examine things more seriously. Especially things I fear. Arms."

Jin lifted her arms back out, feeling the water slide over them. "And what do you fear?"

"Besides arriving at a state function and realizing I'm naked?" He grimaced. "I have that nightmare sometimes."

"You don't have to tell me, Your Highness. I'm sorry I asked." She hadn't meant to pry. But she was genuinely curious about what someone of Tai's station might fear.

For a while, there was only the sound of the water falling into the pool. Then his voice spoke, low and even in her ear. "I fear that no matter what I do, I won't be as good a ruler as my mother. And that even if I'm remembered as a good ruler, it will only be because the officials and court scribes are all narrow-minded conservatives who want a man—any man—back on the throne. I won't be judged for my attributes, but for my sex."

"What you're describing sounds very much like being a woman, Your Highness."

He was quiet again for a moment, then said, "Yes, I suppose you're right."

"You need a crow's mouth."

"Crow's mouth?"

"It's a thieving phrase," Jin explained. "A crow's voice sounds terrible, but when you hear it, you know something has died."

"So a voice that's ugly but truthful?"

"Something like that."

"Then it's decided. You can be my crow," he said, and she thought she detected a smile in his voice. "Though your voice is not so terrible. So tell me, how does a tough crow like you almost drown? What were you stealing?"

She stiffened and immediately began to sink. His hands caught her at the waist and guided her back to the surface.

"You don't have to tell me if you don't want to," he said softly.

"I wasn't stealing. I was being tested." She paused. "By my clan leader. He didn't do it to anyone else, just me. He had me placed in a bamboo cage and submerged in a river."

"By the eight levels of hell," the prince said. "How did you get out?"

"My best friend found me," Jin said, her heart squeezing at the thought of Lu. Would the ache of his death, and how he died, ever go away? "He risked his life and came back. I had managed to break out of the cage, but I'd be at the river bottom if he hadn't come to find me."

She felt a pressure on her arm and realized his hands were squeezing her.

"There are some benefits to being crown prince. I suppose I could have him killed for you if you'd like."

Her throat closed, and she moved away to the poolside, leaning her arms on the cold marble side. "Gao already did."

Prince Tai swam over in two strokes and leaned against the pool side. "I'm sorry. I didn't mean to be callous."

"It's alright, Your Highness."

"You sound sad that he's dead."

"I am."

He frowned. "But he submerged you in a cage. How can you mourn such a person?"

"Feelings are not black and white. Hatred and love are not always exclusive." Not to mention that no matter what he had done to her, Jin knew that he had also made her who she was, and in no way had she ever wanted to cause his death. She drew a breath. "I'm sorry, Your Highness. You didn't ask for a boring list of weaknesses."

"Actually, I did. Besides, having weaknesses doesn't make you weak." He moved next to her. "We can end this lesson early if you wish."

She shook her head. "We're here, and I'm missing training. We might as well keep going until I can do this right."

He nodded and let her lean her head back on him, arms floating out. His heartbeat had evened, though it still sounded faster than hers.

"It's comforting to know you have weaknesses," he said.

"Are you making fun of me, Your Highness?"

"I wouldn't dare," he replied smoothly. "You punched me when we first met. I always try to avoid past mistakes."

"Sorry, I—"

"Don't be. It's ironic. That night, I probably wanted nothing more than to kill you, and here I am, half naked in a pool in the hopes I can keep you alive when you go to battle."

Something in his voice made her turn to look up into his face, but he made a noise to stop her. "Don't move, just—"

He stepped away, and she realized she was floating completely on her own. A sense of accomplishment flooded her, and she grinned.

"Well done. Keep your belly up." His hand rested on the bare skin of her abdomen, making her draw a sharp breath. "And gaze at the sky. That's the secret."

He then showed her the strokes, how the arms went backward instead of forward, and he showed her how to cup her hands to form paddles, just like Aadan had. Though the first few tries had her floundering, she soon had a general grasp of it and could move through the water.

Belly up, head back, arms long. Triumph rippled through her, and after a few days, she was able to make her way up and down the pool at a good speed, her legs kicking and her arms developing a rhythm of their own. By the end of the second week, she could keep up with the other riders, if not outswim them, and the jeers from her first days faded to silence. Even Master Xi, who had at first blustered about her not being able to swim the forward stroke, had to admit that she was amongst the best in the class, especially on the day Prince Tai came to inspect them.

"When you're fighting for your life in the ocean," he said calmly to Master Xi, his eyes on Jin, "no one cares what stroke you do. Just that you survive." He looked back to Master Xi and smiled. "Congratulations, Master Xi, all your students are now proficient in the water."

They all bowed as Prince Tai walked to the doors, and mixed in with Jin's feeling of pride was a pinprick of regret.

Already missing your private swimming lessons? Rayshan grunted in her head.

Just as the prince reached the doors leading out of the pools, they opened, and a senior rider with a messenger's insignia entered.

"Your Highness, the king of Khitan has sailed."

Jin's heart lurched, and she felt Rayshan stir at her reaction.

The prince stood very still. "But he's not due to leave for a fortnight!"

The messenger bowed. "Marquis Sanjin believes he deliberately disseminated false information, but they have set sail already. Yesterday, in fact."

Aadan shot a look at Jin.

Already, drums sounded from outside the pool walls, a call to everyone in Dragon Class.

The war was to be fought now.

CHAPTER 31

The Blood Oval was in a fury of activity as Oyang Kang barked orders to riders and grooms, servants and valets. They would fly within the hour, and the new recruits had come out to watch, wide-eyed, from the balconies.

Dragons were already flying from Dragon City to alight in the Blood Oval and find their riders. Jin stood and looked for Rayshan, and didn't even realize the prince was there until she felt a hand on her arm.

"Fly well, Little Crow, and return."

She recalled another day like this when he had seen her off to the test where she had nearly died. She nodded.

"I will, Your Highness."

He made an admonishing sound. "What do I need to do to make you stop calling me that?"

"No one is allowed to speak your name," she reminded him.

He raised an eyebrow. "We'll think of something on your return. I'm partial to Lord Charming."

Before she could rip off a retort, she saw Aadan striding across the field, strapping his daggers to his leg guards. "Take care, *Your Highness.*"

She walked across the field, calling out to Rayshan before she spied him on one of the spires.

I'm here, she called, and her heart swelled as he spread his wings and swooped toward her, pivoting to avoid a low gliding silver. The dragons found their riders and let them mount, then formed into their wings. Oyang Kang was still busy barking orders, his great hulking black dragon behind him, as Aadan and Wanli came alongside her. Prince Tai had retreated to the stands, where a group of generals had gathered in a somber huddle.

A bugle sounded, and the Oval fell silent. Oyang Kang strode over to them, his cloak trailing and his scar livid against his forehead. He looked somewhat improved since Jin had last seen him, but he still looked haunted. He raised his fist, and each squad took to the air, three of them in all, with five dragons in each—except for Jin's wing, and she felt a new pang for the loss of Ezho. Soon, the sky was dark with the cloud of dragons winging their way over the city, then turning sharply northeast.

Not long after they left the borders of the prefecture, pelting rain began sleeting down and slicking the dragon's wings. The water ran off the cured leather of the dragonriders but soaked into the wool coats and saddle pads. The dragons seemed eager to fight, some breaking rank to spout fire or emit roars.

Like the other riders, Jin had studied the maps showing the Bohai pass. In good weather, the trip would have taken a single rider two days of uninterrupted flying, but with a moving army, they needed four.

They flew until light began to fade and camped in a roll of hills two days' flight from the bay where Ulagan was expected to pass through the Bohai peninsula. They slept only until first light before pressing on.

Oyang, Jin knew, wanted them well rested when they arrived at the sea, for they would be attacking at night in order to even the playing field with the invisible dragon.

On the night before the battle, Jin, Aadan, Jao, and Panshalar gathered with the other wings in the hastily erected officers' tent. Riders stood against the walls as Oyang pinned up a map. Emar, looking worn but much better than when Jin had last seen him, stood leaning on a cane at the front, along with several wing leaders Jin didn't recognize.

"Scouts have King Ulagan located here, with a fleet of ten ships," Oyang said. "As you know, we will need to cut them off here—" he pointed to a narrow strip that ran between two peninsulas "—for once they break into open seas, they can scatter."

"Are they likely to?" Jin asked. "Strength in numbers, no?"

Oyang nodded. "True, but they may split into two in an attempt to divide us. If that happens, I want us to break into our wing units. Aadan's unit will go with me, and Yihan's unit will fly with Suling's. Follow my lead. Whoever I go for, Suling will go for the other." Suling, a wide man with a hairy face and neck, nodded.

"Remember," Oyang Kang said, "we need to move fast and strike quickly. Because Ulagan sailed before our ships were ready to leave port, we won't have any, and I do mean any, friendly landing space out there on the sea. Don't fall into the water, and don't exhaust yourselves to the point where you can't make it back to land."

Jin wondered if anyone else noticed Oyang looking more haggard than usual, as if something within him had been deflating.

"Any questions?"

"When do we fly?" Jao called out.

"Just after midnight. Make sure all your tack is ready. Mages, I want all the saddles and gear to be lightened and ready to go by moonrise. Sleep while you can. We will sound the drums at midnight and fly within the hour of the rat."

The mages nodded, and the attendees filed from the

tent to their own bed rolls while Oyang and Emar continued to discuss tactics over the map.

Jin laid out her simple bed roll near Rayshan and curled into the crook of him. Though she was too nervous to sleep, Jin knew Oyang's advice was sound. After she tossed and turned for the best part of an hour, however, Rayshan hummed to her until she fell asleep.

THE HOUR AFTER MIDNIGHT WAS INKY, AND JIN PEERED up at a sky devoid of stars or even a hint of moon. The occasional torch had been lit so that soldiers could find their gear and saddles, but otherwise, the night was absolute.

She sifted the smells of camp, of so many bodies and dragons and leather, of grass and campfire and wood. And the charge of nervous excitement. Most of these soldiers had never encountered Baikalan, only heard his name.

And today, they would have to battle him over open water.

The mages were already circling the saddles, giving them a weight-easing spell that would hopefully last the duration of the battle. Grooms and soldiers scurried about readying the dragons and the riders in the dark, and the squad leaders called out curt orders. Jin found Aadan and the others.

She turned to look at Jao and Panshalar. "Panshalar, you once said that I can't die, so I should go in first. You were right. So no one be a hero, do you hear?" At their protests, she plowed on, determined. "I'm not a hero; I'm simply blood bonded, so I will go first in the wing, and no matter what happens to me, do not risk your own life to get me. None of you die because of me. Understood?"

Jao and Panshalar glanced at each other, then nodded, but Aadan shook his head.

"Promise me," she insisted.

"I cannot. Besides, as wing leader, it's my duty to fly first."

She turned her mind to Wanli. *Take him away if things become too dangerous. I'll be fine, and Rayshan will be fine.*

Wanli gave a reluctant agreement.

"Don't talk to my dragon behind my back!" Aadan said.

"Wait, she can talk to our dragons?" Jao said, eyes wide. He gave Nakkalan a slap on the tail, eliciting a snarl in reply. "And you never told me?"

Leaving them to their bickering, Jin reached out to Rayshan. *Everyone will be relying on dragon eyes in the dark. And smell.*

He stretched his neck, making the ridges there stand out. *I will tell the other dragons if I smell Baikalan.*

It was the best they had. They were the only ones who had battled him before and knew his scent, and in the dark over water, it would be only too easy to miss Baikalan's invisible presence.

Several torches waved in the agreed signal to fly. The squads took to the air, first Oyang's, with Emar riding behind the war hero, then Jin's, then Suling's. The dragons spread out once airborne, which, even at this distance from the ocean, smelled heavily of salt.

Soon, they heard waves on the shore, and then the land below gave way to a long strip of rocky sand before they were soaring northeast over the swells of the Bohai sea. The occasional glimmer showed Jin the water, but otherwise it was a great black void, its sound swallowing all others.

Jin sensed the tension in the dragons at once. Having no land beneath them and not even a ship to perch on was an unfamiliar exercise. They would have to remain airborne for the whole of the attack.

A murmur swept through the dragon bonds, and Jin understood that Oyang's dragon had passed on the sighting of ships to the other dragons.

Soon, a number came back—ten ships in all, traveling two abreast and just entering the peninsula's neck.

A tremor rippled amongst the dragons, and Jin understood: thirty dragons to ten ships were good odds. They could sweep in and destroy the convoy in one pass, two at most.

Where is Baikalan?

Rayshan growled. *I do not smell him. I smell only sea and . . .*

Rotting fish. Jin wrinkled her nose. *That's odd. And why would Baikalan not be here?*

A gull cry sounded ahead, the signal for them to move into attack formation. Rayshan rose higher as they broke out into their rehearsed wedge, using the sound of the other dragon's wings and their keen dragon sight to guide them—for here, their riders were nearly blind.

As they descended, Jin spied dark shapes on the water, their white sails like spectral beacons against the inky night. The lanterns at the ships' sides glowed, and Jin could indeed discern about ten ships in all, cutting silently through the waters.

Another gull cry came. Prepare for attack and ready fire.

Jin leaned close over Rayshan's neck, gripping one of his ridges. She smelled salt, dragons, leather—along with something sharp and familiar, yet so incongruous that she couldn't immediately pinpoint it.

Fireworks.

The first squad was already diving when her mind screamed. But it was too late.

The dragons glided low, their fire hitting the ship decks in a deadly cascade.

And then the night itself was sundered by light.

The first ship to explode sent red, saffron, and green sparks everywhere. Roars of pain and surprise flooded Jin's mind as the fiery missiles shredded the first squad's wings and bellies, their riders toppling as the injured dragons crashed into the inferno.

"It's a trap!" Jin screamed. "Hold fire!"

But the ships had been traveling close enough together that flames from one soon reached the others, creating a chain of exploding vessels that spewed deadly chunks of fire into the sky, puncturing dragon wings and throats.

The squadrons broke rank, trying desperately to escape the whirling sparks. Injured dragons hit the water with resounding splashes, sinking within heartbeats. The squadron in front of Jin's tried to pull up but, in their confusion, had broken all formation.

Hang on! Rayshan cried. He spun, narrowly missing a wave of screaming sparks.

Jin gripped with all her might, a cinder grazing her face. Something hissed as it tore through Rayshan's wing, and the air shifted beneath them.

You've been hit!

Rayshan beat his wings faster, but more sparks rose to meet them, and the world tilted.

The great horned head materialized out of the dark like a phantom. One moment, it wasn't there, and then it was. A flash of green scales and an ear-splitting snap of fangs accompanied an overwhelming stench of rotten fish.

He camouflaged his scent. Jin realized too late.

Her dragon roared in pain, and Jin felt it like a slice of fire across her back.

Rayshan!

They flew dangerously close to the water, flaming ships cracking and groaning on either side.

Up! You have to move up!

If they hit the water, they would be done, for Rayshan could not possibly swim with injuries, and his wings would likely drag him down. Rayshan growled in response, and she felt his muscles bunch as he gathered himself.

There! Onto that!

One of the ships had drifted away from the others, and though flames had ripped through its hull, part of it had broken off and turned belly side down, so half of it was still afloat. If they could climb onto it, they could keep from sinking.

Something slammed into them from the left.

She was falling, spinning through air while Rayshan crashed into one of the ships, sparks billowing like a deathly flower into the water about him. Great, scaled claws plucked her only an arm's length from the sea's surface.

Jin was still screaming for Rayshan as the giant jade dragon bore her away, but she knew no one would hear her. For the screams of dozens of other dragons and riders, along with the hungry roar of the ship fires, drowned out any sounds she made before the claws smothered her.

CHAPTER 32

The ground was rocking. Something salty and metallic surrounded her.

Blood.

The stickiness on her forehead and the itch on her scalp were both from caked blood. The scent flooded her nostrils, and she realized the blood was her own. She tried to sit up, but then her head hit something hard.

Her hands were bound together at the wrists, chafed and numb. She reached out, where hard, cold metal greeted her.

Rayshan?

There was only silence.

Rayshan! She screamed across the bond. But the bond felt different. She ran her hands along her prison, and her heart stilled.

Lead. This must be lead.

And now that she thought about it, she hoped it was lead. For only lead could stop communication between rider and dragon, and if this wasn't lead, and Rayshan wasn't answering, then that could only mean he was out of reach. Or dead.

But if he was dead, then she would be, too, or at least dying. Bonded riders who lost their dragons died within the year, and surely she would feel it if she was dying? This gave her a flicker of hope.

She pounded on the metal, screaming, but her voice only bounced back at her. She listened, straining for sounds that might pierce the lead.

A rhythmic creaking. A slap. A creak and a slap again. What was that? She could feel movement beneath her. A ship?

Jin called to Rayshan again, just to be sure he couldn't hear her, and then forced herself to think. She was imprisoned, so the only way out was to find a clasp. She touched her surroundings, first above her and then to the sides. The box was about the size and shape of a coffin, and several thoughts fluttered through her brain simultaneously like panicked birds.

They can't kill you.

But they can make you feel pain.

And Baikalan can kill you.

Baikalan. Out of desperation, she tried reaching out to Baikalan, but he, too, was absent.

She took a deep breath and forced herself to focus. She had no bond, no dragon, no ability to call the dead.

She would have to rely on her own hands and senses. She turned onto her stomach and began to feel the floor of the coffin. It was just as hard and unmarred as the rest of the container, and she began to wonder whether it even had seams. She felt along the corners, and finally, she detected a small indent that she took to be the latch.

She pressed and scraped, but nothing happened. She wasn't sure what she expected to find, but she'd hoped that there would be some clue as to what her prison was.

Would they leave her here to run out of air? Could she run out of air if she couldn't die? She didn't really want to find out, even if she could be revived. Dying once had been enough for her.

What seemed hours later, as her back began to cramp and her legs started to spasm, she heard the opening of a door and the slide of feet across the floor, though it was not a steady tread, but more as if someone drunk was trying to make their way to her. She heard murmuring, then chanting.

Mages.

What were they doing?

She felt her limbs growing heavy and realized with a start that they were making her heavier. As she suspected, soon her arms couldn't move, and then her legs wouldn't obey her. She tried to shift, but every part of her felt as heavy as a dragon's tail.

Then the lid of the coffin slid open, and dank gloom

replaced pitch dark. She could just make out four figures standing over her, and then the heaviness in her eased, but not enough for her to move freely. The figures bent and took her by the shoulders, then hauled her to a sitting position.

She was in the hold of something.

A ship.

She reached out to Rayshan but still heard nothing, and this time her heart sank. Without the lead coffin blocking her, what could be severing their bond?

"Drink," a gruff voice said, and a ladle pressed her lips. She sniffed, wary of poison, but the figure then grasped her chin in the palm of his hand and forced her mouth open, tipping the ladle's contents in. It was just water, and she swallowed it in relief.

They pushed another ladle on her, then hauled her out of the coffin, having lightened her limbs just enough so she could walk but would have difficulty running. She realized such a charm was taking the mages a lot of work, for they were sweating profusely, even in the cold.

They hauled her up a few steep, narrow steps until she was on a deck. A moody sea of clouds above matched the gray waves that rocked the ship, a long one with great sails the size of ten dragon wings that strained in the wind. She spotted a dozen others spaced out across the waters. These ships were nothing like the ones they had attacked—these were sleek and clearly built for war, with metal plating hammered into the prow and two towers, one at the stern and one at the bow, their slit-like windows clearly used for archers to attack enemies while protected.

Men worked the oars, ten rows on each side of the ship with twelve men to each oar. Two soldiers pounded drums at an elevated deck at the ship's bow, the beat in time to the men's pulls on the great oars that dipped and rose in the gray waves. Banners flapped in the wind, and Jin caught the word "Parhae."

"Welcome aboard, Rider Jin," a familiar voice drawled, and Jin looked around to see Ulagan standing behind her, another man with a wide face and close-set eyes next to him. This man was clearly royal by the way he seemed at pains to appear taller than Ulagan. He wanted to seem in control, she guessed, and not lose face in front of the other king.

"You two have not met?" Ulagan said. "King Do, this is Rider Jin, who killed Minister Gao and is the reason why women are being allowed into Dragon Class."

King Do walked forward. He wore a leopard skin draped across his shoulders and had his beard cut in a harsh foreign style. He spoke Chinese in a rush, the words blending together.

"The famed Rider Jin. It is interesting to meet you."

Jin couldn't bring herself to engage in polite greetings. "Where is Rayshan?"

The king pointed to another ship in the distance, similar to this one, with flapping banners and full sails, carving its way through the waves. "Safely in the bowels of the *Eternal Sun*, unharmed."

Relief mingled with suspicion. "Then why can't I hear him?"

King Ulagan grinned. "I put a lead headpiece on him. Useful things, those." He strode closer and looked her up and down. "Well, well, blood bonded, are you? Never thought I'd see another one."

Jin wondered where Emar was and whether he had escaped, but said nothing.

"Emar's alive as well," Ulagan said, as if reading her thoughts. "The king of Parhae had thought him dead and left him to the sea, which is how he escaped." Here, he turned a contemptuous glance on King Do, who bristled. "But we won't be making that error again. Mengkhis will be very happy to see him. I understand the two have enough bad blood to make a cat and mouse seem like lovers."

Jin kept her face still, but inside, a storm raged at the news of Emar's capture. She looked up at the sound of wings. A great bronze circled, along with a gold. King Ulagan's dragons.

"Where are we headed?" she asked, though she could guess. The more information she had, the better her chances of doing something. Anything.

"The southern kingdom of Champa," Ulagan said. "There, we will free Mengkhis Lai on the acceptance of a deal."

"And what makes you think he will strike a deal with you?" Jin asked.

"He would be foolish not to," the king of Parhae said. "We have the army, we have his dragon, we have Emar. We can offer him the Dragon Throne of China—at a price."

Jin doubted Mengkhis would submit to anyone for any length of time, much less these two, and would figure out a way to rid himself of any yokes. But she knew there was no convincing them. She had seen far smarter men confident of much less. And there was no telling what would happen once Mengkhis was freed, with Baikalan delivered to him. She had to find Rayshan, free him, and then see if they had a chance of freeing Emar as well and getting away.

"But before then, we'll hold a special ceremony tomorrow."

"What ceremony?" Dread coiled in Jin.

He grinned. "I am going to take my rightful dragon back. The jade I was due."

Her heart stuttered. "You would unbond him?"

Ulagan smiled. "I have the mages and nothing else to do on this journey south—might as well gain myself a dragon."

She lunged at him. "You could kill him!"

"You cannot catch a tiger's cubs without entering the tiger's den," he said, then turned to the guards. "Take her below."

The mages and guards seized her and dragged her

back. With her hands tied, she couldn't fend them off, and soon they had her in the lead coffin once more, the lid shutting out all light.

She screamed in her rage, but there was no answer besides the lapping of the waves and the faint beat of the drum, taking them ever closer to Mengkhis Lai.

JIN HEARD A SCRAPING. HAD IT BEEN HOURS OR DAYS? She couldn't tell anymore. She was starting to run out of air and had tried to save her breath, for even if she couldn't truly die, she didn't want to risk losing consciousness as she had when Ulagan had killed her.

"Rider Jin?"

She stopped, listening. It was a female voice, a voice she had heard before but didn't recognize.

"Rider Jin, it's Nomu."

Ulagan's daughter. Was she here to help, or torment?

"I want you to know that your dragon is safe and healthy."

Relief buoyed her for a moment. "Why are you telling me this?"

There was a pause before Nomu said, "Because I think you deserve to know. And because I don't like what my father does."

Hope welled in Jin. If Nomu didn't agree with her father . . . "Nomu, listen to me. Can you let me out?"

There was another pause. "If I do, he will know I did it. I've asked him to let you out, and he has forbidden me from coming here. I'm only here because the mages are taking shifts, and the one on guard right now was a childhood friend."

"Then help me in some other way," Jin said, desperate. "Can you free Rayshan?"

"No, he is guarded on another ship, and we don't dock for another two days, I heard the navigator say."

Jin's heart fell.

"Ever since I heard about you, I've wanted to become a dragonrider. I dreamed I might bond to my father's dragon, Satu," she said. "But life isn't fair, is it? Instead I am now married to the king of Parhae, whom I have only just met."

Jin's stomach turned at the thought of this sixteen-year-old forced to marry King Do, a man well over fifty. This child had burdens of her own and was in no small amount of danger herself. Aiding her father's and husband's enemy would surely result in severe consequences.

"I can't help you," Nomu continued, "but I promise I'll take care of Rayshan when he's bonded to my father."

Jin heard Nomu shuffling to her feet. "Wait! Don't go! I can help you if you let me out!" She didn't know how, but she had to try.

"I am sorry. I wish I could do many things that I cannot. Peace upon you, Rider Jin."

Jin heard the sadness in her voice before the girl's steps, one heavy, one light, sounded up the stairs.

Jin tried to stop the tears from coming, tried to comfort herself that at least she knew from one other that Rayshan was alive. But somehow, none of that worked. All she could think of was that she was in a coffin, and though she didn't know if the unbonding would kill her or Rayshan, it almost didn't matter, for being severed from Rayshan would be worse than death.

CHAPTER 33

News of the defeat hit the court like a hammer blow, and a hushed pall fell over the palace as the empress locked herself and Tai away with Sanjin and her top military advisors.

They heard the account from a messenger who had flown non-stop from the Bohai sea, Tai's heart plummeting further with every detail. They had lost a fourth of their dragons, not to mention Jin and Emar. Oyang Kang had called a retreat, and the remainder of the squadrons were nursing their wounds at a base camp just off the channel. They had no element of surprise, and by now, the actual ships would be well on their way to Champa.

The empress dismissed everyone but asked Sanjin to stay. When Tai made no move to leave, she said, "See to the Dragon Class riders. They will want their leader seen taking action."

Tai frowned. "Respectfully, any decision involving Dragon Class should involve me."

"I will brief you later on what we decide," she promised, "but for now, you should have much to do to make sure the riders return safely."

Tai knew this was an excuse, but he dutifully bowed and retreated. Shortly after, he sent the rest of his staff on, murmuring that he had dropped something in the audience chamber, then doubled back.

He knew of the rear entry from all his times accompanying his mother. This was where he and his mother entered the chamber for ministerial audiences. He slipped into the hallway now but stayed behind the curtain that led to the chamber, out of sight.

"... few options open."

"It's true the window is closing," Sanjin said. "Even a marriage would be too late."

"It's too late to stop them from freeing Mengkhis if that's what they choose to do. And Champa may not even put up a fight. They have their own internal squabbles and won't risk their necks. Most likely, Ulagan or Parhae will bribe them."

"Then what do you suggest?" Sanjin asked.

"My son had an idea," she answered.

Tai's ears pricked.

"He suggested we send troops with Aadan's father so they can help his cousin win back Persia and gain an army."

Sanjin snorted. "That is a roundabout way to get an

army. We will be here until next fall before that happens."

"Of course, I'm not proposing we do that." There was the rustle of silks, and then his mother's voice dropped so that Tai had to strain to hear. "But what if we ally with the Caliphate?"

There was a pause. "You mean give them something they want?"

"Or someone," the empress said.

Tai's heart pounded. Was she really suggesting . . . ?

"They would do anything to get their hands on Aadan and his father, that's true," Sanjin agreed.

"We could have their troops here within the month. They are notorious for traveling quickly. That would help us defend against Mengkhis Lai and whoever is supporting him."

"The suggestion is not without merit, but Aadan and his father won't go willingly, of course."

"Then arrest the father," Tai's mother said. "According to the reports, the son was injured. We can make sure we deliver them within the week."

Tai clenched his fists. His mother would sacrifice Aadan, a loyal Dragon Class rider who had done nothing but serve the empire. His mind raced at what he could do, if anything.

"I will make arrangements, Your Majesty."

"See if the Caliphate will accept this first, and then we will move."

"Yes, Your Majesty. Is that all?"

"For now."

Tai slipped out the way he had come, seething at not just the betrayal of a friend, but what felt like his mother's most recent betrayal of him.

"Throne above all," could go to the eight levels of hell.

Yes, politics meant being harsh. His mother had drilled that into him. But the throne meant nothing if it made you willingly send your allies to the blade. For who would stand behind them in war, if that was how they treated their friends when threatened?

As dusk fell, he watched the guards change shift on the walls. The usual guard number had been doubled. No one was allowed in or out. The plan he was shaping would involve a great feat of smuggling. Sanjin would lose no time contacting the Persians, but in the meantime he would surely want to bring Aadan back here before sending him to Persia. Once he was back in the palace, freeing Aadan would be tricky. Best if his friend was tipped as to the empress's plans and escaped before he could be brought back to Changan.

Flying might be an option, but even then, how was Tai going to convince the Dragon Class to defy orders and give him a bronze and carriage? Though he was head of Dragon Class, he knew his mother's orders overruled any authority he had.

And besides Aadan, whom did he know whom he could trust? Mage Situ Han? He wasn't sure the mage would support his flying to war, seeing as he appeared to have much riding on Tai ascending the throne one day. He couldn't risk it.

Meipin.

Perhaps she would be willing to bend the rules, given their last conversation. She had warned him once about Peilah in a very roundabout way that the younger fool he had been had completely missed, but in the days following the poisoning, he had come to realize that she had been trying to help him.

Perhaps she would help him now. He had no one else to ask.

It was much too late to make a polite social call, but this was no ordinary ask, and Aadan was running out of time. His mother and Sanjin would act straightaway to send an emissary to Persia, and in the meantime, Aadan would be kept under watch.

He slipped out and told his guards he was going for a walk. The guards came with him, as he expected, but then, once he'd walked the perimeter of the outer apartment grounds four times, they grew bored and kept a slower pace. He took his opportunity when they were both distracted by a wing of dragons doing a night patrol overhead.

He scurried on soft feet through a side alley and emerged into the outer palace, then hurried toward the noble apartments in the eastern half. He estimated he would have about half an hour before his personal guards alerted anyone, for they would first thoroughly search the area themselves and delay as long as possible admitting to any superiors that they had lost track of their charge.

The moon was already high when he reached her doors. Guards chatted quietly at the front, passing a pipe. He assessed his options and then decided that a lantern pole on the side of the grounds offered the best solution.

He didn't need gossip about him visiting Meipin at night. And it was best if his mother didn't know Meipin was involved at all if she agreed to help him.

Tai grasped the pole and swung himself, muffling his grunts as best he could. He straddled the curve of the pole where the beam held the lantern, then gauged the distance to the outer wall. He could hear giggling from inside and wondered how he would talk to Meipin privately if she wasn't alone. Too late now.

He leaped over onto the wall, teetering as he regained his balance. He had nearly succeeded when a piece of tile gave way beneath him, and he slid and clattered to the bushes below, cracking several branches.

The house guards were immediately entering the garden, and above him, the window shutters flew open.

Meipin peered out, suspicious. She spied him in the bushes and was about to call out when he shook his head and put a finger to his lips.

The guards were still shouting and had rushed to the area. Tai hid out of sight in the bushes and looked up at Meipin, hoping he had not misjudged.

"Are you alright, honored miss?"

Meipin nodded. "Fine. I'm so clumsy, I simply dropped something."

"We'll retrieve it for you then. We can look—"

"No!" Meipin said quickly. "It's a feminine item. I can retrieve it myself."

Though Tai wondered what feminine item could make a sound like a crashing man, the guards seemed relieved to be excused.

Once the main gate had closed behind them, Meipin hissed, "Stay there!"

By the time she came down, he had disentangled himself from the bush and brushed off the leaves. She hurriedly led him into the apartments and sat him down in her foyer. Tai suddenly had a memory of coming here when Jin was living in these apartments, and giving Jin her dragon saddle. It seemed a long time ago.

"What are you doing here, Your Highness?" Meipin asked, pulling out a stool and sitting to pour cups of tea. She had dispensed with her usual courtly formal speech, and Tai noticed for the first time that there were no waiting women about, which was odd.

"I needed to speak to someone," he answered. "Who else is here?"

"No one, Your Highness," Meipin said, then hesitated. "You can trust Ahlu."

As if summoned, Ahlu, her maid, came into the foyer on quiet, slippered feet. Tai took in the stray strands of hair, the one button on the side of the girl's dress that was in the wrong loop. He remembered a vendor at the Festival of Sevens, where Meipin's stone had glowed between them while Ahlu watched in the background.

He glanced from Ahlu to Meipin, and noticed that they were at pains not to look at each other.

He sipped the cup of tea Meipin had poured and said, "You said you were a friend. I've come to ask a friend's help."

"In the middle of the night?"

He shrugged. "It seems I didn't wake you."

She flushed. "I like to sleep and rise late."

"I am not one who . . ." he searched for a word ". . . judges others on whom they love. I think we can be honest with each other, and though your ravishing looks could keep poets occupied for centuries—"

"We have no sense of fire flowers together," Meipin finished.

He cocked his head. "It appears I can take comfort in the fact that I am not eligible for this particular race."

She motioned for Ahlu to leave. The girl retreated, her face tight with fear. When she had gone, Meipin turned back to Tai. "I do hope Your Highness will be discreet. My birth will protect me, whereas Ahlu . . ."

He nodded. "I understand." It seemed he was not the only one who worried about how his affections might harm others.

Meipin regarded him thoughtfully, and he sensed worry in her voice. "Though . . . will you tell your mother and remove me from the running for empress?"

"I won't breathe a word," he promised, then leaned forward. "I have something else that's actually more pressing. I came to ask for your help with getting Aadan out of the palace to safety. I need to remove him before Sanjin's people do."

Her eyes widened. "Sanjin is after Aadan?"

"Yes, he's—" Tai stopped. "Look, it's safer that you don't know. Just tell me, can you get me a letter from the legal ministry, from your uncle's office, that can get me and a Dragon Class rider out of here?"

It was Meipin's turn to nearly choke on her tea. "You want me to forge a pass? Do you think I don't value my head?"

"It's a pretty head, but I always thought the brains were far more formidable than the looks," he said. "Prove me right."

A grin crept over her face, and he knew he had made the right gamble. "Even if I could get you a pass, how would you find a rider and get Aadan out?"

"I have one idea," he said. "Now, can you help me?"

"Just tell me why you're doing this," she said.

"Because Aadan's in trouble, and my mother thinks she can use him to defend the empire."

"So you are risking your mother's wrath to save your friend?"

"Yes."

She ran a finger around the rim of her tea cup. "You

will make a very likable emperor, Your Highness. Not necessarily the best emperor, but a likable one."

He leaned forward. "So will you help me?"

"Give me a couple of hours," she said, standing. "You can stay here, but I'll need Ahlu to go with me."

He nodded. "I'll be here. But hurry."

s the guard at the perimeter waved them down, Tai repeated mage Situ Han's words for calm.

He had the document in his hand, but even so, apprehension knotted his stomach. He was about to defy his mother in a way he had never done before. And all this after mounting a dragon for the first time.

The wind had threatened to unseat him, and even his chosen rider, a quiet, reliable messenger he knew named Mao, seemed unsure of his ability to ride. Tai had donned the mage's robes Situ Han had given him the day they had left the palace, as the letter said that a mage needed to be transported to a local official's house without delay to see to a breach in mage defenses.

They landed on the wall, and the guard strode up to them, sword slapping his side.

He held out a hand, and Tai passed him the document, trying to appear bored as the guard held it up to the torchlight and read it.

The guard flicked a glance at Tai, and for a moment, he thought all was lost. He had worn a thick scarf over his neck, unlike most mages, and wasn't sure this wouldn't give him away. He had returned to his quarters and made a show to his servants of enjoying a private bath, before sneaking out through the window. But who knew whether some curious attendant had discovered his absence and sounded the alarm?

After an interminable pause, the guard rolled up the scroll and handed it back with a wave.

"Safe journey."

Mao nodded to him, and Tai relaxed, but then tensed again as the great dragon spread his wings and took to the sky.

They flew over the city, and Tai tried not to look down. Riders did this all the time, he thought. In fact, they enjoyed it, he could tell. For the life of him, he didn't know why.

They soared over the temples and slumbering city streets, then banked, making Tai's stomach roll.

"You alright, Your Highness?" Mao asked.

Tai could just hear him over the whistling of night air. "Yes."

"If you feel sick, Your Highness can chew on this," Mao said, and shoved something back against Tai's chest.

He took it and sniffed. "Licorice root?"

"Helps calm the stomach, Your Highness."

"I think it's easier if you stopped calling me Your Highness for now," Tai said.

"Yes, Your—" Mao faltered. "Sure."

Tai knew the rider couldn't bring himself to say the prince's name without an honorific beforehand. To do so was the utmost disrespect. But Tai didn't want Mao accidentally letting slip who his passenger was.

"Why did you agree to help me?" Tai asked.

"Because you're helping Aadan."

Tai left it at that. What had mage Situ Han said? Princes had allies, not friends. Tai was commander in chief of Dragon Class, but that meant that everyone kept their distance, for he was a prince, and not one of them. But Aadan was one of them and clearly well-liked. Perhaps Jin liked Aadan just as much, if not more. He forced away the small stab of pain accompanying that thought.

They flew on into the night, and Tai felt a growing sense of triumph at having slipped past the empress.

He might be a fugitive, but he was no longer a prisoner.

THEY MADE GOOD TIME, WHICH WAS FORTUNATE, FOR Tai didn't know exactly how far his mother's and Sanjin's networks spread. How long after he had departed did it take for his mother to realize he was gone? And how would she handle it? Discreetly, no doubt. She wouldn't let anyone know he was missing and instead send out agents to find him and bring him back. Would she guess his destination?

Tai finished relieving himself against a tree and returned to where Mao was cinching the last hole in his dragon's saddle. He climbed up behind Mao and held on as the dragon took to the sky.

He had grown more accustomed to flying on dragon back, but that didn't mean he enjoyed it. He tried to keep his mind off the ground and simply think of Aadan, of reaching him before Sanjin's agents did.

And when he found Aadan, what then? Would Aadan listen to him? He would tell his friend the truth, at least.

They came within sight of the encampment, close enough to the coast that Tai could smell salt in the air. They landed on the western side of the military camp, where grooms tended to injured dragons, and doctors hurried about delivering supplies and medicines. Mao spoke with a groom, then came back to Tai.

"Aadan's wing is camped on the far side, Your . . ." His words trailed off, and he pointed.

Tai was away before Mao could even call out to wait.

He walked past several tents, where soldiers sat on stools or tended fires and gear. The mood was oppressive, the shock of their defeat not yet worn off. Tai passed tent after tent until he saw someone he recognized from Aadan's year carrying a saddle. The man didn't even look at Tai's face closely when he asked for Rider Aadan, instead pointing at a nearby tent and then hurrying off.

Tai swept the tent flap open and entered a closed room with the smell of herbs hanging heavy in the air. Aadan was dressing a bandage on his arm, and looked like he hadn't slept in days, but otherwise seemed largely unscathed.

"Prince Tai!" Aadan made to stand and bow, but Tai waved the gesture away.

"No time for that, my friend. I am here to get you out."

Aadan froze. "Out? Why?"

Tai drew a breath. There was no soft way to convey the news. "Because if you don't leave, my mother is going to hand you over to Persia in exchange for an army."

Aadan drew back. "She's . . . what?"

"She wants an army, and fast," Tai said. "I am sorry, I flew here as soon as I could."

His friend's mouth opened, then closed, clearly still digesting this news as anger replaced confusion. "The Caliphate?"

"The same. Can you ride?"

"Yes, but—"

"There's no time," Tai insisted. "You have to leave now."

Tai shoved his mage cloak toward Aadan and motioned for the rider to remove his leathers. Aadan was slightly taller than Tai, but there had been no time to source an extra set of leathers or boots. They swapped clothes, then Tai said, "Mao will take you to find your parents."

"My parents?" Aadan's head snapped up. "They're to trade my parents?"

Tai nodded. "I am sorry. I didn't think she would resort to this, but I cannot stand by and do nothing."

"By the Wise Lord." Aadan closed his eyes for a moment, one thumb rubbing at his temple. "It's profit over principles, I see." The words stung Tai, but there was no arguing the truth. Aadan frowned. "But then I am leaving you, leaving Jin—I mean the whole wing. I will look a coward!"

"Better that than falling into enemy hands," Tai reasoned. "Now, move. I will tell your wing the truth when the time is right, but for now, this is your one chance to leave and reach safety with Wanli. You must go."

Aadan looked severely torn.

Tai put a hand on his shoulder. "Don't make me have done this for nothing. Please."

"What of Jin?" Aadan said. "I can't leave Jin with Ulagan."

"He has her?" Tai asked. Relief that she lived warred with worry about her being in the clutches of Ulagan, whose vindictiveness he knew well.

Aadan nodded, misery and fury on his face. "I saw Ulagan's soldiers pull her onto their ship, but Wanli overrode my commands and retreated when Oyang made the call."

"Trust me," Tai said with a confidence he didn't completely feel, "we have plans in place to rescue Jin and get her and Rayshan back. I promise we will do everything in our power. Now, if I need to do it, I will command you to go." His voice softened. "If not for yourself, then think of your parents and how it would kill them to have you sent back to Persia."

His friend's face paled, the fear evident, and he buried his face in his hands.

"Aadan?"

Taking a deep breath, the rider looked up and nodded, grim. "Thank you, Your Highness."

"You're welcome. Now go, my friend."

He watched Aadan leave and pass the guards, then went to seek Oyang Kang.

THE COMMANDER'S TENT LEANED IN THE WIND, AND when Tai entered, he found only a bedroll and stool set up, with no desk or rack for leathers and boots. It was as if whoever had erected the tent had abandoned it mid-task, losing interest or simply not seeing the point in continuing.

Oyang Kang himself looked haggard, and Tai

couldn't help but think of the word broken. The man was writing copious drafts of something on a fold-out bamboo table, spilled ink staining his leathers and several ripped pages lying in a pile next to him.

"What do you want?" Oyang barked, then, seeing who it was, immediately became contrite and scrambled to his knees. "Your Highness, I had no message of your—"

"This was an unplanned visit," Tai said. "Stand, please. What is it you are writing?"

Oyang regarded the sheet in his hand, making no move to rise. "My resignation, Your Highness. You have saved me a trip, it seems."

Tai shook his head. "And I will save you the wait for an answer. I refuse to accept your resignation. Please stand."

The man obeyed. "Your Highness, this was an unforgivable failure."

"All the more reason why you must serve now," Tai answered. "I need you to stop Ulagan and the king of Parhae from reaching Champa. And to save Jin."

Oyang Kang looked up at him. "It's done. We failed."

"Then we will try until we succeed," Tai said firmly. "And this time, with a different plan." He crossed to a travel trunk, where a jumble of large rolls of paper protruded like some unchecked plant. One roll had the corner of a map visible. Tai pulled this out, swept aside the ripped letter on the fold-out table, and unrolled the map. "Part of the reason we failed was because Ulagan caught us out at sea, an environment hostile to dragons and where his ships had the advantage of surprise." He tapped a bay south of Bohai. "This bay is known for its rapid high and low tides. If we drive them in here, we can ground them and take them."

Oyang Kang shook his head. "And how will we drive them there, Your Highness? We have twenty-five dragons left, but some are injured, and we cannot herd the ships like sheep while also fighting enemy fire. It's over five hundred li to the coastline."

"We won't herd them," Tai said. "We'll let the winds and tide do our work."

Oyang glanced from the map to Tai, brow furrowed. "That would take—"

"Incredible magic," Tai agreed. "Or a few powerful silver and black dragons. They could even be injured. They would just have to influence the sea and winds. How many do you have?"

Tai could see he was swaying the man. The chance to re-establish his name and erase the shame of defeat clearly tempted the hero in Oyang Kang. "We have three blacks and four silvers."

"Then we'll make that work. Gather whichever riders are fit for battle."

When the men had arrived and overcome their shock at seeing the prince, he outlined his thoughts to them, using the map to illustrate their movements. He spied Jin's wing at the back, murmuring to each other and casting anxious glances about the tent.

"Jao, and Panshalar, is it?" he called out. "You have a question."

The two of them stopped murmuring immediately, eyes on him. He knew what they would ask, but also knew it was best to deal with it now.

"We were just . . ." Panshalar looked pained at trying to come up with an excuse that would not betray his wing leader as absent from duty.

Tai kept his expression neutral. He didn't want to lie, but telling the truth would only make the men resent his mother. And him. "He has other duties. I have excused him from this mission."

"Your Highness, he is the wing leader—" Jao protested.

"And the commander in chief of Dragon Class has told you he was excused," Oyang Kang barked. "Is that understood?"

Jao frowned but muttered, "Yes, Commander."

Tai turned back to the map. "Does everyone understand the plan? We will distract Baikalan from the ships, allowing our silvers and blacks to drive the armada into this bay, where we can more easily attack and defeat them."

"All respect, Your Highness," Panshalar cut in. "But what of Baikalan? We can't get near the ships if he's patrolling while invisible."

"We'll have bait to distract him," Tai said.

A tall, lanky rider with a crooked nose snorted, but at Tai's glance he had the decency to compose himself.

"Who's going to volunteer?"

"Me," Tai answered. A sharp intake of breath swept the men. "Baikalan won't pass up a chance to capture the crown prince and bring the empire to its knees." Perhaps his mother would give him up the way she'd given him up to Gao, but the dragon wouldn't know that. "Now, everyone, pay attention. We haven't time for me to repeat myself."

CHAPTER 35

Jin couldn't tell how long she had been in the ship, except it felt like days, possibly weeks. She was only let out to eat and drink, the food nothing but dried fish and seaweed, but even this was welcome.

She found the portions woefully inadequate, and the few times they let her up on deck, she immediately sought out the other ships, trying to find a sign of Rayshan. Or Emar. But she saw neither, and the bond with Rayshan stayed silent. She had never gone so long without hearing him in her head, without sensing his heartbeat, and she was starting to feel hollow, like something was slowly carving out pieces of her.

The fourth time her captors brought her up, a palpable nervousness permeated the air, and she stiffened. Was this the day they would unbond Rayshan from her? But from what she could tell, the mages had fallen ill. One was heaving the contents of his stomach over the side, and another looked green in the face. Such mages could not work enough magic.

But then she noticed a familiar smell, and the hair on her arms prickled. There was something eerie about that smell, something she didn't like. She peered through the mist toward the coastline.

Coastline.

She hadn't seen land for days and knew that coming this close to shore was dangerous, unless they were already in the land of Champa. Her gut twisted. If they were already there, then they were nearly upon Mengkhis Lai.

But the weather felt too cold to be Champa, and Jin listened.

Her guards pulled her roughly forward toward the king of Parhae, who stood near the bow arguing with Ulagan. Their raised voices carried through the mist, and another man, small and wiry, stood next to them, a sextant in his hand as he bowed and muttered protests.

". . . nowhere near. Is this a trick of yours?"

"He is the best navigator I have."

"Then why are we nearly grounded?"

"The winds have been unfavorable, Your Highnesses," the man with the sextant said, voice strained. "There was nothing we could do but find port."

"Nothing you could do," King Ulagan snarled. "That's all I hear from your Parhae swine."

"Careful," the king of Parhae barked. "You are still on my boats, and by that, I have rule here."

"Then get us to Champa," Ulagan snapped back. "And soon. Once this weather dies down, we should be setting out to sea where we can't be attacked by Tang counterforces."

He turned to look at Jin. "In the meantime, let's get on with securing my dragon." He signaled to someone in the crow's nest, and there was a flash of light as the lookout there angled a mirror. There was precious little light in this mist, but there must have been enough, for an answering flash came from a neighboring boat, and Jin felt the deck beneath her shift as the ship turned course.

"You could kill him," Jin said.

Ulagan shrugged. "A risk I'm willing to take."

Jin thought hard. She had to save Rayshan, for she could not bear to be unbonded from him, much less have him be like one of the miserable dragons who flew above them now, their eyes empty, a mere shell of themselves.

Perhaps she could wait until they took the metal hood from him and then tell him to fly with her, for they would have to remove any lead device from him before the mage's magic could work on him. Perhaps they would need her as well. They couldn't just unbond her without her there, could they?

As if to answer her question, the guard roped her feet together and bundled her over his shoulder. She swung helplessly over the man's back, and raged, but forced herself to stay calm and wait. If they had to move her to Rayshan's ship, then at least she and Rayshan would have to be brought together. Her heart thudded. Once that happened, they had a chance. She had to believe they had a chance.

The soldier holding her went to the railing, where grappling hooks were already landing to secure the two ships together. Jin saw no sign of Rayshan, but when the soldier stepped across the plank bridge that had been hooked to her ship and he landed on the other deck, she saw a great yawning hole in the middle of the deck, where a set of trapdoors had been winched open.

Bound by chains, with a lead hood covering his head, was Rayshan, and Jin's heart nearly split at the sight of him trapped. He raised his snout in the air. His nostrils flared, and he strained against his bonds. He could smell her.

Rayshan! she cried, though she knew he couldn't hear. But she could tell in the way he moved that he sensed her all the same.

"A beautiful creature," Ulagan said, materializing by her side. "A wonderful addition to my others."

Jin swore to herself that she would tear out his eyes when she had the chance. It occurred to her that Ulagan was about to steal back what she'd stolen. But that was different. She'd stolen Rayshan's egg, but Rayshan had chosen her himself. He would never have chosen Ulagan, not without the forced bond of a mage.

"Bring her down!" Ulagan bellowed. "Have the mages follow."

Three mages in purple robes immediately lined up beside Jin, while another lowered himself down a rope to Rayshan's level. Deck hands shimmied down ropes to tie Rayshan's snout shut, so that he could not snap them in half once the hood came off. For the hood encased everything but the ears and nose, with even the eyes covered in lead.

The mages undid the hood, and Rayshan tried to roar, but it was useless, for his jaws had been bound shut.

Rayshan! she cried.

Jin!

Fight the unbonding when it comes!

I will not be unbound from you. I WILL NOT!

But in her heart she feared it was a futile ask, for no one could withstand mage magic, and the forces of unbonding or bonding. Could they? Could their blood bond be strong enough? Already the mages were circling the dragon, sprinkling a strange ocher dust around him, just as they had when they had bonded the bronze dragon to Ulagan. Only, this time, they would put Rayshan through double pain: that of unbonding from Jin and rebonding to Ulagan.

The mages began to chant, and Rayshan reached out to her.

Jin, do you smell that?

She stilled and let her senses open. *I smell the ocean, the sweat, the fear . . .*

No, underneath, Rayshan said. *I smell . . .*

And then she caught it, the scent of bones bleached by sun, the tang of blood and ash in the sand.

Jimo.

CHAPTER 36

It had taken two nights, and at times, Tai had worried the dragons and their riders might collapse from exhaustion, but they had managed to secretly steer the ships within sight of shore.

The black dragons had tracked, then circled the convoy under the cover of night, before pulling on the winds, angling the sails until the vessels were tacking southwest. Half of the silver dragons had worked the tides, keeping formation just out of sight on the armada's west. The other half had used their water abilities to work up a thick sea fog near the ships, hiding the stars so that any navigators on board would not sense the change of direction until it was too late.

Adjusting so many ships over five hundred li was no easy feat, and Tai had never read of such a military maneuver, but it seemed as if they might just pull it off. Now for the rest of his plan.

Oyang Kang scanned the dawn skies as they neared shore. They had been flying for a night without rest, and the dragons could take no more. They would have to hope that the winds and tides they had set in motion did the rest, and if they did, then the Parhae ships would be appearing on the horizon by noon.

"Baikalan should know something is amiss by now and will come hunting," the war hero said. "Are you sure you don't want me to play decoy?"

"Well, now that you ask, I could use your help. I'll need a ride."

Oyang grinned. "Good. The thought of you getting all the glory is almost scarier than Baikalan himself."

Tai didn't need the reminder of how dangerous this was. Decoying Baikalan so that someone could get an arrow or a shot of flame in to damage the dragon's wing would require precision and no small amount of luck. But it was their only chance of taking Baikalan out of the fight long enough for them to attack Ulagan's ships.

As he changed from mage robes to his imperial yellow ones, Tai caught a hand quivering and drew a steadying breath. He was about to throw himself before two of his greatest fears. He had just finished sliding two daggers into his waistband when a cry went up from Jao.

"Baikalan! Incoming!"

Tai's head snapped up. He caught a flicker of jade

green before Baikalan disappeared into thin air, leaving Tai's blood cold.

"Scatter!" Oyang Kang bellowed, and the squads rushed to obey. Tai vaulted onto a nearby rock, then grasped Oyang's outstretched hand. He had barely settled himself behind the rider when Oyang's black dragon, Heiyan, launched into the sky, wings pummeling.

A scream erupted, and Tai glanced back.

One dragon was trying to stay airborne despite the giant rip in his wing, while his rider tumbled to the ground.

"Come on, you worthless bag of scales," Tai muttered, undoing the sash at his robe so the silks billowed free behind him, a bright unmistakable yellow banner flashing in the sunlight.

Oyang and his dragon climbed, making sure that Baikalan could see them. Once Baikalan knew there was an imperial prince, he would abandon all else, surely. For the jade would know what a bargaining chip a royal prince offered.

But the screams below continued, and Tai chanced another glance down. A silver lay in the sand, trying to defend itself against invisible claws. From here it looked like wounds were magically opening of their own accord, blood soaking the ground as the silver tried to close its jaws on a part, any part, of his unseen foe.

The silver's rider launched himself upward, but an

invisible limb batted him aside, smashing him into the sand where he lay with his neck at an impossible angle.

Tai's gut twisted, but he knew there was nothing he could do. "Bank! We have to distract him," Tai shouted over the wind.

Oyang dove straight into the melee, and Tai almost relished the feeling of impact as they barreled into the unseen dragon. Baikalan flickered back into vision. His muzzle was stained with blood from his silver victim, and his eyes locked on Tai's, recognition dawning.

The dragon loosed a roar that seemed to shake the very sky, and then Baikalan launched himself after them, not even bothering to turn invisible.

Tai gripped hard, willing himself to stay astride as fire blazed a mere arm's length behind them. Oyang's dragon snarled, and Tai detected a whiff of burnt flesh, but then they were diving—Baikalan with them—over rocky terrain that bordered the shore. Baikalan flamed again, aiming for Heiyan, trying to maim the dragon to unseat Tai.

The black rose and twisted, blasting a swirling tunnel of air directly at Baikalan, but the jade dodged and vanished.

"Storm pocket!" Oyang Kang shouted, and the surrounding air shifted, closing in a tight knot around them. Tai had seen this only a few times, as only older dragons who had seen battle knew this trick. Heiyan was creating a storm barrier around them, cocooning them, Oyang and Tai at the center, so that any enemy would have to plunge through a raging wall of air to get to them.

For a moment, Tai relished the feeling of safety. The walls of the cyclone blocked everything from sight and muted almost all other sounds.

Stay with us, Baikalan . . .

He needed to buy the others time to go and attack the ships. But how long could Heiyan keep this up? Tai had heard of Heiyan's legendary strength, but could it—

A hole burst open in the storm wall. Claws locked on Tai and ripped him off Heiyan, while his robes tore in the wind.

The storm crushed Tai's lungs until he couldn't breathe, and then he was flying upside down. He pulled himself up to grasp one of the claws holding him, and spotted several dark shapes in pursuit. Oyang Kang, Panshalar, and Jao.

Baikalan swerved as Heiyan blasted them with wind, causing Tai to lose his grip. He swung wildly, the earth rushing by in a sickening blur, but he forced himself to reach for his daggers. Just as he pulled them out, Baikalan twisted into a steep rise. The daggers slipped from Tai's grasp, spinning away and disappearing.

Tai cursed. His strategy had not included capture, and he would have to incapacitate the dragon for his riders to have any chance of taking down the ships.

He willed his stomach to settle, racking his brains

for a way to make the dragon drop him. He had no dragon, no weapon, and his mage skills were laughable —he could barely freeze a cup of water.

Freeze a cup of water.

By the eight levels of hell, would it work? It had to, because options were as slim as flea hairs right now.

He focused on the dragon's head. There'd be no walking the circle as Situ Han had taught him, no way of focusing on his mai except by pure concentration while flying upside down and facing death.

But his life depended on it.

He blocked out everything, took several steadying breaths, and harnessed the magic he needed.

A gust of fire blew past them, the heat raising blisters on Tai's arms and shattering his focus.

Stop! Tai wanted to shout. But he knew Oyang couldn't hear him, and besides, the man was working blind as both Baikalan and Tai were invisible. He concentrated again, this time urging, *forcing* his magic to flow and pinpoint faster.

A grunt, then a roar from overhead, and Baikalan flickered into visibility. Oyang shouted to the others, and the jade dropped altitude at an alarming speed as he shook his head violently—for Tai's magic had frozen the surface of the dragon's eyes. It wouldn't hold for long, Tai knew, but perhaps it would be enough to—

Heiyan blasted a wicked stream of fire that hit Baikalan in the tail.

And then he was falling.

Tai plummeted, Baikalan writhing in fury above him before swooping away. Tai caught a flash of metal as Panshalar loosed an arrow, before a satisfying scream came from Baikalan. Tai landed with bruising force on an outstretched bronze wing. He scrabbled for purchase, hands grasping a wing bone just as his legs slipped over the side to dangle over nothingness.

"Over here, Your Highness!"

Tai looked up at Jao in the saddle. His bronze had tripled his size to give them the best chance of catching Tai.

"You'll have to slide, Your Highness!" Jao called. Tai remembered the maneuver—he had seen it done but, of course, never performed it himself.

It's just like sliding down an awning, he told himself sternly, *just like sliding down an—*

The dragon tilted hard to the left, and all rational thought melted into terror. Tai's stomach churned at the sight of the ground far below, but some last-minute instinct made him lean into the slant, hurtling toward the saddle.

He reached Jao's outstretched hand what seemed an eternity later. He held tight as Jao pulled him up, and though Tai longed for solid ground, even if just for a moment, he knew they had no time.

He shouted so loudly his throat scraped raw. "To the ships!"

CHAPTER 37

*J*in could still not quite fathom that they were in Jimo.

Jimo, where Mengkhis Lai and Baikalan had massacred an entire city's adult male population and sent thousands of souls to their deaths in the sea. She looked up, trying to spy the great jade dragon, but found only wind-scraped sky.

The mages were marking Jin's forehead with ocher and smearing it on her lips. She tried to spit it off her, but the mage slapped her face so hard spots of light danced before her.

"Stay still," the mage said simply, without emotion, and began reapplying the ocher to her now split lip, the blood mingling with the clay.

The chanting increased in tempo, and already Jin felt strange, like millions of toothed worms were gnawing their way out from beneath her skin.

Rayshan, when I give you the signal, flare as hard as you can.

Who are we summoning?

Everyone, she replied. *Flare as hard as you can, as bright as you can.*

Rayshan's mental bond quivered and then screamed. The mages were shredding his bond.

She drew on every drop of energy. *Are you ready? FLARE!*

Nothing happened.

Oh by heaven. She was too late. The bond had already broken; perhaps Rayshan couldn't even hear her.

But then everything blurred and his glow burst forth, bright and pulsing, its light unmistakable. Hope surged.

Harder!

She focused as Yuli had taught her, ignoring the chanting that tangled around her like ropes, biting into her and stripping her of her bond with Rayshan. She fought them off, concentrating on the memory of Jimo: a belt in the sand, its buckle cracked and caked in barnacles; a rotted wooden clog, buried and blackened in the surf.

Think of the person's essence. If you had to reduce them to one word, what would it be? Yuli's words came back to her.

What was the one thing those men in Jimo had felt? What bound them?

Love.

Love for their children had made those men do Mengkhis's bidding, made them drink the sea until their insides drowned in salt. Just so they could see their children again. Love had united those thousands of men in Jimo that day.

And then she felt them. First one, then a dozen, then more. They materialized on the ship deck, specters at first but then slowly solidifying, their edges sharpening.

"Hey! Who goes there?"

"What—what are those people?"

"Cut them down!" King Ulagan barked.

And then she heard shrieks in the sky. Dragons. Dragons who were not Ulagan's, but who were attacking the ships. There was Bayan, and Oyang Kang on his black dragon, and several other dragons she recognized from the squadron.

Suling shot by on his bronze, with Mao and several other Dragon Class riders.

Hope gave Jin new strength, and confusion swept through the ship at the apparitions and enemy dragons. Suling's bronze breathed a great wall of fire, engulfing the sails of the ship that had so recently been Jin's prison.

Keep flaring! Jin cried. Even now, Satu and Shatang were flying up to meet the attackers, belching fire and giving chase.

Jin opened herself, trembling with the weight of the

souls as they flooded toward Rayshan's flare, drawn by the light.

Yuli's voice came again. *Invite them.*

She inhaled. The dead were not hers to command, just as the past was not hers to change. *I ask nothing of you, but invite you to come if you wish, and take form.*

Jin focused as hard as she could, letting go all her energy and will. The dead appeared to rise from all directions, as if a gate to a dam had been opened. The power of thousands of souls passed through Jin—the whisper of a million fates snuffed in one day, for Mengkhis Lai had killed several thousand, but those thousands would have created another three hundred thousand for whom there now would be no life. Untold lives, hopes, loves won and lost, dreams lived and broken. Countless lives cut short and even more who would instead float away in nothingness, never to be woven into life.

The vessel groaned under the weight of thousands of Jimo's dead. They descended on the Parhae men, and climbed the masts, breaking into the cabins. Someone undid the chains holding Rayshan's head, though the one around his neck held. His head swung, swiping mages who ran for cover.

Jin felt the heat of the souls burning her, searing her nerves as they fed on her and Rayshan's energy to take shape. She was going to become ash herself, surely, as waves of them rose from the water, climbing the ship rigging.

A sky-rending scream sounded, and then Baikalan materialized overhead. He scattered the imperial dragons, then vanished before reappearing above a black dragon. He ripped the rider from his saddle and crushed one of the black's wings with his claws, going invisible again before two silvers could come to their companion's aid. The black dragon and his rider spiraled to the sea, devoured by the waves.

Jin tried to hold on, to keep Rayshan's flare alive. Pain radiated from her head down her neck, but she refused to give in. When the mage who had applied ocher tried to pull her away by her bound wrists, she grit her teeth, locked her fingers together and smashed her bound fists up into his chin, crumpling him.

She looked up in time to catch a flash of green as Baikalan swept down to bathe the risen dead in fire, but this seemed to only invigorate them, until they were clinging to the jade's wings and tail, weighing him down by sheer mass. Someone threw a grappling hook, which tore a ragged hole in one wing. The dragon half crashed, half landed on the ship, and snapped the grappling line with his jaws, but another grappling hook bit into his tail, drawing a roar of pain from the jade.

Rayshan struggled to climb out of the ship's hold, his claws gouging the wood as he tried to free his wings. But the chain around his neck wouldn't allow him enough lead to get his hind legs over the hold's ledge.

Jin! To me!

But Jin was too weak. Already the dead were dissipating, dissolving into ash that coated the planking, the sails, the ballasts. The force of thousands of souls ripping through her had brought her to her knees, a white-hot stake driving its way into her skull. Vomit splattered onto the deck—hers, she realized—and her limbs trembled. She stood shakily, head hammering, in time to see Jao on his bronze—and was that Prince Tai?—wing in along with Panshalar and Oyang Kang. But just then a fighting pair of fleeing Parhae soldiers stumbled into her, sending her head first into Rayshan's pit.

Her dragon shielded her with his body, still calling her name.

Stay with me, Jin! You have to stay awake, fight it!

She tried, but she almost felt dead herself. Devoid of energy, she struggled to stand. Dimly, she noticed water pouring in from the left. A weapons chest had smashed the hull, its contents piled against the hole, and seawater was pouring in. It would only be a matter of time before the ship sank. And she would be with it.

We have to fly, she said. She managed to work the rope off her ankles, then began working at the knots on her wrists until they were free.

Exactly! Rayshan cried. *But first we have to get you out. I can't spread my wings here. Grasp on to my tail.*

She did as he asked, unsure whether she could even hold on. Hearing a familiar voice shout from behind wooden planking, Jin looked around, perplexed. Was that—Emar?

Rayshan, wait, it's—

Watch out!

Rayshan hurled Jin up onto the deck, where she landed in a pile of broken wood and a scattering of bodies. Thoughts of Emar fled as she took in the destruction around her. The sails and crow's nest were on fire, incinerating most of the Parhae men trying to escape and leaving thick clouds of smoke that clogged Jin's lungs. Through bleary eyes, Jin made out the infernos of other ships, where Oyang Kang and the others were raining fire on everything in sight.

At the bow, Baikalan managed to yank free of the grappling hook. But the force of his tail also shattered a burning mast. It leaned, then fell, pulverizing the anchor winch and setting parts of the deck on fire. Metal screamed as the freed anchor chain snaked along the deck, a section snarling around Baikalan's hind leg as it slid over the porthole. The entire ship trembled as the great jade was pulled to the deck, his claws raking deep furrows as he struggled to stay on deck.

Jin fought the steepening tilt of the ship and scrambled to her feet, only to find herself staring into King Ulagan's livid face, his hair white with the ash of the dead.

"I can't kill you," he spat, "but he can."

The king shoved her, hard, sending her rolling down the slanted deck toward Baikalan's waiting jaws.

She tried to stop herself, but her exhausted muscles wouldn't obey. One hand felt the burn of rope, and she grasped at it, halting her tumble toward death. The dragon's eyes gleamed, and a wave of hot air told Jin what was coming.

Jin!

Rayshan's head appeared above the pit ledge, his snout pushing up a burly figure wielding an ax.

Emar.

The man pulled himself over the ledge and stood, then with a surprising strength, launched himself at Baikalan, ax held high. "For Yalongma!"

His blade found Baikalan's left forearm, biting deep into flesh, bone, and deck.

Baikalan bellowed, wings beating. The dragon made a grab for Emar, but in doing so tore his arm, finishing the job the ax had started. Blood slicked the deck as Baikalan scrabbled for purchase. But with only one forearm, he slid into the sea, steam hissing as he breathed fire underwater. Emar watched him go, white eye wild and chest heaving.

Jin heard movement behind her and too late shouted, "Emar!"

A dagger protruded from Emar's shoulder, blood already blooming. Jin pulled herself over to the rails just as the old teacher toppled over them and onto the back of Oyang's swooping black dragon.

Behind you!

Rayshan's warning made her turn around,

summoning what energy she could. There was no time to think about Emar, or anyone. She needed to survive.

Ulagan lunged at her. She dodged, but his sword found her cheek, trickling blood onto her neck. Rayshan grunted at the pain he felt, having slid back down into the pit. Half of the ship was now lilting sideways, slipping into the water as the sea fought to claim it.

Ulagan lunged again, but this time Jin was ready. Ulagan blocked her path to the ax, still stuck to the deck with Baikalan's forearm, so she rolled in the opposite direction. A broken piece of the ship's mast was the closest weapon, and she hefted it like a club, sidestepping a pile of burning rigging.

Ulagan chuckled. "You think you'll best me and my sword with a piece of wood?" He dove in and delivered several vicious sweeps, making Jin stumble over messy snarls of rope and abandoned weapons. The ship was sinking more rapidly now, and Rayshan's chain was still holding. She had to get him out, before he was taken to the seas.

Hang on! she called out as she parried another of Ulagan's blows.

"You can't die, but you can spend eternity at the bottom of the ocean. How does that sound?" Ulagan chuckled, shifting his blade.

"You have to best me first," Jin growled with more confidence than she felt. She had little strength left, so precision was key.

She lunged, timing her blow to smash his kneecap. To her surprise, he merely grunted, whereas most men she knew would have at least dropped their swords.

"Is that all you have, little girl?" Ulagan laughed. "Here, let me show you how a Khitan man fights."

He redoubled his efforts and came slashing. Every blow rippled down her arm, and though she was blood bonded and had Rayshan's strength, Rayshan was weakened from fighting his own battle, and she was not nearly recovered from summoning the dead of Jimo. She sensed the water was already up to Rayshan's chest, and soon, his head would be under if she couldn't get Ulagan off her.

She caught movement from Rayshan. Ulagan used the distraction and launched himself on her, sending them both crashing into a supply room below where boxes floated in seawater and bits of sailcloth swam amongst the debris. She couldn't see Rayshan and realized she must be in an adjacent chamber. Jin couldn't touch the ground here, and she had lost even her paltry club. Panic seized her at the memory of a cold river, of being tied and going underwater, of darkness taking over.

"Oh, can't the little girl swim?" Ulagan laughed. He easily stood above the waterline, and now he seized her by the hair, forcing her head into the water.

Jin! Where are you!

She couldn't reply, as water was rushing up her nose and her lungs were burning. Panic spread through her like a living thing. Suddenly the wall of the cabin cracked, splintered, and caved as Rayshan's tail burst through it. The water level only surged higher, however, and Ulagan kicked her savagely as he tried to swim while holding on to her.

A shriek came from above, and Jin sensed Ulagan's dragon winging near.

"Satu! To me!" the king bellowed.

She was being lifted up, Ulagan gripping her by the hair as she thought he would rip her scalp off. She grasped his forearm to lessen the pain. Ulagan's other arm clung to Satu's tail, which the dragon had lowered like a rope.

Rayshan, I'll come back for you, I swear it.

She closed her eyes and reached out to Satu. This was her last hope. *Satu, I am sorry for what I did. For all of it. But you deserve better. You do not deserve Ulagan.*

A flash of anger seared her mind. She pushed past the painful buzzing, determined.

You have every right to be angry. But this man is the reason you had to be taken away, and he hurts you, wants nothing but to hurt you.

She recalled the day in the Blood Oval when the hatchling Satu was taken to Ulagan and bonded to him. She showed Satu the memory of Ulagan complaining about Satu's size and reactions, like meat at the market.

Defy your bond. Think of Nomu. Nomu, who loves you. This man does not love you.

A searing bolt of anger blazed, jagged and raw,

along with Ulagan's angry voice. "What are you doing to my dragon, you little whelp?"

Listen, Satu, he doesn't value you. Let him go. Let him go and drop us . . .

Satu hovered, wings beating. His head snaked back, jaws open, eyes furious.

Jin prepared to be ripped in half.

She heard a wet gasp.

Blood spurted from Ulagan's neck where his head should have been. His fingers clenched, then slackened. With a splash, Ulagan's head hit the water, and Jin followed closely after.

The salty sea enveloped her. Icy water seared her lungs, and she scrabbled desperately for the surface. Just as she was about to give up ever finding air, the ocean seemed to buoy her up, parting until she broke the surface and was momentarily airborne. Silver flashed, and then a hand pulled her up onto the dragon skimming by.

"Aadan?" she breathed, hardly daring to believe her eyes. Though dressed in mage robes, it was definitely Aadan.

"Are you alright?" he asked, holding her with one arm as if he would never let go.

She nodded, shivering. "But Rayshan—"

"Hang on."

They swept up and back toward the ship. By now, most of the vessel had broken apart, and the hold imprisoning Rayshan was almost completely submerged. They were just in time to spot Rayshan's snout disappear beneath the water.

She dove before Aadan could stop her and heard his curse before he followed. She swam down, kicking furiously against her panic, against the numbing cold, until she reached the chains that held Rayshan to the boat's beams. It had been looped through a thick iron ring, and down here, Rayshan's fire was useless.

We need a gold dragon, she said.

No time, Rayshan said, yanking against the chains.

You can't die. Just stay with me. But even as she said it, she knew that he was shutting down. And if he shut down, she would lose her bond with him, and if he sank too far below the surface, how would she find him again?

Aadan appeared next to her, his arms floating and his hair waving in the water. He pointed up and closed his eyes.

The water shifted. It was not pulling them down anymore but pulling them up, albeit erratically.

Wanli spoke to her. He could slow down the water's drag, but he didn't have the strength to make the water lift the entire ship and Rayshan to the surface. They needed to break the chain.

A gold. Who had a gold?

Bayan!

She heard an answering roar, and then the metal was lifting, straining. Even in the water, Jin could hear it groaning, and then it snapped. The chains snaked through the loop as Rayshan broke free, bubbles streaming from his nostrils as he reached out, grabbing Jin with one free forearm and Aadan with the other. His tail lashed like an eel as he fought for the surface, his wings tightly folded. They broke through, gasping.

All around them, ships were sinking, many still on fire, the sails billowing curtains of flame against a smoke-filled sky. Baikalan had disappeared into the sea, while dragons circled overhead. Jin spotted Jao and Prince Tai on Nakkalan, Panshalar on a triumphant-looking Bayan, and Oyang Kang on his black dragon, one arm around a weak but smiling Emar.

She looked over at Aadan. "Thank you."

His hand found hers beneath the water, and he squeezed.

Wanli created a current, bringing a section of ship decking closer to them. Rayshan clawed his way on, Aadan and Jin holding on to his tail. He shook the water from his wings and breathed fire to clear his throat and lungs.

The dragons were circling down when she noticed her wing mates' faces contort with horror. "Jin!"

She turned.

The great green head broke the surface an arm's length from Jin, and then claws held her. Baikalan pulled Jin with him back into the waves, the anchor chain still tangled in his legs.

If I am spending years in the ocean, you will spend it with me, Baikalan said.

She reached out for Rayshan and heard his anguish as she sank beneath the waves, Baikalan's grip squeezing the air from her lungs in clouds of bubbles that slithered away from her.

Then the voices died away, and darkness closed overhead.

CHAPTER 38

Tai watched in shock as the dragon disappeared with Jin. Aadan shouted her name, then dove off the decking into the water after them.

Tai leapt off Jao's bronze, the cold shocking his body and making his skin feel on fire. He swam out to where Baikalan had disappeared and searched the depths. Aadan bobbed to the surface, but the frantic look in his eyes told Tai that he couldn't reach them.

Just then, Rayshan flew high into the air, spiraling.

"What's he doing?" Tai asked.

"I don't know. He can't have given her up—"

Just then, Rayshan turned, flipping head down, and folded his wings.

"By the Wise Lord, he's—"

Rayshan cocooned himself and dove toward them.

"Move!" Tai shouted, and he and Aadan swam hard

to get out of the way as Rayshan plummeted toward the water like an arrow. Wanli parted the water so that the jade could dive deeper.

Rayshan hit the surface like a spear, with barely a ripple around him as he sliced through the water and into the depths below.

Aadan and Tai waited, along with the other riders, trying to see. But the reflection from the clear skies above and the churned water made seeing anything impossible, and they could only hold their breaths. A moment. Two.

Tai's heart pounded as he tried not to give up hope, tried to ignore his limbs growing numb with cold. But as the time crawled by, he couldn't think that Rayshan would ever find Baikalan and Jin. They had sunk to the bottom of the ocean, and surely even a blood-bonded dragon wouldn't be able to go all the way to the ocean floor?

Aadan shouted, pointing. Some distance away, Rayshan had burst through the water, clutching a limp figure. The other dragons flew over, and again, Wanli moved a large piece of debris over for Rayshan to climb onto. The dragon drew himself, claw by claw, onto the shattered half of the ship deck, and Tai saw the figure he clutched. Tai struck out toward the deck immediately, Aadan in pursuit.

They clambered aboard, both soaking and shivering, but more intent on the rider in Rayshan's clutches.

Jin lay inert under her dragon's chest, with not even

a hint of breathing. Rayshan himself, Tai noticed, seemed shaky on his legs, as if he would collapse from exhaustion, and was coughing up seawater.

Aadan immediately rolled Jin onto her side, opening her mouth and pressing hard on her stomach. Some water trickled out, but still, Jin did not stir.

"You cannot die, Jin," Aadan muttered. "Not like this."

But Tai knew the rules of blood bonding. She could die, as Baikalan had been the one to drag her into the sea.

"Wanli!" Aadan screamed.

The dragon's wings beat the air as he pulled close, and Aadan looked at the dragon pleadingly. Wanli bent his head over Jin's, the great snout only breaths from hers, and concentrated, hovering above her.

Jin's body trembled, and water began to flow out of her mouth and nose, running over the sides of her face and onto the wooden deck.

"She's freezing," Aadan said, resting a hand on her cheek. It was indeed a disturbing shade of blue.

"Here," Tai said. "I can help." He focused his chi and let it warm his hands, then brought them against Jin's collarbone and along her neck. He focused, making the warmth flow from the mage-induced chi into her body. Wanli continued to draw water, and her pulse fluttered under his hands.

"Where'd you learn to do that?" Aadan asked, astounded.

"Being a caged prince means I had a lot of spare time."

A spluttering interrupted him, and Jin sat up, water rushing from her and onto the deck. She coughed and threw out a hand to clutch Aadan, who crushed her against him. Jealousy clouded the relief Tai felt at her being alive, but he locked it away.

"What—" Jin looked around frantically, but at Rayshan's tail curling against her seemed to calm down. "Rayshan says he dove after me."

Aadan nodded. "And Wanli took the water out of your lungs." He glanced at Tai. "Though if Tai hadn't stepped in, you might have died of cold."

Jao's dragon swept alongside, and he dropped a cloak from a saddle pouch he had with him. "Here, use this."

Aadan wrapped the cloak tightly around Jin.

"I know you love the water," Tai remarked. "But perhaps you're ready to make it back to shore?"

Jin nodded.

Rayshan flexed his wings gingerly, then let Jin climb on. He took to the sky, and Aadan helped Tai climb aboard Wanli.

"Didn't take my advice about leaving?" Tai said.

Aadan shook his head. "It didn't feel right."

He was glad to see his friend, but as he watched Aadan staring at Jin as if afraid she would disappear, Tai hoped it wasn't too late for the Persian to escape the empire.

THEY REACHED THE SHORE AND DISMOUNTED, JIN'S HEAD pounding from the salt and sea she had absorbed. Her feet sank in the sand as she half stumbled, half walked to where Panshalar and Mao had propped Emar up to make him comfortable. Nomu was sitting to one side, hands bound. The gold and bronze dragons lay wary but silent next to her.

Jin knelt next to Emar. His shoulder had been roughly bandaged and his hair had come loose from its tie. His white eye moved along with his good one, a sea of pain evident there.

"Master Emar," she said, "I'm sorry."

He closed his eyes. "You wouldn't happen to have poppy and wine on you, would you?"

She shook her head, chest tight.

Prince Tai stepped forward and leaned down. "Let me help."

Emar grunted. "I was meant to go twenty years ago. And I held on, for some false hope. I've been a foolish man." He grimaced, then clutched Tai's forearm in a gesture of familiarity that would have been punishable by anyone else. "And Your Highness, remember you are noble. It's something no one can write away with a pen."

Tai frowned, clearly as confused at his words as Jin was. "Save your strength," Tai said gently.

"We'll find some poppy," Jin promised.

"You and the riders will be just fine," Emar coughed. "Baikalan is at the bottom of the sea, where Mengkhis will never find him. All is safe for now."

"There must be something I can do," Jin said, but Emar fluttered his fingers.

"Don't bother. There's nothing anyone can do. I now go to death. And Yalongma."

We cannot save him. Rayshan craned his neck. *But there is one thing we can do.*

Jin looked at him. *We have never tried it.*

But I know I can.

Jin nodded, her eyes tearing but willing her strength to return, if only for this one feat. She had already taxed Rayshan and herself to the limit, but now she would ask for one more.

Flare, she said.

She placed a hand on Emar's arm and said, "What do you think of when you think of Yalongma?"

A smile split Emar's face, and he whispered, "Freedom."

Jin nodded. Rayshan's flare radiated outward as he stretched his wings and called out.

Jin took his flare, absorbing it and channeling it, reaching out with her being for the one they sought.

She knew she had succeeded when Emar's eyes widened. She followed his gaze into the sky, and a dragon's call split the air.

"It cannot . . ."

"It is," Jin said gently.

A great black dragon winged overhead, then landed in the sand. Rayshan and the others made way for him as the dragon walked forward and bent his head to push his snout against Emar, at first tentatively and then with greater force.

"I . . . have I died?" Emar asked, his face crumpling like a child's.

Jin shook her head. "Yalongma has come to you." She held out a hand to Emar. "Can you ride?"

Emar's white face almost moved in its determination. "By every Buddha on every altar, I'll ride."

She pulled him up but found he was surprisingly strong. Yalongma bent, angling himself so that Emar could find his footing and fling one leg over, sliding between two golden ridges that marked the black dragon's back. Jin touched the foreleg, the black scales there scarred and chipped, as the dragon's golden eyes turned to look at her.

Soar.

The black dragon spread his great leather wings and then leaped, showering everyone below with sand. He drew up into the sky, and even from the ground, they could hear Emar's long, low whoop of ecstasy. The dragon wheeled over the ocean, and at one point, as he circled back, Emar held out his arms and tilted his head to the setting sun, his hair streaming loose behind him, no longer straggling, but a banner in the wind.

Tai and Aadan stood with Jin as they watched him

weave through the clouds and dive, then rise again, the movements sinuous, joyous.

Jin wasn't sure whose heart ached more when the dragon finally came and landed back on shore, quiet and spent, lying down so Emar could dismount. He slid down, his hair wild and his eyes full of tears. But Jin knew it wasn't from the salt wind.

They gave Emar and Yalongma privacy while Emar murmured to his dragon and laid his hand on Yalongma's neck. The great black dragon began slowly fading to gray and then dissolving, his body turning to dust. Emar was still holding his head as Yalongma's eyes closed, and the ash sifted through his rider's fingers.

"I am sorry," Jin said. "I cannot do more. I'm sorry I could not save your life."

Emar turned to her, his lined face full of surprise. "Rider Jin, I died twenty years ago. You just gave me several precious minutes of life." He smiled. "Thank you. And now I really will go and join him." He leaned against the mountain of ash that had been Yalongma, watching its dust swirl away over the ocean. His breathing grew shallow, but he turned to her and motioned with one hand.

"Rider Jin, a favor, if you will."

"Of course," Jin agreed.

"Tell the empress that she was right." He turned back to watch the last of his dragon's ashes float over the ocean.

"Right about what?" Jin said gently. When he didn't answer, she ventured, "Master Emar?"

But he didn't answer, and sat propped, smiling into the sunset as strands of his white hair blew in the wind with a life of their own.

Tears stung her eyes, and she could see that Aadan, Prince Tai, and the rest of her wing were struggling with their own emotions.

"Walk well," Tai said, putting a hand on the old man's shoulder. "Uncle Emar."

Aadan bowed three times in the formal fashion and said a prayer in what Jin assumed was Persian. The remaining dragons raised their heads, and a high keening sound rose from them as they mourned the passing of a rider. And a friend.

Jin wanted to simply sit with Emar's body, but there were other things to attend to, not least the other riders who had fallen and the survivors from the battle.

She turned to Nomu, who had watched from the sidelines in silence, her young face stoic despite the loss of her father and so many of her people. Satu and Shatang were lying protectively next to her and snarled through their muzzles when Jin approached. She stood a safe distance away.

"Can we trust you?" she said to Nomu.

The girl nodded.

Jin pulled out her dagger, telling the dragons she meant to free rather than harm the girl, and cut Nomu's bonds, which had chafed her skin scarlet. Nomu stood on shaky legs.

"Everyone speaks of widows as unhappy people," Nomu said. "Yet I am happier today than yesterday."

The girl looked so small and fragile that Jin didn't want to ruin her relief, but she had to temper her expectations. "I do not have the authority to free you, but I'll do everything I can to protect you. You will need to come with us to Changan."

Nomu smiled wistfully. "How quickly our situations reverse."

Jin nodded, feeling absolutely no joy in this unexpected price of her own freedom. "The dragons will obey you?"

Nomu turned to place one hand on each. "I think so. I cannot speak to them as you do, but we understand each other somehow."

"Good." Jin expressed her thanks to Satu and told them both that once they had reunited with mages, they could take away the muzzles in favor of binding spells.

Oyang Kang and the remainder of the Dragon Class force watched the bonfire consume the bodies of their enemies. There was no time, or even strength, for burial. Tai was readying the other riders and survivors for transport back to the capital, and Jin found Aadan by her side as she looked out at sea.

"Wanli told me what happened, that you were to be bartered," she said.

Aadan looked down. "I don't want to go."

"You have to." She turned to him, anger at the

empress welling in her. "The empress has shown that she will sacrifice you if it works in her favor, and now that you've defied her by escaping, she will always view you with suspicion. You can't live your life that way."

"I also can't live my life away." He looked at her, and she felt that familiar swoop in her stomach, which made it all the harder to try to persuade him to leave. She wanted him here, not a thousand *li* away, but if staying meant that he might find himself betrayed or, worse, killed, then she'd rather he be safe. Even if it meant never seeing him again. Even if it killed a piece of her.

"You have to," she repeated. "The only safe place for you is in Persia, having won back your army, your kingdom. Then Empress Wu will have to treat you as a prince and not as a bargaining chip."

Aadan's eyes darkened. "It's hard to fight for a land you've never seen, especially if what—" he paused, seeming to wrestle with himself "—or who you love is here."

She swallowed, the ache in her chest making every other injury on her seem like a scrape. "I would rather have you gone and safe than here and always having to look over your shoulder."

"I will think about it, how about that?" he said.

"Don't think too long," she replied. "We have to return to the capital soon, and if anyone here changes their mind about you, they may decide to turn you in for a reward."

Aadan looked around at Panshalar and Nakkalan using their metalworking skills to repair broken saddle buckles, Jao organizing what remained of the weapons washed to shore so that they could arm themselves for the trip home, and Tai organizing the burial for Emar. "I trust them. They had my back when I most needed it."

They gathered that night around the funeral pyre for Emar and watched the flames take him. Aadan had explained that he would have wanted a fire funeral like those of his home rather than a burial.

To go in flames and fly to the sky was a proper way to honor him, unlike the Han people, who believed a desecrated body prevented one from entering the afterlife. Jin made a note to ask the dead whether that was true, though somehow she doubted it. And though Jin could have called Emar back, something in her heeded Lu's advice. The dead were not to be called without very good reason, and on their own terms.

She had found a flask of wine in one of the Khitan soldiers' belongings, and she tossed it on the fire to honor Emar. She missed him, for with him burned away the only other blood-bonded rider she knew besides Mengkhis Lai. She had so many more questions, and she would likely never be able to ask them.

Rayshan nudged her through the bond. *With any luck, we won't be meeting Mengkhis Lai.*

THAT NIGHT, THEY ATE WHAT THEY COULD, PACKED what they could carry, and prepared for the morning. Jin noticed Aadan growing increasingly somber, and Wanli's mood echoed his. She'd also seen him talking to Tai, in what appeared to be an intense consultation. Jin knew the morning would bring goodbye.

Her chest tightened with the impending loss, and she walked away from the fire to seek the isolation of the sandy dunes around them. Despite having told him to leave, somewhere she'd held out hope that Aadan, the smartest man she knew, would think of a way to stay.

Instinctively, her walking brought her toward a high jutting cliff that overlooked crashing waves below. She stood and let the bracing wind whip the long tussock grass around her, grateful for the distraction of the salt air and the icy sea spray on her cheeks, anything to drive out the smell of sandalwood and longing.

But even here, she could smell him, warm in the cold. And when fingers touched hers, she looked over to see Aadan standing there, his eyes on her.

"Tai agrees with you that I must go," Aadan said.

Though she knew this advice echoed hers, her heart still squeezed. Like a child, she had hoped for the impossible, that Tai would say he could protect Aadan, shield him from the empress.

"I don't want to," he continued softly. "I want to stay

wherever you are, fight your battles with you, die next to you if that's what comes."

Jin laced her fingers with his, the gesture both unfamiliar and natural at the same time. She had never experienced this feeling with anyone, and she still wasn't sure what to make of it, except that she wanted more. Still, there would be no such feelings if Aadan was killed, and she didn't want to be constantly worrying about his safety.

"I understand." He was a good deal taller than Jin, and she leaned her head against the side of his shoulder, giving in to the intoxicating smell and the feel of him. "You risked everything to come back."

"Because everything I cared about was here."

His words dissolved the last walls of her defenses. Tomorrow, she would be headed for Changan, and Aadan would be a fugitive. Already was a fugitive. She didn't know how long there was between now and her joining Emar and the countless souls in the darkness beyond, but if Emar had taught her anything in his last moments, it was to live fully.

She faced Aadan, her back to the sea, her face upturned. His breathing seemed to hitch, and a range of emotions swept across his face. She ran her fingers over his beard, over his neck, and before she could think, her mouth was on his and his hands immediately circled to the small of her back.

Though she had never bedded anyone in her life, she had taken advantage of couples' distractions to lift items and had fought off more than a few drunken and not-so-drunken advances. But never had she felt desire, and certainly not desire like this, which seemed to incinerate all rational thought in its path. Everything about Aadan attracted her, from his green eyes with their black-lined pupils, to his luxurious beard, to the distinct olive color of his skin.

Somehow, they found their way into the long grass, and as she pulled him to her, he hesitated.

"Are you sure?" His intense expression made her pulse surge.

She nodded, but then a thought occurred to her. "Unless you don't want me." The thought sliced her to the core, but she couldn't bear anyone's pity, least of all Aadan's.

"I'm not sure there's a word for what I feel for you," he said softly, then sighed, head bowed. "But I won't do this."

The burning in her died, and now the cold wind cut past all her clothing, chilling her. "Why not?" The anger in her voice surprised even her. "You leave tomorrow, and—"

He pushed himself off her and sat. "You're grieving. If I'm honest with myself, I'm grieving. I don't want this to be an act of comfort or, worse, mourning."

Jin tried to tame the whirlwind of emotions and longing in her, but it felt as impossible as yoking the sea.

She wanted to strike him for coming here and

saving her, for making her very soul want to wrap around him but then refusing her on this literal precipice. She wanted to rage at him for not slaking this unfamiliar feeling that seemed like it would rip her at the seams. Anger, desire, and confusion boiled inside her. Jin wanted to destroy something, beat her fists into a target that would crumple and break the way she felt her emotions were breaking her.

She looked into Aadan's eyes, ready to scream, and saw everything she felt reflected there.

Like a bottle shattering, sadness washed over her, sweeping away the desire and everything else. His arms were around her, tight, while his jacket suddenly felt wet, and she realized it was from her sobbing.

"It's unfair," she said at last when the tears let her speak. "If I hadn't stolen Rayshan, none of this, none of it—would have happened. And now I can't keep you."

He kissed her on the top of her head. "I know. But if you hadn't stolen Rayshan, I wouldn't have met you. And that's not a world I want either."

The warmth of his arms and chest lulled her as exhaustion took over. The stars moved in their set patterns in the sky, mockingly cheerful despite the fact that come morning, she would lose him.

And though she vowed to stay awake as long as she could, to etch every detail of him in her memory, his steady breathing slowly lulled her to sleep, the drumming of his heart the only sound that mattered in the world.

SHE WOKE TO WANLI'S VOICE IN HER HEAD, TELLING them it was dawn and time was short. Jin knew there would be talk if they weren't back down when the others awoke, though she found it hard to care. All she cared about was the man looking at her now as they lay curled in their meager bed of grass.

"I'll come back," he said. "Do you trust me?"

She did, she realized. Haitao had taught her to trust no one, but Aadan had risked his life to return for her. He would do it again. "Go and bring back an army," she said.

Aadan kissed her on the forehead, then the lips, before sitting up to look at her. "Wait for me," he said.

She smiled, fighting back the tears. "Just come back."

He squeezed her hand and then kissed her eyelids. "Keep your eyes closed."

"Why?" she whispered, wanting desperately to see him for every moment that she could.

"Because I don't want you to remember me as walking away from you," he said, his voice tight with the unspoken knowledge that they had no idea whether they would be apart for days, months, or years. "Do that for me. Please?"

Jin nodded, though it took all of her willpower to keep her eyes shut.

He squeezed her hands gently, then let go. She tried

to memorize the scent of him, the brush of his beard against her when he had kissed her.

She lay there for several moments, not wanting to open her eyes. For maybe if she kept them shut, he would still be there. But she knew this was foolish. The scent of sandalwood was nearly gone, and she could hear faint voices from below as the other riders greeted him.

By the time she reached the camp on the beach, Aadan was already a spot in the sky, Jao and Panshalar standing on the shore watching him go. She thought she saw Panshalar wipe a tear, but her own eyes were too blurred to know for sure.

"We've lost two in our wing in less than a year," Panshalar said.

"We haven't lost him," Jin said, though the words were unconvincing.

I feel your sadness.

Is it sadness? she asked. It felt like something more. A piece of her was disappearing with Aadan.

She smelled agarwood and incense.

"You look like you've lost your best friend."

She glanced at Prince Tai, who had silently joined her, then looked back at the empty sky. "Perhaps I have."

"That makes both of us."

She nodded, strangely comforted by Tai's presence. He was, after all, the only one who knew Aadan as well, if not more, than she did.

Impulsively, she said, "Would you ride with me on the way back, Your Highness?"

He hesitated.

"Unless you'd rather ride with Oyang Kang, Your Highness. I understand."

"No, I'd be honored."

They packed the rest of their supplies, made sure the few Khitan and Parhae prisoners were bound and placed securely in the crude cages they had built, and then mounted their dragons. They flew over the landscape heading northwest, passing countryside slumbering under a new layer of glistening snow.

CHAPTER 40

For the first time in his life, Tai didn't feel nervous on a dragon. Perhaps it was the way Jin rode, so sure of herself, as if she grew from Rayshan.

She rode with a rhythm that was in time with Rayshan's beating of wings, and Tai quickly grew used to it as well. He rose and fell with the movement, gradually learning to bank and shift his weight as she did.

He glanced in front of them at Oyang Kang leading the squad on his black dragon, followed by his wing and the two dozen dragons left from the attack, as well as the girl Nomu, who rode on her father's bronze, the gold flying alongside. They seemed content to follow her and left others alone as long as they didn't threaten the Khitan girl.

Rayshan dipped slightly as they angled further west to head toward the hills bordering Changan. As Tai leaned closer to Jin to keep his balance, he noticed a dark mark behind her ear, then realized it was a scar, a circle enclosing one single word.

Precious.

"Can I ask you a personal question?"

"Your Highness can ask anything he wants."

He wished he could break down Jin's acute awareness of social barriers. But water couldn't pierce stone in a day. "Let me put it another way. I'd like you to answer something if you are willing. Where did you get this mark behind your ear?" The word "kway" could mean either precious or expensive. Had she been branded as a slave?

She stiffened, tucking a strand of hair behind her ear to cover the scar. "I don't know. It's been with me since the day I was born."

"Is that how you came to be named Kway Jin?" he guessed. "Precious Gold?"

"My clan boss Haitao thought I'd bring great wealth by giving me that name. He thought the mark behind my ear was lucky."

"Perhaps your parents gave you that, so it would be true."

He could tell his comment surprised her. "I've never thought of it that way."

The scar on his neck twinged. "Since that night you saved my life, Little Crow, I sometimes think our scars are there to remind us of how lucky we are."

They flew on in silence after that, the wind making

talk difficult. But Tai was strangely content to just sit on the back of the dragon with Jin in front of him, and for the first time in his life, he was enjoying flying on a dragon. Up here, the world was far below, and a couple of times he was reminded that he could easily fall to a bone-shattering death. But then he'd remember the rope around his waist, the fact that it was attached first to the ridge in front of him and then to Jin's middle, bound in dragonrider leather and warm beneath his arm.

Although Emar's death was enough to have weighed on him, seeing Aadan follow Jin to the cliff had guaranteed him a sleepless night. He had also noticed Aadan's return just before dawn, and the sharp claws of jealousy shredded him all day long. It was an unfamiliar and absolutely foreign feeling that debilitated him, for no one, even Peilah, had ever made him jealous. No girl at court ever thought to endanger her position by suggesting a rival—not even Peilah, who had been so eager to create strife.

He cursed the fates, sure they were having a good laugh that though he was as physically close to Jin as a man could be, her heart was far away, winging toward Persia.

By the time they sighted the outskirts of Changan, news of their return and the battle at Jimo had reached the capital. A line of dragons waited to greet them, and as they landed at the roads that led into the capital, one of the riders came forward with an entourage of carriages, horses, and men.

"Peace upon your afternoon," the commander said, leaping from his dragon and taking in Prince Tai with some surprise. "Your Highness, we took the liberty of preparing a welcoming entourage. Your mother felt you should ride through the city on horseback."

Today, Tai couldn't fault the logic. A victorious returning party seen riding through the streets would give time for the people to celebrate and take part in their ruler's victory, whereas a dragon flight over the city would take all of ten minutes and deprive the city of a spectacle.

"I brought your steed, Your Highness," the commander said, gesturing a groom forward, "as well as an official robe so you are more presentable." Tai realized he was indeed a mess of shredded mage robes and mud-spattered boots. He was gladdened to see his horse, Leiyu, who nipped him softly in greeting.

Oyang Kang had slid to the ground. "Your Highness, might I suggest you lead the way with the riders and prisoners coming behind?" He glanced at the carriages. "I assume the dragonriders will be riding on horseback while the prince rides in the carriage?"

The commander was about to speak when Tai interrupted.

"I think it best if we are all seen on horseback." He turned. "Riding in a carriage might be too sedate."

Oyang Kang bowed, while Jin looked like she'd prefer to climb in the carriage and draw the curtains. "Including Rider Jin," he said. "The heroine of the hour cannot be locked away from view."

She frowned, as did Oyang Kang. Tai lowered his voice so only Jin could hear. "Moping won't help. This will distract you." She grimaced but bowed low, accepting.

"But, Your Highness," the commander said, "we didn't bring enough horses for everyone. Some of the riders will have to ride in the carriage."

"Very well." Tai put on the robe the groom held out for him, then mounted his horse before reaching down and holding out a hand to Jin. "We will ride together."

With a small sigh, Jin pulled herself onto the saddle behind him. Now that they were back in the capital with a palace full of gossip-mongers and intrigue artists, he would be wise to take care how he treated Jin in public. But he couldn't help make today an exception.

He noticed Jin trying to find something to hold on to. On Rayshan, he had been the one to hold on to her. But to touch a royal person uninvited was forbidden.

Tai wordlessly reached back and pulled her left arm around his waist, keeping it there with one hand as he nodded to the commander and goaded Leiyu into a canter. It felt good to be on horseback once more, the solid earth beneath hooves. The rest of the entourage fell into line, including Princess Nomu and her Khitan men. The commander pulled abreast as the dragons, including Rayshan, circled overhead, following the slower earth-bound mortals in steady swoops.

As they rode, he felt something warm in the inner pocket of the robe the commander had given him. He absently reached in and pulled out a stone, confused. But then he recognized it: it was the oval rock the magician had given him at the Festival of Sevens. It had changed from its original dove white to a bright, unmistakable crimson.

By the eight levels of hell.

He pocketed it, sighing, then lowered his hand once more over Jin's arm at his waist.

The sound of the bugles and drums on the walls deafened all thoughts, and then they were passing through the central Gate of Shining Virtue, its great doors having been thrown wide in welcome.

The Avenue of Vermillion Birds that ran from the main southern gate all the way to the palace at the north end was crowded with civilians, the imperial soldiers having set up silken ropes to hold the throng back so they wouldn't impede the horses now making their way down the city's largest thoroughfare. The people threw seeds, waved scarves, and flew serrated banners over every shop, chanting. The dragons flew overhead, circling back every so often to stay with the slower retinue on horseback.

He heard Jin's intake of breath and deciphered the words people were shouting: "Ten thousand years! May the Prince and Princess of Dragons live ten thousand years!"

Tai smiled and waved, thoughts swirling in his mind. Where had they come up with that phrase? Had mage Situ Han fed them this term, or could it be the crowds had made it up on their own, knowing the events of the past week? Knowing he, the head of Dragon Class, and Jin, the only female rider, had helped bring down the feared Baikalan?

He didn't know the truth, but for the moment, he also didn't care. Impulsively, he laced his fingers through Jin's hand at his waist and raised it into the air. The reaction was explosive, as a ripple of sound swept the crowds, its force startling even the dragons as their formation faltered momentarily.

"Do they think . . . you and I . . . ?" Jin ventured.

"You can try to tell them they're wrong," Tai shouted to be heard over the roar. "But I don't think they'll hear you."

"TEN THOUSAND YEARS! TEN THOUSAND YEARS! THE PRINCE AND PRINCESS OF DRAGONS!"

No, for the first time in his life, Tai relished a rumor. He was riding into Changan as the returning Prince of Dragons, with Jin's arm around him, the people hailing them like a ruling couple.

If only his mage skills included stopping time.

Their return was celebrated for a full seven days and nights, with the palace pulling out every luxury to ply their heroes with feasts, dance parties, giving of honors, and also a day of mourning for Emar.

Through it all Jin barely had time to herself, which might have been fortunate, as she found that time alone meant time thinking about Aadan, especially when she retrieved the orange silk scarf from under her pillow, its contents of nuts untouched.

She sat on her bed and held the gift, then gently opened the ties. Nestled inside were black melon seeds, green pistachios, ivory-white almonds, and raisins with the exact same shade of green as Aadan's eyes.

Jin stared at the pile in her hands. She had put his gift aside, unwilling to eat it. And despite how foolish she felt, she closed her eyes and whispered what she wanted most beneath her breath.

She opened her eyes and ate the gift one piece at a time, but she couldn't say how any of it tasted, for her throat and nose had closed with tears.

In the following days Jin tried to go flying with Rayshan, but the influx of officials and the full itinerary of celebrations kept her away even from Meipin, with whom she had insisted she continue sharing accommodation despite the multiple offers of a private residence for her.

The only person she saw much of was Tai, as she found they were often summoned together to events, seated at the places of honor. She tried to substitute Oyang Kang in, as she noticed he looked out of sorts at this sudden shift in his own fame, but no one would even entertain it. Least of all, she found, the organizing mages and household valet.

Even Sanjin insisted on displaying her like Tai's indispensable companion, and so she dutifully went, dressed in new shiny leathers, silk gowns, and fur cloaks, to attend the temple ceremonies thanking Buddha for their safe return, praising the gods and goddesses of the different altars at all four corners of the city for granting victory over Baikalan.

Rayshan accompanied her to some of them, where they were expected to swoop in and awe the spectators with a brief show of fire breathing. The stories of their ability to summon the dead had also spread far and wide, for the palace had disseminated pamphlets with images of Jin and Rayshan leading an army of the dead to bring down their enemies.

Is that the empress? Jin had asked Rayshan when she showed him a copy.

As a Bodhisattva, it seems, Rayshan had huffed. In the upper corner of the images showing Jin and Rayshan and Prince Tai fighting the Parhae ships, a glowing Bodhisattva floated on a cloud behind Jin. These pamphlets were freely distributed through the streets, and the story was retold on every corner and in every inn, where embellishments about the empress's holy strength and Jin's divine gift multiplied daily. Even Panshalar and Jao seemed happy to pitch in to this version. Panshalar eagerly regaled anyone who would listen with stories of the battle and how Bayan had freed Rayshan in his hour of need, while Jao was happy to back him up with grunts of agreement or snide remarks when the giant's tales grew too tall.

Jin had asked Prince Tai about Nomu and her dragons when she had a chance, and was relieved at the prince's reply.

"She's in good health and has a small suite of private apartments within the palace." Prince Tai had given her a rueful smile. "She's a valuable bargaining chip with the Khitans, so we will keep her and the dragons here to make sure her brothers don't do anything rash."

"Do they care whether she lives or dies?" Jin asked, dubious.

"Regardless of whether they have any sibling affections, a royal princess is still an asset for them in forging alliances."

Jin tried her best to have a private moment with the empress, but her promised meeting times kept getting postponed. After the third such delay, Jin mustered her courage during a walk with the empress to a Buddhist temple to attend a ceremony, knowing she had but moments.

"Your Majesty, I would have died, and Baikalan would have won if Aadan had not come back."

The empress continued to walk, eyes forward, between the rows of monks who had come out to line the boulevard leading to the main temple, their chants filling the morning air.

"I don't doubt the man's courage," the empress said, "but he has fled the empire of his own volition. Those who leave Dragon Class without permission are expelled."

Jin's anger flared. "He left because he felt threatened, Your Majesty."

"We all feel threatened. It does not mean we desert our posts," the empress said, glancing at her. "Do you love him?"

The question took Jin by surprise, but she knew better than to reveal such things. "I simply wish to do what's right by my wing mate, Your Majesty."

"It's in his hands. If he returns and accepts his punishment, he can rejoin Dragon Class."

"His punishment?" The word twisted in Jin's stomach. Aadan had risked everything to come back. He should be lauded, not punished. "And what punishment would that be?"

The empress slowed, as they were nearing the entry to the temple, and their conversation would have to end. "I will deal with that if and when it happens. And I advise you to do the same."

And with that, the empress swept ahead of her, the monks in the temple bowing like grain before a scythe. But before she was too far away, Jin called out. "Your Majesty."

The empress turned, impatient.

"I forgot to give you Emar's last words. He asked me to tell you that you were right."

If Jin didn't know better, she would have sworn the empress looked stricken, but then drums sounded, and the woman's face was once more an imperial mask as she nodded and turned back toward the temple.

Jin spent the rest of the ceremony wondering what Emar had meant and whether she would ever see Aadan again. The thought dulled even the brightest colors, and everything smelled wrong because there was no hint of sandalwood and him anywhere in the empire, she knew.

The one small highlight that Jin anticipated, along with all the other riders who had graduated, was their submission of applications to which banner of Dragon Class they wished to join. Though it was an open secret that the applications were formalities and that preferences were often not honored, the halls were filled with riders discussing the benefits of each banner and which ones they hoped to join.

Jin remembered her conversation with Aadan what seemed a lifetime ago, but what she had said then still held true: she wanted to be a messenger, to travel and be with Rayshan but avoid battles. She had more than enough death to last a lifetime, and she didn't wish to invite more into her life.

And so she filled out the application's sections, including an essay on how her special skills could be of benefit to her chosen banner. She wrote of her and Rayshan's ability to travel long distances and needing little sleep, though she was careful to leave no hints as to her blood bond. She argued that Rayshan's ability to flame could help recover messages from those who had died in service.

Her writing skills still left much to be desired, and so it took her longer than most to write her essay, then rewrite it to correct the mistakes and splotched ink from her first few tries. Therefore, when she reached the Blood Oval, it was to find the space already crowded with riders. The traditional training grounds had been converted into a processing station, with clerks seated at long tables lined end to end. Queues had formed before three clerks, who were noting down the names, years, and applicant details of each rider who came forth.

Jin passed all the curious stares and whispers, making straight for Jao and Panshalar at the end of the third line. She nervously tapped her scroll against her thigh.

"Everyone was asking me which one you were joining," Panshalar said.

"And what did you tell them?"

"That I didn't know," Panshalar said truthfully. "I think everyone expects you to join the warrior banner. Applicants will triple this year."

Jin frowned. "Surely they have a quota? Besides, how much weight do our preferences really carry?"

"If the ministers are split, they look to preferences," Panshalar said.

Jao nodded. "And only the best get into the warrior banner."

"Well, they'd be mad to not take you both after the Bohai battle."

Panshalar beamed, his large fist nearly crushing the scroll in his hand. "They would, wouldn't they?"

Jao motioned to her scroll. "So what about you?"

"Messenger."

"No jest?" Jao said, surprised.

Panshalar frowned. "You were crucial in Bohai. They'd want you for the warrior banner."

They stepped forward in the line, and Jin sighed. "That did occur to me. But now that the threat is over, and Baikalan is at the bottom of the sea, I'm hoping they'll feel the warrior banner no longer needs me."

They each took their turns handing over their scrolls and noting down their own and their dragons' names before walking back to the mess hall together.

"It'll be strange," Jao said. "I've gotten used to being on the woman's wing."

"There are more women joining, remember?" Jin said.

"True. Let's hope the ones in my wing are better looking."

"But then you wouldn't have a chance with them," Jin said sweetly. Panshalar laughed, and even Jao let slip a grin before reverting to his usual scowl.

THE NIGHTS WERE ONE LONG CELEBRATION OF DRINKING and feasting, with platters of roasted quail stuffed with ginkgo, river fish fried in hot oil and sprinkled with scallions and almonds, and stewed turtle with black mushrooms the size of her palm, along with every vegetable and sweet she could imagine. She grew weary of the food, despite her appetite, and everything tasted the same despite her heightened senses.

It's because you're pining, Rayshan admonished her matter-of-factly one day.

I suppose I am, she admitted. *If you know it, then I suppose everyone does.*

It's natural. Perhaps you can do what a dragon would do.

I thought dragons don't love their own kind like we do? You don't mate for life.

We don't. Because it results in pining. That's why I suggest you do what we do, find another for the time being.

Jin poured a bucket of water she'd been using to scrub his nails over his foreleg, making him snap at her in mock reprimand. *Well, I'm human, not a dragon. Besides, even if I wanted to, there isn't exactly a line of suitors.*

Rayshan grunted, his breath steaming in the frigid air. *That's not true. But you're right, I'd prefer you stay away from the other option, personally. He's not even a rider.*

Who are you talking about?

The crown prince.

She cleaned off his scaling brush and hung it up. *That's ridiculous. He and I wouldn't be together in a thousand years.*

But Rayshan's words made her think of their ride back into the city, how the crowds had chanted "ten thousand years" and hailed them like a conquering couple. And Tai had not dissuaded it. But then again, he wouldn't. As Aadan had once told her, Tai would do anything to strengthen his grip on the throne and win the support of the people.

As she left Rayshan's cave, promising to bring him even more oranges now that feasts were happening every night, she knew she would be counting the days until Aadan's return.

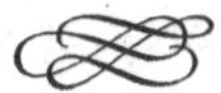

The empress didn't look up from her papers as Tai entered the office and bowed. Her long golden nails made soft scratching noises as she shifted the scrolls.

Tai watched her, preparing for the storm he sensed was coming. Copper burners as high as his waist lined the room, the warmth from their bellies full of coal bricks a sharp contrast to the snow falling outside, and his mother's icy expression.

The empress put aside her documents and looked up at him, examining him for a moment. "I know the last while has been frustrating for you. You have felt powerless and wanted to act out."

"I simply did what I thought best," he answered.

"And luckily, you are still alive," she said sharply. "You have been reckless, disobedient, and absolutely witless in a way I didn't think possible of you. I know you disagree with my methods, and Gao's coup has made you question my lack of mercy at times. But to go behind my back and alert Aadan? Instead of coming to me?"

"I found consulting you wasn't working. Besides, it wasn't about lack of mercy. It was about due process and fairness."

The empress folded her hands in her sleeves. "You want to be loved, and I understand that. But the people of China don't want someone to love. They want someone with an iron fist, preferably holding a sharpened sword that will keep them safe."

"How do you know, Mother?" Tai countered. "Have you asked the people what they want?"

The empress smiled. "A wise ruler doesn't have to ask. A wise ruler knows because history has proven it for thousands of years. China is too vast to rule through love."

"Yet the sage Lao Tse said that a ruler should rule as you would cook a small fish: gently and carefully."

His mother smirked. "Spoken like a true man who likely never cooked a fish in his life."

"I don't see how I am to learn to rule," Tai insisted, "if I'm on indefinite hiatus from duties and not even permitted to leave palace walls." He paused. "I am beginning to suspect it's less for my protection and more because you don't trust me."

"And why should I trust you?" his mother replied.

"After you alerted Aadan behind my back and disobeyed orders?"

"But my actions helped defeat Ulagan and Parhae." He watched her, unflinching. "You fear I'll be a figurehead for another Gao who wants you off the throne."

He caught her telltale flinch. His words held some truth.

"I would never want an enemy of my son," she said softly. "Then I would have failed as a mother." She sighed and stood, her dress whispering as she came around to stand before him. "I know you long to take a more active role in the government, something higher than Dragon Class and with more responsibility."

"I simply feel it is time I stretched beyond my current duties. Especially as Baikalan is no longer a threat."

"I agree." She regarded him, her immaculate features like a mask.

He tried to find where he had gotten his eyes, his nose, his cheekbones, but could find only a possible similar expression on her face. She looked saddened, he realized, and he noticed a puffiness around her eyes. Despite himself, his heart softened.

"I am at a crossroads. I can either trust you completely or cut you from me out of fear that you'll let what happened with Gao divide us." She paused, and the moment stretched between them. "I can't let that happen. So I'm making you Minister of War."

Tai blinked, unsure he had heard correctly. "Minister of—but—"

"You wanted responsibility. This will be your responsibility. You will take over the financial accounts and bring the army and navy back to its previous strength. You disobeyed my orders, which I still have in no way forgiven you for. But you proved yourself in Bohai, so my opponents cannot say you lack experience on the field." She paused. "I trust no one else with this, because putting anyone else in this position would be asking the wolf to guard the sheep."

This had not been what he had expected. He had acted as commander in chief of Dragon Class for some time, but that was also with Emar's guidance. "Your Majesty, are you sure I am qualified for such a position?"

There was a rustle of skirts and a tinkling of gold as his mother came down the dais and placed a hand on his arm. "What you don't know, you will learn. Right now, I need people I can trust over those with experience but no courage and even less loyalty. You won't disappoint me."

She turned and took her seat again. Tai noted that it was a statement, not a question.

Tai bowed. "I am honored, Your Majesty." He stood and noted her prolonged gaze out the window so that he wouldn't see the tears in her eyes.

"Mother," he said softly, "what troubles you?"

"Now that your role is empty," she said, "I'd like you

to select a new commander of Dragon Class, as well as head trainer."

Emar's loss had struck him hard, but perhaps it had struck his mother in a way that he didn't fully understand. She had lost a childhood friend in the old huren, and Tai began to suspect it might have been something more.

"We all miss Emar, and he can't be replaced," Tai said, drawing closer. "I will do my best. Did you and he have . . . a special friendship?"

His mother looked down, rubbing a ring in what had become a familiar gesture when she was emotional.

"He was a friend," she said simply. "Nothing more."

Tai sat down in the chair next to her. "Some might say there is nothing greater than a friend."

She closed her eyes, as if pained, then leaned her head against him, the hair decorations tinkling gently and her face powder smudging his robe. "I know you think I was wrong to send for Aadan, but I did it so you wouldn't have to."

"I wouldn't have made the same choice."

"I know. Which means you are not ready for the throne." She sat up, sighing and straightening her hair. As she did, he caught sight of the ring she had been rubbing and frowned.

"Where did you get this?" he asked, reaching out and holding her hand.

"The ruby? It was my mother's."

"No, this one," he said, pulling on the gold band that adorned her smallest finger.

"I forget," she said. "Either your father or one of my sisters. It's been so long."

Something in her casualness made Tai think the question shook her, but it was so fleeting he wondered if he had imagined it.

"I shall see you at the winter solstice feast tonight," he said, bowing.

"Good," she said, turning back to her papers. "Make sure to regale Minister Han and Minister Rong with your stories about fighting Baikalan. They would do well to remember the new Minister of War has defeated a dragon."

Tai nodded and retreated from the room, his mind still digesting what he had seen on his mother's ring. The word carved there was "kway," like the mark on the soft skin behind Jin's ear. It was roughly the same size and shape. Many concubines had similar rings or necklaces, for "kway" was used to denote a special concubine of great favor. It could be a coincidence, but a small seed of suspicion nestled its way into Tai's mind.

THE PALACE SEEMED TO BE ON FIRE WITH LIGHTS.

Music blazed from every corner as the court gathered to enjoy the royal bounty before disbanding for a week-long winter solstice holiday with families. But Tai was watching Jin, thoughtful. She and Meipin had dressed in conservative high-waisted gowns with low fur-lined bodices, and Jin wore her dark amber hair loosely tied to one side. He hadn't missed the latest court fashion of streaking hair with a mix of ocher and crushed chestnut in a shade similar to Jin's. The empire's first female dragonrider had aged, yet that seemed to only add to her power and allure.

"Admiring your future wife?"

Tai turned to see mage Situ Han, a full cup of wine in one hand and a bowl of bean paste dumplings in the other. The mage had clearly sought him out, as Tai had been careful to find a secluded balcony overlooking the courtyard in order to escape the party.

"You really do believe this fairy tale, don't you?" Tai asked, resigned.

"I like this particular fairy tale," Situ Han replied, slurping at the sweetened rice wine the dumplings swam in. It was a southern food but had recently gained popularity at court. "And people love a fairy tale with a happy ending." He leaned against the balustrade. "I have not had a chance to congratulate you on your Bohai expedition. I am hurt you didn't think of me in your hour of need. Next time you need to escape the palace, you can always come to me."

"I remembered you said you prefer feasts to work. I assumed you wouldn't want to be in danger."

The mage chuckled. "A little danger adds spice to

life. Don't underestimate me, Your Highness. I'm a man of subtle talents, a crouching tiger, hidden dragon, as they say." He gave a deep, rolling belch. "And it's an honor to provide my services to the new Minister of War."

Tai gave him a sharp look. "That has not been announced."

Situ Han grinned. "The Ministry of Mages has the empress's confidence. Were your mage skills useful during the battle?"

Tai glanced at Jin. "Yes, they were, in fact."

Situ Han followed his gaze and watched Jin speaking to a group of noblewomen. "The people love her," he said. "They'll adore her as empress. Which means you should make her yours."

"And what about what she thinks?" The only thing worse than the thought of a loveless marriage, he realized, was a forced marriage. Not to mention all the complications of his own feelings and his friendship with Aadan.

Mage Situ Han smiled. "She'll be persuaded."

Tai bristled. "If you are thinking of using threats or force—"

Mage Situ Han scoffed and took a large mouthful of wine. "Your Highness, are you telling me that the crown prince, who also happens to be the most charming man in the land, can't win over any woman he wants?"

Tai looked back at Jin, sighing. *That's exactly what I'm saying.* "I think you underestimate her."

"Oh, not at all," mage Situ Han said, finishing off his dumplings and placing the bowl on the balustrade. "I simply have faith in you. And, of course, I will make sure she hears about all your incredible attributes. Aha," he said, his eyes lighting, "they've brought out the silk thread buns."

He left Tai, whistling a cheery tune as he sauntered toward the servants bearing the platter of crisp white pastries, but Tai couldn't share his enthusiasm. The thought that he needed the mage's help to win Jin's favor wouldn't sting so much if he didn't genuinely wish she would look at him the way he'd seen her looking at Aadan.

When Jin returned to her chambers that night after the feast, she found an envelope on her bed, the seal of the Ministry of Justice marked in crisp black ink on its creamy surface. Despite her conversations with Emar and her determination to not let the past define her, her curiosity burned. She tore it open, hands shaking, and read the note.

Thank you for your inquiry with the Department of Records. We regret to inform you that no records of a criminal named Lan Ming during the First Year of Empress Wu's reign exist. We have checked all three halls of records and can find no evidence of such a person. With Full Respects, Office of Clerks and Records, Imperial Ministry of Justice.

Jin sat down on her bed, frowning. This was impossible. She had seen the seal, and certainly, Gao had seemed to think the record was real. Where had he found it? How could there be no copies? Of course, he could have been lying about its validity, but she didn't think so. Thieving had taught her many things, and she had a good sense of when someone was lying. Gao had truly believed the record was genuine.

Someone is tampering with the records, perhaps, Rayshan growled in response to her question.

Clearly. But who? And why?

"Lady Jin?"

Jin looked up to see Ahlu peering at her from the doorway. "Yes?"

"Marquis Sanjin is here to see you."

Jin folded up the envelope and put it in her sleeve, then followed Ahlu out to the foyer, where tea had been set and Sanjin was already sitting down.

"Kindly close the doors," Sanjin said to Ahlu without looking at her, and the maid bowed and obeyed, hastening out.

"I know you have been digging into records about your birth," Sanjin said, glancing at her sleeve as if he could see the letter there.

Jin resisted the urge to hide her arms. "Is that a crime?"

Sanjin smiled. "Not yet. But I do want to ask that you don't look into it any further."

"Why is that?" Jin's throat tightened, and at that moment, she was sure Sanjin had something to do with the records being unattainable.

The marquis looked at her with emotionless eyes.

"Because you are the daughter of a criminal. You know it. I know it. Gao knew it. But your fate is now tied to the empress's, and it would not be beneficial for the general public to know that you come from murderer stock. There are many who would wish to tear down the empress, and this would add fuel to their pyre. Do you understand?"

"How do you know it is the truth?"

"That is neither here nor there, but as the Royal Veil, it is my business to know things others do not."

"I deserve to know the truth."

He laughed outright, the sound far more disconcerting than a snarl. "Really? And why is that? Why do any of us ever deserve the truth? You have gone far above your lot. I'd say fate has been kind to you—" At her look of protest, he held up a hand. "Think about the extraordinary luck you must have—a thief, a murderer's child, a female who bonded to a dragon, and here you are, sitting across from me, Marquis Sanjin, having tea." He smiled, but the look in his eye was wicked. "Really having tea, Jin."

Her stomach turned.

"Don't push your luck, Rider. Now, on another note." Sanjin pulled from his sleeve a sheaf of paper tied with silk, and Jin recognized her application to join the messengers. "I'm afraid I come with both exciting and disappointing news."

She stayed silent.

"The disappointing news is your application to join the Banner of Communications has been rejected."

"And the exciting news?" Jin suspected that what was exciting to Sanjin was far from desirable for most.

"You will be joining a much more interesting and, if I might say so myself, esteemed department." He smiled. "Mine. The Royal Veil."

Her throat went dry. She had heard of riders being hand-picked for the Veil and had hoped to avoid it. "That's not even a banner." Her shock was so complete that she hadn't even been able to form the traditional answer of being too lowly to accept such favor.

"It's not. But it's far more elite."

"Why me?"

"Because your empress needs you, and the empire needs you—for a very special task. But the good news is, once you've completed this mission, you'll be allowed to choose whichever department you like. Including the Banner of Communications, should you still wish to join." Sanjin smiled. "Though I think the empress has something much more prestigious in mind. Head of Dragon Class one day, even."

She had, like everyone in Dragon Class, heard the rumors of Prince Tai's promotion. But never in a thousand years could she have fathomed she would be asked to take his place, never mind if she'd even like to take it. And posts like that did not come without a price. Usually a high one. "And what mission is this?"

Sanjin made a noise of disappointment. "I thought you would have guessed. It's a mission you are uniquely placed to carry out." The marquis leaned across the table, and his smile hid a thousand blades. "Kill Mengkhis Lai."

Pre-order your copy of "Dragon Rogue", Book 3 in "Riders of Jade & Fire." Releasing 2025!

FAQS

Why Tang China?

I've always been fascinated by Tang China, as it was considered a "golden age". Many of China's most famous stories and historical figures come from this period–including the Empress Wu. It was a time of relative openness and booming trade, where women were able to hold office, wear men's clothes, travel, and play polo on horseback. Many of these things were forbidden before, and restricted again for several dynasties afterwards. It was also a time when the capital had a large population of foreigners, and so became a melting pot for religions, fashion, food, and the arts.

How much of the history in this second book is true?

I've been inspired mostly by fact, but I've also given myself a lot of creative freedom.

The Empress Wu did exist, and actually ruled in her own right as an emperor (not just through her husband or son) from 690 to 705. The capital city, Changan, which is near today's Xi'an, was the biggest in the world at the time, with a population of 1 million people–many of them huren like Emar and Aadan, or of mixed heritage like Jin. Empress Wu reformed the imperial exams to make them more merit based, and gave certain government offices to women. I like to think someone like Meipin was one of them, pushing for the advancement of women where the empress might have been more motivated by power.

The part about the Empress Wu portraying herself as a Bodhisattva from heaven is based in fact. She encouraged depictions of herself as Buddha's reincarnation, to bolster her status and infallibility.

The Khitans were also a real people, and often fought with the Tang. They had a separate language and distinct culture from the Han Chinese. Their women had a bit more power than I've portrayed them here–for instance, women generally had more say in their spouses. But then again, kidnapping one's bride was also a traditional marriage custom.

The reindeer tribe is inspired by the Tsaatan people of northern Mongolia, whose livelihood depends almost solely on their reindeer. These do often live in tents with their herders. The Tsaatan are nomadic and have their own Turkic language.

Aadan is loosely modeled on a real Iranian prince,

Narsieh, who fled to China in the mid 650s with his father Peroz III when his kingdom was invaded by the Arabs. He was in China during Empress Wu's ascent to the throne, so it's quite probable they knew each other.

Sanjin is a fictional character, but based on the very real secret police force Empress Wu kept–and which I've renamed the Royal Veil for the ROJAF series. Many of the department officials were ruthless and corrupt, fabricating crimes and confessions when it suited them.

The Festival of Sevens is a real festival that still goes on today in China, and is a celebration of love.

Here are some other things in the book that really existed:

• Fireworks: fireworks were a Tang invention, but it wasn't used as a weapon until the 900s. I had the Khitans use it here as a weapon of sorts.

• Pools: swimming was popular amongst the nobility, and the palace had elaborate heated swimming pools.

• The Great Wall: this wall was built long before the Tang Dynasty, but the Tang emperors did indeed let it fall into disrepair, as their trade and influence was sufficient to keep invaders at bay for a time.

What language did they speak in Tang China?

The Chinese of the Tang Court was known as

Middle Chinese, and was the precursor to languages like Cantonese and Hakka. I took great liberties mixing and matching Mandarin and Cantonese pronunciation for names and places. I did this because Chinese is a tonal language, and therefore a lot of words sound exactly the same on the page when translated into English. For ease of distinguishing names, I decided it was best to not strictly follow one dialect or another, and thereby allow a greater breadth of name choices.

The poem "Farewell" that Meipin recites is a real poem by the Tang poet Du Mu. This translation is my own and I've taken some liberties in tweaking the original meaning. All translation mistakes are mine.

Rayshan and all the other dragons seem like "western" dragons. Why not use "Chinese" dragons?

In Chinese culture, dragons are not traditionally seen as fighters. They are mystical, wise, and connected to nature, traditionally found living in seas or lakes. In imagining the world of Dragon Class, the dragons seemed more of the air and of war, more like the aggressive fire breathing dragons of western folklore. So I went with what Rayshan and the story was trying to tell me, rather than bending the Chinese concept of a dragon to fit Jin's story. But who knows, perhaps I will write a story with Chinese style dragons in future.

Thanks for reading! If you enjoyed this, why not subscribe to my newsletter? You'll be first to know about upcoming books, plus you'll receive free:

* *Night of the Black Dragon* - the prequel to *Dragon Class*, with the events leading right up to Jin and Lu's heist;

The Queen and the Dagger, the prequel to my other series, *Book of Theo;*

* exclusive previews and bonus stories. Join now at www.melanieansley.com/subscribe

Enjoyed *Dragon Flame?* Please consider leaving a review on Amazon and Goodreads, or elsewhere. You'll ensure many more of Jin's stories follow.

ACKNOWLEDGMENTS

First and foremost, thanks to my family–Sam, Artemis, and Evander–for putting up with my daydreams.

A huge thank you to the editors who helped shape this into its better version: Stacey K (@Grammargirl), and Maryssa G. from Pocket Editing. I also couldn't have gotten this manuscript to where it is now without the help of awesome beta readers: thank you Hannah Greer, Jordan Trippeer, Laura Daleo, and Rari Rajesh.

Huge gratitude to my ARC team as well, especially Cecilia Sutton, Tanvi Chandra, Eric Herbaut, and John Saxon. Chere, Sara Rosevear, Kez Sharrow, Ken Miller, Tara Bolden, Birdie Berlanga, Mattia, Andrea, Judith Jenkins, Marcie Walters, Kristin Ann Conroy, Linda, Lisa, Tiffany Ewald, Toni Foreman, Karen Hewett, Krystina Roupe, Joe, Jeanette Deacon, Trevor T O'Brien, Deb, Carl D. Poellnitz, Jennifer Macaulay, Vicky Hopkins, Allan Gillard, Prenscella, and Sandy, thank you for reading and championing the book through its last stages! You are all rockstars. Lyn Ducich, thank you for all your support and for introducing me to the BookLounge.

Last but not least, thanks to all the readers and subscribers who have joined this ride with me. You make this not only possible, but much more fun and magical.

Melanie was born in Canada but raised in China, and now lives in Ballarat, Australia with her husband and two children. She loves to read, write, and laugh. She also makes movies.

The *Book of Theo* series:

Theo and the Forbidden Language

Theo and the Secret of Elshon

Theo and the Stolen Library

The Queen and the Dagger

(a prequel novella)

The Lost Child of Willago

(a prequel available only to subscribers)

The *Riders of Jade & Fire* series:

Night of the Black Dragon (prequel novella)

Dragon Class

Dragon Flame

Dragon Rogue (2025 release)